SARA WILL

SARA WILL

SUE ELLEN BRIDGERS

1817

HARPER & ROW, PUBLISHERS, New York

CAMBRIDGE, PHILADELPHIA, SAN FRANCISCO, LONDON
MEXICO CITY, SÃO PAULO, SINGAPORE, SYDNEY

Designer: Barbara DuPree Knowles

LIBRARY OF CONGRESS CATALOGING IN PUBLICATION DATA
Bridgers, Sue Ellen.
Sara Will.

I. Title.
PS3552.R4543S2   1985   813'.54   84-48139
ISBN 0-06-015385-7

FOR BEN

In Memoriam

Annie McGlohon Abbott
1887–1983

Nancye Smathers Haire
1938–1981

AUTUMN

1

✦ Sara Will came down the road, quick steps deep in shadows, her head lifted to the autumn air. Through the six o'clock light, haze hanging close and bringing night damply in to weigh down the brittle leaves above her head, she went along, her rake over her shoulder, cotton gloves tucked into her belt, skirt heavy with leaf dust. No one was in the world but her.

Formed out of the iridescent colors of this half-light, she was a good-looking woman, tall but rounded at her edges as if her layered clothing had softened her strong angular frame into a more nebulous shape. Her skirt swished on her bare cool legs.

Her hair, its natural shade of burnished leaves catching new snatches of color, hung loose down her back, bits of stem and broken leaves caught in the curling ends. She moved her head a little, rolling it on her shoulders as if she were playing with a shiver, a warm new hand on her throat, when actually she was just now noticing the freedom of her head without the tightly coiled bun she usually pulled to the nape of her neck.

She was in the middle of her life, too old to have this head of hair not cut in more than forty years, as thick as a girl's. Even winding it tight and hard every morning, she almost never lost a strand. Her comb was as clean as a whistle.

Now she came down the little incline, at the bottom of which her house formed a dull whitish shape in the gloomy twilight. She could see into the parlor window, dark except for the blue glare of the television screen, a flickering artificial light that offered no welcome in its distant glow.

She knew her sister Swanee Hope was watching a game

3

show, jumping and clapping in the dark while some poor sucker went momentarily into another tax bracket. Swanee Hope didn't care about taxes. It wasn't just the money that mattered. Swanee Hope relished the spontaneous victory, the burst of applause, as if she herself had done something spectacular. She wanted the thrill of mouth-gaping disbelief transformed into joy on a stranger's face, a display of astonishment so apparent that she would want to hug herself, unable as she was to get to them. The fact was that Swanee knew most of the answers, and she jabbed her finger at the screen, pointing the way to flights to Amsterdam, second homes, hard cash.

Sara couldn't get excited about it. Those contestants must be people on vacation, she'd decided long ago when Swanee first tried to entice her into watching. Why else would they do something so stupid as get themselves on television, pancake makeup and all?

Sara Will leaned the rake against the house, coiled her hair expertly around her hand, and fastened it to her head with pins from her pocket. Then she peered into the window.

"Swanee Hope," she called softly so as not to frighten her sister. "It's me, Sara Will, come home from the cemetery."

A face came to the window, eyes along the edge of the summer sheers. "Tell me what Mama's full name might be and what year she was laid to rest," a voice purred back.

"Sara Hope McElroy Burney," Sara Will said to the cold dusty pane. "Nineteen sixty-three."

"That's the right answer," the voice said. "Come on in the house, Sara Will. It's dark out there."

It was darker inside, a solid kind of dark shaped by the sagging angles of joists and warped studs. The house seemed to need propping up. Sara Will could feel it leaning a little, straining down the slope as if it were answering a call beyond the woods, bending its ear to the sound of trees.

Just a year ago, she'd begun to notice it was slightly gray, moldy and dust-dingy, but now the house seemed to be giving in. It surprised her that it could change without her noticing,

4

although she knew she was apt to wear clothes long past their use, remembering how a shirt looked when new rather than examining it, as the seasons changed, for pinhole tears or a frayed hem. When she felt comfortable she saw no point in disturbing things, and she had always been comfortable in her worn clothes and her aging house. Safe, she had thought, locked in against any modern danger, protected by the structure of her uneventful days and by the house itself. Yet she couldn't deny that the porch roof leaked in a hard rain; she put a rag rug over the spot of dark, softening wood where the bucket always spilled over before she could empty it.

Now, coming in, she stepped over the soft place and moved silently beyond the parlor where Swanee Hope stood between the window and the television, her mind between them too as she decided whether to join her sister in the kitchen or watch the rest of the program.

"Sara, come in here a minute and see this," she called, although she knew the futility of such an invitation. Sara thought television was foolish. Swanee knew her sister thought she was foolish too, but she didn't care. Television was at least an alternative to Sara's quiet.

On the screen the prize was six thousand dollars and a Colt automobile. In the kitchen, it was some kind of supper, whatever Sara Will could find to fix—three eggs in the fridge, a pot of steaming grits, biscuits made from a box mix. Swanee shook her head irritably, blue light catching in the gray streaks as if it were an instant, miraculous rinse, and kept on watching.

The question was the name of Romeo's friend.

"Mercutio!" Swanee Hope shouted at the set. A high school question.

The man looked solemn while the electronic ticker sounded off the seconds. He seemed to want to touch his face, maybe press a throbbing sinus cavity or run his finger over an itchy eyebrow, a familiar anxious habit. But he sensed the makeup would betray a sham. He twitched his nose. So did Swanee Hope.

"Mercutio," she said softly. "'A plague o' both your houses!'"

"Tybalt?" the man said into the silence. He seemed to be asking Swanee for advice, testing his answer to her.

"No, you fool!" she cried, stamping her foot, fist shaking. "Mercutio!"

"So sorry," the emcee was saying, elastic smile of sympathy snapping across his handsome face.

"Sorry. Sorry, stupid," Swanee mimicked and slapped the button that turned off the set.

Such an easy question. She should be up there herself instead of trying to yell the answers across three thousand miles. She might as well have two tin cans and a length of cotton twine. But she could win if she ever got the chance, and someday she would. She could imagine herself on the screen, and anything you can imagine you could make happen.

The room was truly dark now. No moonlight yet. She could hear her sister stirring in the kitchen. Water ran, clanging through the old pipes under the house. Swanee thought she could hear the crack of eggs, shell against glass bowl, the sizzle of butter on the stove. They were the kinds of sounds she heard in the house when the television was silent, almost imperceptible noises she had to strain her ears to make out amid the twitches of the house itself. She wanted to hear human noise, not the inanimate moaning of weakening joists. The television provided at least a facsimile of interchange. People talked, if not to Swanee then at least at her, and she intended to enjoy it whether Sara did or not. Sara didn't need noise.

Well, I do, Swanee thought and hugged herself. Needing anything at all—a glass of water in the night, a cough drop, a sharpened pencil—reminded her of other, more crucial needs: her husband dead long years now, her son who didn't come home often enough, almost never since she'd moved back here to keep Sara Will company. Her son didn't have time to travel this far. It was hours by plane; then he'd have to rent a car. Or days by car, all the way across the country from California.

Well, he'd gotten as far away from her as he could. She knew it was intentional. You don't go to California without intentions.

Anyhow it was her husband, Jonathan, she missed. Still. After ten years. She'd rented the house in town because of missing him, sold belongings that didn't fit into Sara Will's scheme of things, gotten Buster Collins to help her load up a U-Haul and drive it these fifteen miles out into this little hollow where she'd been born and raised. She'd sat in the cab next to Buster, him smelling like a pig, dust sticking to his grease-smeared arms, and looked out at the unfamiliar landscape of her childhood home through a blur of unexpected tears. Once moved into Sara's house, she'd polished all her furniture to get Buster's grimy prints off. Then she arranged the pieces as best she could without moving any of the other furniture, which hadn't been disturbed in thirty years. Sara Will had stood silently watching the few empty spaces fill up, her arms crossed at her long waist, not helping.

"Is this all right?" Swanee would say, watching for an impatient flicker of disgust to strike a glancing light on Sara Will's brow, but she never saw it.

It was body language, not face, that said everything. When Swanee had sent Buster Collins off in the empty U-Haul, twenty-five crisp dollar bills in his grubby hand, the sour, oily smell of him lingering in the closed-up parlor, Sara Will had released her tightly folded arms, opening them to her sister in welcome. They embraced in the hallway, afternoon light pouring through the dust around their heads. It was the last time they ever hugged each other, up to this very day. Never again had there been a greeting or a parting, just doors closing softly at eleven o'clock, opening again at seven, and, in between, the long still night enfolding them in arms of soft worn quiet, quiet that seemed to have been used before on other evenings. They slept with Mama's down comforters tight to their chins.

"Swanee!"

Sara Will was calling her to come out of the dark parlor into the hall, then down the passage to the kitchen, where the electric cookstove would be pouring off easy heat. Sara Will hadn't wanted the electric stove, but she hadn't made a fuss when Buster Collins came two weeks after Swanee's arrival and moved Swanee's fancy appliance out of the barn where he'd put it in storage and set it in the place where the wood cookstove had been. It was shiny white and small, stupid-looking.

But Sara Will didn't protest, not wanting to resist a change she knew would make life easier for them. After all, they were getting older now and wood had to be split and constantly tended in the stove. Still, she wanted a little woodstove just for heat, and so Buster came once more, a dull black stove roped to his truck bed. He spent the afternoon connecting it to the old stove flue and there it had set all summer, a cold black rectangle on heavy squat legs next to the white and polished-chrome shine of the electric contraption. So they each had a stove; each retained pride and made adjustments.

Now, this late in autumn, the woodstove was cold—no one to split the logs—but the kettle sang on the electric eye until Sara Will lifted it away, cutting the whistle to a white spurt of steam.

"I'm cooking us a couple of eggs," she said, not turning from the stove. She had felt the little rush of cool air as Swanee came in, displacing Sara's natural silence with her sighing.

Swanee always seemed to be sighing, little bursts of air rising from her pursed regretful lips, filling up space when it was the hours that were empty. She spent her days watching television, reading from the cache of library books the sisters got off the bookmobile every month. She hardly ever moved except to make a marble cake or dust or sweep the front porch. She liked to cook sweet things: puddings smooth with patience; angel cakes folded slowly, rotating bowl easing its circle against her curving rubber spatula.

Sara Will hadn't the patience for it, or the desire. That was the main thing. She didn't want to make an angel cake, all white air and crusty brown crown. She'd take her blackberries plain or mixed with a little sugar and poured over a hot sweet

8

biscuit she didn't need a mixer to make. Her kitchen was full of gadgets now, so many that Swanee Hope was all the time blowing fuses, putting them momentarily into unexpected dark. Swanee Hope would never understand that the radio, washing machine, stove, and mixer all going at the same time was hazardous, so Sara Will kept a box of fuses handy, protection against the dark she constantly anticipated. She prided herself on being prepared, covered her early azaleas against a cold snap, kept her butcher knife sharpened to cut collards after the first frost, her baskets clean and mended to gather the windfall of apples behind the house. A grocery list grew daily on the back of a used envelope for her one trip into town each week.

Now she scraped the eggs out of the skillet onto their plates, dividing equally, spooned stewed apples beside the eggs, forked old biscuits, split and toasted in butter, in the empty spaces.

Swanee poured steaming water over instant coffee in their cups. They made coffee in the morning, sipping at it until the pot was empty at noon, but at night they drank instant, more expensive but not wasteful. She put the cups on their mama's round oak table and sat herself down while Sara Will brought their filled plates, heavy cream-colored dime-store plates because Sara had packed away her mother's dishes and refused to use Swanee's good china. She didn't want to wash the slick plates that could slip out of her careful hands, smashing into the enamel basin. Sara Will knew that no matter how often her sister urged its use, Swanee Hope would mourn each lost piece.

Swanee even knew the origin of each one; who had given her the meat platter, the divided vegetable bowl, each bread-and-butter plate. She remembered the lost pieces, too: the creamer Jonathan dropped in '65, splattering yellow cream at fifty-three cents a pint on the dining room rug. She like to never got it out.

The rug would, of course, remind Swanee of its purchase, how she kept Jonathan awake one entire night, explaining to him their need for the rose-bordered twelve by fifteen she'd discovered marked one third off at Broydan's Store. In the dawning hours she had finally pounced on him as he tossed groggily

9

between quiet and the testy whine of her demanding voice. She put her lips to his ear, testing his endurance, his fallibility. By the time her wandering, purposeful mouth reached his warm bare belly, she could see his signature on the blank check and the pale green and rose of the carpet rising off the bare floor of her soon-to-be elegant dining room.

Sara Will didn't want to hear it, already yielding to embarrassment, the cold wet flood of dread she'd come to feel when she sensed Swanee's reminiscences coming on, ravaging her brain like crimes she'd committed and must confess. Sara Will didn't want to hear; she braced herself against listening to tales of female wiles, her own sister's cunning.

She shut her face and ears to it, although Swanee didn't seem to notice the tight biting lips, hands grasping flesh in her lap as she pinched her thighs. Swanee Hope seemed to think that because Sara Will was her sister, she should know everything: had some right, even a need, to know the intimacies of Swanee's marriage. How Jonathan had always given in— succumbed, it seemed to Sara. Well, he ended up dead, that was for sure, although Swanee Hope hadn't exactly killed him. The culprit was the six fifty-two freight train skimming down the hill on schedule, whistle blowing like always, Jonathan's 1954 Nash Rambler stalled on the tracks. What Swanee should have finagled was a new car, and maybe she'd have Jonathan to cajole yet. Then Sara Will would be alone in this house where she'd always lived without a television or a Mixmaster or an electric stove humming and clicking as it cooled.

They bowed their heads for silent prayer and then Sara Will clicked her spoon into her coffee, stirring and watching Swanee's bent gray head. Even still like this, so quiet, Swanee could draw attention to herself. She knew the advantage of silence as well as the excitement of drama, books, life itself, and she took advantage of it.

Sara forked a bit of egg into her mouth, tasting the dull flat flavor. "Needs salt," she said and pushed away from the table. The screeching chair brought Swanee's head up.

"I know it's a bother to you, not salting things," she said, "but the doctor told me—"

"You swell up, I know," Sara Will said, doctoring her eggs generously.

"Well, I do."

"I appreciate his opinion," Sara Will said. "I'm not complaining."

"But you're in a snit, I know you are," complained Swanee, poking at her apples to separate the cooked peel from the fruit. "You're always in a state when you come home from the cemetery. You ought to leave it to somebody else."

"And just who might that be? Nobody's ever taken an interest except myself."

"I know you're referring to me, and it's not that I don't take an interest, Sara Will. After all, Mama and Daddy are out there. My family's all out there, including Jonathan, God rest him, but I can't see how a few leaves are going to hurt anything. Listen!" She stopped, fork raised as if she were pointing toward the sound. "A wind coming up. By morning, nobody'll ever know you spent the entire day raking that cemetery."

"I'll know it."

"And you'll rake it again."

"I suppose I will." Sara Will pressed her napkin to her mouth and placed it carefully beside her plate. "I was thinking out there, Swanee, about Serena."

"I knew you were. You always do, Sara Will, and then you get all worked up and start taking it out on me! I mean, it's not my fault Serena's buried across the lake. Nobody knew they were planning to dam up the river and put a body of water between us and the departed. I mean, nobody thinks their community cemetery is going to end up on an *island*, now, do they? It's ludicrous."

"Nevertheless, all the Burneys buried before 1945 are over there, lost to us. There's nobody to sweep away over there. No respects paid. I just can't stand knowing our sister's over there and Mama and Daddy are safe with us. That's the way I see it, Swanee. She's deserted over there."

"She's resting in the Lord," Swanee said, eyes turned toward the bulb with its fluted glazed shade above the table.

"She was seventeen years old and didn't know what she was doing when she married Clement Jessop," Sara Will said.

"She was in love, Sara Will. You weren't but a girl at the time. How could you remember the details the way I do? I tell you, a person remembers when her younger sister gets married first. Why, I was mortified. I reckon if I hadn't been courting, anticipating a big wedding and all, I'd of just died of mortification over the whole thing. But I knew she was in love with that boy, although who's to say it would of lasted? Who's to know? But I promise you this, by every word she wrote to us she had fourteen months of a good time before she left this world for the next. Fourteen months as opposed to nothing."

"And what does that mean?" Sara Will asked, getting up to put the kettle on again. The room was growing chill now, the dark invading through the long narrow windows that faced the woods. She would have to warm herself with coffee.

"Nothing like you imagine, Sara Will," Swanee said. She closed her mouth around a crisp buttery round of biscuit.

Outside, dead leaves rattled and turned in the wind. They blew across the tin roof, skidding and rustling as they settled along the gutter, where they would rot if they weren't cleaned out soon. She would have that to do, Sara thought, seeing herself on the ladder which Swanee held to the ground.

Swanee never held the ladder solidly enough, and so Sara always felt it floating away from her, her feet and hands losing hold, knees trembling. But once secure on the roof, she could stand up and see the world, look up the ridge to see the circle of smoke from the next house making its thick morning spiral, could look past the barn and the pond to a tiny plot of dried and withered summer crops, a row of purple asters, then on toward the cemetery, at least the top of the maple and the edge of elms and the tulip poplar, leaves hanging resolutely on so she'd be raking at Thanksgiving against the threat of first snowfall.

Up there above Swanee's head, she would imagine the town miles away, hidden from her by the hills. She could see all the places between here and there, the narrow road winding blindly, following its nose, sniffing out industry and shops and supermarkets and entertainment, all the things Sara had never cared about. She would look in the other direction, then, toward where she knew the lake was bottled up against a floodgate, a concrete wall in the middle of a wilderness. A wild place it was now with Serena in it, out there in the middle of what, God be praised, had once been a high place.

They had promised a new road to replace the one underwater, that and a bridge. Access, they had called it. Men in boots and business suits had come to explain how the valley needed electricity—how the Burneys in particular needed it. Her parents had been wary, nervous, noncommittal. They had gathered on front porches of other farmhouses in their community—Sparrow Creek, it was called then—wondering if they shouldn't protest, complain to someone somewhere. But they didn't want to cause trouble or stand in the way of progress. Besides, construction of a dam meant jobs, and there was the promise of access.

But there had never been a bridge, not even a cleared gravel path along the ridge that would take them to the only place where a bridge could possibly connect the island to the mainland. Now, over thirty-five years later, Sara was yet to see her sister's grave, or the graves of her grandparents on the Burney side, or her granddaddy's brothers and their families. Only in her mind could she know how the place looked, weeds grown up, ferns thick in the damp shady places, tangled briar bushes weaving their spiky arms across the etched names and dates, hiding in their bramble the only tangible evidence that these particular lives had even been lived.

Sara Will found herself staring into the lively, open face of her older sister, who licked preserves from her upper lip with a flick of her tongue. This was all the family she had left, Swanee Hope and that obnoxious son of hers and his children who, God help them, were growing up in California, probably on some hot white beach like the ones she sometimes glimpsed on Swanee's television set. Those children, brown-skinned and heathen-looking, were the only ones still carrying McElroy-Burney blood, and as weak as the strain was, she could only be grateful for it. At least Swanee Hope had done that much.

Sara Will pulled her cold eggs closer. They had lost their fluffiness, turned dark and solid on her plate. She forked the apples, which were edible cold.

"Tomorrow I'll gather the rest of the apples," Swanee Hope said to break the silence between them.

"You needn't do that," Sara answered gently.

"I want to do something." Swanee released one of her slow puffs of air that lingered above them like a sigh of wind. "I think I'll stir up a mess of apple butter. Or maybe applesauce. Which do you think, sister?"

"Whichever strikes you," Sara Will said.

"But tell me your *preference*," Swanee said. "Which do you prefer?"

"Applesauce," Sara Will said.

"I was intending to make the butter," was what Swanee Hope said last.

2

✦ Sara Will saw it coming, a truck once black now caked with mud on its fenders, dust stuck to the hood, the load on the back covered with dirty blankets and an old mattress pad, jostling. From where she stood on the roof, slanted, the broom's ragged broken bristles curved hard on the silvery tin to help her keep balance, Sara Will watched uneasily as the truck took the curve onto her narrow bumpy lane, and she leaned a little with it, sucking air between her teeth.

She had heard the vehicle coming. Twice already she'd stopped her broom mid-stroke, leaves skittering on down the tin, to listen to the faint engine sound rising to her. From her vantage point on the roof, she had squelched the edge of panic that always rose in her chest when anyone invaded her property and replaced it with hostility. Whoever it was, they'd get short shrift from her. Then she'd heard a slipping clutch slapped hard and the roar of second gear taking hold. Whoever it was, they sure weren't sneaking in.

"Who is it?" Swanee Hope called up from the side yard. She had been gathering the leaves Sara sent down to her on the broom, dropping armloads into the wheelbarrow, where they fluttered noisily, crackling and spilling from her overload. Her face played with excitement, a wide-eyed anxious look toward her fiery sister and a quivering smile in the direction of the truck.

"I can't tell yet," Sara Will called back. "I certainly didn't invite anybody, did you? You didn't, did you, Swanee?" Because Sara wouldn't put it past her. "You better come here and hold the ladder for me."

But Swanee was already on her way down the yard to the front, where the truck had no choice but to stop. She spit on her hands, then wiped them across her crown to bring discipline to her windy curls. She felt trembly with excitement. On the roof Sara Will sighed irritably, with no choice but to wait.

The truck stopped, blowing dust toward the house and the spot where Swanee Hope stood smiling, hand to breast in welcome.

"Why, it's a man and a child," she called to Sara Will, who frowned down at the truck and her sister.

"Why, it's a man and child and an infant in arms!" Swanee

called again happily as she peered through the dust into the cab. "Strangers every one!"

"Swanee, come here this minute and hold this ladder!"

Sara Will looked down on the heads appearing from the truck. She saw a man's head first, a thinning spot, pink scalp on top surrounded by thick brown curls, shaggy, undisciplined hair that curved too long around his ears and into his collar. He looked short to her—short at least for a man, although he could easily be as tall as she. She couldn't tell, seeing mostly the tops of things: head, one broad shoulder, the other more narrow, damaged-looking, drooping a little. The crease of dusty Sunday pants breaking at the top of unpolished black loafers.

Then a young woman came slowly around the front of the truck, weighted and waiting as if she believed she were outside the event and had no responsibilities. Blond head—no, yellow—a hard, bright color, brassy. Caught in her arm and resting on one jutting hip, a baby: bald at this distance but probably with white fuzz. A perfect circle of a head. A fat bare baby arm held to the woman's neck, fingers curling under the straggly bleached hair. The woman looked compact, somehow, as if she had blown all her air out and then just stopped breathing. Everything inside her was still and calm as though she didn't have a worry in the world, even when she was approaching absolute strangers like this. Sara didn't see a thing about them to like.

"Why, I do believe it's Fate!" Swanee Hope called out and tripped right down the double stone steps to hug him.

"It's who?" Sara yelled back.

"Lafayette Jessop, Sara!" Swanee let the man go and he leaned back toward the truck, pulling the young woman to him with his right hand. "Clement's brother, Fate! Remember, he came up here to Serena's funeral all those many years ago! It goes to prove I never forget a face!"

"Swanee, come get me down from here right this minute," Sara Will said, more furious than ever.

"What's she doing up there?" the young woman asked Swanee.

"Cleaning the gutters," Swanee said, not moving an inch. "Else the leaves clog them up and rain drips off the roof and makes a little trench along the house."

"Swan, the ladder! Right now!" Sara Will shouted.

"I'll get it," Fate said, looking up at Sara for the first time.

Her inspection of flyaway hair changed to view of a good-natured, almost gentle expression, but there was something undisciplined about his face, too. He was grinning as if he thought his looks would have a happy effect on her.

Sara stared right down into his dancing eyes and said stonily, "Swanee can do it, thank you."

"Don't you worry about my arm," Fate said, coming toward the house as though he hadn't heard her right. "My right is strong enough for two."

"What happened to him?" Swanee asked the girl.

"Car fell on him. He heard the jack going and he got everything out but his left arm, right about here." She extended her free arm and, balancing the baby more heavily on her hip, pointed to a place just below the elbow. "Mashed it flat."

"Good heavens," Swanee said.

"They just about cut it off right there in the hospital. They wanted to," the young woman continued, swinging the baby slightly on her hip, "but Uncle Fate was cussing and hollering and so they decided to see how long they could let it go. It's been over twenty years now." She looked down at the baby as if she were surprised by her. "This is Rachel," she said to Swanee. "And I'm Eva. Eva Jessop."

"Clement's child!" Swanee cried, hands up to cover her open mouth. "Why, we knew Clement got married again, but that was years ago! And he's got a child your age? Why, you don't look sixteen up close, except for that hair. What did you do to it, anyhow? Looks God-awful cheap to me."

17

"I'm growing it out," Eva said, dropping her head slightly so Swanee could see the beginning of brown roots.

Fate was settling the ladder in the soft mulchy dirt along the side of the house. He pushed against it with his shoulder, then weighted it down with one foot firmly on the bottom rung. His good hand got a grip higher up.

"Swanee!" Sara Will called, stepping back farther from the edge and the ladder sticking up at her.

"Fate's getting it!" Swanee called back. She had taken the baby and was patting it happily to her shoulder.

"Swanee! You come here this minute!" Sara Will screamed, pulling the gathers of her skirt forward around her knees.

"Well, I certainly will shut my eyes, Miss Sara," Fate said, still smiling up at her. "I will do that."

"Oh-h-h!" Sara Will groaned and dropped the broom, which clattered down the tin and stuck against the gutter. "Oh, oh, oh."

"Look, Miss Sara," Fate said, "you're not scared to come down, are you? I know there are people like that. Going up don't bother them, but they can't seem to take coming down. Maybe you ought to be the one shutting eyes."

"I have been on this roof countless times, Mr. Jessop, and I have never suffered vertigo or panic of any sort," Sara Will said. To prove it, she released her skirt a little, getting ready to ease down the slope of the roof. Her tennis shoes moved in tiny slanted steps to the edge, where she turned around and put one foot over the gutter to catch the rung, one hand on the roof, bent over as though she'd been commanded to take a whipping. The other foot took a solid hold, and she crawled on one hand down the tin until her palm reached the gutter and jumped it to find the ladder support. She started her descent.

Less than halfway down, she found herself peering into the second-story spare room, the windows dusty, curtains half closed against the fading properties of the western light. Seen from this unusual perspective, the room was foreign to her. She felt like a voyeur looking in, expecting a scene to unfold be-

18

tween the enclosing walls. A bed, white iron with a faded quilt spread over it, bare pine floor, an armoire stuffed with boxes, bits of Christmas and birthday wrap and ribbons, old patterns and oddly shaped scraps of cloth. A rocking chair that matched the one in her room—well, almost. At least, made at the same time and by the same hands.

In a split second she took the room in, surveying the familiar contents, and yet everything seemed strange to her. Her heartbeat quickened as if she had suddenly sprinted forward in time and now stood gasping at the future. She closed her eyes against a vision of Fate Jessop in that room, the armoire lined with his peculiar belongings, the lamp casting rumpled light on the unmade bed. Her knees trembled slightly and she pushed them hard against the rung, making a bruise. She wanted to get away from the sight of it and so, still holding her skirt tightly to her legs, she felt her way toward solid ground.

Near the bottom she sensed a hand coming up to meet her, felt fingers gripping at her waistband. The ladder grumbled a little under her weight. She stepped off, releasing her skirt, and found herself still encircled by the arm of Fate Jessop, who she saw was opening his eyes slowly, one eye at a time, as if to mock her. He was taller than she.

They came in. Swanee left her wheelbarrow, the leaves blowing up on a sudden gusting wind, to lead them up the porch and through the front door with Sara Will following them, her face pinched and colorless, her heart thumping no. They went into the parlor, a room crammed tight with Swanee's things, the accumulation of her married life stuck in corners, nailed to walls, and spread over chairs, lacy, fragile doilies of memory scattered here and there.

Sara Will hated the clutter of it, and now the room seemed even more crowded, stuffed tight with people she didn't know or care a fig about. People who had come in a truck loaded down with God knows what—their belongings, more than likely—junk they would push through her front door, heave up her stairs, scatter in her kitchen and parlor. She could feel them pushing at her even as she stood in the parlor doorway, seeing them wait, hesitant to sit but expecting to. She could tell that. They expected her to ask them to stay awhile—an hour, until next week, some undetermined length of time. She could see it in their faces already, shadows of conspiracy crossing the darkening room before Swanee could circle them, switching on lamps.

"Well, you all sit," Swanee said, having lit the corners against any misunderstanding of her hospitality. She looked up at Sara Will's closed, stony face and said it again. "Sit, sit. Make yourself at home."

The emphasis on "at home" caused Fate and Eva to drop immediately into the closest chairs, leaving Swanee and Sara Will standing. They looked at each other across the room.

"You'll be staying for supper," Sara Will said, not an invitation but an acknowledgment of their intentions. Where could they go this late in the afternoon? Where could she send them, anyway? She didn't know why they had come, but their reason would be irresistible, she knew that; undisputable. Her anger was no defense against them.

"Thank you, Miss Sara," Fate said, slapping at his pantleg with his hand. Dust sparkled, springing into the light.

"And you'd like to wash up," Sara Will replied.

"We're all right," Fate said, brushing at the other leg. "Just our hands before we eat."

"But Mr. Jessop, the soil of travel is clearly on your person," Sara said, provoked again. She had a vision of other people's dirt in her house, their disarray spilling into her life.

"I need to wash the baby some," Eva said calmly, as if she didn't notice the tension. "Uncle Fate, will you get the baby's things—the crib too, if you don't mind? I think if she eats and has a bath, she'll go right to sleep."

"She's a precious thing," Swanee Hope said, coming to take the baby again. "Whose is she?"

"Why, she's mine," Eva said.

"Yours?" Swanee held the baby away from her chest to get a good look at the two of them. Her eyes found resemblance. "Just how old are you, my dear?"

"Rachel's nine months and I'm sixteen—well, sixteen and a half."

"And where is the father of this precious child?" Swanee Hope asked, unwilling to waste a moment in her interrogation. She would know everything. Intimacy with strangers was so easy. It was people she expected to be close to who kept secrets.

"There isn't one," Eva said. "I mean, he doesn't know a thing about Rachel. She's my baby alone."

"God help us," Sara Will said from the doorway.

"I'll go get the crib off the truck," Fate said, trying to ease by Sara Will unnoticed. She moved slightly to let him pass.

"I'll help him," Eva said. "He has a hard time doing things like that with one arm." She looked from Sara Will to Swanee Hope for a glimmer of sympathy.

"Go right ahead," Swanee said helpfully. "I'll just cuddle this sweet thing."

They heard the front door shut, then the clatter of objects being pushed and pulled on the truck bed. The sisters looked at each other and then at the baby, who, thumb in mouth, pulled with her other fat hand at one of Swanee's curls, wrapping it around her pudgy finger. They stood there waiting as if they were no longer in control and needed directions.

"What is happening here?" Sara Will said finally, hearing the scratch of wood on the porch and then the door flying open, banging into the wall.

"Up the stairs!" Swanee called, coming back to life. "In Serena's old room!"

The baby tight to her shoulder, she hurried past her sister to show them the way while Sara Will stood in the silent parlor, stunned and trembling, undone by her inability to make the sounds above her head go away.

21

3

✦ Nobody asked Fate Jessop how they got there. If they had, he wouldn't have been able to tell them in any kind of sensible fashion. The past year had been too full of emotions, too dense with feeling, for him to make much sense out of what he'd done and why. But there in Sara Will's house, ensconced in that cold spare room which seemed so purposefully plain, he forced himself to remember, as if it were necessary to give the events a chronology, to create a past for himself and Eva which could eventually serve as a defense against the interrogation of the sisters.

That day when Eva arrived at his door, he had failed to show up for work and so he hid when the doorbell buzzed, shattering his self-imposed silence like a little explosion. Well, not really hid, he told himself now, but what else can you call falling face down behind the sofa, and it not more than two feet from the wall? All because he didn't have curtains at the windows, and none on the glass-paned door either, this being an upstairs apartment he'd rented when he lost his wife and sold his house years ago to slouch wearily back into a single life.

He'd thought it was Ira Roth, come to fetch him to the nursery, where he spent hours on a daily basis spraying houseplants with mist from the hose or loading funeral wreaths in the van or pinching yellowing leaves off leggy scheffleras nobody wanted to buy. Ira would do something like that, coming to get him, because he didn't want to give a man a day off, ever. Plants don't take time off, Ira would say, waving his thick butcher's arm at the jungle he kept enclosed in hot, moist plastic. Who else was gonna give a one-armed man a job, he'd like to know. And doing what?

Ira said everything, never holding back for politeness or charity and especially not for wisdom's sake. Ira was certainly not wise, which would account for his storming up the steps beside Swift's Pharmacy to peer into the dingy glass of Fate's door. He would be hoping to find his only employee stretched out on the sofa, tiny earphone wires circling his bushy head while he listened to Kenny Rogers mellow and close in his ears.

Fate was the smart one—that was why, when he laid out of work like this, he didn't put on the earphones at all. He didn't even come into the living room except this once, looking for a Louis L'Amour paperback he'd started the night before.

Searching for the book among the litter of cracker boxes, TV dinner trays, and R.C. Cola cans, Fate had glimpsed something moving on the stair, a form unidentified in motion but scary enough to send him flopping to the floor, right behind the dilapidated green and orange floral sofa he'd dragged up the steps single-handed, thumping one of its legs so hard it came all the way off so that now a stack of old Louis L'Amours were rammed under that corner to keep it steady.

He waited, breathing the dusty floor, his good hand webby against the dangling rusty springs of the sofa, his lifeless hand curled under his heaving chest. He waited a long time, expecting to hear the thud of Ira Roth's tread back down, the cold muttering of his curse because now he knew Fate wasn't sick at all or else was dead in the bedroom, out of sight. Either way, it was trouble for Ira.

Minutes passed, long enough for Fate to get impatient for a look. He could literally feel someone there, only the glass separating them, but what was the person looking at? There was nothing in the room worth a second glance. One battered, cigarette-scorched table, a rummage-sale chair, the sofa, a lamp with a split shade and no finial to hold it straight. His tape player deep in the corner away from this week's worth of litter, a little oilstove sticking out of what had once been a fireplace opening. All of it dingy, drab, and temporary-looking.

He pulled himself into a crouch, then edged forward a little, crawling on his good arm, the other dragging against the splintery, dusty wood, and peeped around the end of the sofa, a quick look. Then a slightly longer glance because he didn't believe what he saw the first time. A girl was standing there, not looking in but giving him her profile as she stared out at the sky behind the building. She looked as if she was deciding what she should do next. He knew she was thinking, but she didn't seem especially worried or upset. He liked the quiet way she stood, as though concentrating on something specific, paying attention to whatever message she expected to get.

He looked again, more carefully this time and with less apprehension about being seen himself. He could see the slope of her breasts; heavy, they seemed, for a girl with so young a face and such thin shoulders. There was something odd about her. Something familiar, too, but he didn't know exactly what. He got up on his knees, intending to be standing whenever she happened to look his way again, but when he was half out of his crouch she looked toward him, straight through the glass as if she'd felt his movement. Before he was standing his full height, he knew who she was and why she'd come.

She looked like him, just a little, across the nose and cheekbones, which he considered the best of the Jessop features. High Indian cheekbones, smooth and leaving a slight hollow below like she had sucked in on a sourball. A straight short nose, hers perhaps a little too short but nice on a girl. Her face looked a little full when he got closer, swollen maybe around the eyes. Her breasts, too. And her waist. She was pregnant. No doubt about it. Eva Jessop, his niece who couldn't be many days past her fifteenth birthday, was standing on his landing, looking dully in at him, her hand lying on top of her bulge, waiting. He wished he'd gone to work.

He opened the door and pulled her in before he could think up an excuse not to. He knew her coming meant trouble for both of them. She was already in trouble, the evidence preceding her, pressed between them as he hugged her.

It must have been three years since he'd last seen her. At Christmas he'd ridden the bus two hundred miles to her house, the family home where he'd grown up and which now belonged to his younger brother, Clement.

He remembered how she looked then, eleven she would have

24

been, maybe twelve, a slight little thing with brown hair tied back with a paper ribbon. He remembered the red glints in her hair as she knelt before the tree, tiny blinking lights making a carnival of color around her as she handed out the presents. She called the names softly, so that twice her daddy told her to speak up. The family from the other side was there, Harriet's two sisters and their husbands. They were loud, jovial people, intent on enjoying themselves and very unlike the Jessops, who had all been taciturn, even shy, except for himself.

As a boy, Fate had been the bumbling idiot, always subject to family ridicule, defiant about education, ignorant of the social graces his mother claimed were the key to success. He'd been as irresponsible with money as with the family reputation and only later, when he'd left home for good, had he seen any value in the solemn, puritanic life his parents had tried to force on him. He'd seen himself become conscientious and thrifty, had settled down with Vickie and set goals for himself. Still, he'd never felt comfortable at home again, as if it were the scene of all his obnoxious behavior, the setting of unforgivable zaniness.

So he held himself aloof, being careful on his occasional visits not to play the fool anymore. He wanted to look respectable as he unwrapped his socks, a string tie, a jar of green-tomato pickles Harriet's sister had wrapped at the last minute when she'd heard he was coming. They all wanted him to have something. They tried to draw him out, to make him a part of their good cheer, but he never was.

Neither was this little girl, Eva. At least, that was how she'd always seemed to him. She seemed to be holding back a little, her eyes darting secretively, lips curled in a detached, bemused smile so she could always pretend she wasn't smiling at all. Harriet had conceived her late in life, then clung to her like a girl clings to her last doll, surreptitiously and with defiance against outgrowing important things. Eva seemed to know that and held herself back from the natural process of growing up as if to oblige her mother in every possible way.

But Clement and Harriet did get older and so did Eva. Obviously their efforts had counted for little, because there she stood in his shabby living room, hand to belly, embarrassed smile hovering on her dry colorless lips. Still, she looked contained to him, in control, as if her hand lightly resting was all the assurance she needed.

"Uncle Fate," she said, and her voice sounded just like it had when she called his name off the tag of a holiday package. "It's me, Eva."

"I know it," Fate said and hugged her again, clutching the thick, rough jacket that hung off her narrow shoulders.

She was wearing pants of some sort—denim jeans with the front cut out?—and a sweater loose at the neck and then stretching down over her stomach, barely covering. They weren't really maternity clothes, he didn't think, more like her old things forced into this peculiar use.

"Sit down, sit down," he said, because she seemed to be wavering in his arm, as light and willowy as a sapling. He was afraid she might faint.

"I don't want to bother you," she said, easing into the chair. Her belly rose to meet her breasts, all her weight concentrated in front while her small feet and arms were flung out to the sides and her small face rested on top. She could have been a child playing dress-up, pretending pregnancy with a pillow under her shirt.

"No bother," Fate said, sitting down on the sofa carefully to avoid the popped springs. "Lucky I wasn't at work. I didn't feel very good this morning, so I stayed home from the job."

"I hope I didn't wake you or anything," Eva said. She sighed and looked around the room. "This is nice. I mean, it's simple and all, but it's nice."

He could tell she was being polite. He knew what she was used to, the frilly bedroom, tiny print fabrics everywhere and coordinated pictures grouped on the papered walls. Cozy. Shag carpet throughout. In the living room, a sectional sofa and a glass coffee table about half the size of this room. He could remember the dark cumbersome furniture and the stiff, uncomfortable upholstery his mother had had, but now Clement and Harriet had redone the house in modern. Nothing spared and most of the family furniture discarded along the way.

"I came to see you," Eva started, still looking at the room. She was beginning to cry. The room was making her cry. This is what it's come to, she was thinking. Here with an uncle I hardly know in a dump like this—no curtains at the windows, no furniture that isn't Goodwill or worse except for that boogie box in the corner, probably a cheap one bought at a discount house, and those tapes they advertise on TV. This is what being accommodating comes to; one unsuspecting night of making out on the Dillard Farm Road with Chet Armstrong is all it takes to put you in a place like this or in a home for unweds or locked in your room with your own mother banging on the door, screaming how it's going to be.

Eva took the handkerchief Fate offered her and pressed it over her face, hiding her eyes from him. "I'm going to have a baby, Uncle Fate," she said, her voice muffled in the cloth.

"I see that," Fate said to help her.

"In two months," Eva added.

"That soon?"

"Well, it's been seven months already." Eva squeezed the handkerchief into a ball and held it on top of her belly. "Day in and day out for seven months, I've been pregnant." She sighed. "Of course, I didn't know it right away. I didn't feel funny or anything. I've never been real regular like a lot of girls are. And then it was too late." She seemed to be reciting a memorized monologue. "A girl I knew at school, I heard she'd had an abortion so I went to her and she told me where to go, to this clinic that sees women—people like me—and so I went and they said it was too late. There was nothing else to do, was there? I went home and told Mama and Daddy and it about killed them. I know it did. I kept apologizing and apologizing, but how much can you say? It didn't do any good, anyway. They were hurt and then they got mad and then they got this steely way about them, this determined look—stubborn, you know—and they

27

said I had to put the baby up for adoption. I could go to a home for unwed mothers they knew about or I could go to my mama's sister in Asheville. Those two choices. But there wasn't any choice about the baby. Well," she said, looking suddenly and closely at Fate so as not to miss a twitch of his reaction, "I couldn't do it. I can't do it. I want to keep this baby."

She waited for him to say or do something, to take on an expression like her daddy's. This would be the moment of truth. Right then and there she'd find out where Fate Jessop stood, no matter what words he spoke. She'd know from his expression, so familiar to her because it was like her own. The moves of that face were known to her, its ability to disclose with a twist of mouth, its caginess, its delight sparkling off blue eyes, round and wet now like her own.

"And you came to me," Fate said slowly and reached for the handkerchief in her hand. "Well, well." He dabbed at his eyes, then folded the damp cloth to a dry spot and reached forward to touch her cheeks. "You came to the right place, girl."

"My bag's on the landing," she said, pulling herself up. "I didn't bring much, sneaking out like I did. I didn't want to bring those clothes Mama had made up for me, anyway. Tent dresses to camouflage my condition, she kept saying, like I was sick. I'm not sick. I feel terrible about what's happened. I wish I weren't having a baby at all. I mean, nobody in her right mind wants a baby when she's fifteen. I want to finish high school and go to college, to business school at least. I always thought I'd be a good secretary. My mind works like that, keeping things in order. I can say the alphabet backwards.

"But first I've got this thing to do, you see, because this is what comes first right now. Having this baby and taking the best care of it I can, and then somehow finding a way to go back to school and get a good job. I've got money, too. All my own in my savings account. Most of it I earned, but some was presents. I've got two hundred dollars cash and a savings book right here. All I have to do once I get settled is make little withdrawals, however much I need, and make do with it. I can do it." She turned away from him to go out on the landing for her bag.

He let her go. He wanted a moment alone, one more moment before his life was forever different. He'd have to sleep on the sofa. It would never do for her and probably not for him more than one night. Why did he have a sofa like that anyway? Surely he could do better. Tomorrow he'd get a cot for himself and he'd start looking in the FOR SALE ads for good-quality used furniture, maybe even check the FOR RENT column for a better apartment, something on the ground floor so she wouldn't have to keep going up and down. He would go to work regularly and buy more than the cold cuts, frozen dinners, and cereal he ate at home. He'd get milk and eggs and leafy greens and ice cream and chicken. He'd—he stopped, seeing she was back in the room with him, her flowered canvas bag clutched in her hand, a shoulder bag with her name burnt in a circle of leaves dangling from her arm.

"Is it all right?" she asked him, seeing his expression of confoundment at all he wanted to do.

"It's fine," he said, his mouth working foolishly toward a grin. "Your Uncle Fate is going to take care of everything."

"I knew you would." That wasn't true, but now with her one hope realized, she wanted to believe she'd never doubted him.

"Let's get you settled then," he said, taking the bag from her. "Come right this way." And so he had ushered in his new life.

4

✦ The first thing he bought after a cot for himself was a crib for the baby. It was brand new and still boxed, so Eva helped him haul it up the steps without even knowing what she was carrying. He made her stop twice to rest, although she said she felt as healthy as a horse now that she'd had a few nights' sleep. She reminded him that she'd played softball and swam way into the summer, until her bathing suit got too tight. She'd felt fine and had looked as if she was just putting on a few extra pounds until the days moved toward September, with school starting again. Then suddenly she felt such heaviness in front that she found herself leaning back from it, spine arched in a sway. It had happened overnight, she said, surprise still surfacing in her voice when she thought about it.

Fate opened the carton in the living room, tearing out the giant metal staples with his pocketknife. He pulled out the pieces one at a time and examined them as if they were parts of a puzzle. Pale yellow side rail, curved headboard, wire springs. Eva was sitting in their one chair, face puffed up with excitement and exertion, watching as though she'd never seen a crib before and was just beginning to relate it to any need of hers.

"Hold this," he said and pushed the footboard into her hands to hold steady while he screwed the permanent side of the railing to it.

"Why, it's a baby bed!" Eva cried, as if she'd identified it by touch alone. "I thought I could use a cardboard box or a drawer or something, at least at first."

"No need now," Fate said, watching the turning screw bind the frame together. "Next week we'll get the mattress." He paused, then went on quickly, not wanting to contemplate how his weekly paycheck would have to stretch. He didn't want to touch his little bit of savings until he had to. "Then some sheets and a blanket. We'll make a list of things a baby needs."

"It's too much," Eva said. The footboard was wobbling in her hand. "It's enough that I can stay here with you, Uncle Fate."

"Live here," Fate corrected.

"But you don't even know the circumstances," Eva protested.

"I know you're here. Who would have thought it, an old geezer like me having folks come to him?"

"Still, you don't know—" Eva began.

"And you don't know much more about me, do you, honey? Like how come I'm not still married. Did you ever hear that I had a wife once? I reckon you didn't, but I had a wife. Vickie. Nothing so special about her—just a girl I met and started taking around. She had a job at the courthouse, a good position although she didn't seem to do much. Good money, though. I was working at the Chevrolet place. I'm a natural-born mechanic. You show me something once about a motor and I know it for life. At least, it used to be that way. I intended to buy myself a station—full-service place. Offer free coffee with a fill-up, keep windshields so slick they'd look invisible. Lubes, alignments, major and minor repairs, road service, the works. We were putting money in the bank toward it, had the right station picked out, everything set. Got a little house, too. Nothing fancy, but nice. Better than what Vickie was brought up with. Then this thing happens with my arm. Folks say I couldn't of heard that jack going, but I know I heard it—a cracking sound at my head like a hammer smacking a black walnut—and I slid out, free right to here." He gripped his lifeless arm with his good hand midway of his forearm. "They wanted to cut it off but I wouldn't let 'em. They got Vickie to begging at me, pleading. I turned my face away from everybody, even her. I did exercises, though. I did everything anybody said except that one thing, and here I am. Got this worthless appendage. Looks terrible, too. I know it. Useless things look terrible, people look away. But it's better than a stump and hard pain with nothing there."

Eva watched him go around to the other side of the crib, where he got on the floor to attach the railing on that side. She held it steady.

"Meanwhile I'm giving Vickie a hell of a time. I mean, I was in a bad mood every minute, fussing and fuming because I could see there wasn't going to be any service station, not with one hand and all that money going for doctors' bills. We were fighting and carrying on. We just didn't seem to have the right things between us anymore—that prospect of a future, you see,

31

or maybe it was ambition that had kept us together all along. Anyway, she finally got tired and up and left. She and a man at the courthouse. Left me six hundred dollars in savings and forty in checking. That wasn't all she took—fifteen thousand dollars between them out of county funds to get themselves a new start in life. Never caught her, either. I sold the house to support myself. Got different jobs, menial work a one-armed man can do. And here I am."

"I don't have a lot to tell," Eva said, as if it were her turn now. "Anyway, I can't talk about it yet."

"Then you just hold onto it, girl. And right now, hold this too." He motioned to the other end of the crib. "One thing, though, Eva. I've got to tell Clement and your mama that you're all right. I'll get him to promise not to bother you any, but I feel like I've got to tell them."

"But they will bother me. They'll be right over here ranting and raving at the door, harassing me!" Eva let go the headboard to clap her hands over her face. The crib slid sideways, assuming an odd, empty shape while Fate held onto it with one hand the best he could.

"Hold this dern thing, Eva!" he shouted, feeling it go, and she caught up her end again and stood there, mouth quivering, shoulders trembling, as still as she could be. She wouldn't look at him.

"Aw, come on, Eva," he said softly, setting the screwdriver into the Phillips head and giving a quick turn. "They're worrying about you. You know that. What else can I do?"

"You can not tell them where I am," Eva said. Her voice was icy, and Fate felt a shiver as if she'd touched him with it.

"We'll see," he said, getting up and standing back from his work. "Trust me, girl."

"I can't seem to do that with anybody," she said, still refusing to look.

Fate ended up not telling them where she was, just that she'd passed through. He'd seen her and she had money and was all right physically, he said, while Harriet wailed into the

32

phone loud enough for the customers in Roth's Nursery to pause and look around to see what punishment was being inflicted on what victim. He turned his back to them and said "sh-h-h-h-h" into the phone, as if that would make Harriet calm down and get the full benefit of his assurance.

"She spent the night with me, Clement," he said to his brother, who finally wrenched the phone out of his wife's frantic clutch. "She was on her way—to Florida. She said she had friends where it was warm and they were going to take care of her and the baby." He couldn't believe he'd made up such a lie right there, hanging onto the receiver and hearing his brother's frustrated, angry breath snorting at him.

"She doesn't know a soul in Florida," Clement barked in his ear. "How would she know anybody from Florida, I want to know?"

"I can't answer that," Fate said calmly. "I can just tell you what she told me."

"Wait a minute, hold the phone!"

He could hear an anxious buzz like a blowfly trapped in a bathroom; then the voice came back. "Harriet says it's those Hardestys. They lived here, just down the street, about two years ago. Moved to Florida. A houseful of kids. Brats. We were glad to see them go. I reckon that's who she's talking about. They'd do something like take in a runaway. No more sense than that." He seemed more content, almost satisfied that Eva had made such an unfortunate choice. "Well, thanks for calling, Fate," he said. "If you hear from her again, let us know."

"Goes without saying," Fate replied and hung up.

He was sweating. The moist air of the greenhouse hung on him, sticking cloth to skin. He looked at the faces edging past him, suspicious eyes cutting over spiky bromeliads or beneath the fluff of hanging maidenhair ferns. They all knew he had lied. Probably Clement knew it too and was already in his Buick, accelerating into the flow of traffic that would put him on Fate's landing in three hours' time.

He had never been good at lying. He had taken a lie detector test when Vickie embezzled the county funds to prove he wasn't a liar. The man at the sheriff's office read his pulse and respiration rate racing on the graph, watched the marker swooping up and down even when he was asked to give his name, his age, his address. The graph was no different when he answered questions about Vickie and her whereabouts.

Did he know about the money? Did he know about her relationship with this Larry Dixon? His heart was broken and yet it raced on, blood pounding in his throat, as he told the terrible truth. He knew nothing.

He wondered now what he would have done if he'd known something of significance to tell the sheriff. Even what clothes Vickie was wearing. What she had carried in her suitcase. He didn't even know that. The closet looked full to him. The missing lingerie and jewelry he could not describe and probably couldn't even identify if he saw it again. He was not, he admitted, an observant man. What he remembered was the shape of her thigh under his hand, the taste of wintergreen on her tongue, the sound of her coming out of sleep in the morning, head crackling and dry with allergy, the noise of her clearing her throat in the bathroom, the honking as she blew her clogged nose open into a wad of toilet tissue.

He didn't say any of those things to the sheriff's deputies as they slouched about the office, leaning against the walls and hanging off the edges of desks. They looked sluggish and bored. He irritated them with his consistent lack of expeditious information. Didn't he know his wife?

He explained about his arm, still in a sling. They nodded but not with sympathy. They didn't seem to understand that he had abandoned his ambition, a dream stunted in an instant of crashing metal, the rim of a Chevy cutting him off like a blade severing a towline. He was sinking, wifeless, jobless, lifeless. He got tears in his eyes, but they didn't notice. The haze of smoke in the crowded, dismal little room was making his eyes water. They'd let him go. . . .

He hurried home to Eva, the truck tearing down the gravel road from the nursery to the highway. He had learned to shift and steer at the same time; during those moments of transition, he leaned his left side into the wheel, forcing it steady against his dead arm. Someday he would have automatic transmission. That, rather than a sticker announcing his handicap. He refused to display the sticker issued him by the license examiner, who didn't know it was Ira Roth's automatic Ford he was driving.

He drove defensively, though, cautiously, always prepared to suddenly gear down, his shoulder swung slightly forward in readiness. Now he scurried across town, the old truck grumbling and rattling, getting home to Eva before any harm could come to her. He had felt vibrations of alarm shooting off the telephone wire, seeking her out. Harriet's hysterical pitch would alert local police, sheriff, juvenile authorities that a fifty-eight-year-old man, practically a derelict but the child's uncle nevertheless, had abducted her, holding her against reason in his shabby walk-up.

He parked the truck in the alley and raced up the stairs, canvas slip-ons pounding the rickety wooden steps he must do something about. He turned his skeleton key in the old lock and found the apartment empty. Bed made, spread pressed neatly under the pillows, the furniture shimmering with polish, the smell of lemon oil thick in the air. The television abandoned and silent, broken knob sticking out, pliers used for changing channels on top. The crib intact awaiting its mattress and the bunny sheets he planned to buy, along with a soft furry yellow blanket.

He went into the kitchen: counter shining, chipped Formica table cleared of breakfast, the condiments and her vitamins neatly arranged in the center, the aluminum coffeepot on the tiny stove half full and cool. No sign of escape, of frantic fleeing, of struggle. A women's magazine on the tank top in the bathroom, her things on the windowsill: Secret, beige liquid in a small bottle, baby powder, a tube of lipstick with a clear top smeared inside with pink so it was opaque.

He went back to the bedroom, feeling calmer now, the panic of his lie settling in his stomach. There were no consequences yet. He saw her shoulder bag on the dresser, ivy encircling a stenciled EVA. She hadn't taken that. He peeped inside—savings book in plastic cover, comb and brush, a soiled envelope folded three times, its edges worn through. Her wallet, an expensive leather French purse with pockets for coins, slots for credit cards and identification, a plastic picture holder.

He thumbed through the pictures. School photos of high school girls, braces glinting under lips pulled tightly down and yet trying to look pleasant, to almost smile. They had sad expressions, caught between embarrassment and the desire to have a presentable picture in the yearbook. They looked like Eva, although none of them was she. All had the same sleek, brushed hair with short wings in front, a recent concession to softness. They all wore those high-neck sweaters that rolled over several times and then flopped in front, a shiny monogrammed stickpin caught in the folds.

Fate turned to the boys, only three of them after so many girls. A long neck, solemn pimpled face, eyes questioning: Do I look all right? Is this my best shot? The next one looked confident; broad tanned face, thick neck, dark wavy hair slicked down a little as if he'd just come from the locker room. Half a smile, as if he were a little pleased with his looks and couldn't deny his conceit. He was the most likely parental candidate so far, Fate thought, studying the heated eyes. If it turned out to be a black-haired baby, he'd know where to look.

Then the last, such an ordinary face that at first glance Fate almost went past it, but then something held his eye, made him peer closer into the faded color. The picture was slightly overexposed. Too much light reached into the boy's eyes and eliminated the shadows natural to his crevices. He looked a little wild without contours, flat-faced and looming toward the surface, although he could as easily be a slight person, a boy not yet grown. He was blond, no demarcation between hair and skin, all washed out. Even his eyes, pale blue and held open to the glare as though he were startled, betrayed nothing. He could have let his lids drop in a quick blink and the camera could have held him there, shut up like portholes closed, and it wouldn't have mattered. The eyes let nothing in, gave nothing out. Were as empty as two dull enamel cereal bowls.

"That's him," Eva said at Fate's elbow, startling him so he clapped the wallet closed.

"The father?" Fate asked, glancing at her to see that she wasn't angry at his snooping. She didn't seem to mind at all. He opened the wallet for another look at the face.

"God, no." Eva sighed. "He's the other reason I ran off, besides Mama and Daddy."

"Him?" Fate asked, nodding at the innocuous, blank face.

"Him." Eva pinched the pictures together in Fate's hand.

He could tell she didn't plan to say any more, just leave him dangling with the memory of the face already drifting away. It wasn't a face worth remembering except that she had given importance to it.

"I called your folks," Fate said, watching her pulling off her coat. Her face was chapped on cheeks and nose from the November wind and her hair looked brittle and electric. "I didn't tell them anything except that I'd seen you and you were heading for Florida. I don't know why I said that."

"You had to say something," Eva said. She didn't seem particularly grateful for his lie. He saw she had already come to expect as much.

"Well, it wasn't easy," Fate said, slightly miffed. "Your mother was hysterical. They might be coming here right now. They might of known I was lying."

"No." Eva hung up the coat in his closet and stretched out on the bed, her sneakers slightly off the edge.

"Why don't you take your shoes off?" Fate asked her.

"It's too much trouble to reach down," Eva answered. "Have you ever had to reach over something like this?" She patted her belly, which sat like a little mountain above her thin legs.

He reached down to pull one dirty string of a sneaker and

then the other. It wasn't always easy with one hand. Sometimes he created a knot instead of releasing one. Now the tie came loose and fell away. He slipped the heel off and dropped her shoe to the floor. Then he did the other one as slowly, feeling her watch him.

"You've got to see a doctor, Eva," he said, watching her curling her toes inside her socks—his socks, they looked like, permanently dingy, with three red bands at the top.

"I want to have the baby here," Eva said.

He looked at her face to see that she meant right there, on his bed. "You can't do that, Eva. Nobody does that. That's why we've got hospitals now, so babies can get born in sterile conditions with all the best equipment."

"I won't go," Eva said stubbornly. She eyed him over her bulge as if she knew it was her weapon, a power over him. "I looked in the phone book downstairs in the drugstore. There's a clinic here that does home deliveries if everything is all right."

"There is not!" Fate said, although he suspected he was up against facts. She had made inquiries, and he could see her determination.

"Is too!" Eva cried. "It's a clinic and I go there for checkups and they do home deliveries. I'm going tomorrow for my first appointment."

"But here, Eva? I don't know anything. I don't even have a big pot to boil water in!" Fate cried.

"We'll get one," Eva said. "You don't have to do anything, Uncle Fate. I promise you that."

He stood staring down at her, appalled by the sight of this person on his bed, her jeans riding up her calves, hands flat and open on his spread. He didn't know what to say to her, seeing as he did around them, spinning like dust motes in the room, all the things he had never done and would now somehow do, for her sake.

5

✦ Sara Will watched the day come in. The solid heavy black of her walls slowly lightened from the center while the edges held the dark in deep ruffles. The gray was thick, a weighted lusterless hue as it pressed on the surfaces of her furniture, obscuring them in dense shadow. While she watched, a pearly tint added its light to the gray, thinning it out like a piece of moiré taffeta, a party dress she'd had years ago when she was still in school and took a vague interest in what she wore. Whatever brought that to her mind? A shimmering gray dress and Mama's pearls, a single strand with a slight pink cast to them when held to light. She had looked good dressed up like that, silver shoes, nylons, her hair swooped up high in the back although the sides dipped to her flushed cheeks, softening her face with loose wisps the color of copper. She had been like a jewel when she fixed herself up like that, hard and contained. She had sparkled on her surface but she had known, even then, that it was all surface. The person she was stayed hidden underneath.

She lay flat on her bed, trying to turn her mind back to the dawning light which now settled on her bed, slowly brightening the disarray in her room. Her unsightly clutter, clothes flung over a chair, pins dropped on her dresser, caused her to close her eyes. After a moment she opened them again to stare at the ceiling, that undisturbed realm above her head where only spiders reached, spiders and moths drawn to warm light. Lingering there, between her head and the ceiling, was a slight haze, almost diaphanous, into which her mind could escape.

Just then she heard a noise; she found herself listening intently to it. What could it be? she wondered as she stared at the light floating below her ceiling on the still air. She wasn't alarmed by the sound. Surprise was done with because during the night she had snapped open her eyes to the compressed dark of her room to stare at the sound of a baby's wail. She had thought she was dreaming, a nightmare of some abandoned infant left on her doorstep, and had blinked herself awake, thinking, whatever will I do? Then she realized the baby was not on her doorstep at all but already in the house, across the hall in Serena's room. There was nothing for her to do. Not now. Yesterday, however, that baby had been on her doorstep and she had done nothing. Swanee Hope had been the one to bring them in.

It was a mistake, too. Sara Will knew that. She'd known she was in for trouble from the first moment, when she'd looked down on their heads from the roof. She'd known just by the look of them that there wasn't a share of good breeding between them, no sense of the appropriate gesture, the polite but firm refusal to be a bother. But Swanee wouldn't know trouble until it scratched her eyes out. Swanee was silly, frivolous, an aggravation, a constant nagging pain like the ache following a gallbladder attack that reminds you it will strike again. Swanee bothered the quiet, punctuated every silence with her foolish chatter and the racket of her modern conveniences.

Sara Will closed her eyes, holding them tight as she frowned at the ceiling. This was all Swanee's fault, these people in the house, a baby disrupting her sleep, and now this noise below. She waited, not wanting to get up although the autumn light on her walls told her that it was after seven. She didn't want to confront the noise, which creaked and stumbled below like a burglar.

Wasn't it better to feign sleep than to risk a thump on the head, a pistol wound, a hand at the throat? No, she said to herself, eyes popped open again. It was better to protect what was yours. It was better to take the offensive, carry your own club, sound your own alarm.

She got out of bed, touching the cold floor as lightly as she could. She pulled on thin anklet socks and stepped into her house shoes, old ragged terrycloth things she'd washed the life out of. The chill caught her at shoulders and chest and she slipped into a chenille robe, hem dragging the floor in back. She pulled it tight to her neck, then knotted the frayed belt. She went downstairs.

Fate was tending the woodstove. He had put the kindling in and was loading the wood. He wore different clothes from yesterday—old jeans and a plaid shirt unbuttoned over a T-shirt, work boots with laces hanging and tongues protruding. The heavy open shoes seemed obscene to her, so she moved her eyes upward toward his wild head, dry and frizzy in the cold. She saw he had shaved. His face looked clean and new, open to her like a child's face.

If he hadn't seen her, she would have ducked away from the door and gone back upstairs, but it was too late. He was smiling at her and she felt herself smiling back. It was all because she'd been taken by surprise, she reasoned. The whole idea of people in the house had befuddled her.

"I woke up," Fate said apologetically and struck a match on the metal stove. He held the fire to a rolled-up scrap of newspaper, and the flame sizzled along the edge of the print, sliding blackly toward his hand. He pushed the burning paper under the kindling. "I wanted to have the fire going, the coffee made. Get the house warmed up for you." He smiled again.

"We have oil heat," Sara Will said, clutching her robe tightly under her chin. "I just haven't gotten the furnace going yet." She refused to smile at him again. This was serious to her and she must show it. She disapproved of his being here, especially of his being in her kitchen and tending her stove. "I can do that," she said, nodding toward it.

"All done," Fate said. He peered into the opening where orange flames sucked at the air, and then shut the latch. "It's going good."

"The coffee, then," Sara Will said. "I'll make the coffee."

"It's on. See?" He nodded toward the pot on the back eye of the electric stove. "I found the coffee up there. I didn't know how strong to make it so I just did what I do at home. Come in," he added, because she was still standing in the doorway.

She was looking away from him, focusing on the last yellow leaves of the gingko tree outside the window. Sunlight shone through the veins, shimmered off leaves lying momentarily flat. The tree had always seemed mysterious to her, exotic among the ordinary dogwoods and hollies that grew up wild in the yard, although the gingko with its oddly carved leaves was as familiar as the others. Suddenly now, as she peered across the room at the golden gingko, everything in her life seemed fraught with newness. Peculiar specters had appeared on her horizon to change the shape of things.

She straightened her shoulders and turned her head to stare straight at the core of the trouble. Fate was putting cups on the table, two cups in their saucers on two woven place mats, one at her place, one opposite.

"Straight up," he said, motioning for her to come.

"What straight up?" she asked. The sound of his voice disturbed her. She longed for silence, and yet she had asked a question. "What?" she repeated, inviting reply.

"Your coffee," Fate said warmly. "No milk or sugar. You see, I remember from last night." He grinned and brought the perking pot to the table to pour. The liquid streamed down, letting off its rich steam. "Here it is."

She sat down at her place, her hands tight in her lap. Her robe fell open a little at the neck, showing the plain edge of her gown, the decorative little buttons down the yoke. She felt exposed and yet she didn't move her hands, which clutched at each other in her lap. She thought she might cry out. She could hear the sound: angry, plaintive, strangled.

But no, she couldn't even do that. She was mesmerized by the smell of the coffee, the warmth pressing on her from the stove, the presence of this man across the table from her. He sipped at his coffee, testing for heat and flavor, then gulped down a scalding swallow. "Good," he said, looking up at her.

She brought her hands to the cup. It was hot. She could feel the heat for seconds after she drew her fingers away. She curled a finger into the crook, her other hand at the rim, and slowly, carefully, lifted the cup to her cool lips.

"Yes," she said, setting the cup back into its saucer, where it seemed to tremble a little, rocking slightly as if to betray her unsteady hand. "It's good."

Fate carried Eva a cup of coffee laced with milk and sugar. It was a habit begun soon after she'd arrived at his apartment. He'd gotten up early those first days, fixing himself a little breakfast, dressing for work, using the bathroom as quietly as he could. He would have to pass the foot of her bed, and he did so soundlessly, trying not to look at her.

At first, early in the morning, he even tried to pretend she wasn't there. He would squint against seeing the rumpled, burdened old bed. He refused to see one hand outstretched over the edge, dangling lifelessly toward the cold floor. She seemed too vulnerable even for his caring eyes.

But one morning she spoke to him. "It's all right," she said into the pillow, and he heard the bed creak as she swung her arm over and lay flat on her back, a round mountain of baby rising between her pale face and his. "I'm awake."

And so he brought her coffee, amends for having awakened her. After that, he frequently thought she was awake before he was. Sometimes she seemed so alert when he came into the room, so wide-eyed and anxious that he thought she'd been waiting for him to bring her out of some kind of predawn panic that afflicted her like the tingling pain of a sleeping limb suddenly coming awake. Surely she must be afraid sometimes. He was.

He got so he'd sit down with her a minute, his coffee on the table beside her. Sometimes her hand would be outside the cover, resting on top of the baby mound, and once he reached over and put his good hand on top of hers. He didn't know exactly why he did that because he really felt a little embarrassed at being in the bedroom with her. It seemed inappropri-

43

ate, and yet his hand went up spontaneously and touched hers and just then the baby moved. He felt a quick hard thrust of muscle and bone—a foot, maybe a hand—coming into his palm through hers. He started to pull away. This was too intimate, too far beyond his sense of propriety. But she lifted her fingers between his and held his hand there so that when the baby moved again, he was prepared for the life springing under his hand and was able to smile a little at Eva, acknowledging the quick movement.

Since then he'd always brought her coffee. After the baby came she was up at night, usually alone because there was nothing he could do to help her with the nursing. He would lie awake through it all, though, waiting for the bedroom to grow quiet again, listening to her sing softly, crooning an out-of-key tune like a weary insomniac in the dark.

But even with so little sleep, she always awoke to have the coffee. Tiny Rachel would be in the crib beside the bed, Fate between mother and daughter. Some mornings he had to force himself up and out, although by then he always went to work, knowing they needed the money he earned.

Now he knocked on the door of Eva's room, the steaming mug held out from his chest. He heard her moving in the bed and so he pushed the door open a crack with his foot and peeped in. She was waiting for him but she looked tired, frail and unkempt with that terrible bleached hair stringing around her face and her cheeks and eyelids swollen.

"You didn't sleep," he said. "I heard you up with Rachel."

"She fussed all night," Eva said, taking the coffee and drinking deeply. "Probably because I was so worried she would. I've never had to worry she'd disturb anybody before—except you, of course."

"She's never bothered me," Fate said, sitting on the edge of the bed.

"That's a lie," Eva said, but she was beginning to smile. The coffee was warming her, and just looking at him seemed to comfort her.

44

"What we've got to do is talk about the future," Fate said. He looked over at the crib where Rachel was sleeping peacefully now, her face away from him, knees tight under her so her bottom stuck up under the yellow blanket.

"Remember how I was going to go back to school, maybe even to college? Remember all those fine ideas I had?" Eva said, her voice a hoarse whisper. "I didn't know anything, Uncle Fate."

"You're still going to do those things," Fate said softly. "It's just taking a while."

"I ought to go back home. I know that. I ought to have gotten on a bus one day, me and Rachel, and gone back there and suffered the consequences." Eva sniffed and stared into her coffee.

"It would of broke my heart, Eva," Fate said, "and that's the truth."

"Well, we can't stay here," Eva said defiantly, still not looking at him. "I know you thought this was a good place to come to. It's out of the way and all, just like you said, but these women aren't my relatives like you are. They've got no reason in the world to care about me and mine."

"They're your daddy's first wife's sisters," Fate said, as if that could possibly be a reason.

"Uncle Fate," Eva said, looking up at him with weary eyes. "Sara Will and Swanee were your sisters-in-law for fourteen months, isn't that right? That's all there was to it. I'm surprised you could even find this place after all these years. My God, it's in the sticks just like you said it was."

"And that's why we've got to arrange to stay, Eva. Because it's in the sticks and he won't ever find you here."

"Maybe he won't. There's no telling about him. But I can't stay where my baby and I aren't welcomed. Can't you see that?"

"I don't see that we're not welcomed, girl. You're here in this nice place, all cozy. I've got that room down the hall to myself. There's space enough. I intend to withdraw my savings all along

45

to help pay our keep. I can fix up around here a little. I didn't get much of a look yesterday, but I suspect this place is half falling down. Winter's coming on and there's a mighty lot of wood out there to be split. They need us just about as bad as we need them, Eva. We've just got to show them that."

"Well, you better get at it." Eva handed him the empty mug. "It's up to you, because I don't see any way I can look like anything but a nuisance to them, and I'm not staying here unless I feel welcome."

The mug had lost its heat in his hand, and he put it down on the table. "You've got to tie my shoes before I can do anything," Fate said. "I felt like a dern fool down there in the kitchen with my boots untied in front of Miss Sara. She noticed, too. She notices everything she don't like, I can tell that about her. I knew I shouldn't of let you talk me into these fool things. A one-armed man with laces to tie."

"I told you I'd do it," Eva said, motioning for him to swing his foot onto the bed. She fixed a quick tight knot and waited for the other foot.

"You might not always be around," Fate said irritably. Having to face how she had so completely invaded his life always frustrated him. He had changed almost everything about himself because of her.

"Then ask Sara Will to tie your shoes," Eva teased him.

"I'd as soon ask a bear for a lick of honey," Fate said.

"Swanee Hope, then." Eva giggled.

Fate couldn't help but grin. "Now that, my girl," he said, "is a real possibility."

Swanee Hope got completely dressed before coming down to breakfast, although it was not her custom. She liked to lounge a bit in the morning, gradually slipping into the day so that by the time the coffeepot was dry she was ready to exert herself a little. Stir up something in the kitchen, crochet a few rows on the afghan she was making for Sara Will's Christmas present, or maybe dust the pictures in the parlor where she could pause at each face, telling some part of their story in her head because Sara Will didn't want to hear. Sara Will wanted everybody to keep quiet.

Sara Will, still in her robe, was at the sink washing up a few things.

"Where are they?" Swanee whispered, coming close to Sara's shoulder.

"Upstairs," she answered, holding a cup under the spigot.

"Where upstairs?"

"In Serena's room, I believe."

"All of them?"

"I believe Mr. Jessop took Eva a cup of coffee. It seems that every morning he takes her coffee in bed," Sara Will said, not looking at Swanee's blustering face.

"Well, I never! Who would of thought of such?"

"Not you, Swanee. You never think, that's the whole trouble. What are they doing here? I ask you that. Last night at supper, you had opportunity. You could have asked them why they've come. After all, even *they* should admit this is peculiar. More than that, Swanee, it's intolerable. They have to go." Sara Will straightened her shoulders and set a saucer in the plastic drain.

"But Sister, what if they are destitute?" Swanee Hope asked. She came closer to Sara Will, her voice croaking out an excited whisper. "What if they have no place else to go?"

"Eva has parents, we know that. And Mr. Jessop is a grown man who can take care of himself. If they need money, I suppose I can spare a few dollars, but that's as far as it can go, Swanee. Do you understand me?"

"There's a poor infant up there, Sara," Swanee said, lifting her eyes to the ceiling. "There's a sixteen-year-old mother. Don't you feel the least bit sorry for them?"

"They slept comfortably last night," Sara said, wiping her hands on a dish towel. "They had a good supper, and they can have breakfast this morning. That's all I have to give them. That's all, Swanee."

47

It was true while she said it. Hearing the words seemed to give them validity. They took on power in the still kitchen air. The woodstove popped and sent off raging heat. She felt the heat under her skin, seeping like oxygen through her veins. Her anger seemed indigenous, as natural as breathing. She stared at Swanee, who, mournful with regret, had already turned down the corners of her mobile, flittering mouth preparing to cry.

"Don't, Swanee," Sara Will said. "Don't you dare." But Swanee was sending the flow of ready tears down her trembling cheeks.

Sara Will turned back to the sink while her sister quivered and made soft snorts into her handkerchief. She could feel the morning suddenly spreading out. It glared at her, some inner light in the house, blinding and hot. She stood at the sink, her straight unyielding back to her sobbing sister, and felt a new heat, like the possibility of some momentous and monstrous change in her life, glowing in her chest. It nauseated her with unexpected warmth as it churned there like a spring. Sour water floated into her throat and she swallowed hard.

"Stop it, Swanee," she said, surprised at the calmness of her own voice.

"I can't," Swanee wailed. "I can't stop thinking about that poor little baby."

"Until tomorrow, then," Sara Will said, surprised again. She had not expected to give in. She seemed to be losing so much. It frightened her, and yet she admired her new hospitality. It was like suddenly remembering what to do with a third spoon or the play of cards in a complicated game.

"I'll tell them," Swanee Hope said, patting her face, "and then I'll make a custard, something the baby can eat. Everybody likes a nice custard, don't they, Sara Will?"

"Everyone within my acquaintance," Sara Will said. But these were not people she knew.

6

◆ Fate found the go-devil, an ax, and a sledgehammer under the shed beside the barn. In the heavy shade of the lean-to, he crouched against the rough board wall, feeling the frigid morning air plunge into his lungs. It hurt. Cold had always hurt him. It made his ears ache clear down into his jaws. He felt his lungs exploding with frozen air and he pounded his good hand solidly against his chest as if he could knock the pain free. His arm hurt too, sympathizing with the frost-curled leaves and the skim of icy, glinting light which reflected as if off glass as sunlight slipped through the open boards between the shed and the barn.

Reflected off what? he wondered and, suddenly revived by curiosity, stood up to put his eye to the slit. He knew it was none of his business what Miss Sara Will Burney was hoarding in there which held the sparkle of light, but finding out might just be pertinent to his situation. Anything he could know about the woman might help him.

Probably just rows of empty Mason jars, he thought, squinting so the light in the barn grew furry, then expanded into milky rays that refused to come into focus. Well, he would just have a little look-see, payment for inflicting this bitter cold on himself. He put the tools against the barn and pushed on the door. It moved slowly, creaking on its ancient hinges, complaining in the cold.

It was a car. A white car. With plates on it. Good tires, a recent wax job. It was a car somebody drove. By God, he said to himself as he slid his palm along the clean cold surface of the hood, Sara Will Burney is somebody to reckon with. Why, she's got herself a '65 Mustang! He knew it was her car, not Swanee Hope's. He was absolutely positive. Only Sara Will would have bought a car like this.

He could imagine her down at the Ford place looking sternly bored while the dealer showed her Classics and Corsairs with velvety upholstery to guarantee her a comfortable ride, automatic windows, a trunk opener in the glove pocket. All the while she would have been looking around the man, over and beyond his shoulder, while she stood with her hands tucked under her elbows, pocketbook caught in the lock of her crossed arms. She was seeing the white Mustang, small, fast-looking, a jaunty red stripe running down its nose.

"What about that one?" she probably said, cutting the salesman off mid-sentence.

"Where?" The man would follow her pointing hand to the far side of the lot where the Mustang waited. "Why, Miss Burney, that's the sports model, the newest thing in the line!" He would pause, waiting for her to turn her attention back to him, but she would move around him toward the car.

"We'll just have a little look at it, then," he'd say, hurrying to catch up with her. Five minutes showing cold vinyl upholstery on sporty bucket seats, automatic transmission on the floor, and he'd have her back with the Classic, the comparison having added spaciousness to his list of luxury car attributes.

"You couldn't transport many of your friends in this," he'd say, leaning against the side of the Mustang. "Now that Classic over there gives you the room you need."

"For what?" Sara Will would have asked, peering into the window at the slick red wheel, the sparkling instruments on the padded dash. "I don't carry anyone but myself." She would have opened the door and gotten in.

Fate could imagine her sitting there, knees up high, her body tilted back a little as if she were in a rocking chair. The salesman was probably smiling as he leaned against the door, not looking in at her but grinning into the sunlight.

This would be something to tell: Miss Sara Will Burney pretending to drive a Mustang, the first one he'd gotten on the lot. It wasn't the kind of car his customers were supposed to want, at least that was what Detroit had told him. They were sending

50

these sporty cars to suburban areas, places where young people had money and few restrictions. "But we'll send you one and see how you do," they'd said. Well, he was doing all right.

"What do you think, Miss Burney?" he'd ask, squeezing a smile between his lips as he bent down to look in at her.

"I think I'll take it," she must have said.

Fate was laughing. He pushed the door handle release but nothing happened. Locked. Another of Sara Will's barricades against him. Well, he wanted to get in that car and he intended to. He wanted to sit there in the cold where nobody had probably ever sat except Sara Will for fifteen years. He wanted to drive, too, and he could because it was an automatic. He wanted control over that car. It was something he knew about. He could check out the engine, tune her up, change the oil, rotate the tires, flush out the radiator. Whatever was needed he would do. How he'd missed working on cars! He had forced himself not to think about it for a long time. All these years he'd closed off the part of his mind that understood motors. He had cooled the senses that sniffed oil and heard a dissident rumbling under a revving engine. His fingers had grown stiff, denied the tactile comfort of a wrench warming in his hand.

He put his good hand on the car, rubbing gently like an experienced horseman calming a colt. It was himself he was calming. The cold slick metal sent shivers up his arm, straight into his chest. One thing at a time, he said to himself. First split the wood, ingratiate yourself to buy some time, a day or two at least. Then instigate a quick look under the hood, next a little spin, just down the road and back to check her out.

He breathed deeply, although his lungs still ached from the crisp air of the chilly autumn morning. He would have to be patient. He could see that. He would have to pretend no interest in the car if he were to succeed in his wooing for time. Well, he had learned to wait. He had taught himself patience after Vickie left, while he was still expecting her to come back to him. He had let himself believe that the embezzlement and disappearance were mistakes or that she was the hostage of a crazy man.

The authorities had kept asking if that were possible, as if he could have read Vickie's mind and known the truth. He didn't know if she was clever enough to carry off such a crime. He didn't know her capabilities.

But the experience had taught him something about his own abilities. He was capable of doing nothing, of waiting. That was what he'd been doing for years, until Eva came. And when she arrived, he'd found out something else about himself. He was capable of action, too.

He had run away from home because of Eva. That was what they'd done. Why, he'd packed up that truck at three o'clock in the morning, Eva anxiously watching from the window while Rachel slept in her arms. They'd driven off, the streetlights casting an eerie bluish glow on the pile of junk in the truck bed and on Eva's drawn, narrow face. She'd looked ghostly, like a shadowy, lifeless spook. If he'd let himself think at all, he'd have known what they were doing was stupid.

They drove all night in the wrong direction. It took him that long to decide where they should go. They were almost out of North Carolina, going west on spiny two-lane roads, when it occurred to him that taking Eva and her baby across the state line was probably a crime. He didn't know for sure, but the possibility scared him enough that when they stopped mid-morning to get breakfast, he pulled out his only map, one so old it was split at the folds and lacked the major interstate system. He traced his finger over it, searching for something, anything, a message, directions to some hidden, unimagined place. His hand skimming the foothills to the south had suddenly come to rest on Tyler Mills. He had squinted at the dot, his eyes weary from the night driving, his head throbbing for caffeine.

Tyler Mills. He could see the bleak little town, one straight narrow street of brick storefronts, their canvas awnings rolled up like eyelids over vacant eyes. He remembered how the hills rolled right down toward the street as if they threatened to push the town even closer into itself, isolating it completely in a crevice below the brown shelves of scrub oaks and scruffy pines. That day when Clement brought his young wife's body home, people stopped on the sidewalk with their hats against their chests and averted their eyes. They were private people.

So were the Burneys. They hardly noticed Clement, ignoring his young raw grief, and paid even less attention to the other Jessops, Fate included, culprits all who had come along to offer an explanation. They wanted to tell the story of how Serena died, but the Burneys wouldn't hear it. They wouldn't alleviate the Jessops' guilt by listening to it, so they simply sat in the parlor around the coffin, which had been placed on three sawhorses, hardly speaking to anyone and wiping the random tears evoked by some small, unspoken memory. They were waiting for the trip down the road and across Sparrow Creek to the cemetery. They wanted to be done with it and then left alone. They had already shared Serena and look what their generosity had come to.

But one of the sisters cried out: the younger one, Sara Will, with auburn hair, who looked like Serena had but more angular, taller, half grown, her body straining against the wool of her hand-me-down dress. She screamed out just once, as if suddenly and for an instant her imagination had taken hold and she could see her sister's laborious death, her heavy pain and quick breathing, the rushing blood at the end that soaked into the thin bedding and dripped, unstoppable even in the cool air, through the slats to the floor.

Nobody moved to comfort Sara Will, and the girl composed herself without another sound except the hard shuddering of her breath as she bore down against her terror.

Staring at the map in the diner, Fate remembered Sara Will Burney's face. He saw the house, remembering its size and isolation. "This is where we're going," he said to Eva, who sat across the booth from him, her own face stunned and plain in the weary, endless aftermath of their escape.

She nodded to him, not bothering to answer. Back in the

truck, they turned southeastward, out of the mountains toward a hiding place.

Fate went out to the woodpile where he balanced a short fat log on end, gave it one solid whack with the go-devil to settle it in the slit, and brought the sledgehammer down on it. The log fell in two. Then he split the halves, sliding his hand down the smooth ax handle. He could split dry wood with one hand, although he knew he'd have a sore arm tomorrow. It was the toting and stacking that would give him trouble. He decided to let the splits lie until Eva could come out and help him.

The sun was moving above the barn, melting the frost and warming his shoulders. He pulled off his wool jacket and flung it on the ground. This was what he needed, a good sweat and honest work to do. He didn't have to think when he chopped wood, could just fall into the rhythm of the ax and feel the tension in his muscles letting go as the metal sank into the wood.

"Yoo-hoooo!" Swanee Hope was calling to him from the back door. She stood under the little roof of the landing, her body pitched slightly forward as if this were as far as she should go. "Yoo-hoooo! Mr. Jessop!"

"Yes, ma'am," Fate called back, leaning on the ax. He gave her his most welcoming smile, so big the movement of his jaws made his Navy-surplus toboggan ease up over his ears. He took the cap off altogether, crammed it in his pocket, and was attempting to smooth down his wild, electric hair when Swanee Hope came tripping across the damp grass. She bounced lightly, as if she could avoid any contact with earth. Stopping in front of him but slightly distant, she pulled her sweater tightly to her chest, holding it together instead of buttoning it.

"Mr. Jessop," she panted at him, "this is not at all necessary. Sara Will said for me to tell you that she has someone coming— I don't know exactly who, but someone—to split the wood. She's called somebody, she says, and so it's unnecessary."

Swanee Hope blew out one of her warm little puffs of exasperation at him.

"You tell Miss Sara that calling somebody to split the wood is what's unnecessary," Fate said, hoisting the go-devil.

"But you only have one arm, Mr. Jessop!" Swanee Hope cried.

"It's less of a handicap than your sister realizes," Fate said patiently. "Tell her to call and cancel her woodcutter."

"I don't think she will," Swanee Hope said, getting worried now. She rubbed her hands on her arms, plucking nervously at the wool. "You have to understand about Sara Will, Mr. Jessop," she began cautiously, a frown drawing tiny furrows at the bridge of her nose. "She's used to doing things her own way."

"She has a particular way she wants the wood split?" Fate wanted to know.

"No, no, no. She's not being critical," Swanee said. "Not at all. She just doesn't want our guests to be working." She brightened a little, having latched on to a satisfactory, even logical, motive for Sara Will's actions. "That's it! She'd rather pay."

"She wants to pay me?"

"Of course not, Mr. Jessop," Swanee Hope cried, visibly shrinking as she waved her hand at him. "Sara realizes, I'm sure, that you are not for hire."

"I might should take the money. I'd better go talk to her myself," Fate said, slinging the go-devil into a log so that Swanee Hope jumped backward in fright. Damp seeped into her soft house shoes and she swayed lightly from one foot to the other.

"Oh no, Mr. Jessop—Fate!" Swanee Hope now put her hand to her throat, her fingers embracing her left jaw. There was something seductive about her as she stood there, stretching up and away from the damp ground, hand to skin, the sunlight ripe on her anxious, baffled face. She was glowing with exertion, with thinking about how she might save this dreadful situation without embarrassing anybody.

Fate could see he had her going, but he also felt his own attention wandering. He could feel his pulse responding to Swanee's physical presence when he was supposed to be swaying her mind, winding her into a conspiracy that would give him leverage against Sara Will. Still, he couldn't help but see that she was a pretty woman, if a little girlish in her pink makeup. She looked frivolous, with lace trim hanging everywhere and peeking above the neck of her old sweater.

She was the kind of woman a man could make light of, even joke about, until he took the time to know her. He saw already that her good intentions could outmeasure her flightiness. She would be worth pinning down. He wished he could remember how she'd looked years ago. He would like a past connection with her, some memory to link them now as they conspired, without Swanee Hope even knowing it, against her sister.

The trouble was that what he remembered about that afternoon of Serena's funeral was scattered in cool fragments: the stormy March sky, the raw clay heaped at the foot of the grave, the meager winter flowers. Just those separate images, as silent and empty as the open field. It was as if they had been trapped, caught in a vapor lock, immobile and mute except for Sara Will's scream. Sara Will was what he remembered, that one searing, wide-awake moment when she had screeched out her fear, her loss, her acute bursting acknowledgment of what dying meant. That was what he remembered, one single instant of irrevocable comprehension that had stayed like a live thing in his head all this time.

"You mustn't," Swanee Hope was saying to him, and Fate looked at her again. She was panicking. Her soft clear forehead wrinkled again, her eyes melted to gray-blue as she pouted at him, hand now reaching solicitously to grasp his sleeve. She would pull him into her confidence if need be and have him understand that nobody messed with Sara Will. Nobody questioned her or argued with her beyond the initial exchange of opinion. Sara Will wouldn't have it. It was as simple as that. "You mustn't," Swanee Hope whispered.

"Why, Miss Swanee?" Fate asked softly, risking everything on one gently put question. "Why mustn't I talk to Sara Will?"

"She isn't partial to company, Fate," Swanee Hope replied, weighing her words. "It's just her way. Nobody's spent the night in this house in years." Her hand was outstretched to take his damaged arm.

He could see she was feeling sorry for him. There it was, trapped in her features, her anxious frown, the way she bit at her pink lip. He could also read behind her words, the way she pushed out little puffs of worried air against them so that "company" fell into a whisper and "years" became a tiny sigh between them. Sara Will intended to get rid of him. And soon. The plan to run him off was working already—Swanee Hope out here at the woodpile telling him to stop. *Don't touch* was Sara Will's message to him. *Everything here is mine.*

Fate dropped the go-devil on the last splits of seasoned oak. "Forgive me, Miss Swanee Hope," he said, bringing what little contrition he could muster into his act because suddenly he found himself actually performing. He had dropped off true feelings just as surely as he'd reached deep into his bag of old tricks, fingering first one ploy and then another, rejecting what obviously wouldn't work, clinging to a few, until suddenly the right approach popped into his head. He put his fingers over Swanee's as she pressed her regret into his withered flesh.

"You must forgive me for bringing trouble to your door. I know we've become a burden to you just in this short time. Let me tell you I understand your meaning as regards Miss Sara Will. I surely do. And there's no hard feelings attached. Rest assured of that, Miss Swanee Hope. No hard feelings. Now." He paused to give her a trembling little smile. "I'll go tell Eva to get packed up because we're leaving this morning, although if the truth be known, I don't know where I'll take her. We wouldn't be bothering you at all except that this right here was the only place I could think of. That's the truth. This was the only place that came to me in our hour of trial, the only place where I knew she'd be safe from that boy." He released her hand, which had grown warm and relaxed under his.

Swanee felt a sudden chill. "What boy?" She leaned forward, ready to embrace whatever he was willing to tell. The morning air was suddenly full of her warm smell, as if something baked had at that moment been set out on the window ledge to cool.

Fate moved backward out of the scent to pick up his jacket, which stank of age and abuse. He felt he was moving too quickly. He could ruin everything now if she sensed how alert he was to her sympathy. And yet the risk was twofold. His own emotions couldn't afford her earnest concern, a woman's care so long denied him. He felt himself pulled toward a genuine response, a desire to take her fluttering hand again and calm it until her pulse was slow and even under his fingers. He had intended to lure her into his plot, and now he felt the possibility of being trapped himself. It would be so easy to get involved with a woman like Swanee Hope, to embrace her innocence and find comfort.

He tried to shift gears in his head. He needed her sympathy more than her arms. Eva and Rachel needed him to be sharp, to construct a future out of this minute. He would go slowly, then, acting his part. He would let Swanee Hope tear his story from him bit by bit so that when she finally heard it, she would already be a participant in the action. If he could achieve that, their story would belong to Swanee Hope and she would be tied to them, a willing compatriot and accomplice.

"Michael," he said.

"Michael who?" Swanee begged, her hands flurrying. "No, no, that's not the important thing. I don't suppose I know him anyway. But what's he got to do with Eva?"

"He's been harassing her," Fate said meaningfully, hoping to embellish his voice with appropriate concern.

"Harassing her? That's terrible!" Swanee Hope paused, mouth open, to gather her senses around this dreadful news.

"Harassing her how?" she asked after a few seconds of unsuccessful imagining.

"Well, he came to my place all hours of the day and night."

"He did! But what did he come for?"

"Well, to talk to her."

"Talk to her? That's all he wanted—to talk to her?"

"Well, that's what he *said*," Fate answered.

"But what did he *mean*?" Swanee asked hopefully. She was perched on her damp toes, expecting the worst.

"He wanted to marry her," Fate said.

Swanee Hope let her hands fall to her sides as if she'd just regained her balance. "But, Mr. Jessop," she said with some disappointment, "Eva's situation does seem to indicate that she's in need of a husband."

"She likes him, too." Fate nodded pitifully. "At least I think she does."

"Then she should marry him, Fate." Her plaintive fingers actually took his sleeve again. "Whatever is wrong with that girl, getting herself in the family way and then not becoming a family when the opportunity arises? Why, I'm appalled." Swanee's voice churned. Fate could actually see the clicking behind her eyes. "Whatever are we going to do?" She paused and turned to look at the house. "Do you know what I think? I think Eva needs a woman's advice right now. Someone she can pour out her little heart to. Not that you haven't been good to her, Fate—I could tell in a minute you have been. I know you've done all you could, handicapped as you are by not being a woman or a mother. I'm a mother, Fate, did you know that? I have a son living in California."

"Why, no, Miss Swanee Hope, I certainly didn't know that," Fate said, truly amazed at this turn of good fortune.

"It's the truth! A son, his wife, and three precious grandchildren. I have raised a child, Mr. Fate Jessop. I have surely done that."

"Then you'll talk to her?" Fate asked, pressing her hand again. "I think that's just what's called for. There are things I just can't seem to put right to her." His hand moved away from hers to rub his paralyzed arm, reminding her of his uselessness. "She needs some time to think, Miss Swanee. Time and an experienced woman's influence."

"I'll talk to her," Swanee Hope said, delighted with the challenge. She smiled happily, eager to put her mind to work. So little happened anymore. Everything interesting was so far away, encased in solid state.

"But what about Miss Sara Will?" Fate wondered aloud. He moved back another step as if the invisible figure of the stern, selfish sister had come between them.

"I'll talk to her too," Swanee Hope said. There was nothing she wouldn't do.

7

✦ From her room, Sara Will could hear the intermittent whacking of the ax. She listened for a moment; then, determined to close her ears to the noise and get on with her day, she slipped out of her robe and stood for a moment in front of the mirror. The warmth of sunlight reflecting on the glass seemed to reach out to her and she moved closer to the mirror, looking at herself as if, for the first time, she were seeing her own frown, the hard exasperation in her eyes.

But her attention was still below. She knew she could look down from her window on Fate Jessop splitting wood. Five steps into the light and she would be framed by the sash, peering down while he might be looking up, catching her in a blur of sun on dusty glass. She would be frozen, fearful of any movement that would betray her curiosity. How did he manage with one arm?

She absolutely would not look. She pulled the gown over her head, snapped her bra fastened, and slipped a T-shirt over her head. Over that she put a shirt with a long tail, layering her clothing in anticipation of the early afternoon sun. She pulled on old wool slacks, the knees picked and the seat bagging. Then she put a jacket on top of everything. Her sneakers were by the back door.

The relentless hacking of the ax continued below her. It had once been a gratifying sound—the noise of work being accomplished, Sara Will's animal instinct intent on foraging, storing for winter—but today the sound made a flush rise to her cheeks, and her fingers brushed against the heat as she pulled her heavy hair back from her face. She pushed the pins against her scalp, scratching clumsily as if she hadn't had years of experience with combs and pins.

I have no reason to be nervous, she said to herself, but her face in the mirror looked pinched, as if she had a nagging pain somewhere, a twinge of irritation like a festering splinter or a raw heel. The wood splitting had stopped. Finally, she said to herself, and approached the window cautiously, on tiptoe. Swanee Hope was delivering her message. There is a woodcutter coming, she was saying. You may stay one more day.

That was the message passed from Sara Will to Fate Jessop by way of the sister, who now leaned forward to rest her hand on his withered arm. Consoling him, Sara Will reasoned, and what harm could that do? It was the reason she'd sent Swanee Hope out there in the first place.

Swanee Hope is kind and I am not, she thought. Besides, if Swanee succumbed temporarily to his charms, what harm was done? It certainly wouldn't do Mr. Jessop any good because Sara Will herself owned the house, free and clear. She would say who went and who stayed. She would have the final word.

Eva was talking to the baby. They passed in the hall on their way downstairs. The baby talk was muffled, as if Eva was nuzzling while she spoke. Then silence. No clanging of metal in the yard, no voices rising out of the tomb of her house. Well, that was the way Sara Will liked it.

She went downstairs and into the kitchen where Eva was mixing the baby's cereal in a china bowl.

"I hope you don't mind my using a little milk," she said, holding out Swanee's china dish for Sara Will to see. Rachel sat on the floor at her feet. "I'm trying to start her on solid food. Fruit and cereal to begin with. Then she'll nurse less and I can start offering her a cup." She tested the consistency of the cereal by dripping it off the spoon. It slid down the edge of the bowl. "I don't suppose you're interested in babies." Her laugh was short and awkward, a "ha" that stuck in the air.

"I've had no reason to be," said Sara Will sharply, but immediately felt a prick of regret. "She's a very pretty child, Eva," she said to make amends.

"Thanks." Eva scooped up the baby and sat down in a kitchen chair. "Uncle Fate bought her this little spoon," she said, holding it up for Sara to examine. "It came in a set. A fork, knife, and spoon in a little box. Stainless steel." She pushed the filled spoon between Rachel's lips and the baby began sucking on it. "I had a silver spoon when I was a baby, but nobody has that anymore. See, she likes it." The cereal oozed out of the corners of Rachel's mouth and Eva caught it with two quick licks of the spoon.

"Your Uncle Fate—you've been with him a long time?" Sara Will came into the kitchen and made herself busy tidying the already spotless counter.

"Since the seventh month. He got Rachel a crib, and if we hadn't left like we did, he would have gotten her a high chair, too." She pushed the spoon into Rachel's mouth. "I thought when I went to him maybe I could stay a little while, until the baby came, but here we are, still together."

She sighed, more, it seemed, at her predicament than at the mess Rachel was making.

"You see, I had to get away from Mama and Daddy. They were hysterical most of the time, and I was so upset. I wanted to decide what to do for myself, you know. I hardly knew Uncle Fate but I thought he'd let me do that. You can tell he has respect for people and their opinions. From the very first day, he's treated me like a grown-up person, even when I don't act like one." Eva concentrated on feeding the baby while Sara Will sponged the countertop.

Sara Will knew this was her opportunity to ask why they'd come but she couldn't. It was as if knowing would weaken her resolve. She would let them stay if she knew, and so she was determined against it. She must build a defense against Fate Jessop's conniving charm, against this child's invasion, because she knew that in the days to come she would resent their presence more and more.

"I'm going to the cemetery," she said. "I'm the caretaker of sorts. It's the least I can do."

"Could we come too?" Eva asked, twisting in her chair to look at Sara.

She might as well have been asking for safe passage to the moon. "It's a good walk, a hard walk," Sara said, turning cold with dread. She couldn't imagine anyone in the cemetery with her; the sound of voices or a baby crying in that quiet was intolerable. She wanted to go alone.

"Oh, I don't mind the walk. In fact, I need the exercise," Eva was saying. "And I have a carrier for Rachel. Uncle Fate got it for me."

"Uncle Fate certainly is generous," Sara Will said.

"Yes, he is." Eva put the bowl in the sink and ran water in it. "I'll just be a minute." She was smiling at Sara Will, brightened by the prospect of doing something.

"Eva," Sara Will began, although she still hadn't discovered the words with which to politely dissuade her. Oh, she knew how to be rude. She could say "I don't want you" easily enough, but that kind of defiance seemed more a threat to herself than to Eva. By admitting her connection to the cemetery, her need for it, she would be saying more about herself than she wanted known, even by this pathetic little creature who obviously didn't know a proposition from a proposal.

The girl was still smiling at her. Then she bent her head to kiss the baby's fingers. There were the dark roots showing through the brittle, streaky blond. Her disheveled hair struck Sara as evidence of rashness, a decision with no more thought of consequences than their decision to come to Sparrow Creek. Everything about this girl looked temporary.

She'll walk all the way to the cemetery and then turn right around and come back, Sara Will thought. She won't stay down there with me when Swanee Hope is here to make over her. When there's a television, and her precious Uncle Fate.

"Well, let's go then," she said. This was little enough concession when they'd be gone tomorrow. In twenty-four hours she'd have their sheets on the line, the rooms aired, solitude restored. She went to the back door to pull on her tennis shoes. Outside all was quiet, the ax dropped to the ground and Fate Jessop put in his place.

The cemetery was no one's property. Years ago the land had belonged to one of the Sparrow Creek families, and when the TVA dammed up the river below the creek, flooding the valley where the old community graveyard had been, the owners had given the Sparrow Creek Baptist Church this little piece of ground along the ridge for a building and a cemetery. The church had been a frame building constructed in three days by the men and boys of the community. When it burned down in 1965 they had not yet managed to get a steeple on it or collected enough donations for a bell. The few families who had been appearing on odd Sundays when the circuit preacher came were glad to move their memberships to the large brick church in Tyler Mills, where there was a recreational program for the children, three choirs, and a fine organ already paid for.

Since then Sara Will had gone nowhere, refusing to join the exodus out of the country. She had the Burney family Bible and the valley and so she tended the neglected cemetery, offering her care not only to her own relations but to the deceased of the deserters as well. Over the years, she'd grown attached to the names. Her mind, so often turned to practical matters, released her into a dream world in the cemetery as she worked, and she recalled the histories of the Paxtons or the Averys, connections drawn in stone: wife, daughter, son, sister, husband.

The land seemed to belong to her since no one else showed it any concern, and gradually she came to believe that the people belonged to her too. When she occasionally found a wreath against a tombstone she was both gratified and resentful. She was glad she never had to see those people who parked their big cars close to the narrow gate and clucked to each other that while the place wasn't exactly growed up, it could do with a little organized care. They should form a committee to look into it. It would be cheap enough to send someone out. Of course, were they to form a committee and call their benevolent purpose to her attention, Sara Will would never volunteer. Instead she would relinquish her duties silently, stoically, and leave the meeting before punch and cookies could be served.

Now here was an intruder in the cemetery with her—Eva— with a baby who crawled in the dry stubble of grass, grabbing at brittle leaves with her clumsy fingers and shoving what she caught toward her mouth.

Sara Will didn't like babies very much. They distracted her. In the supermarket, they were always leaning dangerously out of carts toward the vegetable bins or the jelly jars. They had runny noses and too much clothing on. Their legs dangled out of the cart seats and their fingers curled on the metal grids, waiting to be mashed. She'd seen them try to stand up. Grabbing the air as they passed gum and sweets at the checkout counter, they got their hands slapped, then found themselves cuddled and consoled. These encounters were her only contact with children, and she had tried buying her groceries at different times of day, hoping to discover a lull in the baby traffic. There never was one. Even at two o'clock in the afternoon, when any decent mother would have a child down for a nap, the aisles were ajumble with garbled, mindless baby talk, whimpers, and spilled Cheerios.

Now Sara Will was determined to ignore Rachel by turning her attention to the tulip poplar, which was baring fast. Her rake scraped, an empty, vibratory sound. Swanee Hope was right. The raking was futile. She did nothing to really improve the cemetery. It was Sara Will who was ministered to. She felt the stretching of her back, the loosening of shoulder blades as she scratched through the leaves to the cool, mulchy ground.

Eva was brushing dry grass off a footstone with the broom they had brought. Then she knelt to shear the standing edge of brown weeds with the clippers. Sara paused for a moment to watch the girl on her knees, inadvertently in an attitude of prayer. What does she want? Sara wondered. Rachel crawled toward her, wanting to get at the shiny clippers Eva was using. Eva put the tool down to gather up the baby and brush the stray stems from her damp hands and hair. Eva didn't say anything; instead, she pressed the baby's head to her shoulder for a moment, rocking her body as if Rachel required comfort.

A little breeze lifted around them. It seemed to come up out of the earth, rattling the leaves and sweeping up into Sara Will's clothes. Eva held Rachel's head close, protecting her face from the airborne debris.

She could be my niece, Sara Will thought suddenly. But she isn't. If Serena had lived . . . if she'd borne her child . . . but that daughter wouldn't be here, kneeling in a cemetery with a baby cradled in her arms. She wouldn't have hideous bleached-out hair like thatch. She wouldn't be traveling around the country with a one-armed man making a nuisance of herself. She wouldn't have had a baby without getting married first. No. Serena's child would be like Serena herself, innocent and auburn-haired, with milky skin and a quick, whispery way of speaking, as if the thought she was expressing had occurred to her spontaneously and then simply spilled out, happy thoughts constantly bubbling up. Swanee had a similar way about her, but because Swanee hadn't been so pretty or so innocent, she'd ended up acting foolish more often than not. Swanee Hope had been downright wayward, if Sara Will remembered correctly.

But maybe memory failed her, or at least played tricks. Somehow her recollections of the dead were soft, photographed through a mist, vignetted in sepia. But the living had little innocence about them, especially Swanee Hope, who didn't mind, even now, telling how she chased Jonathan Calhoun all over Tyler Mills until she caught him. She took pleasure in recounting it, reliving romance, her body fluttering as if she felt that same excitement now, just by recalling the look of Jonathan, who from Sara's point of view had had very little to recommend him besides a college education.

"Miss Sara," Eva was saying to her. "I think we'll walk on back now." The girl had risen and was moving forward, forcing herself into Sara Will's vision.

Sara had a little smile on her lips when she looked at her. She had been right all along. The girl had no staying power. The invasion had been temporary, just a little skirmish into Sara Will's territory. No reconnaissance, no plunder, no captives.

"That's good," Sara Will said and turned back to her raking. She didn't stop to watch them go.

And yet when the crunch of gravel had vanished, when the air was filled with that pure silence she usually relished, Sara Will rested her rake again and stood there, stone-still like a piece of ancient statuary among the gray monuments.

Space was almost visible around her, heavy, pressing air that confounded her with its stillness. She turned her head slowly against the tight-collared quiet, then moved her whole body westward toward the lake, where Serena lay, inaccessible to her. She could envision the narrowness of that confinement, the cramped putrid bed where hair and nails had grown with fierce denial. Perhaps that was all that remained. How long did decaying take? She could only think that water had seeped in immediately—there were no vaults in those days and the coffin, although factory-made, had seemed unreliable to her, more a carton than a casket. Surely substance was required to contain the weight of such a death, with the burden of lost youth so heavy in it.

Everything had seemed fragile then, tentative, except for the excruciating fact that she would never see Serena again. Not ever. Not if she lived to be a thousand. Not even if the Second Coming really came, she didn't expect to see those creamy fleshy arms, those brows plucked defiantly in a thin arched line, the eyes below them bright blue and spirited, forever denying any unpleasantness in what they saw.

There was something of that in Eva. Like Serena, she seemed to think whatever was best for her was bound to be good for everybody else. But they had more in common than just youth. Eva was earthy the way Serena had been. Sara knew because Eva gave her the same feeling, a familiar trembly sensation that reminded her she was slightly puny, out of sync, differently made, even alien to them.

I've never had their courage, she thought. Never, not once have I known what it is like to be Serena or Eva, even Swanee. How could that be? she wondered. What obligation had been so overwhelming, what fear so great, that she had abdicated herself, all her yearnings squelched into a bitter silence that had lasted all these years, until she was old and stodgy? When had there been a moment's release except for her scream the day of Serena's funeral, a sound that haunted her still with its closeness, the echo of it trapped forever in her throat?

We were all so close to death that day, Sara remembered. I was on the edge of it, peering down. If no arms had held Serena back—Serena, who was beautiful and determined and good—then surely there was nothing that would save Sara Will.

In the cemetery, Sara tossed her head like someone shaking off grogginess. She didn't want to think about the past. No matter where her memories began, they always ended with Serena dead and buried, lost to her except in her childish, terrified memory of the cemetery terraced into the hillside. Lost to her by water. What good did thinking do when her letters to the TVA had meant nothing, when she had not been able to accomplish the simple task of access?

At first she had sent polite letters reminding them of obligations. After all, they had been the ones to make promises. There will be a road, they had said, at the very least a logging trail cleared of boulders and traversable in good weather, and a bridge. So she waited, anticipating earthmovers, the racket of chain saws and rough smoky voices in her valley. She expected concrete pilings to rise out of the water, a steel trestle laid. She found a book on bridges and studied the pictures, read the details, imagining the structure that would take her to Serena.

Gradually her letters became anxious, carried a nagging tone; then irate, demanding, vengeful. Over the years, sporadic replies had fallen from her meager parcel of mail. "An investigation of Sparrow Creek Dam access is now in progress" or "Your inquiry is being given the full attention of such-and-such a department." Her letters continued to go out, typed on an old portable that left extra spaces and raised t's. She did not understand, was not appeased; she did not forgive. Eventually their corporate impatience surfaced. Who was this crazy woman who demanded a million-dollar bridge to a useless ten acres of scraggly woods in the middle of the lake?

Finally, men came to see for themselves. It was Sara Will they came to see, not the lake to the edge of which she dragged them so they could look out at the ragged but solid plot on the horizon. "There," she said to them, for they did not seem to understand that the cemetery truly existed. Their language was vague to her, heavy with engineering talk and never touching on the issue, the island itself, her sister's lonely untended rectangle of earth. She pointed, her eyes shaded with her other hand against the western sun. Her outstretched arm seemed to lengthen, to rise to a curve above the water. She felt herself reaching, her body straining, her heart pulling forward out of her pounding chest. If she could only bend with the pull, stretch every muscle to the limit, she could reach her sister. But she drew back, tottering at the damp, lapping edge of embarrassment. She would be cool, standoffish, even abrupt, while the men peered after her, their eyes hidden behind tinted glass. She could never be sure what they saw.

But after that, the letters from the TVA were more conciliatory, even patient, as if they now knew for certain they were dealing with a madwoman. They tried to pacify her with letters that began "We appreciate your situation," but there was no commitment, still no acknowledgment of their promise.

More and more convinced her battle was hopeless, she nevertheless went to the courthouse in search of the names of the people buried there. "The cemetery itself provides the record," the assistant clerk told her. She was a snippy young girl with long arms made strong from lifting the oversized books. Sara Will didn't even reply. What good did it do to explain that the cemetery was lost to her, desecrated by a man-made flood? The cemetery wasn't all that was lost. Think about the farms, she could say to the ignorant girl. The houses, the roads, the buildings, flower gardens, fences, acres of fertile land and timber under water. Don't you care about what's hidden from you? Instead she said to herself, we should have moved the bodies. She had been thinking that for years, long before her parents died, but she never spoke of it. It didn't change anything to blame Mama and Daddy, who had believed the story about the bridge.

She knew the Sparrow Creek church records had gone up in flames when the church burned. She would have preferred reading records in private rather than making personal inquiries, but eventually she bristled to the task, edged on by the TVA's stilted, uncooperative replies which now came only two or three times a year. She called on her neighbors. Who was buried in the old cemetery? she wanted to know. People remembered a few: their great-grandparents, ancestors removed from them by generations and not really worth the hassle. Of course, if Sara Will accomplished something—got a road and a bridge—they wouldn't mind going over from time to time. But wouldn't such convenient access turn the little island into a recreational area? Wouldn't young people build fires and drink beer and carry on there if given the opportunity? Better leave the dead in peace. At least nobody was breaking tombstones or littering the place.

But Sara Will felt no peace. Through all the years while she gave more obvious attention to other things—her job, her parents' failing health, a disjointed, uneventful social life—she fumed about the bridge. The neighborhood's apathy triggered in her mind the possibility of the island as a recreational site. For a while, she eliminated any mention of the cemetery from her letters and wrote of the other attributes of the island, all visionary and hypothetical. It could be partially cleared for campsites. A small dock could be constructed at what seemed to be a natural harbor, a slight curve as if a spoon had been dipped along the edge. They could bring the road out at the narrowest stretch of water, the only place a bridge was feasible. She was not a crazy woman. Her demands were not unreasonable.

Their replies met her new tactic with one of their own. Such a plan had already been considered and abandoned. The island was too small for adequate parking. More feasible sites for recreational purposes were already being developed along the upper edges of the lake, but many thanks for a pertinent and thoughtful suggestion.

She wrote to her congressmen. Their responses were sympathetic but as noncommittal as the TVA's. A secretary added a handwritten note to the bottom of one of them, asking if she'd considered hiring a boat. The idea appalled her. She would be terrified. Besides, she didn't want alternatives or suggestions. The battle for the bridge had become a solitary business, lonely and full of rage.

I am sick to death of it, Sara Will thought, her hands gripping the rake handle as if she would expend her last strength into it. She saw where she was. Her hands ached as she pushed the metal bristles of the rake into the earth, bearing down against a pain.

She had lost Serena. She felt, as she had many times before, the necessity of giving up before the past strangled her completely. Too often now, memory made her gasp. The air she breathed was thick and moist with regret. It clogged her up and rattled in her chest. But today there was something different. What it was, she didn't know; she just knew there was a sudden shuddering coolness near her heart, a loose place where the breath came easier.

I have lost Serena, she thought again, ready to mourn, even eager for the old tightness. Instead, her breath sang out almost audibly as her chest heaved up. But Eva and her baby are here, her breath said. And for the first time in years, Sara Will cried.

8

◆ It was after midnight when Fate heard it: just a slight sound, like a distant whistle of breeze, noticeable only because it kept on coming. Then it was more like an insect, a mosquito zooming across the dark room, searching out flesh, a soft cheek turned from the pillow, a shoulder bared to the house's slow dying warmth. It was a motorcycle.

Fate lay absolutely still, thinking what he should do. There were, he figured, these possibilities: he could get up and put on his pants and appear on the front porch, letting the headlight catch him in its yellow searching glare; he could hurry farther down the yard and into the dark path, where he would stop the intruder short and send him packing by whatever means available, probably the rough edge of a two-by-four; or he could keep on lying there in bed until the sound woke the rest of the house and the women were up and about, seeing to whatever mischief was happening in the middle of the night. Maybe that was the best thing to do. After all, if he weren't here, Sara Will would take charge. She'd probably call the sheriff's office before she even peeked out the window to see who the stranger was. She certainly wouldn't be warm in her welcome. She probably had a gun somewhere, or a billy club. He knew she had a kitchen knife.

So it was possible that she might kill Michael or at least wound him, and that would get them all in trouble. He sighed, hearing the mosquito alight. At least Michael had sense enough not to come roaring up to the front door. He was obviously pushing the Honda along the rutted path, sneaking in. How had he found them anyway?

Fate got up and pulled on his pants and loafers. He would meet the boy halfway. He'd explain for the hundredth time how Eva didn't want to see him, how he should just give up and go back home, finish his education or get steady employment, something better than night clerking. He'd taken that job because it included a room in case Eva came to live with him. Well, it was high time he went home to his own mama and daddy, who must be thinking he'd gone crazy chasing around all over the country after an unwed mother, trying to get her to marry him.

It was too late. He could hear stirring down the hall. Sara Will was up. A light swept beneath his door: Sara Will going downstairs, her narrow flashlight beam tight to the stair. He cracked open his door and peeped out. The light was even in the dark, marking her steady, purposeful tread. Then another light caught him full in the face and he clasped his good hand over his eyes.

"What is it?" Swanee Hope whispered behind the light. Her beam danced away from his face, running up and down his body, hitting wall, ceiling, her own feet, as if she expected to find the cause of the disturbance right there in front of her.

"I heard a noise," Fate said. "And your sister just went down."

"What did it sound like?" Swanee Hope asked. "I thought I heard a motor. Was it a motor you heard?"

"Maybe." He came out into the hall. "Maybe it's Michael," he said. "Michael has a motorcycle. It sounded like a motorcycle to me, but then the sound died and I wasn't sure."

"Sara Will is going to have a fit," Swanee Hope said, wagging the flashlight so the yellow ball of light bounced around them.

They could hear her opening the front door. The lock released slowly, almost soundlessly, but they heard it. The house was still dark. No porch light went on, just the solid dark of a moonless night buffering them.

"We ought to go down there with her," Swanee whispered, but then they heard her speaking.

"I know you're out there," she said sternly into the dark. "I heard you coming and I've already called the sheriff."

"She has not," Swanee Hope said softly. "She'd about as soon get murdered in her bed as have the sheriff out here snooping around. That's the truth. She'd rather die."

"I hope I didn't frighten you, ma'am," a voice came back. "I was being as quiet as I could. I've just come to see Eva Jessop. You know her, don't you? I know you know her uncle, Mr. Fate Jessop. He's the brother of your late sister's husband. I believe I have that correct. It's information from a newspaper obituary. I found it in Mr. Jessop's apartment. It was the only lead I had and I've been desperate to find Eva, so I rode all the way over here and I couldn't find a single place in town to stay the night so I thought I'd come on out here and maybe sleep in a barn or somewhere and then talk to Eva in the morning. I didn't mean to wake you up, Miss Burney. You are Miss Burney, aren't you?"

There was silence. The quiet took on weight compatible with the dark and pressed on Fate's chest. If Michael left now, he'd surely call Eva's parents. The truck was right there to confirm his suspicions. He'd have nothing to lose. Swanee Hope was holding her breath too, but he could feel her mind working, that earnest clicking of romance against reason, of Sara Will's ire against having purpose in her own vacant life. Swanee wasn't about to let that boy go, no matter how crazy he was.

Fate felt her starting to move before she actually did, as though he had pushed her. In a way, he had. He'd primed her for this moment when she'd take a stand against Sara Will, because she was the only one of them who could afford to. Now she was racing down the stairs, her light flinging splotches on the wall. He heard her swing out the screen door, pushing past her sister. She stopped mid-porch, beaming her light this way and that until it caught a solid object, a white face with circles of glare gleaming back at her. His glasses, as thick as fruit jars.

"Yes, she is Miss Burney," Swanee Hope said on a shudder of chilled breath. She was shaking with excitement. "And I'm the other sister, Mrs. Calhoun. And you are Michael what's-his-name. Come in."

"Swanee!" Sara Will cried, truly anguished.

"He can sleep on the sofa tonight," Swanee Hope said. "In the morning we'll decide what to do next."

"I know what to do next!" Sara Will turned away, leaving Swanee Hope to usher the boy in. She cast her light on the stairs, each medallion of golden wood showing her the way. "I know exactly what to do," she was saying as she passed Fate's room, while he, pressed against the other side of the closed door, listened intently, hoping to hear a tiny hint of resignation in her voice. There was none.

The early light seemed to have been born exhausted. Damp and smoky, the gray air embraced the timber of the house, seeped around window jambs, invaded the warmth of heavy quilts pulled tight. Fate had hardly closed his eyes, and so they burned and itched as if he'd been tending a fire all night. The bed seemed the wrong size for him, too small one minute, too large the next. He flung his good arm out of the quilt's close heat and gripped the edge of the old mattress. The bed was old.

75

That was what irritated him the most. Everything in the house was old and damp and creaky. He could hear people coming and going no matter how stealthful their movements. It was a house that wouldn't allow secrets. Conversations slipped through walls, Rachel's whining echoed in the folds of curtains. All night he'd listened to the house forcing itself into quiet as if it were grabbing sound by the throat and choking it into submission. He heard movement determined to be contained: eyelids held open in the dark, necks tense on soft pillows, locked fingers squeezing and releasing as knuckles cracked and teeth ground. He heard himself and Sara Will and Swanee Hope awake while Eva and Rachel slept their innocent, lip-parted sleep, almost content. Michael probably slept too, from exhaustion if not with satisfaction. He had finally found Eva and was under the same roof with her. He was probably dreaming that she leaned over him so close he could see the faded sunburn freckles on her shoulder even without his glasses. Fate knew what Michael wanted.

The problem that kept him awake had to do with what Fate wanted. He wanted Eva to be happy. He pulled at the ridged seam of the worn mattress, tightening muscles up his arm and shoulder into his chest. The strain made his heart hurt. He wanted Rachel to have everything she would ever want or need, but was he supposed to be a part of that? Or had he just been hanging on, protecting himself from losing them by keeping Eva away from Michael? He didn't know. He just knew he couldn't think about life without the two of them.

Even now, with Rachel almost a year old, he still thought, with a frequency that alarmed him, about her birth, remembering it in simplistic images as if her coming had been like turning right an inside-out sleeve. Eva had seemed inside-out to him, all raw edges, swollen and pulsing, after the pains started. Her face had contorted abruptly, startling him with its petulance. Her cutting eyes were wild and angry, her mouth pinched tight to hold back a howl. Somehow the hours had passed, night fiercely formed under the hard light of a ceiling bulb, until the baby fought free and Eva was smooth and healed and perfect again.

He knew it wasn't really that way but the image stuck in his mind, a way of coping with the pain he'd watched her suffer when she was just a girl herself, skinny legs and arms sticking out from her quickening bulge on the bed. This is ordinary, it is normal, he'd said to himself during the long night. This is as natural as a sleeve turned right.

The women did all the work. Two midwives or nurse-practitioners. He didn't know exactly who they were, these people Eva had found at that clinic of hers. He didn't know a thing about them except their phone number, and after the pains were coming regularly he dialed the number from the pay phone down the block (it was one o'clock in the morning when Eva finally decided there was no avoiding this being the real thing), and the sound of the woman's voice—sleepy, then abruptly alert, listening, questioning, taking control—seemed right to him. Having babies was women's business, work that was more their responsibility than any other task on earth, he reckoned, and he would leave it to them.

But he couldn't. He messed around the kitchen, doing what he was told, offering coffee and grilled-cheese sandwiches. Eva asked for music, and so he brought his tape player into the bedroom and set it up on the dresser. She wanted to hear Christmas carols, although Christmas was a couple of weeks past; a choir sang "O Little Town of Bethlehem" and "Hark the Herald Angels Sing" all through the night while Eva panted and sweated on his bed.

He wandered from stove to window to the bedroom door while the women, with everything in readiness around them, talked quietly together until a pain came. Then they moved into action, still quiet and firmly efficient, each taking a prearranged role as if they had memorized specific parts for which he was the only spectator. He stared out the window a lot, saw the sun begin to come up. It was after seven, the long winter's night turning gray and snowy close to the shabby toy skyline of

77

the town, when Eva screamed out. He went to the doorway, not wanting to see but knowing he would. He had to; he'd come too far to turn back now. He was as committed as Eva and there was no way out but this one: to be present, to see with his own eyes the terrible struggle going on between Eva and this bawling unknown, a skinny, cheesy object finally laid on her sheeted stomach. He had seen!

It was as though he'd peered into a chasm between Eva's white knees and discovered all forms of life there, a narrow valley teeming with movement. Quivering, involuntary spasms shook her down to her toes and she was still. He turned away from the afterbirth and thought instead of a sleeve, his coat caught inside itself and suddenly released. Righted. That was it. Eva was right now, her guilt no longer attached and obvious to the eye. The baby could be her sister, her cousin, a neighbor's child.

The choir sang "It Came Upon the Midnight Clear" and there was the baby, its cord tied and cut, separated from Eva, who had closed her eyes and lay as still as death, frail and shrunken. He watched the water in his sink change color as the screeching baby girl was washed. The water drained away.

When the women finally left, there was no evidence of pain, no cries hanging in the still, warm heat that poured off the living-room stove. The baby and Eva slept. The silence compressed around Fate, pushing him down. He felt drowsy, almost unconscious with weariness. He stretched out on his cot in the living room. It was beginning to snow outside. The snow was as gray as the sky, as dull and smoky as the building next door, but when he awoke an hour later the world was white.

They got along. Surviving the birth had linked them even more tenaciously to each other. He was the protector, the provider. He paid the women. He paid for everything because Eva was afraid to make a withdrawal from her savings yet and wouldn't approach the social services people. She was afraid of having her name recorded anywhere or of showing need. She dipped into her small supply of cash to get the baby a bunting for winter. She bought a new lipstick, a blouse, and a print skirt she hoped would fit by spring. On Valentine's Day, Fate brought home a plant for her. It hadn't a single red bloom, but it was living. She hugged him. She was always hugging him now. He knew she needed someone to touch her, to make her feel safe and loved because so much of her time was taken with holding the baby, with being Rachel's comforter when she had been so unprepared to soothe anyone. One night with her jeans caught around her ankles hadn't prepared her for much.

She needed friends, but Fate didn't know how to find any. He didn't know any young people, much less ones with babies. Eventually she met a girl at the clinic. Linda was seventeen and married since the summer. She was five months pregnant when Eva asked her to hold Rachel while she went into the examining room for her six-week postnatal checkup. Linda didn't want to.

"It was written all over her face." Eva laughed later, when the three of them were sitting at Fate's kitchen table drinking hot chocolate, which wasn't allowed on the nursing mother's diet.

"Well, I'm scared of babies," Linda said, rubbing her stomach. "I don't know what in the world to do with them."

"I tell you all they want is to nurse," Eva said. "That's the truth. Just taking care of that gives you time to get to know what else they need. I just sit here holding Rachel while she nurses, and all the while I'm looking at her cheek or her ear or her hand. I can look at a fingernail for the longest time. You wouldn't believe how long." She stopped, embarrassed. Her fingers were shaking around her mug. "I ought not be drinking this," she said suddenly and rose, scraping the chair hard, to pour the chocolate down the drain. "How could I drink something that will give her colic?" She had her back to them, leaning into the sink as if she hoped to throw up.

Linda looked at Fate nervously. She didn't even know these people. But Fate was looking at Eva and his eyes were tearing.

79

They seemed to enlarge, spreading round and flat to meet the expanding liquid surface. He blinked and the tears washed down onto his cheekbones, minute trenches of wet he didn't brush away.

"Aw, Eva," he said, pulling out his handkerchief as if he expected someone other than himself to need it. He didn't get up. "She'll be all right. You'll both be all right. You're doing fine."

Eva straightened her shoulders but was unable to control a shiver that shot down her back, as quick and penetrable as if she'd touched a live wire. "I love chocolate," she said, turning to give Linda a little smile. "Mama used to forbid it—she claimed it caused every zit in the world—but I ate it anyway. I mean, what did Mama know?"

"It's just while she's nursing," Fate said to Linda. "No onions, cinnamon, chocolate. What else, Eva?"

"I don't know. You're who memorized the list." Eva came back to the table and sat down. "It was only a couple of swallows I had."

"She'll be all right," Fate said again.

And Linda just looked at them both while she warmed her hands on the mug and wondered if she shouldn't get on home to the trailer park. It wasn't much of a place but it was as nice as this and Denny was there, a young man, a lover, to share whatever happened to her. At least her baby was going to have a daddy. She pulled her coat around her and went home, leaving the spotless little apartment that smelled of baby oil and Pine-sol and warm chocolate.

Fate felt relieved knowing Eva had a friend, even a friendship based on convenience like theirs was. Linda had quit school, breaking completely the already fraying ties with most of her old girlfriends who were stuck in the drafty old building from eight till three writing senior term papers and planning the spring dance. These girls checked the mail every afternoon for letters from college admission offices while Linda worked at the local movie house in the concession stand collecting dollars for warmed-over yellow popcorn and overpriced candy bars.

With her days mostly free, she'd come to Fate's apartment and the two girls would take Rachel for a walk or sit in the drugstore downstairs or go to the library and thumb through the paperbacks while Rachel lay sleeping in the crib the patrons had provided. They read the covers of romances, giggling together over the torrid descriptions of passion advertised there. It was always on the high seas or in abandoned cabins overlooking waterfalls or in harems. Never in automobiles; rarely in motels or deserted rec rooms while parents slept upstairs. It was never sticky or cold or fumbling or boring. Well, Eva didn't know anything about the boring part. She hadn't had time to get bored. She hadn't even felt a lingering stab of pain or seen the fateful spot of blood, tampons having taken care of that a couple of years before in the pristine privacy of her gleaming yellow bathroom.

Linda, on the other hand, admitted experience: ten times, before she and Denny escaped into South Carolina and got married on the Fourth of July weekend. She knew because she had marked each time in her diary, using a code she'd initiated in the eighth grade and which had grown more elaborate in time. At first, in the right-hand corner, a simple dot for tongue kissing. Then two dots, one above the other, to describe heavy petting, partial undressing, hands groping inside elastic, mouths pressed to random, dark, unfamiliar places. Three dots to form a triangle for services rendered, handkerchief ready to catch the spill. And then finally a star made with a red pencil. Stars on ten pages, but most of the rest systematically decorated with what would appear as careless doodling to her mother.

"And all that time, no accident?" Eva asked, amazed at Linda's luck and her own fecundity.

"Well, we thought so," Linda said. They had stopped in front of a ladies' store window and were looking at the pastel collection exhibited in anticipation of spring. Their own expressions overlaid the fashions, two pale small triangular faces looming out of dark hair and knit hats and dreary coats. They focused on the clothes, not wanting to view themselves. "Look at that pink sweater there. Isn't it yummy?"

"You thought so?" Eva asked, moving on.

"I missed two months." Linda sighed, turning away from the window. "So we went to South Carolina. The next week my period started. A week of screwing loosened the action. That's what Denny said. Sometimes Denny's so coarse. I said it was all nerves. I'd been worried about getting pregnant all that time."

"Did you take sex education at school?" Eva asked. She nestled Rachel closer to her chest, out of the wind.

"Mama and Daddy wouldn't let me. They said I didn't need to know that stuff yet. Shoot. I was already doing it when they said that. What about you? You must not have taken it either."

"I did. I took notes and everything," Eva said. "I just didn't think it applied to me. I was too busy with other things. I didn't have a boyfriend, just Michael, who I'd known forever. He was the kind of guy everybody likes but nobody gets serious about. I mean, I didn't feel anything for him except as a friend."

"And it was him?"

"No. We never even dated, which doesn't mean he didn't keep asking me. We just talked at school and stuff. We were friends. I didn't date much anyway. My folks were so particular—snobbish, I guess. They didn't think anybody was good enough for me. And I didn't feel ready for all that dating stuff, so I just wrote down everything in class and made an A on the test and forgot about it. I guess I always thought that when something important happened to me, somebody would be there to take care of it for me."

"Some asshole sure will, too," Linda said.

"Chet Armstrong."

"God, he sounds like a cartoon character."

"Well, in a way he was. He never even asked if he was the one." Eva sighed and put her gloved hand gently against Rachel's lax cheek. "What happened between us didn't matter a whit to him. I knew that right away. He never thought about it enough to think it could have any result. It was Michael who always took me seriously. He wanted to marry me."

"And you refused?"

"She's not Michael's baby."

"She's hardly Chet Armstrong's either, to hear you tell it."

"That's right. She's just mine. Mine and Uncle Fate's."

"Eva, an uncle is no substitute for a husband, that's for sure."

"Well, he loves us."

"And Michael doesn't?"

"Michael is crazy."

"I think he sounds pretty nice."

"Believe me, Linda, he's a nut. Look." She fumbled over Rachel's back to pull out her wallet and open it to the blond, flat-faced, overexposed visage of Michael Logan.

"So. He looks kinda weird. It's not a good picture." Linda shrugged. "He also looks nice. And clean-cut. Actually, I think he's sort of cute. Anyway, beggars can't be choosers."

"That's why I'm not begging," Eva said firmly and slapped the wallet shut.

Knowing all this, Fate had thought Michael Logan was out of Eva's life. But now he was back, sprawled on the sofa, arm across his face, one socked foot dangling across an embroidered antimacassar. He looked dead and yet Fate knew how determined he was, how willing to do anything.

This was what Fate attempted to tell Swanee Hope as they lingered over breakfast in the quiet kitchen. It was after eight and Sara Will was yet to appear. She's giving me time, Fate thought, and she doesn't even know it. The kitchen had a glow about it, light glancing off the polished pine floor, diffused on the pale leaves of infant plants Swanee was nursing on the sill, filtering through the soft gray curls that stood up around her head. The light seemed to be there at Swanee Hope's bidding, and she moved her hand in it, fingering a silver spoon near her coffee cup as if that were where all the action was focused.

Fate watched the hand, nails carefully filed and glazed with pearl. While he talked about Eva, explaining how she came to have the baby in his apartment, he watched the hand, waiting for the moment when he could take it, press the fluttering fingers still under his own warm strong fingers, and feel through the soft flesh a hard unyielding structure, bones, the solidity of her commitment to help him. He was patient as he listened to her softly troubled, commiserative offerings. She consoled him, complimented, brought Christianity into it.

"You did the Christian thing," she said several times, never realizing how selfish he had been, how Eva meant more to him than any person in his life, even Vickie, simply because she needed him. What he had done, he'd done to keep her.

Maybe Eva should get married. Maybe Michael was the answer. But he hadn't been able to think about that, not when things had been going so well for them. He'd gotten a little raise at the nursery once he'd convinced Ira he had additional responsibilities. Linda had helped him get a night job cleaning the theater. He went at eleven, just when the second show was letting out, and scraped up bits of Tootsie Roll, Goobers, and gum before they had time to set on the upholstery. He sponged away soda spills already drying stickily on the concrete floor, swept up overturned popcorn, collected garbage bags full of cups, wrappers, filthy tissues. It took him a couple of hours and then he was back with Eva and Rachel, both of them sleeping, undisturbed by his absence because they were confident of his return. They knew they could depend on him.

He took Swanee Hope's hand simply by resting his over it. She was trapped, her fingers limp and yielding. He curled his thumb into her palm, as soft and warm as a nest, and pressed a little.

"I saw there's a car in the barn," he said softly. She leaned slightly forward to make sure she heard right. His voice was a murmur to her. "A Mustang," he said. "I'd been wondering how you got places, to church and such."

"It's Sara Will's. She's a fanatic about the care she gives that car," Swanee Hope said, frowning a little at this turn in the conversation when she had her mind fastened on Eva. She didn't withdraw her hand, though. "She doesn't go to church."

"Then I'll take you on Sunday," Fate said, smiling. "In the truck."

"Neighbors pick me up," Swanee Hope said, her own voice a murmur. She could see herself at the end of the lane in her hat and coat, shoes dusty from the road, waiting. She'd never liked standing out there like a hitchhiker, but she couldn't ask anyone to come clear up to the house. The Daltons were always running late and besides, she was obliged for the ride. "But I'll go with you this Sunday."

That was four days. She was giving them four days, although Fate wasn't sure she realized it yet: through Sunday, when she'd sit in the truck, washed by then and the bed emptied of the remaining junk they'd brought. The truck could look pretty good if he got Michael to help him with a waxing. Of course, he expected Michael to be gone by then. Sent packing. Now that he'd come to complicate matters, they'd probably all be gone.

"If Sara Will lets us stay that long," he ended and released her hand. The sun struck it, freckles, a ribbon of vein running down the knob of her wrist to her fingers.

She rolled her wrist, exposing the empty palm, fingers curved slightly as if to receive a gift.

"I want to stay, Swanee Hope," Fate said, and she drew her fingers closed around the words.

"And you will," she said.

9

✦ At first she thought she just wouldn't go down. She would skip breakfast and attack her dresser drawers, discarding underwear that should have been in the ragbag years ago. There was old lipstick, too, and foundation makeup as hard as stone in its little milk-glass cup. Bright blue eye shadow in a plastic case.

An eyebrow pencil with tiny dry brown rods for refills. How long had she had it? Years. Ten years, maybe, although she couldn't remember ever using it. She didn't wear makeup anymore. Her skin was good, tanned in spring and summer, ruddy with wind and cold in winter. She had never been without natural color, had never been sickly or pale, had never felt palpitations and aching clenched jaws. Not until now.

So she would withdraw: a minor, probably unnoticed retreat to take care of business long overdue. First she would discard the makeup and then she'd work her way through the closet, eliminating dresses still hanging there, misshapen and styleless since the fifties. Shirtwaists with lace collars, tucks down the front, and cloth belts with plastic buckles. Sheath dresses with skirts too straight to sit in. A sack dress Swanee had insisted she buy, although Sara Will had felt foolish in it even in the confines of the little dressing room at Broydan's Store. She wore the dress only once; the tiny pleats flapping at her knees embarrassed her. She didn't know why she kept such aberrations except that she had room for them. She rarely bought anything new, and so the slow accumulation of many years had never caused an overflow. Still she would pack the useless items today and take them to the hospital auxiliary thrift shop on her next trip to town.

She stood at the dresser, hands on the knobs ready to pull, but looking at her own face made her lift her hands slowly, as if she were about to touch something unusual, so fragile even the pressure of a fingertip created a risk. It was a look she'd seen often lately, a knotted, thorny expression as if the frazzled threads in her head had suddenly twisted themselves into a gigantic tangle that pushed against her forehead, wrenching her with pain. She squeezed her eyes shut as if the pressure of eyelids straining deeply could straighten the threads. Her ears ached; a ridge along her neck rose painfully, working down into her shoulders. She opened her eyes but the face was the same, full of dread, drained white as if blood were accumulating to clot in her throat.

I am not myself, she thought suddenly and covered her mouth with her hands. I am locking myself in this room as if I have some reason to be afraid. I am churning inside with anger. She felt flushed with it. The knot unraveled, and her face turned hot with rage. This can't go on, she said into the mirror. Her silent language was as loud as a scream. I will not have it! she cried. She went downstairs.

The boy was still sleeping. He had put his glasses on the table at one end of the sofa. His duffel bag, dirty canvas with a ripped-out zipper, was on the floor at his feet. More clutter. She stared at him from the doorway and then went down the hall to the kitchen, where she stopped again, this time with true surprise because Swanee Hope and Fate Jessop, facing each other across the kitchen table, offered her their undisturbed profiles. They were looking at each other, and seeing them there—Swanee Hope's hand open on the table, Fate leaning slightly forward as if he'd just touched her somehow—made Sara Will gasp. She caught the flood of air in her mouth, swallowed hard on it, and stood in the silence while fear grew quietly in her stomach, filled her lungs, moved through her bloodstream into her brain, where the knot of dread collected itself again, pinching behind her eyes which spontaneously teared. It was desolation that enveloped her as she stood there, seeing her sister and this man. Without her. Separate from her, as if there were a veil through which she couldn't pass, a shimmering screen as impenetrable as glass.

She had never minded being alone, had even relished it, but it had always been a self-induced privacy. She had been the one doing the rejecting. She had built the barricades because loneliness had seemed a good alternative to the irritating habits of other people. After her mother's long illness, she had wanted to rest. She'd wanted quiet, and between her mother's death and Swanee's arrival, she'd taken pride in her ability to accept her circumstances and even find pleasure in them. She hadn't really objected to Swanee Hope's coming, but she hadn't encouraged it either.

But this was different. She saw Swanee Hope becoming one of them. Three days ago she would have told anybody she didn't care what Swanee Hope did and would have meant it. But this is different, she thought again. What made it different?

She backed silently away and went down the hall and up the stairs toward her room. But on the landing she stopped. She wouldn't give up this soon. They were the invaders, not she! She marched to Serena's room and rapped on the door, then went in.

Eva was on her back, the loose covers crushed around her feet. Her gown was thin and old, with missing buttons down the front and a tear under the arm that was raised above her head on the pillow. Asleep, she looked older than she was. Trapped in sleep, she looked like a woman, her face frowzy and full, her relaxed body more sexual than anything else Sara Will had ever seen.

"Eva," she said, to stop herself from looking, and watched the eyes snap open, the hand above the ragged hair come down to her stomach, legs twist themselves straight.

"What is it?" Eva asked. She brought herself into a sit in one movement and pulled the sheet up over her. "What?"

"Michael's here," Sara Will replied. "He's found you."

"Oh, damn." Eva clutched the sheet tighter and fell back on the bed. "Where?"

"He's asleep on the sofa. Swanee Hope let him in."

"Why did she do that?" Eva moaned. "Does she let everybody that comes along march right in here?"

"Obviously," Sara Will said.

"Oh, why did this have to happen?" Eva whispered to the ceiling.

"I believe he broke into your uncle's apartment."

"He didn't! Why, that's terrible! That's against the law!" Eva twisted onto her side, away from Sara Will.

"So is trespassing," Sara Will said. "I could call the sheriff right now, I suppose. After all, he came onto my property uninvited, scaring the wits out of innocent, law-abiding people."

88

She could imagine the boy being hauled into the deputy's car, his bike and belongings confiscated. How much peace would that give her? It certainly wouldn't get Fate and Eva on their way and could even prolong their stay. They'd probably have to borrow money from her to bail him out. They'd do something like that, with Swanee Hope out in front quoting the Bible and looking mournful. No, it wouldn't do. She'd just have to be patient until something else occurred to her.

Eva rose out of the bed again, coming to her knees in front of Sara Will, sheet still tight to her chest. "Don't do that, please don't. I'll get rid of him. I promise. I've always been able to handle Michael."

"Then see to it," Sara Will said, turning to the door. "This is your responsibility, Eva."

Less than five minutes later, Eva and Michael were shouting at each other.

Finally, Sara Will said to herself from the landing, toward which the parlor sounds easily drifted. She sat down on the step to wait it out.

In the parlor, Michael had already patted the table for his glasses, pushed them on, and put Eva in focus. She was still in her gown, a wrinkled, yellowish rag that hung off one shoulder and dipped unevenly to the floor. She looked terrible.

"How did you find me?" she wanted to know.

"I broke into Mr. Jessop's apartment," Michael said. The truth seemed more foolish than dangerous to him, and he took off his glasses to wipe his hand across his bleary eyes. He didn't want to see Eva looking like that. She looked old to him, used up. It was a look he'd seen coming over a year ago, ever since she'd told him she was pregnant. Gradually she'd turned pale and lifeless, as if she harbored a disease, not a baby. When she ran away from home, he'd thought she was like a wild animal searching for a place to die. It had scared him that bad. He'd been so frightened all those months looking for her, expecting to find her in a morgue somewhere. He'd actually checked hospitals regularly, methodic in his search for an unidentified pregnant girl, a nameless baby, a corpse kept cold while he searched, going from town to town holding out a limp school picture and repeating, "She doesn't really look like this anymore." He hurt when he said that.

Now he put his glasses on again and forced himself to look at her. "I went by to see you, Eva. I just wanted to talk to you, to tell you not to worry about anything, but you were gone."

"You knew I couldn't stay. It was your fault, Michael."

"I looked in the window and the crib was missing. That's how I knew. So I broke in and there was this box of junk under the bed—pictures, news clippings, things Mr. Jessop had saved."

"You did what? Miss Sara told me but I couldn't believe it! That makes you a common criminal. Here I am dealing with a burglar." She had her hands on her hips, her breasts pushed forward in defiance.

But Michael wasn't going to let her stop him. "I found an obituary notice about his sister-in-law in there, and it gave her name and said she'd be buried in Sparrow Creek Cemetery near Tyler Mills, and so I came. I couldn't think of any other place to look. I wasn't going to call your daddy, Eva. I know I said I would, but you should of known better. I just got so frustrated with your not letting me see you and Rachel. I miss you."

"Well, you shouldn't! Nobody's asking you to. I don't want you to. I just want you to leave me alone, Michael. I don't know why I ever told you in the first place. It certainly was a mistake." Eva covered her face with her hands so he'd disappear, but when she looked again he was still there looking mournfully at her. "We didn't leave just because you threatened to call Daddy, Michael. That was only one reason. We left because of you, too. To get away from you. Can't you understand that?" Her voice had fallen to a hiss.

"I guess not," Michael said and stood up. His clothes were as wrinkled as hers.

"You're disgusting," Eva said, getting a second wind from just seeing a full view of him. "You look like you haven't had a bath in days. You make me sick, Michael, do you know that? I'm so sick of you. All I ever wanted was to have my baby in peace without being hassled by anybody."

"I never meant to hassle you—" Michael started.

"Well, what exactly would you call it? That's what it is when one person won't leave another person alone!"

"I guess I would have left you alone—I could—if I thought you were all right."

"I was all right, you just wouldn't see it. Uncle Fate and I were fine together and then you came, and from then on it's been trouble. You know it has. What I don't understand is, if you care so much about me, why don't you do what I want for a change? Why don't you just go away and leave me alone?"

"I can't." Michael slumped back on the sofa, too tired to listen. He did smell bad. He couldn't stand himself. He had no defense.

"You have to, do you hear me, Michael? We could have stayed here. It would have been all right, for a while at least, but you've ruined it. What am I supposed to do? These people don't know me. They don't care. We got to stay this long just because we took them by surprise. But they won't put up with you, I can tell you that, and neither will I."

She was beginning to cry. Muscles that had throbbed with anger and held her tender face tight abruptly released to set her mouth quivering. She felt awash with regret. She wanted to be home going to high school. She wanted her own room and food her mother cooked and the sound of her daddy humming in the bathroom. She wanted to have a date and kiss somebody full in the mouth with her arms tight around him. Instead she had Michael and this ramshackle old house and a baby.

"Miss Sara is talking about having you arrested," she began, but just then Rachel screamed out as if startled out of sleep by the events transpiring beneath her.

"Oh, my God," Eva moaned and fled, running past Sara Will on the stair, her gown at her knees, tears streaming as she panted upward to her child.

Why did I ever think she could handle anything? Sara Will wondered, although, were the truth known, she didn't know exactly what tack to take with Michael either.

She went down into her parlor where he still sat, rumpled and dingy with yesterday's grime. "I assume you'll be going now," she said, playing her aggressive, up-front approach first. She saw his eyes framed by his glasses. They gave him an innocent babyish look. He didn't seem any older or wiser than Eva.

He sniffed and ducked his head away from her stare. "If I had time, I could win her," he said softly. "That's always been the problem, you see. When she told me she was going to have a baby, I wanted to marry her, but she wouldn't even talk about it, and before I could figure something out—make plans about where and how we've live, the money and all that so I could convince her—she was gone. Just vanished. It was in the fall she left; I had graduated from high school that spring before, so I started looking. I worked at odd jobs, anything to get enough money to keep on looking. My folks thought I was crazy, but they kept on feeding me when I turned up at home. Finally I found her, almost by accident, although I guess there was a method to it. I started checking on the relatives. Who would have thought she'd be with someone like Mr. Jessop all this time? Someone who should have let her folks know? But there she was. So I got a job, night clerk in the hotel there, and I tried to see her and the baby. That baby's growing up without even knowing me." He paused to see Sara Will still staring at him, her face slightly perplexed by the implication of his story just dawning on her.

"You're Rachel's father," she said finally.

"I sure am," Michael breathed.

"Take a bath, young man," Sara Will said. "You can use the bathroom upstairs while I scramble you some eggs for breakfast." She was as surprised as he to find that she was smiling.

It wasn't going to be easy, Michael knew, as he sprawled in the bathtub up to his chest in warm water. He dragged his fingers through the water and up to his neck, where the drippings off his fingertips slid down his skin, making him shiver. He should hurry so as not to keep the lady with the eggs waiting, but the bath felt so good. He was relaxed for the first time in days, although there was no easing the permanent tension in his chest, not until he'd accomplished his mission. Still, he felt the best he had in months, knowing Eva was down the hall, defiant but at least under the same roof with him. That was something. And the woman with the eggs seemed interested in his situation, maybe even willing to help him. It was simply a matter of convincing her that he and Eva belonged together. Convincing her now seemed equivalent to convincing Eva herself.

But it wasn't going to be easy because it required a certain willingness to believe the unbelievable—a suspension of disbelief, he thought it was called—to accept his dilemma. He was the father of Eva's child, but Eva didn't believe it. When he tried to tell her about it, as he had many times, she pulled her senses tight, refusing to hear him or consider the possibility of what he saw so vividly. He could describe every little detail. He knew how her eyes had looked, how her mouth felt, her teeth against his tongue, her breast under his lips, her heels digging into his thighs as she locked her legs around him. He remembered the frenzy and then the heavy quiet, her breath on his shoulder, fingers pulling at his flesh as if she were not ready to let go, then her sleepy body pressing on him, her damp hair limp on his chest. Their bodies had sucked and popped together imperfectly, he knew. Awkwardly. And yet there had been a completeness in it that he'd always known would be there. They had loved each other. Really loved. She was everything he would ever want.

The bathroom door opened and he sat up and then sank lower in the water, the soapy washcloth protecting him. It was Eva with Rachel on her hip.

"Who let you in here?" she asked, turning away from him to the lavatory. "Who said you could use this bathroom?"

"The tall one," Michael said. "I'll be out in a minute." He lathered his shoulders with the bar of soap.

"Where to? Where are you going now, Michael?" Eva glared at him while water ran into the lavatory. She was too angry to be embarrassed. Besides, his body had always been insignificant to her.

"Downstairs to eat breakfast."

"No." Eva twisted the water off and splashed Rachel's feet in it. "No, no, no. You are getting your things and getting on that stupid bike and you are leaving here."

"You're coming home then?" Michael baited her. He wondered what she'd do if he stood up. The idea appealed to him but he lacked the courage. He was always afraid of going too far with her. He abandoned the impulse and leaned back against the tub. "Now that I know where you are, you might as well. Your Uncle Fate is going to lose his job, Eva, if he hasn't already. Ira Roth was pretty upset. I guess I've lost mine too, but I'll get something else. I'll get us someplace to live, too, or you can stay with your uncle a while longer and I'll help out with the groceries and take care of Rachel's needs. I ought to be supporting you, Eva. You know that."

"I don't know any such thing, Michael Logan." Eva patted the baby's face and hands dry.

"Look at her, Eva," he said. "She needs a daddy. She needs a family."

"She has everything she needs." Eva turned to go.

"And you, Eva? Do you have everything you need?"

He saw her back tremble. It was a tiny shudder, shoulders momentarily lifted to ward off the cold.

"Please go, Michael. Please. Go back home and get enrolled in college like you always planned. Make something of yourself. What kind of person gives up everything and chases another person all over the country?"

"I love you, Eva," he said, but Eva didn't wait to hear.

The faucet dripped into the drained lavatory, a solitary splash recording loss. Michael slid underwater, submerged for as long as his breath held out. Surfacing, he pulled himself up, tossing water like a dog before he rubbed himself dry with a towel. He dug through his duffel bag to find clean but wrinkled clothes. Dressed, he stopped in front of the small mirror just to look at himself. Through the fog on his lenses, he saw a weary face, still night-worn, a slight weakness about the mouth that meant he had to bite down to show any determination. He clenched his jaw. That was better. He went downstairs to put his intentions to the test.

10

◆ That evening, Swanee Hope and Fate sat over coffee while Sara Will scraped the supper dishes. Swanee Hope had spent the entire day cooking. The hours had magically passed without her once thinking to turn on the television. Instead, she'd been up and doing, showing Eva how the washing machine worked, rocking Rachel, glancing out the window from time to time to watch Fate and Michael stacking the split wood against the house. They were using the old Western Flyer wagon she'd found in the barn.

Fate had put some sort of battery-operated music device on the back stoop, and the sound spinning off the tape was coarse and unfamiliar to her. Young people's music, probably what was referred to as acid rock. Sometimes she could only hear the bass parts thumping as if dull blows were striking the side of the house. She was surprised that the confusing noise didn't irritate her in the least. She even felt content with it as she rolled a piecrust and stirred corn pudding on the stove.

Her only worry was that Sara Will was going to hate the tape player; she was literally going to despise the sound and the idea of it. She was also going to be mad as a hornet when Swanee Hope started begging to let all of them, Michael included, stay. Through the week, she had decided, while turning the sputtering chicken in the frying pan. Sara Will was going to have a hissy-fit and Swanee knew it. Still she intended to ask—no, to insist, as if this were her house too and she had some rights in it. Well, she did have rights, didn't she?

To begin with, she was the oldest. Six years on Sara Will ought to be worth something, even if you didn't count experience. Of course, one must count what you'd done in your life, what you'd accomplished. Sara Will had never lived anywhere except in this house, had not had a suitor in the thirty-odd years since Frank Settlemyer gave up and married a girl eighteen years old who pressed clothes in the dry cleaner's. Swanee Hope used to see her, the steam rising into her face from around the edges of the presser as she creased pants and flattened lapels. She was pretty and eager and damp. Swanee Hope always thought Frank Settlemyer did the wise thing, but she never said that to Sara Will, not even for spite.

Sara Will had a job for a while—years, actually, although Swanee Hope remembered those same years, when she was first married and starting her family, in a blur. It had all been done with so fast. It seemed to her she'd been young one day and old the next. Even in her mid-twenties she'd felt matronly, pudgy with what she was convinced was some kind of hormonal swelling, undiagnosed of course because she never questioned the doctor about what in reality was fifteen pounds of solid weight put on during her pregnancy. Figure or not, she'd wanted more children, a daughter to confide in, someone she could buy expensive dresses for and depend on when she was old.

Her son grew up, locked the bathroom door, was sullen and affectionate in fits and spurts she could never understand. Then he was gone: college-educated, married, a parent himself but no longer a son, certainly not her child. Soon afterward Jonathan died so unexpectedly she was stupefied, aged by endless hours of simply existing while she waited for the loneliness to go away. It never did.

It was hard for Swanee to remember that Sara Will had had a life too. She had been gainfully employed for years as a bookkeeper—part-time, but for several small businesses, which ended up making her work full days. She had a head for numbers, was cautious and exact. Her print was exquisite and her honesty beyond question.

Then their daddy died and they suddenly realized they were worth more in land and timber than he'd let on. Mama wasn't well after that, and gradually Sara gave up her jobs until she was doing only the bookkeeping she could do at home. Finally the inconvenience of it—she had to make frequent quick trips to town—caused her to give in to her hermitic nature and she stopped working altogether. She turned her full attention to her mother's care, the house, the garden. She sold small tracts of land and acres of timber to give them an ample living income. She made careful investments, her motivation never wealth but security.

She began her battle with authority over the road and bridge surreptitiously, restraining herself from mentioning it to their mother, who was feeble and nervous, her stamina drained by the constant care she gave her dying husband. She didn't even tell Swanee.

It was no time for confidences even after their father died a slow, malnourished death from cancer, which left everyone feeling frail and sickly. All the while, Mama's heart jumped and raced, making her clammy with fear. It was heart disease, not cancer, that eventually took her.

Through it all, the prospect of a bridge made Sara Will impervious. She held on to the challenge of it as if she needed something to be angry about. The fight hardened her; she never seemed to change at all. She refused to get her hair styled, to put aluminum siding on the house, or to trade in that car of hers.

Now Swanee Hope sat across the kitchen table from Fate, hoping the car wouldn't come up again. Surely he knew that mentioning the Mustang would be asking for trouble. He'd known to put the tape player away when Sara came home from the cemetery. He'd stacked the wood under the kitchen eaves, inviting gratitude. He'd taken a bath and left the bathroom sparkling. Up till now, Swanee Hope thought, everything had gone perfectly well even though the house was clamoring with sound, which Swanee knew could make Sara Will more than a little contentious. Michael was in the parlor, where cars screeched across the television screen. Eva was giving Rachel her bath. The bathroom was above them and they could hear the floorboards creaking, water running for a few seconds, even faint musical sounds as if Eva was singing between the squealing tires on the TV.

Swanee Hope played with her spoon in the dirty pie plate, turning it over and over in her hand, clinking each time on the glass. "Sara Will," she said finally, "I've been hearing a little about Eva's history. Fate has been kind enough to tell me something of their situation."

Sara Will sprayed water on the plates, her back to them. The china dishes were Swanee's, and the sound of her sister's voice—what she heard so clearly in it—made her want to smash one of them. This oval serving bowl which Swanee treasured; Sara wanted to see the shattered fragments in the sink, a rose petal here, the curved edge of a leaf there. She would do it, too, except that she knew it wouldn't change anything.

"The truth is, they need to stay a few more days. You see, Eva's parents wanted her to give up the baby so she ran away to Fate, here, who out of the goodness of his heart took her in and did everything for her, paid for everything. Why, she actually had the baby in his apartment with him right there helping. It's an inspiring story, Sara Will." She glanced at Fate. He looked strange to her, as if he were truly out of place. Well, he was. But she was trying to fix that.

She gave him an encouraging smile. She felt encouraged herself. Sara Will hadn't stopped her yet, so she continued.

"Unforeseen circumstances—the appearance of Michael and his veiled threat to expose Eva's whereabouts—forced them to flee from their home. Fate could have stayed, of course, but he chose to help Eva and her baby. Now Michael has arrived, the father of the child. They're all together here. I think it's the best thing that could have happened—their all meeting up like this in a restful place where they can have a few days of quiet and make plans for the future. So we have a choice concerning them, Sara Will. You and I have to decide whether to extend common courtesy, whether to open our home like Mary and Martha did to those in need of a place to lay their heads—"

"Hush," Sara Will said. Her back had stiffened as she listened. She was like a sculpture just begun, the features chiseled on the surface but still locked in the stone. "You can't help but go too far, can you, Swanee? You just can't help it. Mary and Martha, my foot. Don't you throw scripture at me. I may not go to church every time the doors open, like you do, but I read the Bible about as often. I know what's written in there."

She turned so quickly both Swanee and Fate jerked backwards as if to avoid being struck.

"I know as many examples of Christian charity as you do, but I have something to say to Mr. Jessop and it's time I said it." She looked straight at Fate. "I don't know you. I didn't invite you here. I don't understand why you're gallivanting around the country with these children. I don't even want to know. I do, however, want to know this: What are your intentions?"

"His intentions?" Swanee Hope gasped, hands pressed to cheeks.

"I am talking to Mr. Jessop," Sara Will said, "because it appears that my efforts to be polite, to avoid a confrontation such as this one, are impossible. I told you one more day, which then slid into two, and now that is not enough, is it? Now they want to stay through the weekend. Is it, Mr. Jessop, your intention to stay forever?"

"Sara!"

"Swanee, shut up!"

"My intention, Miss Sara Will, is to do whatever I have to do to take care of Eva and her baby."

"That is all well and good for you, Mr. Jessop. I expect you'll see stars in your crown, if that's of interest to you. But it is unfair to expect the same of strangers. We are strangers. Strangers."

She was so angry. Her body was clutched tight with it. Fate thought all her color had drained away; no blood was moving as she drew up every muscle, heart included, to explode against him.

"I heard you cry out once," he said softly, because suddenly her face reminded him of it so acutely he couldn't help but tell her. "The day of Serena's funeral I was sitting in there in the parlor. It was so awkward that day with everybody holding on so tight, like you are now, afraid of feeling anything. And then you screamed—you were just a girl, Sara Will, and I wasn't all that much older, but all my life I've remembered it. That's why we came here, because I remembered you.

"As for my intentions, I don't have any, none except what you know already: to take care of Eva and her baby the best I can because I don't want anything bad to ever happen to them. You stay in your fine house back here in this hollow and you don't have to think about all the bad things happening out there, things people can't do anything about. There's grief coming at every side, Sara Will, and I want to protect Eva from as much of it as I can."

Sara Will looked at him, fingers still clenched, face drawn white and narrow, and then she released her hands and turned back to the sink, where she looked down at Swanee Hope's china vegetable bowl. "Through the weekend," she said softly and picked up the bowl with great care.

Eva leaned over the edge of the claw-foot tub in Sara Will's bathroom, her hand grasping Rachel's shoulder to keep her steady. The baby seemed ready, even eager, to bobble on the water. She seemed to think she could lie there like an infant sea beast, weightless appendages at home in the rhythm of waves, so Eva grasped firmly in the slippery water, holding on to the tender neck, the tiny shoulder that fitted under her palm, bone smooth with baby fat. She had heard about bathtub drownings, those split seconds of face enveloped in silky water, then the slow floating up. Perhaps babies believed they could breathe under water. Maybe some ancient urge caused them to slip under the bubbles, eyes opened to view once-familiar sights as if embryonic memory held more power than light and air and Mother's voice.

Drowning and crib death—these were Eva's greatest fears other than her constant apprehension about her parents. Not because they would take Rachel away. She knew they wouldn't even try, not after all these months, not when they actually saw her. But they would want an explanation, wouldn't they? They would expect to be told everything. She didn't want to have to describe her flight to Uncle Fate's door or the care he'd provided, which they would never consider adequate no matter how glowingly she recalled it. She didn't want to tell them anything, for their knowing would invade her most private life, would make her accountable for feelings she couldn't possibly explain.

She dripped warm soapy water down the baby's back. The soap clung and she dipped the cloth into the water and, holding it at Rachel's neck, squeezed to flood the suds away. Rachel shivered, her chubby body reacting to the tickle. She liked the water, had never cried during her bath, not even when she was very small. Now she slapped the surface, spraying her blinking eyes and chuckling to herself.

Next summer I'll get her a swimming pool, Eva thought, lifting the baby so her feet churned the water. Eva wrapped a towel around her and drew Rachel close. But where would they be next summer? She didn't want to go back to Fate's apartment, although her memories of that place would always be dear. But they had left there now and she knew there was no going back, at least not for her and Rachel.

Anyhow, she wanted Rachel to have a swing and a sandbox, a yard like at home, not a concrete sidewalk and a flight of steps off an alley. It surprised her that she wanted for Rachel what she'd had herself. A comfortable room, wallpaper and lacy curtains. Toys—bright, tested, educational toys—and dolls too. Dolls and stuffed animals with silly faces. Miniature furniture, especially a rocking chair, in the French Provincial style.

This would be a good place to stay, out here in the country with this lawn sweeping down into the woods. Through the low narrow window she could look down at the thick browning grass that in spring would be soft underfoot. There was a creek along the forest edge—she had heard it—and she could take Rachel wading there in the cold water, smooth rocks for stepping stones, the bank spongy with moss and thick with wild violets and bluets in spring. Rachel could learn to ride a three-wheeler and then a bike on the dirt lane, which would be safe from traffic. Eva could watch from the front porch. They could even fence in part of the yard to make her truly safe. It was possible.

She had realized that when, in the cemetery with Sara Will, she'd knelt at the footstone of a girl of her own age. CLARA CHILD OF ADELIA AND CLAUDE was chiseled in the stone in such small letters Eva had to trace the etching with her finger to be certain of them, and yet it was a name, a relationship defined there for everyone to see. This valley was a place of families: it was where people could stay forever if they wanted to, never budging, safe against small-town worries about what the neighbors would think. It was where a girl could have a baby and nobody think the worse of her as long as she did her best by it. Unforgivable sins were crimes of abandonment, of ignoring need and giving up what belonged to you.

And just then in the cemetery, Rachel had crawled into her arms and held on much as she did now. Holding Rachel, Eva had heard the scraping of Sara Will's rake, the painstaking, monotonous toil of fierce commitment to what was hers. I feel that

102

too, Eva had thought. She still felt it. That was why all day today she'd been adjusting herself to Michael's presence. His finding her didn't matter as much as she'd thought it would. Not that she wasn't angry with him, but what good did it do? She was worn out with being angry when all that really mattered was Rachel. She would do what was best for Rachel.

She stood up in the bathroom, the baby against her chest, and looked at the two of them in the mirror. They looked alike, both rosy and moist with bathroom heat, both blond although unnaturally so. Rachel would lose her fine white baby hair just as Eva had before her second birthday, when soft brown took root. Eva would let her bleached hair grow out so they could be brunettes together. It would take a year or more because the dark roots were only an inch long, a row of weeds at her part. Maybe she would dye it brown. That would help. She wanted to look like herself again, get her figure back, squeeze hips into size seven Levi's and button blouses without a safety pin to keep the gap closed between her breasts. She wanted to have her old face, too. Thinner than this face, her cheekbones high and colored with blush, her hair thick but soft and properly shaped to bring out its hint of curl.

She had regretted the bleaching from the moment she smelled the vile chemical odor in the bathroom and felt Linda's gloved fingers on her scalp as she worked the warm liquid into her hair. She had hated changing one more thing about herself, but it had seemed necessary. Uncle Fate had heard from her father, a long painstaking letter describing all they had done to search for her: the contacts in major cities and with Florida juvenile authorities, with hospitals and obstetricians, with highway patrol stations and sheriffs' departments. Her picture was in circulation, Clement had written. All over the eastern seaboard there were these floating images of Eva Jeanette Jessop, age fifteen, blue eyes, long brown hair. No distinguishing marks, a capped tooth in front broken in a bike spill, five-four, 105 pounds.

The hair was what she could change. Linda had cut it with

dull scissors, pulling every strand until Eva screamed at her, as much from frustration as from pain. She had hated what she was doing to herself. No. She hated what was being done to her. She was just beginning to see the pattern of her first fifteen years. She had always been so accommodating, had never rebelled against the food on her plate, the dresses in her closet, the ballet and violin lessons. She had always been conscientious, even grateful, because that too was expected.

And yet as her fingers were pressed firmly to the strings, head adjusted to secure the instrument under her chin, she had felt bitterness. She had longed for dissent. It wasn't that she didn't like to play the violin or the bits of classical melody she gradually learned by rote. It was that there was never time or place to abandon structure, to experiment without guiding hands and determined instruction. No time or place for creating. Well, she'd created now. But shouldn't a person make a poem before she makes a baby? Shouldn't she have one little piano phrase to call her own, one thought that didn't parrot her mother? Shouldn't she, just once, have stepped out of Miss Davis's corps de ballet to pirouette to a movement of music only she heard?

She remembered a line about marching to your own drummer. She didn't know where it came from, but she knew it had to do with being your own person and doing what was right for yourself. It meant not being done to.

Rachel struggled in Eva's arms, reaching out for the glass. Her short fingers touched her image and drew back, then slapped at herself, laughing. Eva caught her hand and held it close to her body, the baby snug against her.

What I want is to stay here, she thought. At least through Christmas, past Rachel's first birthday. She wanted Swanee Hope to bake a cake and Sara Will Burney to wear a silver paper hat. Well, maybe that was too much to ask for, but a party wasn't more than Rachel deserved. Neither was this house to have it in.

"We're going to be all right," she whispered into Rachel's

clean hair. But Rachel was pushing away from her, flinging herself toward her own baby image in the mirror. Eva didn't try to hold her back. She didn't intend to hold herself back, either. Never again. She snapped off the light and stood for a moment in the warm dark. Then she pushed open the door, on her way to make something happen.

She went past the parlor without even looking in at Michael. She had nothing to say to him. Whether he went or stayed didn't matter to her. He was totally insignificant. It wasn't even Uncle Fate who mattered to her now, although she loved him, would always love him. But at the moment, he wasn't involved. Yesterday she'd expected him to take care of her, but not now. Now she was the one to give care. All her attention belonged to Rachel and to the women she found in the kitchen.

"Uncle Fate," she said from the doorway, "would you excuse us for a minute?"

She knew she'd startled him witless. The tone of her voice even surprised herself. Fate was up and out before the women could object if they'd wanted to.

"Oh, she's all nice and clean. You sweet thing," Swanee Hope said, reaching out for Rachel.

But Eva held on. She wanted them to see mother and child together. Baked in their memories would be this young haggard girl with a soft, clean, innocent baby in her arms. If they said no, they'd always have this image to go with it.

"I'd like to talk to you," Eva said, nodding toward the table. She was surprised again to see Sara Will promptly fold her tea towel carefully over the drying rack and come to take her seat. Eva sat down too and then wished she hadn't. She felt like a child at their table, but it was too late. The women were waiting.

"I wanted to ask you—" Eva began and then faltered. She pressed Rachel to her shoulder, a shield against Sara Will's cool stare. It was for Rachel that she'd come begging, and the baby's fine head at her chin reminded her acutely of obligations. This was more than just showing up for lessons or being home by eleven. It was even more than carrying another person in your uterus and doing what you could to bring it safely into the world. This was a day-in and day-out responsibility she had here. For the rest of her life, no matter what else she did, she would always be a mother.

"We've just been discussing it," Swanee Hope gusted, unable to hold her tongue a moment longer, "and it's been decided that you should stay with us through the weekend. You and Rachel and your uncle. Even Michael if he wants to." She was beaming.

"I grew up in such a nice house," Eva said, accepting this rerouting for a moment. "It's the house Uncle Fate and my daddy grew up in, but it's been remodeled. It's a big house like this one. I've always wanted Rachel to have a house, not just an apartment like Uncle Fate's. Of course, it doesn't matter much yet. She's just a baby. But I have to be thinking about the future. It comes so quick." She looked from Swanee Hope to Sara Will and back again. Her eyes were tearing, an aggravating predicament when she was trying to be unwavering and polite at the same time.

"What is it, Eva?" Sara Will wanted to know. Her voice wasn't stony and impatient. Looking at Eva, it occurred to her she must be prepared for anything.

"I want to stay here though the winter," Eva said. "I know that's a lot to ask, more than a stranger could possibly expect, but I have to ask it for Rachel. She's my child and there's nothing I won't do for her. I've thought about going home, but I know that's not the right thing for me so I can't think it would be right for Rachel. I want her to be a year old, at least a year, before I take her there. I want one year of being her one true mother before Mama takes over. Mama won't mean any harm, but it will work out that way. I'll go back to school and she'll keep Rachel and I'll never have her again, not like now. And then there's Uncle Fate. He's going to be in trouble over me. And Michael."

"But Michael is her father," Swanee Hope urged plaintively.

106

"I know that's what he says. Why, he even tells me that, so I know he's convinced himself of it somehow. But he isn't Rachel's daddy, I swear it. Michael and I never even held hands. We went to the ball games sometimes. I went to the Sweetheart Dance with him when he was a senior because he wouldn't go without me and who wants to be responsible for somebody missing their senior dance? But that's all. Nothing ever happened between Michael and me."

"Well, I declare!" Swanee Hope puffed at her. "What do you think, Sara Will?"

"I think Eva's telling the truth," Sara Will said.

"I know I'm asking more than anybody has a right to ask," Eva said, finding courage in Sara's conciliatory tone. "I don't have much money, but unless we were to get sick, we'll just need food and keeping warm. I just want to stay here with Rachel through the winter. That's all I'll ever ask for. I'm not ready to go home yet, and I can't keep on dragging her around."

The silence loomed around them. They felt it pressing down, sucking their breaths.

"Then you'll stay," Sara Will said.

"Why, sister!" Swanee beamed and then clamped her mouth shut as if she'd been struck.

They sat there, none of them quite believing, while the baby slept on Eva's shoulder, oblivious of her newly determined future. The two women were quiet, Swanee Hope stunned by her sister's sudden generosity while Sara Will felt resigned, not just to the presence of the baby in her house but to a new unsettled feeling inside where everything had for so long been simple, unruffled, and austerely plain.

"What about Fate?" Swanee Hope asked as they sat, eyes averted so as not to focus on their new situation.

"We'll see," Sara Will said, her voice floating above them, an audible whisper in the quiet. She felt tired, muscle weary, as if she'd been splitting wood or had taken a long hike. It was a welcome exhaustion, one she had always willingly carried to sleep. "I'm going to bed now."

"But what about Michael? Where can he sleep?" Swanee Hope asked, wanting to get plans made while Sara Will was compliant.

"There's a rollaway bed in the storage space under the eaves. He and Fate will have to make do."

"That's fine," Swanee Hope said. "That's wonderful, sister."

But Sara Will was already leaving the room, treading the worn path of the hall, past the parlor and along the stairs, up and away from them. In her room, she undressed and got into bed, hair and teeth unbrushed. She felt too tired to bother, but then she lay there, eyes wide open, listening for the new participants in her life to stir. They were silent—fearful, she suspected, of her sudden raging. They expected her to catch fire, spontaneous combustion as possible in her head as in an attic of smoky rags.

Well, she wouldn't explode. Strangely, she wasn't angry with them anymore. She wasn't even thinking about them at all, although her mind clicked furiously. She would have to turn the water heater up and get the furnace going. Put fresh gravel on the lane so there'd be traction in case of snow. Get a hook for the bathroom door. Beg or borrow a high chair. Buy a new bathrobe. Her mind raced while her heart lay leaden in her chest. She seemed to have no pulse, no sensation of breathing at all. Only her brain worked, demanding that she stare into the darkness and contemplate the future. She saw the dawn before she slept.

WINTER

11

✦ The winter would bring snow to her valley. Sara Will knew that at least one heavy gray morning would press clouds to the treetops, holding back the sun so there was never really dawn, just a thickening haze turned soft with flakes as big as quarters. At first they would melt. She would watch them slip damply down her windowpane or disappear in the brown tufts of grass in the yard, but then a light patch would appear to the north of that old oak at the curve in the lane. Slowly the grass would take on a crystal look, strangely pale as though coated with thin sugar syrup. The stubs of autumn asters would stick up defiantly, rattling in the damp muffled air. By noon, the snow-flakes would be small, hard, and fierce. She wouldn't be able to see past the porch.

This thought, a cold vision of her world contained so tightly by the snow that she felt insulated in it, was what she held on to those late days of October when there were people in her house. She picked a natural phenomenon, an event totally beyond her control and yet inevitable unless the entire universe had slipped: changing sunspots, jet streams, whatever brought the weather to her from some unfathomable distance. Siberia, she thought it was. She closed her eyes to see the snow, shut her ears to hear the silence of its falling, pulled her sweater tight to her shoulders against the thought of continuous chill. Surely the snow would come by January, burying the house and barn, camouflaging the truck, hiding her lane, bending low the dogwoods and the gingko. Unretractable cold would settle in with the snow; the slow afternoon thaw would freeze again at nightfall. The bend in her lane would be like glass for perhaps a week, then raw slime to spin in, finally hard and dry, frozen solid but traversable. At that perfect moment of cleared lane and sunny cold sky, she would send them away. They would be eager to go.

"What are you looking at?" Swanee Hope asked from behind her.

Sara was looking at the truck Fate had pulled up close to the house. The truck looked like a derelict, its grill a smirk, the windshields smeared in a grimy fan shape where the wipers had failed.

"Oh, that." Swanee sighed, blowing a puff of air toward Sara Will's neck. "Fate said he was going to wash it before tomorrow. We'll be going to church in it."

"Surely not," Sara replied without a second's hesitation. "You've been riding with the Daltons all these years."

"Not by choice, sister," Swanee said. "And tomorrow I don't have to. Fate said he'd take me."

"And go in? He's going into church with you?"

"Of course he is, Sara. Mr. Jessop isn't a chauffeur, for heaven's sake. He's a Christian man, a churchgoer."

But Sara Will didn't believe it. She stood looking out the kitchen window—staring out, she would have said, could she have looked in at herself. She stared so much lately, not just because what she saw confused her but because all her thoughts seemed to come in visions, posed like the living pictures she'd seen once at a Christmas program.

She remembered sitting completely still, hardly letting a breath escape as the Sparrow Creek Sunday school children held a Nativity pose. Mary was unblinking in her gaze across the manger into the glazed eyes of a bearded Joseph who, not yet sixteen, hid his own fuzzed cheeks beneath a scraggly Santa Claus beard hastily colored with coal dust. They had seemed absolutely trapped. Their awkwardly draped clothing was prison garb, their stiff faces were masks held fast against any twitching, a sudden itch, a slight curl of lip that could at any moment send them into irreverent gales of laughter. Sara Will had known what their condition was like, the restless, scratchy urge to do something pressed down by the fear of exposure. If they moved, they would betray themselves. Sara had been like that herself, and so she'd held her breath with them, understanding their dilemma.

Now, as she faced the old truck, she felt that same breathlessness. She could imagine it at the center of a tableau, a picture that captured her household like a snapshot taken at an outing in which the picnickers leaned on fenders and hood to prove how they got there. She would be the one frowning.

Beyond the trees the wind was lifting, sweeping long strokes into the woods. The heavy sway on the tops of the pines arrested her thoughts, sending a small shiver of alarm down her back. Fate and Michael were on the roof securing a sagging gutter and repairing the flashing around the chimney. They had made squirrel sounds all morning, their tiny maddening racket following her about the house, reminding her that they were there and doing something useful when she would have liked to have their idleness to complain about.

They weren't lazy but she doubted their experience: whether Fate could balance with one arm, if Michael was capable of anything but persistence. They didn't know her roof as she did, having clung there year after year with her broom. She thought to go out and warn them of the wind, but why should she? She was not responsible. She hadn't had responsibility for anyone but herself since her mother died.

And that seemed so long ago. I have been alone so long, she thought. Too long to change. Yet her unyielding nature wasn't something she was pleased with or proud of. She hadn't intended to be unbending; one doesn't plan from birth to be set in one's ways. A person simply takes hold of those attributes that seem most reasonable, like picking a wool coat in preference to a cotton sweater when going out in the cold. But she had continued to wear the coat when shirt sleeves would do. There was no denying that.

"Swanee," she said, still facing the window. "I could take you to church tomorrow."

"That won't be necessary, Sara, as I already have an invitation." Swanee Hope had returned to the piecrust she was making, and she banged the rolling pin on the counter hard enough to make Sara Will start. "I'm not ashamed to be seen with Fate Jessop. I'm sure he's a fine figure of a man when he gets dressed up."

"I'm not questioning his appearance, Swanee. It just seems to me—"

"I know what you're thinking, Sara. You want to keep them hidden out here so nobody will know you've done such a generous thing as to take them in. Or maybe you're worried about what people will say seeing me and a man together. Is that what's bothering you? Well, I thought of that myself and that's why I'm taking Michael and Eva with us." Swanee was beaming.

"And what about Rachel?" Sara asked, although she was afraid to hear.

"I'm sure you can manage for an hour or two."

"I'm expected to keep the baby? I shan't do it, Swanee. I flatly refuse."

"And deny Eva and Michael the experience of worship together? Why, Sara Will, it could be what finally draws them to each other. It could open Eva's eyes to the importance of family. It could be the beginning of salvation for everybody."

"Coercion," Sara said.

"No, Sara," Swanee said, pricking the pie shell daintily with a fork, "fighting sin is all it is."

So Sara stood on the porch with the baby in her arms while they piled into the gleaming truck. Michael couldn't slam the door shut against his shoulder. He leaned in across Eva, squishing her till she squealed. Fate, looking exasperated, avoided Sara Will's stare through the sparkling windshield. His bad arm was turned into the wheel so he was almost sitting sideways. Sara didn't see how he could drive like that. Only Swanee was unperturbed, burrowed in between Fate and Eva and wearing her navy blue felt hat from which one stark feather stuck straight up like a signal. Michael worked the half-latched door open and fell out, catching his feet just as he touched ground. He climbed onto the bed of the truck and stood there facing the cab, looking straight ahead as the biting morning air ruffled his hair, struck bone beneath his windbreaker, flipped the ends of the hand-painted tie Swanee had found in a box of miscellaneous belongings under the eaves. He looked embarrassed so Sara averted her eyes, not wanting to share his misery. Eva waved out the window, but Sara could only nod because her hands were taken with the baby. Swanee Hope was a blur of color where sunlight struck the windshield. Sara couldn't see her face.

So they went, leaving her on the porch with Rachel cradled to her chest. She pulled the blanket snugly around the small body everywhere cold could seep in and walked out into the yard. The baby was quiet, fed, groggy, content. She didn't seem to know or care in whose arms she nestled. Held out at arms' length she would have screamed, panicked by instinctive fear of falling, but secure within a boundary, any boundary, she was at peace.

It's the same with me, Sara thought. Here in her front yard staring at the receding bubble of dust behind the truck, she felt herself standing on the edge of her life looking out into what she had always imagined was a rocky place, treacherous with slippery boulders and rising water.

She had seen the valley flooded, had stood alone on the ridge every evening for a month and watched the rising water enveloping familiar places. The water had been alive and powerful. She had been careful not to slip. It was the same with her life; she had thought she would drown out there among people, pushed under by obligations, held fast by concerns she would collect like stones. She had hung back, clinging to the old and familiar which, although chipped, faded, practically useless, offered no resistance. She had fashioned the shape of things, her life here, Swanee's there, the two connecting only at mealtimes or when some minor dilemma faced them simultaneously. She had controlled all the possibilities except natural disasters, illness, and death and had not wanted to look beyond the solitary confinement she faced each morning.

Now, expecting the worst, she was forced to see in place of her dark vision, her own landscape painfully ragged and in need of repair. She saw dilapidated gates, the dry pond bed grown up, the scraggly garden. She saw things Fate Jessop and Michael could do. These intruders might have brought the world with them to ravel her seams, but their damage seemed slight, almost imperceptible, amid the oversights she'd made herself.

Still, she didn't regret her old life. What had been wrong with it? She couldn't think what. She had earned a living, had salvaged her family heritage in ledger books, photographs, household goods, cemetery markers. She had kept the land safe, drawing from it only those resources essential to its maintenance. She had repaired and refurbished when nothing else would do. She had had good friends once, before family took precedence. She had had her share of dates, all local boys she'd been in school with who remembered the awkward girl she'd been and didn't expect any handholding or obligatory smooching, just a screaming ride on the county fair bullet or a willingness to sit through a double feature of gangster movies. She had liked to dance and to play bridge. She had liked Frank Settlemyer but not enough to marry him. Was that true? Had it really been a lack of affection that made her hesitate until it was too late? Surely she had once dreamed of a life different from the one she now led, but she couldn't remember the particulars of it. It had been, after all, a dream, a fantasy saved for sleep. She hadn't let foolishness interfere with the day-to-day practicalities of her life, and she'd managed to accomplish all she'd intended, except for a road cut through the woods and the bridge.

But now the boundaries weren't so clear. Lately, she'd awakened shuddering on the edge of fragile dreams, and the days were dense with emotion. She couldn't quite identify the dread that followed her about, pushing against her, prodding until she felt as though she were again leaning from the ridge toward the dark water. She recognized the panic, though. Its dark familiarity clung to her like a cloak knotted at her throat. Resignation spread across her shoulders.

What was even more strange was the tenderness she had begun to feel. Seeing her life becoming different—every day of this week had presented itself embroidered with a new quirky stitch in someone's personality, some unforeseen glimpse into past lives that astonished her with their richness—she felt only slightly unhinged. She had expected peculiarities. That had been her most persuasive mental argument against letting them stay. What she didn't understand, what truly baffled her, was the feeling of tenderness, of melting inside, that came when she was least prepared for it and which released her briefly and without warning from the tightly held terror she'd felt when she first saw the truck bouncing up the lane.

This morning she'd felt that tenderness while Swanee Hope stood in the hall before the speckled mirror and nervously tucked gray wisps under the edges of her ancient hat. She was wearing her finest, but even that seemed tattered and shabby, out of fashion. Swanee was pretty—why had she always tried to deny that?—but the drab fading blue of her coat and hat defeated her gentle baby features. Swanee is a person meant for pastels, Sara had thought, watching her sister lift on her toes in excitement, poised like a dancer anticipating the sound of music.

At that moment, Sara Will had felt something. Love, perhaps? Surely she had always loved her sister, yet she couldn't bring herself to speak of it. How could she? How did you say I love you to someone you'd known all your life? It would seem so sudden, so impulsive, wouldn't it? Such an embarrassing oversight of feeling all these years. Besides, she couldn't undo, could she, make amends for neglect, for all the years of belittling sarcasm Swanee had seemed to ignore? Swanee had probably deserved every derogatory remark Sara Will ever sent in her direction. Still, Sara regretted cattiness and jokes made at Swanee's expense. With all that, perhaps even because of her sister's endurance, she knew she loved her. Surely she always had.

The baby stirred under the blanket, stretching into sleep. I need to finish dinner, Sara Will thought, moving toward the house. The roast was in the oven but there was corn to put on, fruit to chop for the salad, the table to set. She had plenty to keep herself busy while the house was empty. If nothing else, she could work one of the crossword puzzles she'd been saving from the paper.

But instead of doing any of those things, she sat down in the parlor with the baby in her arms and pushed back the blanket from Rachel's head so the soft fuzz was under her hand. The baby's cheek was against her breast as soft as cotton. Her mouth bubbled a film of moist milky breath onto Sara Will's dress. The warmth seeped in. Sara sat there in the silence, not thinking about anything, not moving.

She'd never felt this calm before, although she'd always considered herself a staid person, reserved, even locked inside herself. This was a new kind of quiet. It seemed to flow between herself and the sleeping baby. After a while she stood up as if startled by her own heartbeat and, cradling Rachel's head against her shoulder to keep the child steady, went up the stairs to put her in the crib. I have to finish dinner, she thought, folding the blanket over the sleeping infant. I can't just sit about all day.

Rachel, startled by the cool flat bed after Sara Will's warm closeness, tensed in a shiver, and Sara touched her back to comfort her. What brought you here to change me? she wondered. The baby relaxed, fingers unclenched, lips parted, eyelids still. I don't want this to happen, Sara Will said silently, but then she could hear the words in the room. They seemed to echo around her, bouncing off the papery walls, resounding as they struck the pine floor, dull from so many years without wax.

She had neglected so many things. She had never even listened to her own voice until now.

"I don't want to care about you, Rachel," she said, this time aloud, as if the spoken words could free her. She knew they could not. There was no way to be free again. She turned away from the sleeping baby, went softly to the door, left it partly open so that from the kitchen she could detect the slightest sound. Going down, her arms felt empty.

Their homecoming provided a flurry of activity. Eva rushed up to look in on Rachel. Fate switched on the television to catch the end of a sports program. Michael came into the kitchen to ask what he could do. Sara Will put him to setting the table and saw with surprise that he could fold napkins into little pockets in which he inserted the silverware at each place.

"I worked in a restaurant once," he said, seeing she had noticed. "I worked in a paper mill one summer and in an ice-cream parlor. Worked for a roofer for a couple of days but couldn't take the sun. Got poisoning. Eyes swelled shut, nose disappeared, nothing to hang my glasses on."

He was nineteen years old and had lived. Sara Will turned back to the Waldorf salad she was mixing. "Why do you want to marry Eva?" she asked, to put him in his place. Here was something he hadn't accomplished.

"Why not?" he replied, and they looked at each other while Swanee Hope rushed in, having discarded coat and hat on her way to them. She was wearing a print dress, pink and yellow flowers mingling with green foliage, too summery for October. Under her solemn coat there had been another person all the time, a cherubic sprite, a flighty, self-indulgent sibling.

"Don't you want to change?" Sara Will asked, knowing the wound she was inflicting.

Swanee Hope began to frown, then shook off the knife before it could do more than crease her surface. "Such a good sermon," she said and slipped an apron over her head, tying the strings under her bosom. Color flashed around the white edges but it was nothing for Sara to complain about. "Didn't you think so, Michael? Mr. Barlow preached about Jesus walking on the water. Did you know that it's only in Matthew that Peter walked with him? He couldn't do it, of course. He didn't have the faith for it. But imagine trying at all."

She began pouring tea into the glasses.

"I introduced them to Mr. Barlow, didn't I, Michael? He was so cordial. He's a lovely man, Sara Will, so bright and attractive. I said to him, 'Mr. Barlow, it renews my faith every time I hear the words come out of your mouth.' And what could he say but 'Mrs. Calhoun, that means a lot to me.' Of course, he meant it. He's sincere. Anybody can tell you that. Isn't that right, Fate?"

Fate was wearing a brown suit with wide lapels, double-breasted like a gangster. His withered arm and hand were tight to his waist as if to conceal a weapon. Sara Will couldn't bear to look at him. Staring at the cupboard in front of her, she saw him in church instead. She knew they had been late arriving so they would have been forced to sit near the front. Swanee Hope studied the hymn board, then located the number in the book. She had arranged to be on his injured side so he could help hold the hymnal between them with his good hand. It was more than that. Swanee was both protecting and acknowledging his deformity. The congregation behind her nodded to each other, more smiles than frowns in case one of the four looked back at them. It would be Fate who looked, feeling eyes at his neck. He would turn, nodding himself and flashing a nervous smile as if to ensure their welcome. He would look innocent and fervent and mischievous all at the same time. Over dinner all the Baptists in Tyler Mills would be asking about him, wondering among themselves if he were a local boy they had forgotten or a relative of the Burneys. It didn't matter what they said. They would all be talking.

"Call Eva," Sara Will said through pinched lips. She brought the salad to the table, turned the platter of roast beef to a different angle, studied the arrangement of dishes for a moment, then moved the biscuits to the other end, away from the men. She would control the meal, passing dishes on request, bringing the food full circle so it always returned to her.

Eva appeared and they sat down.

"Will you say grace?" Swanee Hope said to Fate suddenly as though inspired.

Sara Will saw him swallow hard, throat catching in panic while the others bowed their heads.

"Bless this food to our use," he began, then hesitated, as if his mind had completely failed him. Sara Will glanced up to see it had. His face was a blank among the bowed heads. She waited a moment longer, watching his features drain, become weary and pained.

And us to thy service, she mouthed in his direction.

He repeated the words quickly, fearful of another lapse of memory. The heads came up, the serving dishes began their rounds. They were halfway through the meal before she could bring herself to look at him. He smiled a little, not quite at her but in her direction, as he answered a question Swanee had just put to him.

Sara Will felt herself smiling back. It was as if she were taking her first step onto the water.

12

✦ Sara Will had grown weary of holidays. Christmas and Easter she observed faithfully, but in solitude and without commercial trappings. Swanee Hope provided trappings enough, insisting on a little artificial table tree in the parlor window, a boxwood wreath on the door, and sprigs of holly tucked here and there—

on the mantel, around the mirror in the hall, in a pitcher on the kitchen table. They had agreed to exchange presents; Sara Will always bought Swanee one nice gift—she was never cheap—and Swanee made and bought Sara Will several, each gaily wrapped and appearing one by one under the tree during the final days before Christmas as if they were being purchased that way, when the idea struck Swanee. Sara knew that wasn't true. All the gifts were under Swanee's bed, had been there since the Saturday after Thanksgiving when Sara Will always left her in town for the day.

Thanksgiving was a holiday Sara had long tried to ignore, its secular nature having lessened her sense of obligation, while Swanee fretted over the roasted chicken which had replaced the turkey and Sara Will's refusal to sit down with her in front of the television to watch the Macy parade. Swanee couldn't accept the general lack of trouble Sara took with the day.

Once in all these years Swanee's son had come, picking this lesser holiday which didn't interrupt his real life. Probably nobody in California celebrated Thanksgiving, Sara thought. She couldn't imagine them going into the house from the beach to eat a rich, hot Thanksgiving dinner when there was no nip in the air, no reason to pad their ribs for winter. Of course there was snow in California and houses with lawns instead of sand. She wasn't ignorant. Nevertheless she had lumped everyone together out there, pushing them under the same umbrella with Bill Calhoun, her truant nephew, an engineer who talked about computers to his mother as if she were capable of more than a nod and smile in reply, always so careful not to offend him with her lack of comprehension. Bill Calhoun was about as deep as a tin pan.

Sara Will was glad he'd left his wife and three children in California, although Swanee mourned their absence and looked longingly at the new pictures Bill brought as if he thought the glossy five-by-sevens should be enough. Swanee needed her arms around somebody, that was the truth of it, and so she spent four days—that was how long he stayed, Wednesday through Saturday—trying to get a grip on him. She never did. He was tanned and trim and slippery. His southern drawl had been clipped into short, quick phrases she frequently missed the meanings of. Swanee Hope smiled for days while tiny furrows of dismay deepened on her forehead. By Saturday when his rented car turned down the lane, she had a splitting headache from wearing two faces. She lay in bed for three days, through Sunday and Monday and into Tuesday, when she rose like a pale ghost of her former self to begin the slow, painful recovery that was inevitable. She had to face the loss of her child, not because he was back in California but because she had no salvageable memory of him. Not an intimate word had passed between them. The perfunctory greeting and departing embraces had been hurried, acts of politeness to be gotten over with. That was the worst Thanksgiving Sara Will could remember until now.

Swanee was planning the menu. For days she fluttered around them, a used envelope in her hand, pen clicked open to write down their wishes. Eva's family always had both rice and dressing. Michael expected creamed onions but had never heard of succotash. Fate and Sara Will were no help to her, although after incessant urging Fate recalled a cranberry relish his mother used to make of fresh ground berries and oranges, cold and tart. Swanee Hope pored over cookbooks searching for recipes. From *Southern Living* she gleaned a chiffon pumpkin pie of gelatin and cream that sounded terrible to Sara Will. "One new recipe, Sara," Swanee pleaded. "Don't you think we should try something new?" as if a pie would bring their puny celebration to life.

"Whatever you want," Sara Will replied, somewhat sullen. She didn't want to think about Thanksgiving, even though it got them closer to January. Every day got them closer.

Fate knew that too. He tried to relax, to take each day at a time, but he found himself noticing the calendar that hung beside Sara Will's telephone in the kitchen. The scene for November was bare trees like sentinels around a farmhouse from which a curl of smoke lifted hesitantly, as if airbrushed in at the last minute for a homey effect. He got through the mornings by working around the place. Sara Will had an account at a hardware and lumber company in Tyler Mills to which he and Michael made frequent trips in the truck, returning with loads of locust posts, a new gate. He repaired the lawnmower, replacing filter and spark plug, sharpened the blade and the ax, cleaned up the truck, supervised various two-handed jobs Michael performed, tinkered with the motorcycle, cast covert glances at the inaccessible Mustang. He tried to leave everybody alone, but it was hard. He longed to sit with Eva as they once had in his little apartment. What had they talked about? The past, mostly. There was so little present between them and they had been wary of the future.

Through Eva's sparse little childhood, he had begun to see his own. He had been a boy in the Depression, a bleak, anxious time. The pervasive memory he carried was of the sternness of his parents who had been caught young and innocent, their fortunes thwarted by hard times. Their slow start was an irritation to them, a sign that life was never going to click along as they had expected. They were never as successful as they had intended to be, and they wore their resentment like weary masks, mouths turned down, their eyes deep hollows veiled in disappointment. Nothing turned out quite right, nothing was good enough for them, not even their children.

He tried to play football because his father liked to go to the games. Three games into the season, he broke his collarbone. One winter he skidded into a tree on a sled and knocked himself out for two days, during which his parents mourned as if he were already dead. They expected to lose things. Of course he recovered, none the worse for it. He worked part-time after school and every summer in a garage. He liked the work and the spending money his father was too tightfisted to provide. Nobody in the family had gone to college; they didn't see much point in learning books beyond high school. Besides, there was the war. Fate joined the Army a week out of high school and, with the war ending, refined his mechanic's skills working on jeeps as a private in New Jersey. The next year his brother, Clement, went to trade school, then spent the winter as an apprentice in one of the textile plants around Tyler Mills, where he met Serena Burney and brought her home with him after three months of courtship. Fate waited a long time to find Vickie. No other girl had ever taken him seriously.

He didn't like to think about Vickie. Her face could still make a stitch come in his groin, like a pulled muscle that responded to a certain movement. He didn't love her anymore, he didn't want her back, and yet remembering her reminded him there was another way of living, just like Sara Will Burney's Mustang reminded him of the work his hands had once done and Michael reminded him of being young and cocky and indestructible.

"Why did you tell them that business about being Rachel's daddy?" he asked Michael one day when they were working on the porch, replacing the rotten boards in the doorway with new ones.

Michael stopped measuring to push his glasses up. "It embarrassed you, didn't it?" He let the metal tape shoot back into its case.

Fate put down the saw and squatted against the wall. "You're the one it should of embarrassed. Everybody knows there's no truth in it."

"What I feel about Eva is true, Mr. Jessop," Michael said wearily. He was tired of having to explain. He adjusted his slipping glasses again over eyes which were bright, glazed with fatigue as if he never slept. "When I found her at your place, I could have called her folks. I thought about it. How many hours would it take, three or four, for them to be at your place dragging her down those steps? I could tell them I'm the father, too, and they'd believe me. Why not? We were together a lot. Besides, they'd want to believe me." He sighed, pulled out the tape a few inches, and let it snap back. "People meet and fall in love every day. They get married or they live together. Even strangers do that. Do you know I've known Eva all my life and I've never had my arms around her except when we were dancing? And that wasn't very often. Have you seen how people dance nowadays? It's either two feet apart or practically standing still in a clinch. At my senior dance they only played three slow numbers the whole night. I didn't even try to kiss her. She went with me because I made her feel guilty—I said I wouldn't go without her. That's no way to get a date, Mr. Jessop. It's inhibiting as hell. I felt like I'd already taken terrible advantage of her. It was always one-sided like that between us. When we talked, she did the listening. At least, I think she listened. Then, that summer, she told me about the baby. I was the only person she told. I didn't even ask who the guy was because, while she was telling me, I was becoming him. I was imagining loving her, and it was so real I felt responsible. That feeling grew and grew until I couldn't think about anything but Eva and the baby. I didn't want anything but her."

Michael was snapping the metal tape in and out. He looked out into the yard.

"Then she disappeared and I started looking. I went crazy looking. I remembered things that never happened. I could actually hear her saying she loved me, weird things like that. 'Come find me,' she'd say. I'd be lying in bed in some dump somewhere, so tired my muscles would ache like they were tied up in knots. I'd be restless, too, so I couldn't shut my eyes or get still. I'd feel wild inside, angry and exhausted at the same time, until I'd see her face right there in the air where I could touch her. And so I would. I'd actually put out my hand and lay it against her cheek." His voice had fallen to a whisper. "She felt so good. She was so real. And so I'd put myself to sleep making love to her. I don't know how to explain it better than that."

Fate dropped to his knees, unable to look at him. He gripped the hammer until his fingers ached, waiting for Michael to turn back to their work. She should have a young man, someone who needs her that way, who can be there when she needs him too, Fate thought. A husband, a man with two good hands who doesn't need help tying his shoes or laying a porch floor. There was a partially sunk nail in front of him. He struck.

"Yoo-hooo! Look who's here!" Swanee Hope called from the side yard. She was coming up from the creek, Rachel in her arms. The baby struggled, pulling toward the ground. "She wants to crawl around, I know she does," Swanee said. "But what would Eva say?"

"She wouldn't mind," Fate said. He glanced at Michael, who didn't seem to object to Fate's authority. "Just make sure there aren't any nails over there."

Swanee set the baby down in the grass and leaned against the side of the porch. "If it weren't so bumpy out here, we could use a stroller."

"She'll be walking soon," Michael said, always thinking about the future.

The baby crawled away from them, down the yard toward the lane.

"Come back, Rachel!" Swanee called. "Come this way, sugar."

Rachel paused, turned on her haunches toward the voice, then looked away from them again. She slapped at the ground, fingers grasping bits of leaves, a tiny branch of red berries. She studied the brightness a moment, crushing it between her fingers, and put the berries in her mouth.

"She sure is still," Michael said from the porch.

"I'll go see," Swanee said.

"I'll go." Michael was already off the porch, leaping the steps, lifting the baby into his arms, cleaning her hands with a quick brush, prying open her clamping jaw. His finger raked into her mouth, tripped over the nubs of front teeth and across the smooth gums. He caught the berries in a slight crook of his finger, pulled them forward while Rachel screamed, retching and gagging as she twisted away from him. The mashed fruit fell down her front, caught in saliva on her chin. "Dogwood berries," Michael said, gripping the screeching baby to his chest. "Poisonous."

"Oh, Lord, and to think I'm the one that put her down!" Swanee cried, trying to hug both of them. "Is she all right, Michael? Should we take her to the doctor?"

"I got them all," Michael said, rubbing Rachel's back as she sobbed. "She didn't have time to swallow. Besides, I bet they're so bitter she'd have spit them out anyway."

Fate stood with them now. He was shaking all over but he put out his good arm toward Rachel. He didn't know what Michael was thinking or what he would do, but he knew he had to try to take the baby. He couldn't give her up this soon. Even if Michael had saved her, he had been the one there when she was born; he had bathed her and watched her nurse. His was the familiar face, the protective arm.

Michael lifted Rachel away from his own chest and placed her against Fate's. "She's all right," he said softly.

"Thanks, Michael."

"Didn't he react quick, Fate? Wasn't he wonderful? Michael, you saved her life! Wait till Eva hears this!"

"That was quick thinking, boy," Fate said. They moved toward the house, the baby's splotchy wet face against his shoulder. He wanted to say more. He wanted to acknowledge Michael's youth, his attentiveness, his willingness to love Eva no matter what he got in return, but he couldn't. The words wouldn't come.

"Let's rinse her mouth out," Michael said.

"Good idea," Fate replied.

They crossed the unfinished porch and went down the hall to the kitchen, where Swanee Hope was already telling the story to Eva and Sara Will, her words coming at them on frantic little gusts of air. She put her hand to her chest as if to still her pounding heart while she told of the speed with which Michael moved, his alertness to the possibility of danger.

"I thought I was going to have a stroke," Swanee cried. "I thought I might as well die right there as have anything happen to that baby. Then Michael saved her. He came to the rescue. Oh, Lord, if he hadn't been there!"

Eva was struck pale. She trembled as she reached for Rachel, who twisted her head in her knitted cap, trying to shake it loose. Eva untied the knot and pulled the cap off to kiss the baby's head. Then she looked up to see Michael standing in the doorway behind Fate and looking sheepish, like a gate crasher inadvertently exposed to the invited guests.

"Oh, Michael," Eva said and put out her free hand to him. It was the first civil word she'd spoken to him.

At Thanksgiving, Swanee Hope cooked the entire dinner, relinquishing only the menial tasks of peeling and chopping to Michael and Eva, who danced eagerly around her, wanting to do something.

The excitement of company in the house which she'd been missing for so long made her wonder why she'd come back here to live. At twenty, she'd wanted to leave badly enough. She'd wanted Jonathan Calhoun, that was for sure. Three years out of high school and chomping at the bit, she was ready to jump the gate for this college man, a teacher who bought items he didn't need just to come into the drugstore where she was working six days a week, stocking shelves and making change.

Jonathan had come to Tyler Mills because it was a little town, a little school district. He was afraid of the competition of a bigger pond. Tyler Mills was a place to get ahead without doing much. A male high school teacher could work his way into the principal's office without doing anything besides being there and behaving himself. Waiting it out. He could wait until the man ahead of him retired or died. Meanwhile he taught civics and sociology to freshmen and sophomores, American history to juniors, and coached the girls' basketball team with more enthusiasm than ability.

At twenty-five, he had begun to survey the local terrain, contemplating the availability of someone like Swanee Hope Burney, who one afternoon peered at him over the laxatives in

Pearson's Drugstore, her feather duster held aloof like a bright red wing. She was wearing a white smock over her homemade dress. Swanee always wore the jacket Mr. Pearson provided, which she believed gave her a professional look.

She had smiled at Jonathan Calhoun, her cheeks flushed pink, and said, "Could I help you?" in such a sweetly suggestive voice that he was bound to buy something. A bottle of milk of magnesia sprang into his hand and from his fingers into hers, and then she was clanging the cash register, opening her palm for his money, dropping change through his trembling fingers so he had to gather it up off the counter, pennies spinning everywhere. She gave him the white bag heavy with antacid and a smile, such a smile that she felt her face exploding with it, blue eyes flashing, lips red and full, yellow hair flying around her burning face. She was like a display of fireworks, hot and crackling.

Several afternoons a week he would drive her home, all the way out to Sparrow Creek, up the narrow dusty lane to the house. They would sit in the car parked in the yard and hold hands. She got to know his hands, every turn and knob, the callus along his thumb where he strummed his guitar, the shape and texture of his nails, the soft splay of his thumb mashed when he was a boy. So well did she know them that when he eventually slipped inside her blouse, pressing fingers under the edge of her cotton brassiere, she felt his hand belonged there against her flesh. Everything seemed natural to her. Sex held no surprises; it became a convenient, easy kind of comfort.

It turned out that Serena got married first, a hurried wedding on the third Sunday in January when the circuit preacher was bound to appear in his long sleek Chrysler. The car was as polished as he was, as refined and slick. He married Serena to Clement Jessop without a single session of counseling, twenty-five dollars pressed into his hand by Mr. Burney, who wanted this smoky daughter married lest passion ripen before his worried eyes. Nobody was surprised when Serena got pregnant that first year. They could all see it coming. Clement Jessop was sullen with sex, his eyes hooded with desire, and Serena was bubbling, her heart racing like a motor. *I'm coming,* her heart thudded, almost loud enough for them to hear. The minister said "Amen," the reed organ blared out, air pumped into its gut by Mrs. Roberts's frantic feet, and they were swept away amid a shower of stinging rice and crying faces calling after them to be good and happy and careful. The next time they saw Serena she was dead.

So much for marriage. Swanee knew that was how Sara Will looked at it. She watched her sister spreading their mother's Quaker lace cloth on the kitchen table for Thanksgiving dinner, her angular hands smoothing with enforced care because she was unaccustomed to such gentle work. Sara Will's hands knew the rake, the Rototiller, the ax. Her arms actually had muscle; her neck and shoulders showed lean strength. But she is soft, Swanee Hope thought, sliding a casserole onto the oven rack.

The heat blew up into Swanee's face. She felt scorched from it but it was a familiar sensation. She had always stood close to fire, believing herself charmed, unsusceptible to destruction. She had thought that until the sheriff's car pulled up at her house in Tyler Mills and she ran out to meet it.

Why had she done that? She should have stood by the window looking dignified as the sheriff and his deputy came. She should have thought to put coffee on, been prepared to entertain these harbingers of disaster. But no, she had raced to them, embracing their anguished expressions, unable to endure not knowing even though their news could break her heart. It broke right there on the sidewalk while Myrtis Long from next door crossed the yard, her thighs shaking in Bermuda shorts she'd never been caught farther than the clothesline in. The mailman, Aaron McPherson, was coming the other way, and he hoisted his bag into his arms like a pitcher of water and ran as if Swanee Hope were on fire. Well, she was. She stood there screaming while the sheriff, his deputy, Myrtis, and Mr. McPherson all stood at arm's length, wanting to embrace and hush her but afraid to. She burned to a crisp while they stood there looking on. She wasn't seeing Jonathan dead or imagining the wreckage. That would come later. Now she was simply burning up. She had taken one step too many, had touched the flame, and it had consumed her. How can I live? she was thinking while she screamed. This is what years of good luck brings you. Who could she trust anymore?

Sara Will was who. The hard exterior, the cold surface of her sister came to her mind. Sara, who had loved so little but so safely. Sara Will would tell her what to do.

But now she knew she had been misguided. All these years of letting her sister rule when Sara Will was soft inside. Mush. A heart like a sponge. Sara Will didn't love because she knew she was so vulnerable to it. That was the truth of it.

They had a glass of wine while Sara Will carved the turkey. Fate held the bird steady with a carving fork as she made thin, perfect slices of breasts rimmed in golden skin. He never said a word, offered no advice or compliment. Swanee's electric knife whirred while Michael poured. The wine was pale and cold but it lit in Swanee's throat and went warmly down.

"Very good," she said to Fate, who had selected it from the grocery store shelf.

"I asked the clerk," Fate said sheepishly. "I'm not much of a drinker."

"That's good," Swanee Hope said and wanted to bite her tongue.

Fate grinned at her. "Cheers," he said.

"Cheers," boomed Michael, clinking glasses with Eva, who was rocking Rachel in a kitchen chair, her body swaying to a mental metronome. Michael gulped his wine and poured more. "At Christmas I'll make punch," he said. "I bet you didn't know I could make wassail," he said to all of them.

"It'll go right to your head," Eva said.

"The Burneys never did drink," Sara said.

"Except for Uncle Lucas," Swanee Hope reminded her, sipping from her little juice glass of wine. "Uncle Lucas had a still," she said to the others.

"Daddy never condoned Uncle Lucas's livelihood," Sara Will said. "I never saw a jar in this house, and I've lived here all my life."

"I'm not talking about Daddy. It's Uncle Lucas I'm on about, and he did have a still, Sara. He used to deliver at church. His legitimate business was carrying the paper, and the Sunday edition was the only one big enough to conceal a pint in. I've seen him myself, leaning against his car after services, handing out the news. Why, the line to shake his hand was longer than the one for the preacher."

"Swanee, that's our family business," Sara said.

"Well, it's the truth, sister!" Swanee slid the rolls into her slightly tarnished bread tray.

"And private."

"Nothing could be further from the truth, Sara," Swanee Hope said, exasperated by this little conflict interrupting their celebration but unwilling to back down. "Everybody on Sparrow Creek, and in Tyler Mills too, knew Uncle Lucas made corn liquor."

Sara Will would stop the spread of incriminating information simply by not responding. She put the platter of turkey slices on the table and stood at her own place, as stern as a teacher prepared to force order on a belligerent class. "Everyone to their places," she said when her gaze moved no one.

They brought their glasses to the table. "We should all say our blessings one by one around the table," Swanee Hope said fervently, "because it's Thanksgiving."

Sara Will looked at her, horrified. Everyone else was eyeing Sara, hoping to be rescued from Swanee Hope's enthusiasm.

But Sara Will was confounded, dizzy with kitchen heat and the wine floating in her head. She wanted to disappear, to become a tiny mote or piece of floating cork, but her head was too large; it ballooned above her stiff neck, swaying gently as if caught in a little breeze. One of Swanee's feverish puffs of wind had put her out of control, tottering in the air.

"I'll say it," Fate said, and Sara Will focused on him to see the beginning of a smile, a hint of mockery but a twist of sympathy, too. He seemed to understand that she felt there was little to be thankful for and it was only fair that, having once been delivered himself, he should rescue her as best he could.

"Our Father," he began as heads bowed eagerly, each feeling gratefully spared, "on this Thanksgiving Day we want to say that we are thankful for our good health, for this beautiful table of food cooked just for us, and for this baby Rachel, who is like warm sunshine in the midst of this hard winter. Especially, Lord, Eva and I want to thank you for Swanee Hope and Sara Will, who brought us out of the jaws of despair into their lovely home. We knocked and they opened the door, and we appreciate it. Amen."

"Excuse me," Sara said and disappeared, slamming the kitchen door behind her. She leaned against the wall in the cool hallway. Her head ached from her sudden movement and her stomach lurched upward, bringing warm sour bubbles of wine into her throat. I just need to eat, she thought, straightening herself to return before Swanee could come to see what was the matter. They would probably all come, surrounding her with solicitude, invading her space with their concern, forcing her to respond.

But no, they were waiting for her, three generations around her table looking like an oddly assembled Thanksgiving photograph, every face missing beauty but holding instead hopefulness, a quaint unassuming kind of joy that made her heart leap with the troublesome tenderness that was so new and painful to her. Standing there in the doorway, she saw for the first time the possibility of loving them.

13

◆ Lately, Eva had had this dream. It wasn't the parachuting dream of her childhood or the wild dogs of her early adolescence from which she raced panting toward wakefulness, raving yellow eyes and mad howls at her heels. She expected dreams of physical fear that followed her to the outer edge of sleep, but this new dream was different. It penetrated the daylight, a recorded message dropped into her brain.

In the dream she saw Chet Armstrong with her parents at the dining room table. She was there too, but they didn't seem to notice her. They were eating. There was a feast laid out on the table, a banquet to celebrate some occasion, and they were laughing and piling their plates.

"Try these," her mother kept saying but never to Eva, who must have been invisible to them. Eva came closer to look into the dish her mother pushed on everyone. It looked like tiny pigs' feet, knuckles, bony appendages, pink dismembered parts which her mother raked onto each plate with a sharp metal fork.

"No!" Eva was screaming but no one could hear her. She tried to tear the dish out of her mother's grasp, then to gather up the pieces from the plate and cradle them in her arms. Rachel! She was screaming the baby's name as she crammed the soggy, greasy bones to her chest.

"Here," a voice said, and it was Michael. He had Rachel against his shoulder, whole flesh, unsevered, protected from harm.

When she put her arms out, she always woke up. Once she actually opened her eyes to stare at her hands outstretched above her, fingers like claws to pull her baby to her. She always got up and went to the crib where Rachel was sleeping, twisted in her blanket so only her head showed. Once Eva even risked waking her by unwrapping the covers to see that the baby had fingers and toes intact. As she touched the relaxed hands in the dark, Rachel curled her fingers around one of Eva's, holding tight for a few seconds as if she too needed reassurance.

One morning after the dream, she almost said "Thank you" to Michael. She stopped herself just in time but he caught her expression, something suggestive of tolerance in her face, and he smiled at her, a question clearly crossing his own face.

What? he seemed to be asking her, as if she'd spoken aloud but he hadn't quite heard. *What do you want?* his eyes asked, and she turned away. She couldn't let him do anything for her. But he had saved Rachel and not just in her dream. He'd raked the dogwood berries out of her mouth. She would always be grateful for that.

But love and gratitude weren't the same. She had never longed to be in love, not the way other girls she knew seemed to. She had listened to them, heard the anxious tremor in their voices as if having a steady boyfriend, or even the prospect of one, was the only essential to their happiness. She had listened, nodding and smiling her agreement; she had even been encouraging but she had not understood. Even in grade school, she'd never been able to sustain for more than a week the kind of friendship with a boy that demanded daily phone calls, her books being carried, her shoulder touched casually and at odd moments as if to remind her she was a possession. She was held too tightly at home to welcome even a light touch elsewhere. That was why she'd hung around with Michael, who never tried to touch her at all but whose presence seemed to eliminate her from the field while keeping her parents content. Michael's attentiveness proved their daughter was attractive and desirable without threatening the protective vise they had her in. She had truly believed she was safe.

So when Chet Armstrong offered her a ride home in his car after a baseball game, she didn't question his motives. Surely he knew the rules as well as she. "Fine," she replied, as if he'd asked her how she felt. She always said fine no matter how she was. It wasn't polite to complain or to refuse a lift.

She went riding with him three times before anything happened. She liked riding in his car, had no objections to speeding down the interstate with the radio blaring and Chet's strong hand so conspicuously in control on the wheel. She felt the speed and the music inside her body, and it interested her as if she were performing an experiment on herself and watching the results, blood spurting into a Vaccu-tainer or her heartbeat making jagged lines on a graph. After the third ride, when he parked on a deserted road to wrap his arms around her, she felt a momentary panic, a sharp wound to her heart that quickly sealed itself, containing her fear. She was still safe. This was, after all, somebody she knew.

"I'll just stay inside a minute," he said and she believed him. His smooth shoulder was visible in the shadowed twilight. He was truly beautiful to look at but she closed her eyes anyway. There wasn't much for her to do, trapped as she was between the scratchy seat and his hot muscular thighs. Wasn't this bound to happen sooner or later? she wondered, eyes closed tightly as she stiffened her spine where it had begun to twitch, a low nagging ache she thought she could get used to.

She saw Chet Armstrong many times after that but never alone. Now he was the one being polite. She knew he was letting her down easy when he brushed against her in the school cafeteria line, his attention diverted for only a second from the crowd he ran with. He gave her a little smile, a rub on her arm that acknowledged past intimacy without inviting more. She knew she had been a conquest but she wasn't really very angry. Instead, she found herself feeling relieved. She hadn't liked him all that much anyway. She didn't want to be obligated to somebody like him who would expect her to get involved with his friends, to be available to him. It would mean obligatory greetings, a smile permanently pasted to her lips, a bouncy carelessness of movement that pretended confidence she didn't have. Her vague position in the school hierarchy, somewhere around the middle, was hard enough to maintain; glowing was far beyond her range. So she sank, with very little regret, into

137

her former place in the scheme of things where Michael still waited, oblivious of any change in her.

"Don't you want to do something about your hair?" Swanee asked her one morning following the dream when Eva was fighting an impulse to look closely at Michael. He sat across the table from her with a cup of coffee. She was certain he'd eaten an hour ago, then hung around the kitchen helping Swanee clean up until she came down. Eva could feel his waiting, could sense herself as the object of all his attention. She didn't mind as much as she once had.

"Your hair, Eva honey," Swanee said. "I could trim it a little. I used to cut my Bill's hair. Then we could dye it. You could go to town and get something to put on it, a rinse or something."

"I'll take her," Michael offered. "I could do some things in town myself."

He was bored. Eva could see that months of traveling around looking for her had left him restless.

"All right," she said to Swanee. "I'll go."

He took her on the bike, although he had only one helmet. Eva wore it, her face hidden while Michael's was exposed. She climbed on behind him, fingers latching into his belt. When they swerved into the lane, she moved closer, huddled slightly forward into the safety of his back.

In the drugstore she selected a brown permanent-color kit while Michael thumbed through the magazines. "I wish there was a shopping center around here," he said, following her through the checkout.

"Me too," she replied. The fact was she could spend all day in a mall. She liked being insulated by it, the mixture of airy light and color, blooming plants that never wilted or faded, the constant temperature, the soft noises that seemed to orchestrate themselves to the piped-in music. She couldn't imagine a loud noise, a carton dropped, a display shattered, an argument in the mall. She knew people who went there for dates—they'd windowshop, play electronic games, have dinner at Chick-fil-A, see a movie, without ever knowing there'd been a change in the weather. She'd gone herself with girlfriends to browse in the record store, take advantage of makeup demonstrations and cheese samples on toothpicks, try on twenty swimsuits without more than a dollar in her pocket.

She'd even heard of a wedding in the mall, held before the central fountain, which was always surrounded by pots of yellow mums. The bridesmaids had worn yellow to match the mums and the groomsmen, white tuxedos rented from Tuxedo World across the way. Top-of-the-Chart Record Store had lent them a tape player and a cassette of the theme from *Masterpiece Theatre,* and the Clear-Shot Camera Shop had allowed the use of an expensive camera, even supplied a photographer and developing service if the couple agreed to have their pictures displayed in the store window through the month of June. According to the newspaper, the couple was delighted. "We met in Sears," the bride said, "and now we intend to buy all our furniture there, starting with a chrome and wicker dinette set."

"I tell you what," Michael said. "Let's at least get a bite of lunch before we go back. We could even go to an early movie."

But the theater only showed in the evening.

"We'll come one night," Michael said.

"I need to get home to Rachel anyway," Eva said, although she'd left juice in case the baby was fussy. She looked at Michael, expecting to see his face register disappointment. There was nothing written there. "We can have lunch if you want," she added.

"Whatever you think," Michael said, leading the way into the little lunchroom on the corner, a cheerfully shabby place with oilcloth on the tables and napkins stuck in chipped jelly glasses. They had the chicken pastry special and ate silently. Michael never looked at her.

"There's got to be something to do around here," Eva said finally, pushing her plate away irritably. Her restlessness annoyed her. She had thought she was used to the boredom that had drifted down on her from the moment she stepped into her uncle's apartment. She had hardly resented it then, for she had expected punishment in one form or another. But now she wondered, Did it have to be boredom, minutes metered out so that hours became days, days weeks? Time expanded but empty? There was nothing to do except watch Rachel, and even that didn't keep her from being lonely as the hours clicked endlessly away. Her mind had become vacant too, without studies, current events, friends to occupy it. Michael had done this to her. Just his presence reminded her that there was a life for her somewhere else.

"It's a nothing place, Eva," he said.

"Why don't you leave then?" she asked, suddenly hurt that he would criticize. But why was that? She didn't care about Tyler Mills any more than he did.

"You know why."

"Well, don't stay on my account. Don't do anything because of me." She watched him sopping the thick gravy with a corner of light bread. He folded the bread carefully into his mouth.

"Maybe I won't." He was looking at his plate and then beyond her, out the window, as if the people on the sidewalk interested him. "I can't remember a time when I didn't care about you, Eva. I've tried not to. I've always known how futile it was, but there it is. I can't stop loving you, but I can change what I do about it. So I've been thinking," he said to the people passing, "that I'll go back home after Christmas, in time to enroll in college for the second semester."

"If that's what you want," Eva said, motioning to the waitress to bring the check. She felt suddenly hollow inside, as if she hadn't swallowed a bite.

Michael took her hand out of the air, captured it under his on the table. "It's not what I want," he said.

The waitress stood over them. "Anything else?"

"The check," Michael said. The green slip floated down, settling beside their locked hands. "It's not what I want, Eva. Don't you see you're just holding on here? You're not facing anything, and you never will if you let Fate Jessop take charge.

He loves you, I know that, but he's so concerned about safety. Prisons are safe, Eva, but I don't want to live in one."

Eva extricated her hand. "It's Rachel he's concerned about, and so am I. She's a poor little innocent child."

"You keep saying that and you're going to end up believing it. You and Rachel have got all the chances in the world if you'll just quit hiding. You had all those dreams, Eva. What happened to them?"

"I've still got them. I just can't do everything at once."

"Well, how about one thing then," Michael said. "Just pick one—a letter to your folks, maybe."

"I can't do that, not yet."

"Then your feelings for me. I know you have them, Eva, and if you don't know it, it's just because you refuse to look at the truth when it's right in front of your face."

She was beginning to smile. This was the old Michael. Come to the dance with me. You'll have a good time, I promise. She laid a bill on top of the check. "Aren't you ever going to give up, Michael?" she asked.

Michael read her smile, saw himself becoming a distraction. Well, she can do her flirting elsewhere, he thought. "I don't know, Eva. Maybe that's what I'm doing now," he said, letting her pay.

What Sara Will wanted was to get through Christmas. She focused on the coming event in much the same way the wise men must have concentrated on the eastern star but without their awe or expectancy. The image of the star itself seemed to dull the effect of the muddle around her, although she felt she was using religion unfairly, even selfishly. Well, that was what some people used religion for—to keep the path narrow, so they didn't have to look left or right, just straight ahead toward retirement or the next promotion or eternal life.

Anticipating Christmas didn't keep her from thinking about Eva and Rachel, though. She could admit an attachment to them. She saw Eva trying. With Swanee's help she was, at this very minute, doing something about her appearance. Swanee had cut her hair with the sewing scissors, which would never be the same again, and now she was lathering in the dark dye. The liquid puddled and smeared at Eva's hairline as Swanee squeezed the strands tightly to her head. Eva looked as if she had on a slick brown cap, and when Michael saw her, he laughed. It made Eva furious when he wandered into the kitchen where she sat at the kitchen table waiting for the dye to take. But why should she care, Sara Will wondered, when just a month ago she'd been in the parlor wearing that old gown that showed everything, as mad as a hornet because he'd come and not caring how she looked to him? Something was happening.

"Get outa here," Eva said to him, trying not to move a muscle so the rinse didn't drip. Swanee dabbed at her forehead with the corner of a stained towel.

"It's almost time, honey," she said soothingly.

"I want it off right now," Eva said furiously, storming up while Michael continued to grin at her.

"Three more minutes," Swanee purred, trying to run the edge of the towel behind Eva's ear while Eva was lunging for the sink.

"I want it done now, Swanee," she said, jerking at the faucet.

"I'm leaving," Michael said, still grinning, "although I don't see what the big deal is. Why, the first morning I was here, Eva came right in the bathroom while I was taking a bath. She stood right there and carried on a conversation."

"That was before you put the hook on the door, Sara," Swanee interjected, to blunt the edge of this appalling news. Sara Will seemed unperturbed.

"Well," Michael continued, "I just came to tell you that Fate and I thought we'd go into town. We won't be back till late, after supper at least."

"But you just went with me yesterday," Eva said, her head dipping under the water. "Dammit, it's too hot!" she screamed.

"Well, I'm going again," Michael said. "See you later." He disappeared around the corner.

"What do you reckon is going on?" Swanee asked, trying to adjust the spigots. She swished her fingers under the spill of water and pushed Eva's head down. Brown color gushed into the drain. "I don't think it took. Look, Eva, hardly any dye is staying on."

"I think that's how it's supposed to be," Sara Will said. "What can't saturate into her hair will obviously rinse off."

"Where do you think they're going?" Eva shouted from under the running water.

"Well, there's Ferguson's Pool Hall," Sara suggested.

"Uncle Fate can't play pool," Eva said, raising her head and turning into the towel Swanee held open for her. "At least I don't think he can. All the time I've been with him, I can't remember his ever going anywhere but to work, but I guess he went out before I came. I know he owns a bowling ball, but he left it in the apartment."

"There's that bowling alley halfway between Tyler Mills and Whitney," Sara said.

"I can't think of anywhere else," Swanee said, "so that must be it." She was satisfied. Jonathan had never gone out like this on Saturday night, but his situation was different. He'd had a reputation to uphold and a wife to stay home with.

Eva had wrapped the towel around her head, but she was pulling one corner down to her face. "Oh," she sobbed into the stained edge.

"What's the matter, honey? Is it in your eyes?" Swanee hovered over her.

But Eva didn't answer, only pressed the damp towel to her face and slumped against the side of the sink.

"If it's not right, I can do it again," Swanee said, still hoping to soothe her.

Eva was sobbing again. Her shoulders shook furiously and she banged the heel of her hand on the sink rim.

"I don't think this has anything to do with her hair," Sara said.

"Then what is it?" Swanee Hope was getting anxious. She could never hear anybody cry without trying to comfort them but she felt defiance from Eva, which prevented her moving closer. "What should we do?" she mouthed to Sara.

Sara Will shrugged but she was a little concerned herself. She hadn't expected such an outburst.

"What's the matter, sweetie pie?" Swanee Hope was practically in tears herself. "We can even bleach it back to blond if that's what you want. It would be a mistake, in my opinion, but I think it can be done."

"It's not my hair!" Eva wailed.

"Well, thank goodness," Swanee cried but then felt quick defeat. "Then what is it?"

"Everything," Eva said, sniffing. She let the towel drop from her blotched, weepy face. Her hair was sticking out in thick dark clumps.

Swanee Hope took a clean towel and approached gingerly as if to trap an animal. She caught Eva's damp hair and began rubbing gently. "Tell us what it is, Eva honey. We can help you, can't we, sister?"

"I have no idea," Sara replied. Nothing seemed simple to her anymore.

"I'm just so bored!" Eva wept anew. She pulled her head out of Swanee's grasp and flung herself into a kitchen chair, forehead pressed to the table as if she'd passed out. "Nothing ever happens," she cried, more angry than morose. "How can you stand it out here? You don't even get but two channels on the TV."

"Well," Swanee Hope started but then stopped short and looked at her sister. "I don't know," she said finally, staring at Sara Will as if she were to blame. "I really truly don't know. We just got used to it, at least I thought I did." She pinched her mouth tight because her lips had begun to quiver. She felt flushed with tears but didn't want to let go. "The truth is I haven't gotten used to it. I had an active life once. I did things. Now I don't know what's happening. Having you here makes me want to do things again, but I don't know what or how."

Eva had stopped crying. She held her head up, short brown fluff surrounding her swollen face.

"Let's go somewhere," she said suddenly.

Something was going on between the sisters. Recriminations passed unspoken in the air. Blame shot by, propelled by Swanee's fervor: We don't have to live like hermits. . . . You didn't have to come. . . . Why can't you be like other people? . . . Why must you be like everybody else?

"Out to dinner," Eva said, although she didn't have money to pay for it. "When Uncle Fate and I were coming here we saw a Western Steak place not far before the exit to Tyler Mills. It can't be more than twenty miles."

"I knew somebody had built that place. That Maxwell boy, the one who's Bill's age, I think he built it. There're several new stores out there with it. Why don't we go, Sara? Get dressed up and go?" Swanee Hope was almost shouting. She rose on her toes, physically reaching for the event.

"What about the baby?" Sara asked, hoping to stall. The thought of getting out the car terrified her. She couldn't imagine driving them anywhere, returning after dark. She hadn't gone anywhere at night in years. Maybe she suffered from night blindness and didn't know it. What if the first car she met blinded her with its headlights and she put them in the ditch, Rachel crushed to the dashboard, the Mustang crumpled like the cardboard she'd always suspected cars were made of? No, that wasn't what panicked her. She knew she could see in the dark and she genuinely liked to drive. She would drive more often if there were anyplace to go, any meaningful occasion awaiting her at the end of the journey. She had always relished the power of the car, the force with which it carried her along, responsive to the touch of her big toe, one clever hand on the wheel. No, it wasn't the car. It was going into the restaurant, ordering food, eating while other people talked and ate around

her. She wasn't sure she'd know how to behave. What if she
were forced by panic to rise and flee to the restroom or the
parking lot? What if they became a spectacle, two middle-aged
women and two children out on Saturday night, four females
looking forlorn and uncomfortable?

"I'll pay," Swanee was saying. "It'll be my treat. And there's
no problem with Rachel, she's so good. They're bound to have
high chairs in a family restaurant." She put the comb to Eva's
hair, smoothing the new brown softness around her face. They
were both glowing feverishly.

"Pl-ease," Eva said to Sara, drawing out the word like a child
would, half-mocking and expecting consent.

"I suppose we could go," Sara Will began, and it was all decided.

14

✦ In the car, Sara Will was surprised by how quiet they were.
She had expected verbosity or at least Rachel squirming and
fussing her way out of Eva's grasp, but the baby leaned contentedly against her mother's chest in the back seat with Eva's
arms loose around her. They all seemed drugged.

Sara Will switched on the radio, but the local station had left
the air at sunset and she could find only an occasional bar of
music interrupted by shouts of static. She turned the switch off
and listened to the car. At night it sounded different, a grinding
insect noise like a dirtdauber building a tube along her windowsill. The engine seemed frantic and she half expected it to
pull away from her, out of control, or else stop short, refusing
to go on. Her hands gripped the wheel heavily as though she

were steering against a wind or into a storm. None of this was my idea, she thought, already exhausted.

"I wonder where Fate and Michael are," Swanee Hope said suddenly in the dark. Her form moved a little in the dashboard light. "You don't think they'd get drunk, do you?"

"And why not?" Imagining them drunk and making fools of themselves suited Sara Will fine. Why should she care as long as nobody associated them with her?

"Uncle Fate got drunk once." Eva's voice drifted from the back. There seemed to be a smile in it. "My friend Linda and her husband came over with two six-packs of beer. Denny and Uncle Fate drank it all except for a couple that Linda and I sipped on. Uncle Fate started dancing. That man can't dance. You ought to see him trying."

"No, thank you," Sara Will said sternly, although the idea brightened her slightly.

"And he said he wasn't a drinking man," Swanee said, almost in a pout.

"Who's the prude around here?" Sara asked. "Besides, what Fate Jessop does is of no concern to us."

They came into Tyler Mills and crossed the railroad tracks onto Main Street. The town was eerie with artificial light. The storefronts, once close and dark with small-paned windows and dull brick, were now all glass and concrete, stripped of familiarity and left starkly illumined. Although she'd watched the renovations taking place over several years, Sara Will hadn't viewed the town at night, hadn't seen the Baptist Church with its sleek spotlighted spire or the bank's glowing automatic teller. The town didn't look old anymore; it had lost the charm of her childhood when the stores had been carelessly maintained but alive, more human than now. Those childhood shops had tugged at her to enter, drawn her into the dark recesses behind barrels, under high glass counters, up wobbly trolley steps.

Why, that's not true, she thought suddenly, because what she really remembered was the fear of entering, of going out of the safe, sunlit street into that unholy dark that smelled of oily floors, ripe bananas, and feed sacks. There were always men hanging about the doorways, their bony raw faces partially obscured by rusting screens, sooty glass, and their own dusty beards. Of course some of the stores had been bright and airy— Mrs. Stone's Ladies Wear, the drugstore with its antiseptic smell and polished tile floor, the dressmaker's, where bolts of cloth stood in colorful rows on the counter, their folds falling softly like skirts. There were rows of thread in hard, bright colors, cartons of buttons sewn to shiny cards, a drawer of loose buttons sparkling and cool to her touch, racks of ribbon, both satin and grosgrain, cabinets of patterns, their descriptive drawings as perfect as any painting Sara Will's young eyes had ever seen. The moiré taffeta for her gray dress had come from there.

But most of her memories were fearful, focusing on the general store, where the displays were haphazard, some madness having flung hard candy beside a jar of assorted nuts and bolts, where house brooms hung next to scythes, cooking pots beside baling wire. Once she'd been sent into one of the stores, a dollar clutched in her hand, to purchase a ball of thick cotton twine, the kind her mother crocheted with. She'd waited at the counter for the man to wait on her, a giant man with a heavy dark face, swollen eyelids, and a drip of tobacco on his lip. She couldn't see over the counter and so she faced the wooden wall in front of her, saw scruff marks where it had been kicked, boards splintered with age and wear. The men sitting on the window ledge were silent, watching her accusingly as if she'd interrupted their talk and as punishment was now the object of all their attention. She could feel them looking at her. Their eyes touched her, flicked at her skirt, burnt her arms and neck. Every exposed part trembled with heat. A paper sack appeared over the edge of the counter. She caught it, flung the wadded wet dollar toward the countertop above her head, and raced out, stumbling down the broken wooden step, the screen door crackling shut behind her.

She jumped into the car beside her father, dropped the sack

on the seat between them, and saw his outstretched hand expecting the change she should have waited for. Then there was another hand uncurling through the window as if to slap her resoundingly or grab her up, pull her straight through the window and back into the store. But no, the fingers held coins which fell into her lap. "She forgot the change," the man said, laughing, in the window. He showed broken gray teeth and a two-day beard, but the hand that brushed against her shoulder was clean and held no menace. She couldn't understand what she had been afraid of.

Of everything, she thought now as she sped through a caution light and out toward the highway connector.

"How many miles?" she asked Eva.

"At least five," the girl said. And yet they were there too soon.

The place looked like a ranch house with its low slanted roof and old bricks trimmed with darkly stained wood. Sara Will turned into the parking lot and sat there, fidgeting with her keys and locating her bag under the seat while Swanee Hope got out and took Rachel through the window opening.

"Come on, Sara," she said, slightly dismayed by the number of cars in the lot. "It looks crowded to me. I bet everybody in town is here on Saturday night. Of course, we don't have a thing to do but wait if it comes to that." She was taking care of all arguments in advance, just in case Sara Will was planning to bolt.

The two women and the baby were on the sidewalk waiting for her. Bright light from the windows and a strip of neon edging the roof framed them. The door opened and a couple sucking on toothpicks came out. Theirs was the car next to Sara's. They eyed the waiting women and then went on around the back of their car, the woman taking Sara Will's side. She stopped with her hand on the door handle, waiting for the man to unlock it from the inside. While she waited, she pushed the toothpick between two molars and looked in at Sara. "It's mighty good." She chewed down on the toothpick, pulled it from between her teeth, and stuck it in another place.

"Grain-fed," the man said as he leaned over to open his wife's door. He was looking at Sara, who seemed to need encouragement.

"I'm coming!" Sara called to Swanee and Eva, although she was looking at the couple. "Just finding my purse," she added with a tight smile.

"Well, enjoy," the woman said, slamming her door soundly.

Sara Will got out as they pulled away. "Do we know them?" Swanee called to her in a half whisper. "I declare, that woman looked so familiar but I just can't place her. Unless . . ." She handed Rachel back to Eva and stood watching the car turn out of the parking lot. "You know, Sara, that could have been one of those Lewis girls. They were all around Bill, just swarming like bees to a comb. He was a good-looking thing. There were a slew of those girls, all pretty the way their mother was. You remember her, don't you, Sara? Libba Lewis, tiny bones and a sharp face, but pretty. Of course, that one's gone to seed."

They were at the door now, Swanee's words having drawn them into a slow march up the walk. In the restaurant, waiting in line to pick up a tray and utensils like the people in front of her were doing, Sara Will was struck with the thought that she'd arranged her life to avoid doing anything that demanded courage. She still had to be pulled out, forced, sent on an unavoidable errand. She studied the lighted display of available dishes—different cuts of steak named Rancher's Delight and Little Partner's Special. She didn't know what she wanted. How could she swallow with her insides so hot? She was a caldron inside, but her folded arms, hands gripping elbows, were cool.

"How about the Ladies' Sirloin?" Swanee Hope was asking her. "I think I'll try that."

"Why, Sara Will Burney, it is you!" The voice seemed to be answering a question. A woman in line behind Eva pushed forward to pat Sara Will's arm. "My goodness, here you are!" She squeezed past, saying, "Excuse me, honey," and put her heavy arms around Sara Will's shoulders, pulling her into a powdery embrace. "I'm here from Cincinnati staying with my sister, and I'd just asked her—just this afternoon, didn't I, Bert?—what ever happened to Sara Will, and sister said she rarely if ever saw either of the Burney girls. Lord help us, it's Swanee Hope right here in front of me!" The woman released Sara to grab Swanee in a hug.

"Helen!" Swanee pulled back, laughing, to get her breath. "It's been the longest time!"

"What do you mean, girl? Since we've seen each other or since high school? I can tell you it's been too long. Of course, Swanee Hope, you'll have to admit you're older than Sara and me!"

"Well, don't tell everybody!" Swanee retorted, more tartness in her voice than she'd expected, although she continued to smile.

The woman pulled Sara Will into her arms again although Sara had been edging backward against the counter, which offered no escape.

"Let's sit together," Helen cried. "There's just the two of us. Bert, isn't that a good idea? What do you think, girls, a reunion right here? We ought to have a high school reunion, Sara Will. You should be in charge since you live here. Still in the same house, aren't you? I declare, some things never change and you're one of them. Why, I'd of known you on the streets of Cincinnati, although I would have been some kind of surprised. A homebody, that's the definition of you, Sara Will."

"We have other people," Sara started, pulling herself away again.

"Where?" Helen asked, looking ahead of Swanee in the line.

"No, here," Swanee said, drawing Eva forward. "This is Eva Jessop. You remember our sister, Serena, married a Jessop. And her daughter, Rachel."

Helen beamed. "You precious thing," she cooed to Rachel. "Why, this makes me homesick! Reminds me how I left a baby

151

just this size at home—my youngest son's child is eleven months and precious, just adorable. I have pictures right here!" She slapped her vinyl monogrammed bag with three secret compartments. "So it's settled, a table for five."

"Your order, please," the girl behind the counter said to Swanee Hope.

"We need to order," Swanee cried. "Is everyone prepared?"

Sara Will had the Ladies' Sirloin, which turned out to be an eighth of an inch thick and cooked too done. She chewed resolutely, letting the women talk around her. At first she could hardly remember Helen, but listening to her voice brought memories of high school. She didn't want to think about the past, although lately she'd felt her mind turning backward to when she was young, Eva's age. She couldn't remember much and yet a feeling for that time seemed to be ensnaring her, unwilling to let her go. It wasn't a sensation she relished; the cold skeletal arms of remembrance told her she'd never been a happy girl, always fearful, always expecting to fail. Especially after Serena died. Suddenly life had taken on a fragility, an uncertainty she felt compelled to escape. Unable to run, confined to the structure of her old life, she had closed herself up. Happiness was no longer the question. Survival was.

The conversation swept around her. Bert still taught fourth grade, but the school was a new consolidated one. Helen had given up bridge for Mah-Jongg, did volunteer work at her branch library, and took care of two of her grandchildren three days a week. Sara Will could feel attention shifting toward herself and Swanee. Soon it would be her turn. But what did they do? How were their days filled?

"Sara's project is the cemetery," Swanee Hope was saying before Sara could stop her, "and not just the cemetery up the road. She's trying to do something about the one out there in the lake, too. You remember the old Sparrow Creek Cemetery? Serena is buried there and a lot of other people—at least a hundred graves we know of—but nobody seems to care. Nobody seems interested in such a terrible injustice except Sara here. She's done everything. She's constantly in touch with the Tennessee Valley Authority and with our congressmen, imploring them to build a road around the lake and then the bridge they promised so many years ago when the dam was built. They promised access, you know. Mama and Daddy would have fought it tooth and nail—everybody would have—if they hadn't believed what they were told. We all go along believing the government is honorable until something like this happens to bring us up short. But Sara keeps trying, although she's rowing against the current, that's for sure. I accuse her of worrying with it too much, but I don't suppose she's doing anything except what's right. She's dedicated, that's all, aren't you, Sara?" Swanee was frowning. Halfway through her explanation of Sara's history, she had sensed her indiscretion. She saw on their faces, even Eva's, that Sara's commitment to the bridge sounded obsessive, compulsive, even crazy. How could she explain that Sara wasn't unreasonable, just belligerent, defiant about injustices done her family? What words would express her sister's courage?

"Well, Sara Will, you have been doing something," Bert cried. "Taking on the government! I, for one, am impressed!"

Helen was subdued, mentally trying to match Sara Will's apparent heroics with some of her own.

"Swanee makes it more exciting in the telling," Sara said sternly, although the truth was she didn't care much what Helen and Bert knew. They would forget soon enough. It was Eva who concerned her. Eva was too close to her heart already. "Anyway, it seems to be a lost cause."

"But you won't give up," Eva said beside her. "You won't, will you?"

Sara Will truly felt it then, as if a soft net had suddenly been flung over the two of them. She sat absolutely still, knowing there was no use in struggling. This child could have been Serena's. There was no real resemblance, of course. Serena had been soft and rounded, almost fluid, ephemeral, and this girl was small and tough, an unwed mother refusing to marry the only available candidate and as stubborn in her refusal as Sara was about the cemetery.

Helen's voice broke into her thoughts. "Where are you from?" she was asking Eva, who had gone back to mashing the soft innards of a French fry for Rachel.

"We live with my uncle," Eva said softly. She seemed shy now, almost embarrassed to be a part of them, although moments ago she'd felt compelled to ally herself with Sara Will.

"And you're a Jessop?" Bert asked.

"Yes, ma'am."

"And you're related to Sara and Swanee somehow," Helen said.

Eva poked a soft bit of potato into the baby's mouth as if she hadn't heard.

"She's our niece," Sara Will said. It sounded like the truth.

"And this dear heart, this lovely infant who's being so good, she's your child?"

"Yes, ma'am, she's mine." Eva was studying Rachel as if seeing her for the first time. "I had her ten months ago."

"And you're just a child yourself," Helen said. "Look at her, Bert. It's two children you're looking at."

"Michael is young-looking too," Swanee said suddenly. She was staring across the table at Sara Will and Eva as if her eyes could burn silence to their mouths. "Michael is Eva's husband. He and her uncle Fate Jessop are at home watching a ball game and so we thought, why shouldn't the ladies have a night out? What's to keep us home when they're glued to the television set? I don't understand a thing about football myself. Never saw the point in it. Besides, it looks painful."

The moment of truth had passed. Swanee Hope had captured it in midair before it struck. Sara Will smiled across the table at her sister. "Tell Helen and Bert about your Bill," she said pleasantly. "Tell them everything." And Swanee Hope, with a smile, began.

Michael sat at the bar in the bowling alley, nursing a beer

and watching Fate Jessop bowl with one hand. It still amazed him how easy Fate was, how he compensated for the imbalance of his lame arm when he released the ball, putting it down the middle time after time until the men around him were looking on with open admiration. There had been no more surreptitious glances at the freak show once they figured out that all the gutter balls belonged to Michael and the strikes went to Fate.

"Great score," one of them had said from the next lane. That was all Fate needed to start talking to them. Between frames his mouth moved fiercely through his grin. He was so glad to be talking; so much had been saved up.

Michael quit playing then and Fate joined his new cronies. They were slapping each other on the back now, bragging about league standings, kidding each other about wives and children, their work at the mill, the quantity of beer consumed on a given Saturday night. Michael could see Fate in his Levi's and flannel shirt becoming one of them. How could it be that easy? Michael wondered, although he knew part of the answer already. Fate Jessop accepted things however he found them.

Why else would he have taken in a pregnant teenager he hardly knew? Bringing her out here in the country to Sara Will's showed what he'd do if he was cornered. But once here, he'd settled into that too, curbing his slapstick just enough to keep Sara Will's ire leashed and Swanee Hope's interest keen. After just a few weeks, he could be taken for their brother, fitting between them like a lovable but seedy sibling who must be both indulged and endured. And with Eva he was wonderful, his affection perfectly balanced with a respectful distance he knew how to keep. Protective but not smothering, knowing just when she needed to be treated like a girl and when she expected to be considered a grown woman. That was certainly more than Michael knew.

He saw how it could go on forever out there—the four of them plus Rachel. He could see them five years from now sending that baby off to school, all of them standing with her at the bus stop, waving frantically after her as if she were putting out to sea. Fate and Sara and Swanee would look exactly as they did now. Only Rachel and Eva would be different, thin and sickly, drained empty of a future by these attachments, suckers attached at heart and head binding them to the land, to Sara Will's inheritance, her cemetery. It would be a life spent in protective custody, and he wouldn't be there to prevent it. They would invade Rachel's life too, make her accountable so subtly that Eva wouldn't even see it. But he knew that unless something drastic happened, they would all live here forever, no matter what Sara Will Burney thought. He had seen from the first days and through all her protests that Sara Will would eventually give in. She was weak like that, so needful herself that eventually the corner she'd been backed into was going to become a comfortable place.

He was the one who would have to go. He was the one who didn't belong. He could leave tonight, go back home to college, graduate, move to Michigan or Wyoming or some other place he'd never imagined going to. No matter where he went, he would always see these people just like they were today, trapped like this, Rachel in a stranglehold of well-intentioned love that robbed her of a childhood just like Eva had been robbed of hers.

And Rachel was his child. In his mind, his heart, in every way that could matter, Rachel was his. Given a chance, she would grow up calling him Daddy. She would get her allowance from him and a kiss good night and a story, and in the mornings he could awaken her by touching her hair so gently it would be like a moth brushing her cheek. He and Eva would give her a brother, a sister. She wouldn't be an only child, a lonely child like he and Eva had been. He had always been reclusive, no more able to let himself go in children's games than he was able to stay with Fate and those men tonight. All he'd ever done was work, menial jobs which he took too seriously. He was too intense for his own good, but what choice did he have when he could do so few things well?

He had played the tuba well, even though he despised the

156

instrument, its weight pressing obligation into his shoulder. Admiring the quick runs, the complicated fingerwork, the effortless, pure sound that had tremored from the bells of gentlemanly musicians, he had longed for a clarinet. But the band director had recommended the tuba—no, had insisted on it—because he needed a tuba player. Besides, there were few notes, and with Michael's poor eyesight . . . The discussion went on and on, turning into an interminable lecture until Michael acquiesced and bore the tuba like an injury. Year after year, marching with his discontentment but playing his best, every *oom-pah-pah* committed to memory, he heard, instead of his own pumping noise, the trills, the harmonies, the bright soaring moments under the field lights when the woodwinds took flight.

Only with Eva had he ever been calm, relaxed, free. He didn't understand how it happened that he loved her, the movement from friendship to love had been so slow, even careless. He had thought he had plenty of time, and then she told him about the baby. He was the only person she told. He convinced himself that meant something. From then on, he'd been sure they belonged together. You could have poor vision and second sight at the same time. He believed she loved him already. Recently, out of the corner of his eye, he had glimpsed it—a softness in her expression, a lightness in her voice that occurred when some momentary joy lifted her away from the humdrum misery of the life she was leading.

Just for a moment, seeing that expression, he could remember the child she'd been. They'd raced on their bikes down deserted roads, their faces glowing with heat, the air around them blowing hot dust, their lungs heaving, sides aching but happy to be out and away, pedaling crazily toward nothing. He had seen her happy. Just a few days ago he'd caught her looking at him in the kitchen and had thought from her eyes that she had spoken to him and he'd not heard. He opened his mouth to say "What?" but didn't. She hadn't spoken. He knew that. Still, the look said something to him, he just didn't know what.

Then this afternoon she'd been so angry with him and there was no reason for it. Surely it wasn't his seeing her with that tangled mess of dyed hair. He'd seen her ugly before. Why, he'd seen her at every awkward age of her life, although he'd never thought of it that way back then when he himself was an aching bag of bones, looking scraggly and half finished, interminably molting. He had seen her angry and sullen, the doomed look of unwanted pregnancy covering her like a dank gray veil. He had seen her bulging out of her clothes, puffed out like a blowfish except for her poor face, which held its bitter leanness. She had shown him her defiance, too, escaping all of them except the baby itself. He had heard of guilt embedded in the brain, lacerating the heart, perforating the gut, but he had never seen it growing, living, protruding so there wasn't a moment of respite or forgetting. But Eva had survived all that. Fate Jessop had helped her when no one else could, and Michael was grateful.

Fate was coming toward him. "I'll have one of those," he said. He grabbed the back of Michael's neck and squeezed. "I might just apply for a job at the mill, kid," he whispered loudly. "Those guys say there're jobs a one-armed man can do. How about that?" He took a long swallow of beer, splitting the foam. He didn't expect an answer. "Drink up, boy."

Michael's beer was warm but he drew deeply on it. "So you're thinking about staying," he said. The beer foamed up in his stomach.

"Maybe so. Hell, I don't know. Not at Sara Will's, I don't reckon, but Eva and me don't have anything behind us worth going back to, now, do we? If I get a job at the mill, maybe we can get a place to live right here. Eva would have Swanee Hope, maybe Sara Will too, for advice and help. I reckon she'd make some friends."

"What about her folks, Fate? How long can you hide from them?"

"Till Eva's ready to face them, that's how long. I'm doing this for her, Michael." Fate rested his cheek on his good hand and looked at him. "You don't think it's the right thing, do you?"

"No, sir, I don't. I think Eva ought to leave here and go back home and finish high school."

"So you can marry her," Fate added.

"I'd marry her tomorrow if she would, but she won't, so that's got nothing to do with it. I just know her folks are going crazy, and here I am knowing where she is and not telling them. Eva thinks that's a threat but it isn't. I just know sometime she's got to stop running and I've got to stop chasing, and I think it's now."

"I know you're right, Michael, but I can't stand the thought of giving her up." Fate looked tearful and Michael looked away. Both of them had had too much beer.

"Neither can I," he said, "But I guess I'll have to. The weird thing is I believe she loves me. I think I'm that close to getting her but I just can't see myself reaching out even one more time. I don't guess it shows, but I've got a little bit of pride. So I've decided to stay through Christmas and then I'm going home. She'll know where to find me."

"I didn't know you had it in you, boy!" Fate slid off the stool and gave Michael a hug. "Let's get out of here and see what's going on at the house. I bet money Swanee Hope's standing at the window right this minute waiting on us." He grinned at the idea.

"And what about Sara Will?" Michael wanted to know. He handed a five-dollar bill to the barman and waited for the change.

"Now there's a mystery," Fate said, suddenly serious. He rubbed his injured arm with his good hand as if he'd just been reminded of his handicap. "An honest-to-God mystery, that's what Sara Will Burney is."

It surprised them both that she was the one waiting. She sat in the kitchen, a cup of steaming tea in front of her on the table, hands folded in her lap while she waited for it to cool.

"We went out," she said to Fate, seeing how startled he was to find her up at midnight. He expected Swanee, she thought, and felt the heat off the tea on her face and throat.

"You did!" Fate plopped down in the chair opposite her and slapped the table gently. "Well, good for you! Where'd you go?"

"Out to eat," Sara said. She rubbed her finger down the edge of the cup handle. "We went to that steak place on the highway. Eva wanted to go somewhere and so we went. I went." She couldn't look at him. She felt as though she was admitting a secret; her fear had been a secret all this time.

"Well, good!" Fate said, grinning at her. He got up suddenly, almost upsetting his chair, and went to the stove. "Water still hot?" he asked, touching the kettle lightly. He was embarrassed. He knew something was happening between them. He could feel it as keenly as the heat of the kettle. Waves of warmth sluiced the air. He put a tea bag in a cup and poured water over it.

"Are you hungry?" Sara Will asked. "Did you eat?"

"We had a burger early on. We went to the bowling alley." He brought the cup to the table, watching it cautiously, and sat down again, dipping the bag by the string. "I met some men there. They work at the mill and bowl in a league. They said there might be work at the mill. Something a one-armed man could do." He concentrated on the tea bag, lifting it high and watching it drip.

"Here," Sara Will said and leaned forward to take the bag from his fingers, her spoon ready. Their fingers touched and moved away too quickly for anyone to have seen, but they felt it, both of them. Fate blew on the tea, pushing the surface gently.

"Michael says he's leaving after Christmas. He's going on to college. I think one of these days Eva's going to marry that boy.

I think she ought to," Fate said. He wasn't sure he felt that, but he wanted to know what Sara Will thought.

She was staring into her cup as if she intended to read an answer there. "She'll have to make up her own mind," she said finally. "There's been too much collusion already. Of course, I know it's hard on Michael when he's so sure of his own feelings." She sighed and looked up. "I have never had feelings like his, so I don't know anything about it." Her own revelation seemed to startle her and she stood up abruptly. "Do you think it's warm in here?" She turned toward the dark, closed window as if there'd be a breeze there.

"I was married once," Fate said. "Her name was Vickie. Everything was fine, and then I had my accident. I guess I was always hard to live with, though."

"I doubt that," Sara Will said to the window.

"The folks back home always thought I was a fool. I was the one most likely to do or say the wrong thing. I couldn't be trusted, was how they looked at it."

"I was always serious. Swanee was the foolish one, although I suppose she was just having a good time. She enjoyed herself. And Serena, now there was the balance. She was so much fun, but understanding and good-natured too. And so pretty. Do you remember how pretty she was?" Her quick turning made the teacup tremble in his hand, and he put it down.

"I surely do."

"I've been thinking that Eva could have been her daughter. Of course, that's not what I mean at all. I mean sometimes I find myself feeling a responsibility for Eva like I'd feel if she were Serena's. Do you understand that?"

"I reckon it's similar to what I feel," Fate said. "She's got a way about her, all right."

"She's such a child, Fate. She's really just a baby herself."

"I know it."

"Do you want a sandwich?" Sara asked. "I could be fixing you something."

"I could stand to eat," he replied, "but I can put it together."

"I'm already up." Sara Will took sliced ham and a jar of mustard from the refrigerator. Her back was to him as she made the sandwich at the counter.

He sat there watching her small movements. Her hair was still up so he could see the back of her neck, strong and lightly tanned. Her shoulder blades made soft ridges in her worn bathrobe. He could see the curve of her hip, the narrow waist where the belt was pulled tight, her hand reaching into the jar with a knife, the blunt nails, slightly protruding veins, sunspots left from summer that would never fade.

He wanted to touch her. There had never been a moment in his life when he wanted so much to move, abandoning reason as he went, until his hand was over hers, then traveling her arm slowly to her neck, the cords softening against the back of his hand until he cupped her cheek in his palm. That was all he wanted, just that touch which would seal this time forever. No matter what else happened to them, he would have held one moment in his hand. But he didn't move.

She turned to him with the sandwich on a plate and reached across the table with it. "Here," she said very softly.

She had known he was watching her. Perhaps she even knew his mind and had willed the moment to pass unused.

"I'll go up to bed now, if you'll turn out the lights." She started to the door but her movements seemed slow to him, almost hesitant.

"Good night, Sara," he said, so quietly he hardly heard himself, but she did because she turned a little, giving him the rounded edge of her face, the best face he'd ever seen in his whole life.

"See you in the morning," she said. He heard it as a promise.

15

✦ Swanee would have a live tree. She knew where a little Fraser fir could be found out beyond the orchard nestled in a place thick with sweet gum and dogwood saplings.

"It got enough sun, though," she said. "Somehow it has managed to become the perfect tree for this Christmas." She was speaking to Eva but within Sara Will's hearing, so she put determination in her voice by lowering the register but increasing the volume. It was the voice she used when returning infested cornmeal to the store or speaking to the tenants who rented her house in Tyler Mills. She looked at Sara Will over Eva's bent head but Sara was off somewhere, maybe listening to Fate's tape player, which whirred out a faint chorus of "Jingle Bells" from the windowsill.

"Two weeks from this very day it'll be Christmas," she said even more forcefully, hoping to draw Sara's attention, but her sister continued to stir the spaghetti sauce.

Sara breathed in the hot garlicky smell, then lifted the wooden spoon to let a drop of tomato sauce run down the trough, where she caught it on her tongue. "Is there a bay leaf anywhere?" she asked over her shoulder. "I think it needs a pinch of sugar, too, to cut the acid. Otherwise it's very good." This to Eva, who was spreading butter on slices of store-bought Italian bread.

"It's the only thing I can make that's the least bit dependable," Eva replied. "Mama wanted me to learn how to cook, she insisted on it, but every time I went in the kitchen, she came and did everything."

"A bay leaf, a bay leaf," Swanee chirped eagerly, searching through the spice tins in a drawer. "Ah, here." She dropped a single brittle leaf into the simmering pot. "And a tree, sister," she said close to Sara Will's ear. "A live fir, dug or cut, I don't care which. With glass balls on it and lights and those silvery icicles like we used to have."

Sara Will frowned and left the stove. She paused by the window to look out at the wintry approach of night. The sky above the trees was steel-gray and solid, but straight ahead she could still see deep into the woods where the fringe of dogwood, poplar, and sweet gum had been picked clean by the autumn wind, opening the forest to its heart. There in the center were the thick shadows of pines and scrub oaks, rough and scraggly, with their dry rattling leaves holding on. She had never let those woods be cut, hardly even thinned. Their depth had always comforted her, the scattered boulders of dead trunks and broken limbs providing a barricade, a maze that protected her from intrusion. But she had been intruded upon anyway, and it wasn't some derelict, an escaped convict stumbling out of the woods toward her smoky light, but a man on the lane in a truck with two children and a damaged arm.

Oh, why couldn't he have been a whole man? she wondered. She had always been so inadequate with handicaps, so quick to look away from children in leg braces or with bobbing heads, to avoid wheelchairs, casts, deformities of sight and speech. Her embarrassment was old, even childish. Will that happen to me? she would catch herself wondering, eyes averted from the slow, dragging steps behind a walker. What would I do, how could I live? she would worry. And now there were new ailments to haunt her, such as this aging disease she'd seen on television, ancient children whom Swanee moaned over while Sara was silent, frozen in fear. Am I like that? she had wondered. Am I old in my mind, brittle, susceptible to infection? What was her reasonably healthy body hiding?

Or else she felt a pang of guilt. What had she done to deserve good health? She'd accomplished so little, not even an access road and a narrow bridge, compliance with an undocumented promise made to her family. Swanee had done more than she. Everyone had. Here she was, trapped in her fifties between youth and old age, and what could possibly be written in the record book to her credit? That she'd taken care of her parents? That she'd tidied a cemetery and not squandered goods left in her care? She had been a caretaker. That was all, and for what? Who was there to leave it to? Who cared about it except her? Wasn't it all accomplished to feed her own ego?

It surprised her to see Fate coming out of the woods. He was dragging a dead log which he pulled slowly to the little ridge at the woods' edge, then dropped it and gave it a push with his foot to send it sliding down the grassy bank into the yard. He followed, slipping on the damp grass, his good arm swinging for balance. He got the log again in the crook of his arm, hoisted it till he was standing, and brought it to the house where he let it fall just yards away from the window where Sara Will stood. She could barely see him now, the light from the window had brought the night that close. Just his moving outline appeared to her. The plaid of his sleeve showed color in the patch of light that fell beyond the window. She stood there looking out as if his whole form, injury and all, were visible to her.

She knew he could see her. She folded her arms across her chest but recognized at once what a protective gesture that was and let her arms fall to her sides. She could tell he was standing there looking in at her, and she wondered how she looked, tried to recall her mirrored image but found she had no memory of herself. Instead she could see him half hidden in the uneven, shallow light, the curls springing around his wool cap, the ruddy cold cheeks, the mouth unsmiling but speaking something to her, soothing her with silent words. It is all right that you are standing there, she heard him saying. It is safe.

Come in, she mouthed. Eva and Swanee Hope were still in the room with her. She put her fingers against the cold windowpane and saw a sleeve and hand appear in the light to wave to her; then the fingers disappeared.

"Fate's coming," she said to the women and went back to the saucepan on the stove.

"And how do you know that?" Swanee Hope asked, wiggling a stubby pencil between her fingers. "I think one fruitcake is all we'll need. A dark one soaked in bourbon whiskey for at least a week to ripen it. I'm getting down the ingredients right here. We need to go to town, sister, and not just for groceries. We've got to do our gift-buying before everything is completely picked over. I'm just glad I've decided to send Bill and his family a check. It's a nice one, too. Two months' rent on the house is what I'm sending, Eva. Of course, you haven't a clue how much that comes to, but it's a nice present, I can promise you that."

"Should we call it a Christmas buffet or what?" Eva asked. She was practicing her penmanship, which was unremarkable but tidy.

"A buffet?" Swanee Hope questioned the air above her head. "Or party. Or open house. Those seem to be the options."

"What are you planning, Swanee?" Sara left the stove to see what Eva was writing. *You are invited,* she had written carefully. "Invited? Invited to what, Swanee?"

"Just a little get-together for the neighborhood. We never see anybody unless somebody dies, and with so many people right here to help, we should just go ahead and ask the neighborhood. Who does that involve anyway, with everybody moving into town like they are? Twenty people or so. Most of them are old, Eva. I don't think there'll be a soul among them for you, but you can serve; that will give you an important function. Serving makes you the most valuable person in the room, plus giving you an opportunity to mingle. Now, we'll have coffee and Michael's wassail, which Eva swears is the best in the world. My fruitcake and your date roll, Sara, for the sweets. Michael said he'd make sausage balls to spear on little colored toothpicks and something called crudities. Isn't that what he called it?"

"It's just raw vegetables with his special curry and herb dip," Eva said. "He knows how to make a real pretty tray from working in a restaurant."

"I don't believe you're serious," Sara protested, but even she heard the hollowness in her voice. She felt drained, completely enervated by their enthusiasm. Wasn't this endurance enough, this claustrophobic, cluttered twilight in her kitchen? Hadn't she given enough already?

"Don't believe what?" Fate asked in the back door. He bent over to pull off a muddy boot with his good hand.

"We're planning a party!" Eva said gaily, ignoring Sara. "I think it should be an open house. That's the term for it, I'm sure."

"Open house," Fate said, as if the idea satisfied him. Both boots rested beside the closed door. He padded into the kitchen in his socks. "Would you mind?" he asked Sara, who was the only person standing. He turned his sloped shoulder to her to get help with his jacket. She pulled it away from his neck without a word but left it for him to work the sleeve over his lifeless arm. "An open house," he repeated, turning to her with the jacket caught between his chest and arm. "It has a nice ring to it. A Christmasy sound, ladies, to go with jingling bells and Johnny Mathis singing that number. What is it, Eva? 'Chestnuts roasting on an open fire,'" he sang, swinging the girl out of her chair. They danced jerkily, stopping and starting with every phrase, singing and laughing together, with Eva's arm tight around his shoulder to keep them close.

"You see!" Eva fell back giggling into her chair. "I told you he can't dance."

"So I'm talked about!" Fate said gleefully. He leaned down to smack a kiss at Eva's cheek but she pushed him away, laughing.

"We're planning a party, Fate Jessop," Swanee Hope said. "Sit down here and help us."

Fate plopped into the chair next to her and boomed, "Christmas is coming, the goose is getting fat. Won't you put a penny in an old man's hat—"

"Sh-h-h, Rachel's asleep right there in the parlor," Eva told him. "Michael too. He was playing with her, and the next thing I know she's asleep on his chest and he's dozing on the sofa. They're a picture." She was smiling to herself but Sara Will saw and, without intending to, looked then at Fate. His face had lost that blustery animation he'd come in with. Now it was the face she'd seen from the window, private, a little sad, touched by something he'd heard in Eva's voice.

"Open house, then," Swanee Hope said. "We'll call it open house. Write that, Eva. Tomorrow we'll get some little invitation cards, then you can write them, and you and Michael can deliver them on the motorcycle. That'll be a nice gesture, won't it, Sara? Hand-delivered invites like we used to make years ago. Oh, we used to have parties then! Remember, Sister? We'd literally roll up the rug in the parlor. It's a big floor space with the furniture pushed back. Refreshments would be right here on this table with Mama's good cloth and candles. We had two or three parties like that a year, but the Christmas one was always the best. Serena planned everything to a tee because she had the best ideas. I would have to say she was the most popular girl in the valley, and I suppose I was second. The Burney girls were something to be reckoned with back then! Even Sara liked Serena's parties—didn't you, Sister?—although on normal occasions Sara went out the back door when a man came in the front." Swanee Hope propped herself up on her elbows, exhausted by the memory of a good time.

"I did no such thing," Sara Will protested, moving back toward the stove.

"I don't see why you have such an aversion to the truth, Sara," Swanee started up again. "You can't deny you sometimes abandoned the house. Either that or you went to your room and turned the key. Many's the time I was sent up there to talk you out. There I'd be whispering and begging, pressed right to the door so nobody could hear, and you never answered me once. Sometimes I wonder that you weren't under the covers with a pillow tight over your head."

"I just sat there in my chair looking out the window." Sara clanged the lid on the pot defiantly and turned to the three faces staring at her. "You have always underestimated my perseverance, Swanee. To this day, you underestimate it. I don't think you understand me at all. But you go right ahead and have your party. Have your live tree in the parlor, your icicles, make fifty fruitcakes for all I care. But if I choose to spend the evening in my room, don't you come knocking and begging. Don't you whimper after me about being polite when right here in this room you have betrayed me, saying things best left unsaid, bringing back the past like it was yours to do with what you like, telling people things—"

"But this is family here, Sara. Besides, there's nobody else to talk to." Swanee sounded tearful, but her ire was up. "Anyway, what you don't want told, you just ought not do. If you'd of stayed about when company came, helping Mama and livening up the conversation like Serena and I did, I wouldn't have a thing to tell. It would have done you good, too." She turned to Fate. "She always stayed through the Christmas parties, though. I'll give her that much."

"Don't plan on it, Swanee," Sara said.

"But what about the date roll, Sara?" Swanee asked, relieved that her sister had turned stony. It was a demeanor she was familiar with.

"I don't see how we can get along without it," Fate said to draw her attention.

Sara attempted to stare straight through him, but he caught her eye. There was something different in his eyes, empathy or at least understanding. He had been embarrassed like this himself, his past brought up carelessly as if his family couldn't see the pain attached. It hurt to know that what he'd outgrown still belonged to somebody, was alive in their memory when he'd killed it in his own. He was hurting for her. She could see that.

"I've got to wash up," he said suddenly and disappeared into the dark hall.

"The date roll, sister?" Swanee asked again, her mind already back on the list she was making.

"I'll see to it," Sara replied, looking after Fate. "It's something I've always done."

"And the sugared pecans? You make the best ones in the world. We'll see to the shelling if you'll just fix them." Swanee Hope didn't wait for an answer. "And tomorrow we'll go to town. There's nothing planned for tomorrow, is there? Just another day rolling by. Of course, we'll get little gifts, won't we? Small mementos. Affection isn't measured in silver and gold. Mama used to say that, and I for one have always taken it to heart. So many people just make themselves sick over Christmas. It shouldn't be like that. When we were girls, we didn't expect much. I remember hearing Mama tell how getting an orange was so wonderful when she was small. Imagine that. An orange! She was a big girl, about old enough to get married, when she finally got a store-bought doll with a china face and a rag body. Sara Will broke it when she was little, threw it down the front steps in a fit of temper and cracked the head down the back. We taped it together but it wouldn't hold. Mama cried. She stood out there on the porch with tears coming down, but she never said a word to reprimand you, did she, Sara?"

"Her crying was enough," Sara said.

"Who's crying now?" Fate sang out softly from behind them. His face looked scrubbed, and he was buttoning a fresh shirt.

"I broke Mama's china doll when I was a child and she cried over it," Sara Will said, looking right at him.

"And so did you," Fate said.

"No, she didn't. I remember not a tear," Swanee Hope replied.

"Inside," Sara said. "All my tears were inside."

Sara Will, Swanee, and Fate went in the Mustang. It was a cold morning, the sun trapped behind a solid wall of snowy sky. Fate offered to get the car out and warm it up.

"I'll let it run a few minutes. It sits too much to respond good in this kind of weather."

So she handed him the keys without a word and watched from the window as he crossed the yard to the shed. Then she turned away, although on the stairs she paused to hear the engine cutting the air, then taking hold. No harm done, she thought, and put on her good coat.

Out in the car, Fate leaned back in the driver's seat, feeling the car purr around him. It was like being in the belly of a cat.

170

He ran his hand around the wheel, then crossed over to the dashboard, still cold and slick. He turned on the radio just to see if it worked, turned it off again because the engine sound was better than music.

"Here we are!" Swanee called, lifting her feet high over the frosty grass. She crawled into the back seat, her list clutched in her hand. "Michael and Eva are coming later in the truck, after Rachel wakes up," she puffed, banging her purse against the back of his seat as she settled herself.

From the back stoop Sara Will could see Fate still in the driver's seat. She should have expected as much. Maybe she had. Maybe the chill she felt when she'd dropped the keys in his hand was proof and she'd denied it, not wanting to have to say "But you can't drive." Surely Swanee Hope had told him. But what? That she had a peculiar attachment to a Mustang, that she was obsessive about possessions, unyielding in her ownership, like a child who refuses to share a toy? If Swanee had told him how protective she was, would he still challenge her? White clouds of exhaust rose around the car. They could be asphyxiated. Warm and content while they waited for her to appear, the two of them could doze off smiling. The car could be her weapon.

Am I completely crazy? she wondered, suddenly seeing how obsessed she was, standing on the back stoop pondering the demise of two of the few people in the whole world she had any feeling for.

Surely he would relinquish his place when she arrived at the car. Hadn't he been thoughtful in other ways? Unspoken commiseration had passed between them during the last few days. Surely she hadn't been misled. She reached the car and stopped at the driver's side.

"Go around!" Swanee Hope called to her through the glass. She jabbed her finger at the opposite door. Fate did nothing.

A month ago she would have been belligerent, defiant, ready to pull the door open and jerk the usurper out. She would have felt justified in filing suit, sending irate messages, defending herself. But what she felt now wasn't really anger, although she trembled slightly as though shivering from the cold. It was more resignation, a closing up of herself against the possibility of any display of emotion. Perhaps he didn't know how she felt about the car. Well, he needn't know. Already he knew too much about her.

"Hurry up, Sara. It's warm inside!" Swanee called, and Sara went around to the passenger side, flung open the door to send a sharp gust of chilled air into their faces, and settled herself without a word in the seat.

"I'll get you there," Fate said, shifting gears so the car changed tune. He backed down the grassy tracks to the gravel lane, straightened up, and sent them forward. "Don't you worry about a thing," he said.

"We're on our way," Swanee Hope cried, patting the top of the seat in front of her.

Sara Will looked out, saw her woods moving away from her. The empty pond bed disappeared behind dried-up winter brush. The car seemed to jump the gate and they were on the highway. How could I have given in so easily? she wondered, holding her shoulders tight as if to take a blow. Her pulse throbbed heavily in her throat. She raised her hand to her temple and pushed on her skull, working against an ache that had begun there.

"Are you all right?" Fate asked, so softly that she was startled by the closeness of his voice.

"Yes," she breathed and let her hand drop. She saw his hand leave the wheel for an instant; his fingers clenched in midair and then took the wheel again.

"I know how to be careful, Sara," he said. "You can depend on that."

How could he know she had never depended on anyone but herself?

Michael's first stop was the post office, where he stamped the letter to the college registrar's office and dropped it in the out-of-town slot. He heard the envelope settle on top of the other mail. So it was done. If everything went right he'd be gone by the first of the year. What happened after that was up to Eva.

She was waiting in the truck, where she bounced Rachel on her lap and rubbed noses, both of them giggling. He could see how excited she was to be doing something. This shopping expedition to a two-bit town had taken on momentous importance; she'd been making her own list, figuring how much money she could spend on each person. His name was on the list, the last name, saved either because the gift must be special or because he would receive the leavings—an off brand of cologne, four handkerchiefs artistically folded in a plastic box, a clip-on tie. Well, he didn't care what she gave him. He was going to buy pearls—two small studs for her ears to replace the plain gold stars she'd been wearing ever since he'd found her.

The two cultured pearls in the jewelry store would take most of the money he had left, leaving enough for small gifts for the Burney sisters, Fate, and Rachel, with maybe five dollars left to get home on. Once there, his parents would come through with tuition. He could live at home and get a part-time job, saving every cent while he waited for Eva to come. But what if she didn't? What if she stayed in Tyler Mills forever? Eventually she'd meet someone and get married. There were plenty of guys who would take a gorgeous stepchild in the bargain. Eva could finish high school or pass the proficiency test for her diploma and go to business school somewhere close by. She could get along without him.

"Where to now?" he asked, swinging into the truck.

"Anywhere," Eva said. "A department store, wherever you want."

"That letter I just mailed, it's to the registrar about my going to school next semester. I'm really going, Eva." He started the truck and nosed out of the parking lot without looking at her.

"I don't want to think about it," Eva breathed, adjusting the edges of Rachel's knit cap around her face.

"These weeks since I found you, they haven't been so bad, have they?"

"I don't guess so."

"Eva, it's been the best time I've ever had in my life." He was too busy looking for a parking place to see her face, but he could feel her tensing up. She held Rachel close.

He pulled the truck into a vacancy on Main Street and cut the engine. They sat in the gray morning silence.

"You know I want you to come with me," Michael said when he couldn't stand the quiet any longer. "This is the last time I'll ever say it, but it will always be true. Now you'll have to decide. You'll have to remember all on your own that I love you because I won't be here to tell you." His hands squeezed the wheel to keep from reaching out for her. "Eva, you can stay out here in the country with those women and your uncle forever. They'll protect you and take care of you and keep you a little girl. You can keep your worries small that way, and your good times, too. But if you decide you want something different, if you want more, you'll have to grow up some. You won't be able to sit around dreaming about going to business school and being a secretary, you'll have to do it. That's what I've decided to do. I intend to make something of myself, and I have to start by leaving here and going to school where I belong. I think it's where you belong, too. I think together we can have a good life, but I can't say how easy it would be."

The silence locked around them, holding them tight.

"This looks like a good place," Eva said finally, nodding out at the gaudy window decorations of the closest store.

"I guess so." Michael pushed the door open and slid out. "Nobody will ever love you more than me, Eva," he said, just before the door slammed between them. He turned away, looking into the store window while he waited to hear her door shut. He was so tired of being on the outside looking in.

Eva couldn't make up her mind. She hoisted Rachel higher against her shoulder, tightened her grip on the shopping bag she held in the same hand, and bent over to peer into the glass case of accessories for men. Rachel leaned forward too, slapping the glass. "Just a minute, honey," Eva said, pulling the baby back so she could look more closely at a row of gold-colored medallions in brown-velvet-lined boxes.

"Could I show you something in particular?" the man behind the counter asked, impatience immediately apparent in his voice.

Eva caught Rachel's hand before it banged on the glass top again. "Those chains," she said.

"Ah, the zodiac medallions. What's his sign?" The man was unlatching the glass door. He stared at her through the glass.

"His sign?" Eva squatted to get a closer look. "Oh, his birthday is early in March."

"Pisces." The man's smooth hand reached for the right box and snapped it up. "Here it is. Very nice. Just the thing for Christmas."

"What kind of metal is it?" Eva asked, afraid to touch.

"Treated. It'll never lose its luster, never tarnish. Better than brass or silver. Go on and look at it. Can't hurt to look."

Eva ran her finger lightly over the raised design of an oriental-looking fish.

"For your husband, I'll bet," the man said. He was concentrating his dour expression on Rachel as if that would prevent her from grabbing the shiny circle.

"I just want to get something he can keep," Eva said shyly.

"Then this is the ticket. Very popular with the young men. I don't think you'll do any better for the price." The clerk lifted the medallion out of the box and draped the chain over his hand. Eva couldn't imagine Michael wearing jewelry but what else was there? The fish swayed magically.

"I'll take it," she said. Rachel was watching the moving medallion as if hypnotized.

"Your baby certainly likes it." The man slipped the chain through the slits in the velvet, arranged the medallion in the center, and snapped the box shut. "Gift wrapping is at the back of the store." He thrust the box in a bag and rang open the cash register. "Fifteen fifty-five."

Eva counted out the money onto the counter. Her last three dollars were in change.

"What are you getting?" Swanee Hope called, coming through the cosmetics department. She was carrying a box wrapped in Santa Claus paper. "It's a doll!" she cried. "One she can play with. Oh, Eva, it's the dearest thing and so pretty. But it's to play with, not to set up somewhere. We ought not buy toys that children can't play with, no matter what they cost. I got Sara Will a jogging suit! Didn't have an idea in my head and then I thought, what would be warm and comfortable and practical all in one? And the idea popped right into my head. She'll look good in it, too. It's forest green with rust trim, the same colors as the afghan I've made her. And I got leather gloves for Michael, fur-lined. Of course, he can exchange them if he wants to. And for Fate, a new jacket. It's lightweight, of course, I couldn't do but so much, but it'll be ideal for coming into town like this when he doesn't expect to be exposed to the elements. Not dressy or anything but nice-looking. And you! Oh, Eva, wait till you see what I got you! I can hardly wait myself!" She was beaming at the clerk, who had just finished counting Eva's change and was dropping it into the compartments of the cash drawer. "Isn't Christmas exciting? I tell you, sometimes I am just overcome with joy. That's what it is, sheer joy at having my health and comfortable means and a family both far and near. And this baby! Have you ever seen such a beautiful child?"

The clerk slammed the drawer shut and handed Eva the sack. "Merry Christmas," he said, without much enthusiasm.

Swanee Hope beamed. "And to you too!" She moved away, pulling Eva with her. "I told Sara Will we'd gather in thirty minutes right outside this store. Then we'll get the groceries and go on home. I bought the invitations, white ones with gold lettering and little sprigs of holly in the corners, and a red pen for you to write with. I know Sara doesn't want to have a party.

She's as serious as a heart attack about everything, but I intend to see it through. Life's just going by us out there, Eva. I've always known it but I didn't know how to change things. Sara's hard to deal with on her own territory, which, of course, she never gets out of. Used to be just looking at her could make me feel bad. There's been no one to smile at besides my own face in the mirror for the longest time. Well, here we are!" She pushed through the glass door and held it open for Eva. The other three waited beside the truck.

"Michael, let's put all the presents in the truck and you and Eva can go on home," Swanee said. "The rest of us will go to the grocery store in the car."

"Why not the other way round?" Sara asked. She was holding three wrapped packages stacked against her chest. "We'll put the gifts in the Mustang. You can go with Michael and Eva in the truck to get the groceries."

"Or," Fate chimed in, "Swanee Hope and I could take the car to the grocery store and you could go home in the truck with Michael and Eva." Laughter edged his voice.

"We're getting cold," Eva said.

"I'll take my car home with the presents," Sara Will said stubbornly. "Eva, you and the baby come with me. Swanee, Fate and Michael will take you to the grocery store in the truck. After all, it's Fate's truck. He should have been driving it all along."

"And the Mustang is yours," Fate said. She was surprised at how near his voice was. It seemed to be inside her own head, although he stood at a distance. He came closer to drop her keys in her hand. They were warm from his pocket.

"I'm going, then," Sara said, and balancing the packages in front of her, she started down the street to where the car was parked.

"You see," Swanee Hope huffed, following along with the others to stow her packages in the Mustang. "Everything always goes her way."

"No," Fate said, coming along beside her and sure to be in

Sara's earshot. "Not everything." He stood beside Sara while she opened the trunk, put his own boxes inside, then added hers. "We'll be along home soon," he said. They were both looking into the spotless trunk, in which their boxes were neatly divided according to purchaser.

"Is there room?" Swanee wanted to know.

"Is there, Sara?" Fate asked her. "Is there room for any of us?"

She didn't have to answer because Swanee Hope had pushed between them, plopping her packages down in the middle. "We'll make room," she said. "Here, children!" Packages fell on top of each other, a pile of bright wrappings spilling over. Swanee slammed the top down on them. "We're off!" she cried, pulling Fate and Michael along to the truck.

Eva got in beside Sara and turned Rachel into a sit on her lap. "Does this mean Swanee pays for everything, for all the groceries?" she asked when Sara had started the car and was pulling into the street.

"Well, after all, my dear," Sara said matter-of-factly, so that there would be no argument, "it's her party."

16

✦ Sara Will awoke with the sun in her face. The room was already warm, the furnace pumping tepid air through the vents. The warmth drifted past her on its way to the ceiling. Fate had turned up the thermostat. She had heard him up before day, had known by the footfall that it was he. Sounds in the house didn't worry her so much anymore; there was no point in lurching out of bed to investigate when almost every night someone was up using the bathroom or Rachel cried out in her sleep or a body turned against a bad dream, disturbing old springs so they moaned.

She could smell breakfast. Coffee, bacon frying. He had said he'd cook this meal. His specialty was eggs combined with slivers of hash browns and cooked in an omelet flecked with bell pepper and green onion. Vickie had taught him to make it. Men are good at breakfast, he'd told her, because they see it as a way of getting control of the day, attacking first. Besides, breakfast was easy.

Thinking about breakfast made her mouth water, but she shouldn't eat it. She'd put on weight in the last two months as their meals had become more elaborate. You didn't offer men a piece of raw fruit for lunch or a scrambled egg on toast for dinner. Now there was sandwich meat in the refrigerator, thick soup and corn bread for supper, a roast every Sunday.

At least five pounds had thickened her waist and was pushing down her hips to her thighs, where she knew it would settle like lard. She hadn't been going to the cemetery either, which eliminated the exercise those frequent treks had once provided. There was nothing to do in the cemetery now that she'd raked the last leaves and pulled up the remaining bits of brush. Nothing but wait for snow to make its own improvements on the landscape, hiding her handiwork with some of its own. There was work she could do here, though. She could start walking about the place this week to investigate the possibility of improvements, maybe even walk down the road to the Burches and pay them a visit. She hadn't been in that house for ten or twelve years, not since the last time she visited them about the bridge and was so incensed by their apathy she swore on the way home she'd never speak to a Burch again. Of course, she should have expected them to have a tolerant attitude toward the dam. The older Burch boy had worked on it, earning enough money and learning enough about pouring concrete to start his own business when the sluice gates were finally closed. Any regrets the Burches had about lost land and neglected graves were buried under poured footings and driveways to new houses in town.

The Burches would be coming to Swanee's party this afternoon and Sara Will would speak to them—she would not acknowledge so long a grudge for it belittled her, not them; she might even give notice of a social call in the near future. She wondered how the homeplace had changed now that Mr. Burch's younger son was rearing his family there. She could remember the old smell of it, that impenetrable musty camphor odor of houses where people had been born, lived out their lives, and died. Every smell seemed trapped in the wood, the drab worn upholstery, the corners of tissue-lined drawers. You could smell sickness in an old house like that even when there'd been no illness in years.

Maybe you could smell it here too, and she'd just never noticed. Beneath the cedar fragrance of the Christmas tree, the scent of bayberry candles Swanee had lit on the mantel the night before, the fresh aroma of breakfast, was there also the odor of age, of decay, of undisruptable quiet that professed the plain truth? There had been no life in this house for years.

"Sara." It was Fate outside her door, his voice barely a whisper.

"Yes." She pulled the covers to her neck and waited to see what would happen. The door pushed open slightly.

He was bringing a mug. "I just took Eva a cup of coffee, and I thought maybe you'd like some too. It's almost nine o'clock." He put the mug on the bedside table and stood looking at her for a moment. She avoided his eyes as she freed one hand from the covers to reach for the mug. Fate turned away too, as if to avoid a glimpse of whatever she might expose. He looked around the room, which was tidy, almost bare. "Why, there's nothing of you in here," he said with quiet astonishment. "Where do you keep yourself, Sara?"

She wrapped her fingers around the hot mug, feeling it burn. "I don't like clutter," she said. Her hand couldn't take any more, and she managed to catch the mug by the handle, took a sip, and set it down.

"I thought you'd have pictures: you know, all those dead people we keep hearing about. And little boxes and jars, dresser scarves, a little glass lamp with a frilly shade." She thought his voice was gently mocking her, but when he turned all the way around and was back to her, she saw he wasn't. "I thought, hidden in here somewhere, I'd find you."

Why would he want to do that?

He rubbed his good hand against the one turned inward to his chest. "Well, I'll go get started on the eggs. Michael and Swanee are up." But he kept on looking at her. She lay still, barely breathing, and wondered how her hair fell around her shoulders on the pillow. She wished she could reach up and test her face.

He could feel her waiting. She was as impatient as he to have something happen.

"What I really came for," he said, clearing his throat slightly on the words, "what I wanted to say to you, Sara, before we get busy opening presents and fixing for the open house—" He stopped, looking dismayed, even pained. She thought he must hurt inside; somewhere deep and unreachable he was wounded, but what could she do about it, she who had spent a lifetime avoiding injury?

He saw her staring at him, a panicked look in her eyes. He hadn't wanted to frighten her. He began to turn away, then looked back at her, too stubborn to relinquish this time alone with her which he'd so obviously instigated.

"I used to be good on my feet," he said suddenly. "Everybody said so. I could get a A-men out of a fencepost, that's what my daddy used to say. What he didn't know was that I never said my true feelings. I kept them hidden so good, Sara, just like you do. My apartment was just as empty as this room. My life was as empty, too, but I wouldn't let myself see it. I was just holding tight to what little I had when Eva came and changed all that. At least on the outside things are different, but I'm still hidden. I know that because lately I've been feeling like I want to tell somebody all about myself. I've got words bubbling up every minute, my mind's full to bursting, and it's you I want to say them to, Sara. Not Eva or Swanee, although both of them are good-hearted and willing to listen. It's you, Sara. But I know you don't want to hear. I can feel how tense you are right this minute. You're lying there scared to death of what I'll say or do. Or maybe it's yourself you're afraid of, I don't know for sure. I just know I have feelings for you that can probably stay just like they are, hidden and small because I'm good at that. I've had practice. Or they can grow. That's something I don't know much about. I'm a real amateur at feelings. But I know this much: If you're willing, Sara, what I feel for you will grow." He turned away from her toward the door. "Now come on downstairs so I can show off my cooking."

"Fate," she said calmly, but the word still surprised her. She hadn't known she was going to say his name. He looked back at her but didn't move in her direction. There was no invitation in her voice, no gentle bidding to bring him near, but there was very little apprehension either. "Merry Christmas," she said.

"Merry Christmas to you too, Sara."

Minutes later, hands trembling, she smeared toothpaste on her brush. Water trickled over the edge of the basin as she sloshed her face. Her fingers collected the knot of hair at her neck but quivered lamely with the pins. She put on a skirt and blouse. The blouse had a tiny trim of lace around the collar but she felt plain, austere, ordinary. In the jewelry box she kept at the back of her bottom drawer, she found her mother's pearls and looped them around her neck and under the collar. She felt foolish wearing pearls to breakfast and took them off, put a touch of lipstick on her lips, blotted most of it away, for a second time decided she was pitifully plain, clasped the pearls on again, and, without another look, went downstairs.

The tree was lit in the parlor, casting its red glow on the room. Swanee had stuck sprigs of holly everywhere imaginable;

at every turn there was a possibility of being pricked. She had hung stockings, too, old hand-knitted ones smelling of mothballs and winter fruit. The one in the middle, Rachel's, bulged with oranges and hard lumps of candy. A stuffed bear with a red yarn grin hung out of the top.

She went on to the kitchen, softening her step, which suddenly sounded like marching. She squeezed her hands together, cracking her knuckles, then stopped in the hall to listen to the raging noise inside herself. Her body betrayed her with its deep rumbling, a burning line of fire in her throat, panting breaths that passed hotly over her tongue. She forced herself to take a deep breath, inhaling the heady air that camouflaged the house's dark smell.

In the kitchen the table was set, unduly burdened, Sara thought, with a collection of candlesticks Swanee Hope had gathered from all over the house, each tied with plaid ribbon and drying holly. There was no place for the food.

"We'll serve the plates from the stove," Swanee said, anticipating Sara's frown, but none was forthcoming. Instead, Sara slipped into her place and waited, the candlelight sending small licks of heat against her face.

"We've got broiled grapefruit coming right up," Michael announced, peering into the oven.

Sara could smell the caramelizing sugar as Michael brought it to her. "Merry Christmas, Sara," he said at her shoulder.

"Merry Christmas, Michael."

"It's going to be the loveliest day," Swanee said. "It can't help but be. Already everything is perfect."

"Eat up," Fate commanded from the stove. "The eggs are almost ready."

"You come too," Swanee said. "We won't start without you."

"She's right, Uncle Fate, we can't eat without the cook." Eva patted his chair.

Sara stuck her spoon into the grapefruit and brought a section to her mouth, concentrating on steadying the spoon in her hand. The pink fruit slid forward, pitching solidly into her lap, where it rested, dripping sugary juice on her napkin. She scooped it up quickly in her spoon and sneaked it onto the edge of her plate. They would notice, if not that infraction then some other. She couldn't get through the entire day without their seeing she was different. How could she hide it when all her energy was taken in resisting the explosion in her chest, the tears and laughter combusting in her throat? How could she avoid his eyes, which had already seen into her heart and now could look again and again? She had not rejected him, had not denied him access to that region of tenderness she now knew existed in her. She had not put a stop to it as she could have this morning. One word was all it would have taken, that simple no which had lately come so hard to her and which now seemed altogether unavailable.

But somehow she must get through the day. She must find a narrow, exclusive focus that locked the future out of view and kept Fate Jessop in a blur. The possibility of exposure heated her face and hands. She must stay hidden, even from him.

"Sara," Fate said to her from across the table, "we're eating."

Forced to look at him, to see a quietly mocking smile, a knowing face, eyes that saw her secret trembling, she knew it was too late.

Christmas Day moved more swiftly than she'd ever remembered. Her recollection was of a long thin day, a narrow white ribbon of time for which she had no expectations. Except for the exchanging of gifts early in the morning and a meal more elaborate than the usual Sunday fare, Christmas Day had for many years been like any other day.

This morning it was almost noon when they left the breakfast dishes on the table to open presents in the parlor. Eva distributed them just as Fate remembered her doing at home, but now she spoke the names out boldly, shaking boxes, hypothesizing about the contents before delivering them. Rachel mangled all the paper but couldn't manage any of the boxes, so Michael held her between his knees on the floor, snipping tape and pulling cartons open for her. Swanee tore into every package that came her way, unable to wait for everyone's attention. Sara Will was secretive, hoarding the nest of gifts at her side as if she hoped to slip away with them unopened. Knowing that wasn't possible, she unwrapped them quietly, but in the end they watched her open the last one. It was one of those times when silence falls unexpectedly, as if somehow the message has gone out that this next moment is one worth noting. It was bath oil, an inexpensive brand but good smelling.

"It's jasmine," Fate said. He was across the room from her, but she felt how narrow the distance was.

"You'll have to have a nice long soak in the tub, Sara," Swanee said, her attention already wavering.

"Yes, I will," Sara replied and replaced the bottle in its box. "Thank you, Fate." She folded the wrapping paper smartly, preventing any clutter around her. She could imagine herself in the tub, the scented water enveloping her in its softness. She would be drowsy there, floating, unresisting. Did he know that? Was Fate Jessop imagining the same thing?

He was opening his gift from her, a pocketknife encased in rippled horn with a finely honed steel blade. "Thank you, Sara," he said, his voice once more magically close. He scraped the blade against his withered hand to test the sharpness.

"Don't!" she cried out.

He snapped the knife shut and put it in his pocket. "I wasn't going to cut myself," he said quietly.

But Sara knew he'd been hurt before, had suffered permanent injury, and it wasn't only his useless arm. Eva had told her about Vickie, how the first months of her disappearance had drained him dry. He hadn't wanted to live, with his hand, his future, his wife all lost to him. He had lost too much blood, was how Eva put it, but he'd been patient, too, and stubborn, unconsciously waiting out his grief until one day he managed to set for himself some small chore that he accomplished. He had to learn how to function with one hand, but once he started trying, he found he was clever that way and, after a while, was even curious to see how he could manage a difficult task.

The social part troubled him most. Speaking to someone on the street, buying a sack of groceries, waiting in line at the bank were ordeals for him. The only public place where he could be comfortable was at the movies and so he went, automatically sitting through two shows on long winter evenings. At first he didn't pay much attention to the stories, simply watched the movement, the colors: scenes of lush jungles, dusty bleak plains, faces larger than life. People talked and ate and smoked and made love right there in front of him. They committed crimes. They cried. They held each other. Gradually he began to notice. He paid attention to how they survived. He took note of the losers, too. After a while he saw a particular movie only once. He remembered what he saw, could play back a certain scene in his head. From the movies he began to see how people lived, and gradually he began to imitate them.

He sold the house, moved to another town, got an apartment and a job, bought a used TV set, an expensive tape player, a bowling ball. He read western novels and science fiction. Once he found interest in his own life, he didn't need the movies so much. He was getting along just fine when Eva came. It was the same with Sara; she had been all right until they came. It wasn't just Fate, it was Eva, too. She had been violated by their needs.

Eva was squealing over the gown and robe Swanee had given her. She put on the fleecy blue robe and danced in a circle around them.

"See how pretty Mommy is," Michael said, hugging the baby to his chest. "But you're my angel, Rachel, you really are." He got up and caught Eva by the arm, pulling her close so the three of them were together in front of the tree.

"Aren't they a picture!" Swanee cried. "If only we had a camera right now! Eva, I could just put a frame around the three of you."

Her happy approval seemed to draw them closer together

and they both bent their heads to kiss Rachel. Then Michael put his free hand on Eva's neck, moving her face closer until his lips were against her cheek. "Merry Christmas, Eva," he whispered.

"Merry Christmas, Michael," she said and turned her face willingly so their lips touched over Rachel's head. She pulled away after a second, her eyes avoiding his, but he wouldn't let her go until she'd looked. "It doesn't mean anything," she said, shuddering on a breath as she took Rachel out of his arms. But everybody there knew it did.

By three-thirty there was a light drizzle. All day, since the sun had struck Sara where she lay sleeping, the clouds had been gathering, bringing with them a damp that now lay on the house like a soaked sheet. Fate went out to bring in more wood for the fireplace.

"Looks like snow coming," he said to Swanee, who was arranging thin slices of fruitcake on her mother's hand-painted cake plate.

"Never mind," Swanee answered. "A little flurry never stopped anybody around here."

Fate's new jacket was damp where crystals had caught on the wooly nap.

"That coat is for wearing to town, not for bringing in wood." Swanee stopped to brush the wet off his shoulders. There were bits of bark stuck to the front. "Hang it there on the back of the door so it can dry."

After shedding the coat, Fate leaned over the steaming pot of wassail. "Smells wonderful. I think I should have a little taste." He dipped the spoon in and brought it to his lips. "Damn, it's hot. I think I've scorched my tongue."

"Serves you right," Swanee said, giving the plate of cake a critical look. "Sara, Fate says it looks like snow."

Sara was waiting in the doorway as if she needed an invitation to join them.

"Come taste this," Fate said, holding the spoon out to her. "It's cool now."

She came forward, leaned toward the spoon, lips pursed to draw the liquid off the rim without really touching it.

"Good, isn't it?" Fate pulled the spoon back.

Sara held the liquid on her tongue. It tasted like spiced cider.

"The spirits aren't in it yet. According to Michael, we have to pour this red wine in at the last minute and just bring it to a simmer again. That'll warm you up."

Did he know, then, how cold she was? All afternoon while the rest of them prepared for the party she had been left to herself. They seemed to be avoiding her, expecting some fiery reprisal if they so much as mentioned the approaching event. There had been no entreaties for last-minute help, no encouragement to join them. Not that she'd expected any. After all, she'd done her part. For two days the date roll had been wrapped in damp cheesecloth in the cool pantry, and the sugared pecans were dry and crunchy in an airtight container. She had been the one to launder the lace tablecloth and sweep the front porch. But today they had asked nothing of her, so there was nothing to do but spend the afternoon out of the way in her room.

After arranging her gifts on her dresser and hanging the jogging suit in the closet, she'd lain down on the bed to sleep. But she didn't. Instead, she found herself listening.

She heard Eva put Rachel down for a nap, the brief struggle between them that ended with Eva singing softly, then falling silent. She heard Michael taking the stairs two at the time when Eva called to him from the landing. She heard a door open, a hushed rumble of movement. What could they be doing? Then Eva said, "Just don't drop it," and she knew he was lifting the glass punch bowl off the top shelf of the linen closet where Sara always kept it.

She had thought something else. Her mind was playing subtle tricks, imagining events she'd never considered before.

They're going to bed together was what she'd thought when she heard them on the stairs. Right here in her house in the middle of Christmas with no evening shadows to hide in, a sleeping baby six feet away, no lock on the door. And she didn't mind. It seemed right to her that Eva should eventually take Michael in. How could a girl not accept love when it was the most important thing in life?

When did I begin believing that? Sara wondered. Well, maybe she'd always believed it. What would have become of her if Swanee hadn't moved in with her? She wondered if she could have lived without the bother of her sister, someone to watch out for, to be angry with. Sharing a life as they'd been doing, that was love, wasn't it?

When she'd heard the rain against the window, she had put a sweater over her blouse and come down.

"I've been thinking about putting siding on the house," she said, stationed with Fate before the steaming pot. "What do you think?"

"I don't know a thing about siding, but we can look into it. I can get brochures at the hardware store, or they can recommend somebody. I'll get on it next week."

"It's just something I've been thinking about," Sara said, alarmed by his quick reaction. She was afraid of sudden decisions.

The doorbell sounded. "I'll get it," Swanee Hope cried, giving the table one last dithering pat. "Pour that wine into the wassail, Fate. I don't know what's happened to Eva and Michael. They just go and come as they please."

She hurried down the hall and they heard her welcome, her apology for the threatening weather and the lack of adequate closet space for their wraps. Sara Will poured coffee into the silver pot while Fate stirred the heady mixture of wine and fruit.

He grinned at her. "I'm getting tipsy just smelling this stuff."

Sara put the coffeepot on the table beside the cups and

helped Fate ladle wassail into the punch bowl at the other end. "Where are those children?" she whispered.

The bell sounded again, and this time they heard Eva being introduced at the door by Swanee. Michael came down. The door opened and closed, filling the house with people who seemed to shed their shyness as quickly as Swanee Hope's addled exuberance touched them. Sara Will heard her sister's laughter, a bit shrill, slightly out of control but contained, too, inside the event, this party she'd longed to have. This was what her sister was good at, the amenities, the daily kindnesses, the questioning concern, the sympathetic replies.

"Swanee's having a wonderful time," Sara said to Fate while they stood awaiting the line of people her sister was urging toward them to be fed.

"Why, Sara," Fate said, grinning as he watched her ladle the first cup of wassail from the bowl, "haven't you noticed? So are we."

17

✦ About five, just as the rain was beginning to freeze, an unfamiliar car turned down the lane toward the house. It hesitated, sending a burst of chalky exhaust into the air, then pulled over to the edge behind the row of muddy vehicles already parked in the yard. The car was a Buick, white but speckled with red clay on the fenders. The windshield wipers pushed a crusty collection of ice across the glass, building up a little ridge of frozen refuse around their sweep.

The couple who got out wore heavy coats, the man a hat pulled low on his forehead, the woman a pink plastic rain bonnet that stood high in the front, too stiff to rest on her hairdo. They held onto each other coming up the lane, which was beginning to ice over; slick patches were forming around rocks where the gravel had been washed away. The woman wobbled on her high heels but the man, peering down to watch their step, held her securely by the arm. She seemed to be walking into him as they made slow, determined progress toward the house.

Once on the porch, they could see through the parlor window that there was a party in progress. The Christmas tree cast its tinsel glow onto the porch, flickering dully as people passed between the tree and the window. The man didn't wait long before pressing the bell, although the woman wanted him to.

"What if this isn't the right house?" she whispered, rounding her body into his side to keep warm.

"This is it, Harriet," the man said through his teeth. He pressed the bell again and stamped the cold from his feet. "Do you think I'd ever forget?"

"Well, they could have moved," Harriet said, pushing her arm through his. Wind whipped sleet in to sting her ankles.

"I don't think the damn bell works," the man said, pushing it hard with the flat of his gloved hand.

"Well, knock then." Harriet was shivering. "Clement, if she's here I don't know what I'll do."

It was Eva who came to the door. Her face flushed with wassail, she stood in the open lighted space, the house heat wafting behind her, the cold sweeping across her front, chilling her like ice touching her chest as she looked into their startled faces.

"Mama," she said, and then Swanee Hope was there beside her, come to see who the latecomers could be.

"Who is it?" Swanee Hope cried, peering out at them. Half in shadow, they were ominous in their dark winter coats. Then Clement stepped forward, bringing Harriet with him, and took off his hat. "Clement Jessop!" Swanee cried and clasped her hand over her mouth. "Eva, it's your folks!"

"I know it," Eva said. She was backing away, but Swanee Hope held onto her.

"Come in, come in out of the cold and join the party. It's the neighborhood come for open house and you might just know some of them, Clement. Why, you were here at least three months."

"It was a long time ago," Clement said, stepping over the threshold. Harriet came with him. She flicked off her rain bonnet, shook it once out of the door before it closed, and stuffed it in her coat pocket. Nobody seemed to know what to do next.

"Well," Swanee Hope said, "the first thing is to get out of those damp coats. You can hang them inside the back door, Eva, so they don't get mixed up with the others." The two struggled out of their wraps. "Take them, Eva honey," Swanee urged, and Eva stepped forward one tiny step and put out her arms for her parents to lay the coats over them. Clement put his hat carefully on top.

"Well," Swanee said again, eyeing them with some satisfaction because they were beautifully groomed and dressed for the occasion. "Let me find Sara. You remember Sara, don't you, Clement, Serena's younger sister? Of course, I can't just leave you all standing in the hall, can I? Come on into the parlor and I'll introduce you round. Then I'll find Sara, who has to be here someplace. The house isn't big enough to get lost in, I don't reckon."

"We didn't come to interrupt anything," Clement said. He put his arm around Harriet to show they stood together.

"Never you mind about that. They'll be going soon anyhow with that sleet starting to come down. You're Harriet," Swanee added, nodding to the woman, who had a sharp little face and was bonier than Swanee liked a person to be. "I don't know why I expected a big woman. Why, you're positively petite. I know where Eva gets her slightness from. Eva's strong, though. Of course, she's young, too." Swanee managed a smile, although she was beginning to feel uncomfortable, forced as she was to carry the full burden of the conversation. "My goodness, what am I telling you about Eva for? You know all about her. So just come on in and meet these other people." She drew them into the parlor where the guests mingled, looking weary. There was an oily glow about most of the faces and the women had eaten off their lipstick. Swanee pulled Clement and Harriet around making introductions, saying that these were Eva's parents. "Now talk to somebody while I tell Sara," she commanded.

But Sara had already heard. She had seen Eva come through the kitchen burdened with the coats, had seen the fearful eyes, the face sunken in grief, the panicked hands that pushed the wraps haphazardly onto hooks. "What is it, Eva?" she had asked, leaving the wassail bowl to catch the girl before she bolted into the hall. Sara knew Eva wouldn't stop there but would race upstairs and slam a door somewhere. Sara had seen that same expression on her own face. "What is it?" she asked again, holding Eva by the shoulder, the other hand stroking her cheek, smoothing hair from her clammy forehead.

"Mama and Daddy are here," Eva breathed into Sara's shoulder. She was shaking.

"What?" Fate was coming to them, alarm in his voice.

"In the parlor right this minute. There's Daddy's overcoat right there."

"So they've seen you," Fate said.

"I answered the door. I opened it right in their faces. I knew who it was just from the shape of them. They look old, Sara. They look terrible." Eva started to cry and turned out of Sara's arms into Fate's. Fate and Sara looked at each other over her head.

"What are we going to do?" Fate asked, truly vexed.

"Nothing until the party is over," Sara said. "Then we'll ask them to have supper and see what their intentions are. Of course, they'll want to see Rachel."

"She's asleep," Eva said, as if that presented a major dilemma. "I knew this was going to happen."

"We all knew it," Sara Will said.

"They're here!" Swanee Hope cried, almost colliding with the huddle. "They're right in the parlor by the Christmas tree looking like two pilgrims. Oh, Lord, I feel so bad!"

"Where's Michael?" Eva pulled out of Fate's arm to ask.

"Here." He came in, rubbing his glasses on his shirt and squinting at them. "I just came through the hall from checking on Rachel and I saw them. I don't think they're here to cause trouble, do you? Anyway, right now we've got this party to look after and it's starting to sleet bad."

Sara took charge. "Swanee, you and Michael start getting coats and saying good-byes. Remind people of the bad weather if you have to. I'll get the two of them in here having something hot to drink. I'm sure they could use it. Eva, you go up and tend to Rachel. Stay up there awhile if you want to. Fate, I don't know about you."

"I'm the one they'll be mad at," he said.

"I suppose you always knew that," Sara said, going to fetch their unexpected guests.

Although there was no place to go, Eva sat on the edge of the bed as if she expected to rise at any moment and be spirited away. Rachel slept in the crib close enough for her to see a bubble of spit that glistened between the baby's lips. She was sleeping in a party dress given her just today by Sara Will. It was a white dress with tiny Christmas trees embroidered across the yoke. Eva thought it must have cost a fortune, not counting the black patent-leather shoes Sara bought to go with it. They were Rachel's first hard-soled shoes, and the sight of them so carefully wrapped in blue tissue in the little white box had made Eva cry. Nothing ever given her was as splendid as those tiny shoes, accessories on which her mother had always put such value. Good shoes were a sign of quality, of attention to detail. Eva despised the cheap sneakers Rachel had been wearing all fall.

She could hear the farewells below, cold engines snapping at the icy air, the sigh of relief that whiffled from Swanee Hope when the door was finally shut and the only sound in the house was the clicking of sleet on the tin roof. What would happen now?

There was a knock on her door, a muffled urgent rapping, and then the door slipped open. It was Fate, with Michael behind him, looking over his shoulder at her. They came in, shutting the door soundlessly behind them.

"We should all go down together," Fate said right off. He rubbed his hand across his withered arm anxiously.

"It was my letter to the registrar," Michael said, coming to Eva. He knelt at her knees and put his hands on her skirt. "One of our neighbors works in the office and she saw the letter and called my folks and they called yours just on the chance that this would be a familiar address. I didn't mean for it to happen like this, Eva."

She couldn't bear to look at him, but she put her hand on his hair as if to bestow a blessing or a pardon. "It doesn't matter, Michael." There were tears in her voice.

"There's nothing to do but go down," Fate said. "I mean, Sara Will and Swanee are entertaining them, for God's sake."

Rachel stirred and opened her eyes as if she'd been beckoned. Seeing the three of them with her, she sat up quickly, her tiny face sagging with sleep. She put out her arms and Fate swung her over the side in one motion.

"Where are her shoes?" Eva cried, swept through with panic. "She can't go without her shoes!"

"Here." Michael stuck them on the fat twisted feet and secured the buckles while Eva smoothed the baby's hair, curling the ends around her nervous fingers.

"Don't worry. She's beautiful. You're beautiful, aren't you, sweet thing?" Fate nuzzled her cheek, but he looked pale too.

"Let's go, then," Michael said. He took Eva's hand and squeezed it, then let go, but she caught his fingers again and held on.

They were in the kitchen. Swanee Hope sat at the table with the Jessops while Sara Will took care of the leftovers at the counter. She laid slices of fruitcake on foil squares and folded them carefully, running two fingers along the seal. The foil crackled. Swanee was facing the door, her mouth turned down in a pout. She had run out of chatter while awaiting the culprits, and she was annoyed by the silence the Jessops seemed incapable of filling. Perhaps she should explain her part in all this, she kept thinking, or give a detailed account of the past two months, but something held her quiet. There was no way to explain how it had been among the six of them. How could she ever put words to it?

When Eva appeared behind them, the Jessops read her arrival in Swanee's eyes and turned abruptly in their chairs to look at their daughter, their faces hesitant to show emotion, as if they had held their mournful looks too long to readily abandon them.

"Here we are," Fate said.

Rachel turned her face shyly into his shoulder and clung to him.

"It's your granny and granddaddy," Eva said to the baby, unable to look at her parents directly. Everybody was looking at Rachel as though she could provide magical release from their communal misery.

"Oh, my God," Harriet wailed, "just look at her! Just look at all of them!" She started out of her chair, then fell back as though the sight of them exhausted her.

"Mama," Eva said evenly, dropping Michael's hand to take the child in her arms. "This is Rachel. She's eleven months old and she's wearing a Christmas dress and shoes from Sara Will. Look at her shoes, Mama. Aren't they the dearest things?" She pushed one little foot out at her mother. The patent leather gleamed, but Harriet was looking at their faces instead.

"I think I'm going to faint," she said.

"No, you're not," Swanee cried. "Sara, hand me a cold wet rag. You're just overwrought," she added, patting Harriet's limp shoulder, "and, pray tell, who wouldn't be?" She pressed the cloth to Harriet's forehead as Clement pulled himself up in

196

one labored movement. He was a big man, thick with middle age and fleshy. With his silvery good looks, he could have been a congressman. Even his sad eyes staring down at his misplaced family had a sturdiness in them, a defiant determination not to suffer too long or without good reason.

"You son of a bitch," he said and had Fate in his grasp. "I ought to wring your neck right here and now!"

Eva shrank against the wall, Rachel's head cradled to her shoulder.

"It wasn't just him, Mr. Jessop," Michael said, attempting to move forward although there didn't appear to be room for one more person in the kitchen. "I've known where she was for months and I didn't tell you. I'm to blame too."

"You're an idiot, Michael Logan, that's common knowledge," Clement said, still holding fast to Fate, who hardly struggled at all, resigned to suffer whatever came to him. "You don't have enough sense to come out of a shower of rain, but Fate here, he's my brother, and he's kept the truth from me. No, it's worse than that, he's lied to me.

"You did, didn't you? That time you called so concerned to tell us Eva'd been to your place, she was still there, wasn't she? She was there from the very first and you let us suffer. You let poor Harriet go out of her mind with grief, mourning like Eva was dead but never knowing for sure. And it wasn't ever going to be over, was it? Was it?"

He pushed Fate off balance, just far enough away to take a swing. The blow caught Fate under the jawbone, knuckles crunching into his neck, and he fell backward, slapping the phone off the hook so it dangled there, clunking against the wall.

Fate leaned backward a moment, his good hand pressed to the pain, then he straightened himself up a little. "I'm not going to fight you, Clement. I couldn't win. Besides, you're right. I did lie to you. I did everything wrong as far as you're concerned, I can see that, but I did one thing right. I loved

Eva." He slumped back against the wall, his head still swung back and throbbing from the blow.

"Are you all right?" Swanee cried, bringing the damp cloth from Harriet's forehead to press against Fate's neck. "I never thought I'd live to see fisticuffs in this house."

"You've seen all there's going to be," Sara Will said sternly. "I know you're upset, Clement, and you have a right to be, but I'd like to think we're all above fistfights."

"I'd beat him to a pulp if it would do any good," Clement growled, but he dropped back into his chair looking like he was the one defeated.

"It's swelling," Swanee Hope fretted. "Michael, put some ice in this rag. Come sit down here, Fate."

Fate stumbled into his regular place while Eva continued to press herself against the wall.

"You come too," Swanee said to her. "We just need to talk this thing out. Why, Eva honey, you haven't even hugged your mama and daddy yet."

"She hasn't written a word in over a year, why should she want to hug anybody?" Harriet asked bitterly. Beneath the strident plane of her voice there was the persistent groan of someone wounded. "I've got a grandchild I've been thinking never made it into this world or else starved to death, abandoned somewhere. All the things you read about—fetuses in garbage cans, babies left to die of exposure in parking lots and on the doorsteps of public buildings—I've had all that to think about."

"You thought I'd do something like that?" Eva cried, taking the offensive as she came forward to claim her chair. "You thought I couldn't be a good mother, couldn't do as well as you? Look at her, Mama!" She turned Rachel frontwards on her lap so the pretty dress showed, the bright clear-blue eyes, the cheeks still heavy with sleep. "Does she look abused to you? Neglected? How could you think that? That I wouldn't know how to love somebody?"

"It's Fate's fault. He's who did wrong," Clement said with

weary resentment. He watched Swanee Hope press the ice pack to his brother's neck. "Eva wasn't herself. She was just a little girl reacting to a bad situation, but Fate here is a grown man who should know a thing or two about responsibility."

"I don't think I'd be one to talk if I were you, Clement, when you took our sister off and brought her back dead," Sara Will said darkly from where she stood apart from them. She seemed to have grown in stature and loomed above them, determined to keep them under control.

"She died in childbirth," Clement said heavily, "and nobody grieved more than me."

"I don't know that's true," Sara said, as cold and unfeeling as she looked. "You got married again."

"He wasn't supposed to mourn forever," Swanee said, irritated that Sara was still attending to the past when the present had problems enough. "We've got a new situation here, sister."

"I'm not going to give Rachel up," Eva said.

"We wouldn't ask you to." Harriet was sobbing. She raised one hand to her temple to press out a pain. Her hand looked narrow, shrunken to child size. So did her face. She looked as if she'd been broken and then carelessly flung back together.

Eva was trying to ignore the tears. "That's what you said would happen, Mama. You said giving her up for adoption was the best thing for everybody concerned. But I knew it wasn't. Not for me. I didn't want to have a baby, but it happened and there wasn't any changing it."

"You could of said no to that boy, whoever he was." Harriet had been saving that sentence for over a year.

"She did!" Swanee Hope cried, warming to the discussion. "Of course she did!"

"No, I didn't," Eva burst out. "I'd never said no to anyone in my whole life, so I didn't know how. The first time I ever said no was when I ran away."

"Well, she's said it considerable times since," Michael said, so solemnly that Fate and the sisters couldn't help but smile.

"Well, what are we going to do now?" Swanee was serious

again. She tested the swelling on Fate's neck with her fingertip and handed him the ice pack. "You hold it awhile," she said. Nobody responded so she continued. "I am of the opinion that we should eat something." She tried to fix a smile on Harriet and Clement, who still looked glum and out of sorts. "I bet you haven't had a thing since lunch, and here it is going on seven o'clock. We had a late breakfast and we've been nibbling on party food ever since, so I think we could all use some nutrition. Let's slice that ham from last night, Sara. We boiled a ham yesterday, Harriet, and cooked some sweet potatoes and collard greens. Not your typical Christmas Eve dinner, but it was mighty good."

"I couldn't eat a thing," Harriet said mournfully. She blew her nose into a discarded Christmas napkin left on the table.

"Of course you can, Mama," Eva said, although she felt herself recoiling. Her parents hadn't turned out to be the threat she'd been so afraid of, but their sadness, the gray, lethargic mood that clung to them now, seemed a more insidious menace. "You sit right here and hold Rachel while I help with supper." She put the baby in her mother's lap before Harriet was prepared, but Rachel settled in as if the arms were familiar ones. "You see, she likes you already."

"She's never met a stranger," Michael said.

"Is she walking?" Clement wanted to know. He was holding out his hand to Rachel, and she slapped at it as he moved his fingers back and forth, tempting her to laugh. There was a red streak along his knuckles where he'd struck his brother.

"Any day now," Michael answered. "We carry her around too much if you ask me. I keep telling Eva just let her go, but there're the stairs to worry about."

"We're getting some gates," Fate reminded him, then talked straight to his brother. "I ordered them weeks ago because they have to be specially sized. When it warms up a little I'm going to put up a chicken-wire fence along the porch rail and a gate between the posts. There and on the stairs."

"When it warms up!" Harriet echoed. She was holding

Rachel firmly now. "Why, there's no need. Eva's coming home with us. That's why we came, to get her and take her home where she belongs."

"And who's to say where I belong?" Eva said. She had the meat knife in her hand, as if this were the fight she'd been expecting. "Mama, I knew you'd say something like that!"

"Wait a minute, Eva," Fate said. "You ought to hear them out."

"Hear them out! That's what I always did, but they never heard me. Nobody ever listened to me!" She clanged the knife on the counter. "Whose side are you on, anyway?"

"Why do there have to be sides?" Swanee Hope wanted to know. "This ought to be a civil discussion, not a free-for-all."

"Well, you all stay here and discuss all you want to," Eva said, grabbing up Rachel, who screamed out during the transfer but then clung to her mother. "But I can tell you right now how it's going to be. Sara Will said I could stay here till spring and I'm going to. After that, I don't know. I haven't planned out my life like it's a week's worth of menus. But I do know what I'm going to do right this minute. I'm going to the parlor and I'm taking Rachel with me. We're going to play with her new toys. We're going to keep on believing this is a perfect Christmas Day, and you people, all of you, can just do whatever you please."

Nobody moved. Instead, they snuck inside themselves, each keeping silent counsel, avoiding each other's eyes. Minutes passed, as empty as their faces, but nobody stirred. Then what had begun as a low tremble, a spontaneous bubble of air in his chest, broke the stern embarrassed face he had been holding onto, and Fate Jessop laughed.

They would spend the night. Swanee Hope offered her own room without even considering where she'd sleep herself.

"The sofa," she said to Fate when the problem finally occurred to her.

"No, I'll sleep there," Michael offered.

"That will hardly do any good," Eva answered, showing her aggravation at the trouble her parents were causing. "Swanee, you can sleep with me."

"We can still go to a motel in town," Clement said halfheartedly. Nobody bothered to answer that there wasn't one.

"I think we can consider the matter settled," Sara Will said, dismissing all their foolishness with one austere gaze. "Did you bring a bag?" she asked Harriet.

"We didn't plan to stay," Harriet said, "but I do have my cosmetic case in the car. I always carry it with me."

"I'll get it," Michael offered, hurrying to put on his jacket. The house seemed stale with old heat and used-up feelings and he was grateful for a chance to escape.

"I'll come too," Eva said, plopping Rachel in Swanee's lap.

"Be careful, it's icy!" Harriet called after her and then fell silent. They all knew Eva hadn't heard her.

Michael and Eva maneuvered the shadowy steps with care and then slid down the dark path toward the hulking shape of the car.

"Get in," Eva said. She sat in the driver's seat and Michael took the passenger side.

"I thought I was going to suffocate if I stayed in there another minute," Eva breathed. She felt warm, although the air in the car was biting cold. She couldn't even touch the steering wheel.

"Me too." Michael reached over and took her hand. The new medallion he was wearing still felt warm on his chest. "You were terrific, Eva."

"I was scared to death."

"I know, but it didn't show. That's what made it so wonderful. You stood up to them without being rude or hurtful."

"I've already hurt them. It's written all over their faces." Eva rubbed her thumb across Michael's knuckles. "Now that I have Rachel I understand more how they felt. I don't agree with them, but I understand that they wanted to protect me however they could. Michael, don't you wonder how it happened or who the father is?"

"No."

"Someday you might. I would tell you, Michael. I'll tell you right now if you want me to."

"I'm her father. We're her parents." Michael moved closer and put his arm around her. They were both getting cold.

"That's not true," Eva said, but she rested her head on his shoulder. A solid sheet of ice covered the windshield. She closed her eyes to imagine summer. "When I come home we can talk about everything, if you still want to by then."

"I don't know." Michael pressed his lips to her hair. "All those college girls."

Eva laughed. "I'll take my chances," she said. "Now let's get Mama's bag before they're all out here looking for us."

"Couple found frozen in passionate embrace," Michael intoned.

"Why, Michael Logan, I'm beginning to think you're a romantic!" Eva pushed open the car door so the light came on. There was her mother's turquoise cosmetic case on the back seat. "Get it," she said, shutting the door.

They started for the house. The air was still now but close and smoky with damp. The bushes clacked with ice. Even the grass was slick.

"I'm falling!" Eva called out, arms swinging frantically as she slid. She was hardly surprised that Michael was there to catch her.

Later, when everyone else was settled in their rooms, Sara Will found themselves still puttering about downstairs. Fate jabbed at the hot cinders with the poker and then put the fire screen back in place. Sara scooped up crumbs from the rug and brushed them into an ashtray. She started to unplug the tree lights but Fate stopped her.

"Let's just sit here awhile," he said, "and enjoy the quiet."

A coal popped behind the screen, sending up a little spray of orange light while Sara settled herself on the sofa. "Aren't you tired?" she asked as he sat down next to her.

"Wound like a top," Fate said, "but I never just get tired. I get exhausted, debilitated, past modern medicine."

"You do exaggerate." Sara was smiling at the Christmas tree.

"Just one of the many things about me you'll have to learn to love," Fate said with a soft chuckle in his voice. He was looking at the tree too. "Who would have thought this would happen?" He seemed to be speaking to the angel perched on top. She had a plastic expression and scraggly blond hair, incredibly cheap.

"Where did that angel come from?" he asked.

"It was a bargain." Sara Will laughed.

"Somebody gave it to you?"

"Paid me to take it."

"Why, Sara, you actually made a joke." He moved closer on the sofa but didn't try to touch her.

"And you thought I couldn't."

"I thought you wouldn't. But you do surprise me. You're a complicated woman, Sara Will. Every day I learn something new about you."

"I feel the same way about Eva," Sara said, not really intending to change the subject. She stretched her legs out toward the fire. "Sometimes I feel like I'm witnessing a birth, I'm actually watching her become a person. It's scary."

"It's wonderful, too. You're wonderful."

"Another exaggeration." Sara could feel herself sinking into the sofa. She'd never felt so relaxed, so near sleep but not in the least bit sleepy. What was the word for it? Safe. That was it. She had never felt so safe.

"I don't think saying you're wonderful is an exaggeration at all." He put his hand on her cheek, gently turning her face toward his.

Sara forced herself to look at him. It took all her strength not to duck her head away from his touch, to rescue herself from whatever folly or joy would come to her next.

"Sara," Fate said, his face almost touching hers, lips almost brushing, "I'm going to kiss you, but I don't think either of us should expect too much from it."

His mouth was painfully soft. The ache of it shot through her, grabbing at nerves that had long ago been anesthetized. She hurt all over from that kiss but she didn't pull away. Instead, she stayed there, unable to resist the ache, not wanting to resist it, even finding courage in it so that in the seconds that passed she gathered more strength than she'd ever known existed and put it to best use. She kissed him back.

18

✦ The next morning turned sunny and warmer. By midday, water dripped like a shower from the trees and the grass sparkled with the thaw. The Jessops left before noon, after nibbling at the hearty breakfast Fate had prepared and saying stiff goodbyes on the porch. Harriet kissed Eva on the cheek, then Rachel but without trying to take her.

"We'll phone," Clement said, giving Eva a loose hug that included the baby. "Just to see how you're doing."

"You'll need the number," Swanee said.

"I've got it." Clement patted his breast pocket. "When that money I gave you runs out, you tell me, you hear?" he whispered to Eva. "I don't want you out here lacking for anything."

"We'll be fine, Daddy," Eva said and tried to hug him with one arm.

They stood on the porch and watched the car start up. "Watch out for that north side," Fate called out. "It's bound to be icy where the sun doesn't strike."

Clement waved out the window and turned the car into the lane. In less than a minute they had disappeared.

"Well, that's over with." Swanee sighed. "I'm worn out."

"You didn't shut your eyes all night," Eva said. "I could tell."

"Then you were awake too. I reckon I was restless, not being in my own bed."

"I slept like a baby," Fate said and grinned at Sara Will. "We're out of bread and milk and I don't know what all, ladies, so I think I'll go on into town for a few things." He went down the steps and around the house where he'd parked the truck before the party. "Sara," he called, and she went to him, feeling her shoes soak through in the wet grass.

"I've got a flat here," he said, pointing toward the left front where the truck slumped. "And no spare."

"You mean—" She stopped short, not wanting to admonish him for the past. She would see to it that he was never without a spare again.

"I'll get it fixed in town and pick up some kind of spare. I know it's foolish not to have one. At least your car's in good shape." He was lifting the jack out of the truck bed. "I won't be gone long."

It was such a harmless plan, an obvious, even necessary arrangement. Why did it make her stomach flop, her pulse quicken? Why shouldn't he take her car when just last night she had given him her kiss, when she had believed she was giving him herself and had been willing to? What was her car compared to that? And yet, standing there strangled with dread, it seemed more than she could do.

"Get a rock to put behind the other tire," Fate said, refusing to read her stony face. Surely he knew what he was doing to her.

"I'll send Michael to help you," Sara managed to say. She bit down on what felt like a sore tooth, her jaw held tight against a screech, and moved away from him toward the house. She sent Michael out and then stood at the kitchen window looking out at them. Fate was loosening the lug bolts while Michael watched. He'll even try to lift the tire off, she thought, just to prove to himself he can. He had so much more confidence than she, so much more faith. She was the one who carried resentment around, always ready to see in any unsuccessful venture just what she'd expected. No one was ever as careful as she.

Fate tugged the tire off and Michael rolled it over to the barn where the Mustang was parked while Fate let the jack down. What could she do?

She would let him go. She cared about him. That was the simple truth of it. No matter how ridiculous it was, how against her grain, how fearful, she had feelings for him and so she would have to trust him. She did trust him, both with her heart and her car. From now on, she would have to depend on his being careful with her life. Last night that choice had been made.

"I need the keys," Fate said through the back-door screen. "My feet are too wet to come in."

Sara took them to him, laid them in his open hand. "Michael's going with me. We won't be long," Fate said.

She wanted to say "Be careful!" but she couldn't. They were words too potent to say.

Swanee and Eva were straightening up the house, which in the light of day appeared in shambles. There was a cigarette burn on the cherry sidetable and a spill of wassail on the arm of a chair. It was the kind of damage Sara Will had expected but she kept quiet, thinking to herself how she could camouflage the burn and scrub away the tacky stain.

She took out the trash, flinging the plastic bags in the barn where they accumulated until she could get them to the dumpster. The missing Mustang made her bang her hand against the door latch when she closed it, and a swift hard pain shot down into her fingers. She had made a bruise.

Back in the house, she switched on the television. The early afternoon news was on. There was no mention of Christmas except for a small item about holiday accidents, fatalities which the newscaster read in his expressionless voice. They should have known better, Sara thought. Those people should have stayed home. But another voice pushed beside her old self-righteous one, ready to scrimmage. Those people had probably been with their families, had traveled to houses like this one. Maybe they were happy yesterday, as peaceful and right with the world as they'd ever been. She switched off the television and sat down on the sofa just where she'd sat the night before. Fate had built a fire earlier, but it was dying now. Red coals radiated their warm comfort to her legs and feet. She felt herself becoming drowsy, overcome with contentment. Soon Fate and Michael would be home. Her life would be intact but fuller, better. What she felt for Fate Jessop—what she now knew she was capable of feeling—made all the difference.

"Sara!" It was Swanee Hope, slamming the front door. "Sara, Michael and Fate are walking up the road. I know it's them. Oh, Lord, what's happened?"

But Sara knew. Already her heart was freezing inside her chest. Blood stopped en route. Warmth faded. Nothing was left of her as she stood there on the porch watching them come, seeing that Fate held a bloody rag to his cheek.

They stumbled along on the sluggish rutty lane.

"What is it?" Swanee Hope cried, going out to meet them. "Tell me what it is!"

"We slid on that bad curve about two miles down the road," Michael said. "You know, right where Fate warned Mr. Jessop it would be bad. It's still covered with ice."

"A sheet of ice, Sara," Fate explained. "No traction at all right there." He lifted the cloth so she could see a fiery skinless place along his cheekbone.

"We can bandage that!" Swanee cried, peering at the wound. "Are you hurt? Anyplace else, I mean?"

"No," Fate said. "We're all right." He was looking at Sara. "But the car's got some damage to it. I couldn't tell how bad because it's laying right up beside the ditch bank. We'll have to call a wrecker to get it out."

"What's wrong?" Eva asked from the front door. "Michael, Uncle Fate, are you all right?"

"We're fine," Michael said. "Just a little fender bender is all."

Fate was still looking at Sara, expecting something from her. She could feel the pleading in his eyes, his need to hear her speak his name, to say she forgave him. But she couldn't. She had never known how to forgive, there was no grace in her, no glance into the future to tell her that this too would pass. She was her old self again. The other Sara, last night's Sara, had been an apparition, a creation of firelight and warm wassail.

She turned away, pushing past Eva to get to the phone. Her fingers fumbled with the phone book as she searched for a wrecker service. Her voice trembled as she described the car and its location. She put down the receiver and went up to her room. There she pulled an old leather suitcase from under the bed, dusted it off with a wad of Kleenex, blew her nose into the clean side of the tissue, and proceeded to pack. She laid the clothes in carefully, then went to the bathroom, where she gathered the essentials from the medicine cabinet. These she laid on top of her clothing.

"What are you doing?" Fate asked from the doorway.

"Packing," she said. How could so much rancor, such contempt, be sounded in one word?

"Where are you going?" The side of his face showed a bruise and was swelling slightly around the raw place.

"I don't know. Into town. I'm going with the car." Her intentions put to words sounded foolish, but she didn't care. What he thought of her didn't matter anymore.

"I'll go," Fate said.

"No," she answered, pinching her mouth around the word, "I'm going." She couldn't believe she was leaving her home. How could she be doing that?

It was to get away from him. But there was an easier solution than this, a less damaging one. He had said it himself. He would go. But she didn't want him to do anything; she didn't want him to have a single chance to make up to her. She would be the one doing something.

"But, Sara—" Fate protested, starting toward her.

"Don't," she said. "Don't touch me. Don't say anything." She slammed the suitcase shut, fastened the strap, then lifted it off the bed. "Good-bye, Fate."

She sped past him, down the steps, stopped to put on her winter coat in the hall but refused to look at herself in the mirror. She never wanted to see herself again. She went out the front door and down the steps while the others stood watching, stunned, afraid to move or try to stop her. Eva had her arms around Swanee Hope, holding her by the shoulders.

Sara felt the cold immediately, although the sun was bright. She trudged on, carrying the heavy case that pulled at her shoulder and sent a dull ache down her back. She would pay for this tomorrow. She was paying already. When she reached the car, she put down the bag and leaned against the back bumper, unable to make herself examine the damage. The car could be fixed, she knew that, but could she?

The wrecker came. She watched the man latch his chain to the rear axle and tug the car away from the bank. Then he attached the chain to the front and hoisted the Mustang until the damaged grill and fender were suspended in the air.

"Can I get a ride into town?" Sara asked when the work was finished.

"Yes, ma'am."

She climbed up into the cab and put the suitcase between them.

"It could be worse," the man said, watching through his rearview mirror as he gave the wrecker some gas. The Mustang moved along with them.

"Yes," Sara said, putting on her stern face to keep from crying. "I suppose it could." But she didn't see how.

SPRING

19

✦ This is her room: a double bed with high ornate head and foot made of solid oak but stained dark to imitate mahogany, no posts, instead curves and scrollwork, clutter; a high chest with broken side lock, the drawers lined with blotting paper and smelling of an old man; a closet with narrow door built shallow in the wall to balance the chimney space; a tiny hearth, the grate set for a coal fire; a club chair turned toward it with gold hand towels pinned to back and arms to hide soil and places rubbed through; a floor lamp wearing a flimsy tablelike skirt.

A man has lived here most recently. In fact, he still does. Mr. Mason is away for the holidays. His clothing has been remanded to the bottom drawers, his summer suits to the chimney wall of the closet. He will not mind, says Mrs. Bloxton, who has rented rooms on the second floor of her house for years and knows how people feel. She is a patter, a sigher. Everybody who lives with her is lonely—of that she is sure. She is alone herself and so, having gathered in an acceptable, even lovable flock, she allows kitchen privileges, bakes birthday cakes, consults about wallpaper and the usefulness of soft worn towels.

"Every room in the house has been recently redone except this one," she explained when showing the room to Sara Will. "Mr. Mason likes the floral pattern. He says it reminds him of spring all year round." She patted the wallpaper, which was flung with rose and blue flowers, hummingbirds hovering intermittently. Sara Will hated it.

"I clean each room once a week," Mrs. Bloxton was saying.

"Of course, I don't expect you'll be here but a few days, will you, Sara?" She was looking at the suitcase Sara had laid on the bed. "I do the bathrooms every other day, but of course I expect cooperation in that regard. There are two bathrooms for six tenants." Mrs. Bloxton sighed and sat down uninvited on the edge of the club chair. Sara stood.

"Oh, dear, I do wish I had a place for you downstairs. If it weren't the holidays I'd so enjoy putting you in my regular guest room beside my very own. But I do have family coming, Sara Will."

"This is fine," Sara replied. She had been afraid to open her mouth. Looking at this room—faded bird prints in chipped frames on the cluttered walls, the worn scatter rugs that served no purpose other than potential injury—she thought she might howl, rise on her toes and screech out her frustration until the room was washed in it, purified, stripped bare of this paltry pretense of home life. There was no home life here.

"I'll take it," she said tightly, intent on holding her distress in a vise. She would not let herself be cajoled into a confession, a baring of the soul. The events that led her to Mrs. Bloxton's door would not be laid out like damaged goods arranged for inspection before being thrown away.

"Oh, well," Mrs. Bloxton said, retreating. "As a rule, I expect to be notified at breakfast when dinner will be taken with us. Breakfast is served between six and eight. Just old Mrs. Holden, who never goes anywhere, comes down for lunch but I generally have the fixings for a sandwich or some sort of fruit to offer if you're here. Sara," she pleaded at the door, "I know something dreadful has happened."

"An accident with the car," Sara said. "But no one was hurt."

When the door had closed, she went quickly to it and turned the lock. The sharp click brought tears to her eyes. She was exhausted, her body limp with grief. No one was hurt, she had said. I am not hurt.

She lay down on the bedspread beside the unopened suitcase, her shoes and coat still on. The window faced east where the light was already fading, settling a purple gloominess on the rented room. She closed her eyes to imagine somewhere else, her own room perhaps, but couldn't conjure it. She could feel this different place on her skin, could smell the dry peculiar air of someone else's existence. It was no use. There was no hiding. She had spent her whole life in secret and now was exposed, her every movement open to scrutiny, visible both to strangers and to people like Mrs. Bloxton, who knew her but did not.

No one knew Sara Will Burney, not unless Fate Jessop did. She had thought he understood her or at least wanted to. Well, the fault was hers. She had thrown herself at him. He had seen her unbend, become pliant; he had read every concession, every pleasant word, as an invitation. Even her hostility had been useful to him. She still remembered the acrimony of their first meeting. She had bowed up right there on the roof, showing by her defensiveness every vulnerable place. It was her own fault that she hadn't been indifferent to him.

Her eyes popped open, surveying in a disheartening gaze the ridiculous room. No! She slapped the suitcase one resounding blow as she sprang up. He wrecked my car! That's what this is all about! Whatever could have happened between herself and Fate Jessop was destroyed now, and he had done it. He had been careless when carelessness wouldn't do. Hadn't he known negligence would be the fatal flaw that could strike her like a scalpel, excising what she believed could have been the beginning of true feeling? Well, she'd never wanted to love anyone, and here was evidence that she'd been right. This room was proof.

She wouldn't stay here. How could she? Within the hour, everybody in this house would know about her. She would exist for people she'd never seen before, people who, under normal circumstances, she would never have spoken to. How could she eat at the same table with them? How could she make conversation or else endure their curious silence? She would not come down. She would go out instead.

But where? She didn't have a car and had never called a cab. She didn't know about eating places. What would be open on the night after Christmas? And money. She didn't have but five dollars in her purse. The first thing tomorrow she'd go to the bank, even before she spoke to the serviceman about repairing the car. She would get herself organized; then she wouldn't have to think about anything, just do. Just function.

Her stomach gnawed. She flattened her hands on her gut, remembering that she hadn't eaten since breakfast. A year's worth of energy had been expended since then. She couldn't think past her hunger; the emptiness reaching into her brain paralyzed any initiative she might have had to escape. The twilight deepened as she sat there on the bed. Gloom fastened on the unfamiliar objects in the room, locking her in shadows. She would have to stay. There was nothing else to do.

She sat there for a long time: hours, it seemed. Then, in the half-light, she opened the suitcase, reached deep into it, under blouses, yellowed cotton panties, and stockings knotted in pairs, until her fingers touched a slick box, rectangular and weighted in her grasp. She started to put the box to her face to whiff the slight hint of jasmine but she stopped herself; instead, she pressed the sharp corners of the carton to her chest, as if such pressure could alleviate the hollowness she felt. It was the first thing she put away.

She went to the table that first evening in a state of sheer emotional exhaustion, depleted like those people who intentionally throw up, never giving nutrients time to work. The meal was more bearable than she could have imagined. She was surprised that, even numb, she could chew and swallow. Everyone seemed to sense her isolation and let her be, or else they simply weren't interested.

The second evening she was truly hungry for she'd spent most of the day walking, seeing on foot the town she'd ignored for years. It was a cold day, the sky so bright that its blue had no depth to it but was shallow and cloudless. The wind blew under her coat and between her legs. She could feel the tension in her pelvis when she started out. Her bones felt locked at the joints, her muscles shriveled. She seemed incapable of responding to even this mild exertion.

She went first to the bank and withdrew a supply of cash, then on to the car dealer, where she was told the parts for her model of Mustang were no longer in stock, not even with the manufacturer. They would have to be ordered from a special dealer who handled "antique" automobiles. Nobody much drives a sixteen-year-old car, she was told. Didn't she think it was time for a trade?

Half condescending, half amused, the dealer droned out his advice while Sara Will studied her image in the glass storefront. She looked eccentric even to herself. Her coat was too short, her feet oversized in old-fashioned shoes with chunky wood-grain heels. Her knit cap was pulled down on her forehead, covering her ears and hair. She had a child's look, impudent but startled, as if she had suddenly realized she might be lost.

"How long for the parts?" she asked, hoping the sound of her voice would change the image she was seeing. Her tone was belligerent, impatient. She watched her old self come back.

"A couple of weeks, three at the most," the dealer said, brought up short by her abruptness. "I'll get in touch with you, Miss Burney. What's the number out there?" Pencil pressed to clipboard, he waited to write.

"I'll check with you," Sara Will said. "No need to call me."

"Yes, ma'am. I'm glad you weren't hurt, Miss Burney." The dealer followed her to the door and caught it as it swung shut behind her. Knowing he was watching her, Sara set herself straight against a gust of wind and marched down the street, denying with every step that she had suffered any kind of injury.

Next she stopped in Broydan's Store and bought a pair of knit stockings made like pantyhose, which she put on in a cubicle in the lounge. Before the mirror, she pulled a few tendrils of hair from under her cap to soften her looks and put Chap Stick on her lips. Because the wind had touched her cheeks, she was not exactly colorless, but she didn't look healthy either. Like someone in chronic pain, there was a dullness in her eyes and a tightness about her mouth. The cords of her neck protruded slightly.

She went into a café and, without shedding her coat or hat, drank a cup of tea at the counter. Even in the new warm stockings she felt chilled, but after the tea she continued walking, incapable of facing the room at Mrs. Bloxton's.

Accustomed as she was to moving swiftly, with purpose, she had to make herself take time. She forced her attention to the store windows, which were still decorated for Christmas. At Broydan's, the tinny melody of "Silent Night, Holy Night" pierced the Thermopane, and she stopped at the window to watch mechanical figures in red-velvet Victorian costumes whose heads nodded and whose hands were raised in constant happy surprise as they circled a lit Christmas tree. How did those things work? she wondered. What were the mechanics of moving mannequins? She wished she could see the connecting wires, the arteries of current that created a facsimile of life in plaster limbs. The empty smiling faces seemed to be aberrations to her, and yet she needed proof they weren't real. The music, a high, hollow one-finger tune intended to evoke all the solemn loneliness, all the watchfulness of that night, shot into her head, a line of sound behind her eyes. It was her own aberrant reflected face she was looking at.

She felt herself crying. Her body shook inside as if she were shivering with a dangerous chill, but she knew it was tears coming up to choke in her chest and spew their bitterness in her throat. She pressed her eyelids hard, but the tears squeezed around them, slipped down in two stinging streams on her wind-burned cheeks. She continued to face the display while rummaging through her bag for a tissue. People pressed behind her, not noticing. Everyone was going somewhere, had business to attend to, family to care for, someplace to be. She had given all that up. She had said no to one kind of pain and now found it replaced with another. Was there no way to live without suffering?

She blew into the tissue and collected herself. It had been the briefest outburst but she was left exhausted, too tired to move another step. She looked about to see where she was. She would rest for a minute in the reading room of the library a few doors down.

But it was closed. A handwritten note wished the patrons a Merry Christmas and reminded them the library would reopen on December 28. Sara Will rested on the stoop for a moment and then went on her way, forcing herself to go slowly. She wandered through a nearby residential section for a while, found herself staring at brown grass, thick beds of mulch, bare dogwoods with hard closed buds, firs strung with lights which would flash on at twilight. The houses were closed up, unwelcoming except for smoke rising from the chimneys, the occasionally banging back door followed by a teenager racing across a yard or jumping into a car and screeching out into the street. The houses themselves seemed to be recuperating. She passed Swanee Hope's old house, had gone beyond it before she realized this was it. Swanee had had it painted last summer with Williamsburg colors, dull gray with deep red door and shutters she had fretted about for months. It was really quite lovely, even with the limp winter shrubbery and dead grass. Sara Will liked it. She would have to tell Swanee. Maybe they would even consider those colors for her own house. She would find out if siding came in gray and she and Fate could paint the door themselves.

How could I be thinking that? she wondered and walked on.

It was almost dark when she arrived at the boardinghouse. She went straight to her room, hung up her coat, and waited behind the door until she was sure the bathroom was clear. Her hair had loosened under the knit cap, and she repinned it into a knot at her neck and applied cream to her cheeks and chin. The bathroom was bright with new porcelain and a gigantic mirror.

She forced herself to find her eyes in the mirror. She looked teary from the wind. There were crinkly marks around her eyes and her bottom lip was torn slightly at the center, but she didn't look conspicuously ill. I am not going to die, she said into the mirror and then looked at herself in surprise. She hadn't known she'd been thinking that but now she saw it was true. Yesterday and through the night, even while she walked today, she had been afraid she couldn't survive. She had believed change was life-threatening. Now she saw it wasn't. Painful, yes. Even terrifying, but not fatal.

She went down to dinner and took the same place at table she'd taken the night before. Only three tenants were there, elderly Mrs. Holden, who smiled at Sara whenever their eyes met, and two men who worked at the mill. Damp, sweet air encircled them as they bent over Mrs. Bloxton's beef stew, talking to each other between steaming bites. She was grateful to be ignored.

After dinner there was nothing to do except watch television in the lounge Mrs. Bloxton had provided in what had once been her front room. Her good furniture had been replaced by wooden-framed chairs with loose cushions. The stain-resistant end tables were stacked with old magazines, and the carpet was worn in an obvious traffic pattern from door to television to the row of chairs. The room felt like a dingy waiting room. Sara Will selected a magazine without even looking at it and went upstairs.

She went to bed early and at first she slept soundly. The hard deep sleep of physical exhaustion pressed into every muscle until she felt as heavy as a stone, but by two o'clock that sleep was over. She surfaced with every nerve on edge, as if she'd been drowning and could only be saved by sucking in air. The room was cool but she was wringing wet.

It's a hot flash after all these years, she thought. She lay there sweltering, not wanting to get up in the chilly room. Finally she turned back the blanket so only the sheet covered her. The room was well lit from the streetlight. She could see where she was, could make out her own form in the bed. Her body seemed too small. She ran her hand over her chest, across her breasts, down to her stomach, reaching to one thigh. She could feel her fingers trembling. It wasn't her own hand on her skin but raw nerves out of control, not recognizing what they touched. She was alien to herself.

You are all right, she thought, but even the imagined sound of her voice was wrong. A whiny note had made it weak and powerless. Pressure seemed to be accumulating in her stomach. Like a gigantic tear, it rippled upward, attacking every bone and muscle, traveling in her blood, filling her chest so she couldn't breathe but was stopped short by it, paralyzed on the strange bed, in the wretched rented room. No one would come. No one cared enough to listen at the door for the sound of her breathing; no one expected her footfall on the stairs.

What is this? she said aloud, but no sound came because there was no air left in her lungs. What am I feeling?

Fear, she answered, this is fear. "Then it will go away," she said, now speaking to herself in a whisper as she collected this one thought out of the frenzy in her brain. Fear does not last forever. Waiting, her hands clasped firmly across her stomach to keep herself from springing into madness, she finally fell into fretful sleep.

20

◆ Every morning she awoke early and lay in bed listening to sounds from the adjacent bathroom. The men, due at the mill by seven o'clock, left a little before the hour. This morning at seven fifteen, the sloshing of bath water told her Miss Emory was in the tub. Miss Emory, who did alterations and clerked when the need arose at Baldree's Men's Wear, always came to breakfast dressed to the teeth, high-necked lacy collars with round pearl buttons on thin georgette blouses, wool skirts that rolled up slightly at her hips and were too short for Sara Will's taste.

According to Mrs. Bloxton, Miss Emory had arrived at the boardinghouse several years ago in pursuit of one Mr. Phillips, a training manager at the mill whose expertise included the workings of a new piece of equipment capable of spinning filament into thread twenty times faster than the old machinery. She had obviously been following him from mill to mill because she had a dusty, homeless look; a frantic expression of hurry quivered on her face when she looked at him, as though she suspected he might bolt before she could catch up. It was on Mrs. Bloxton's front stoop that Mr. Phillips finally informed Miss Emory of his intention to return to his wife and two sons, where he hoped to recover from the miseries of transient life—chronic indigestion, athlete's foot, and lower back pain—which had plagued him for years. In response, Miss Emory slapped him so hard Mrs. Bloxton thought by the sound of it he'd been shot. She got to the door in time to see the man staggering backward, blood pouring from his nose onto his shirtfront and coloring the air as he flung his head back and frantically sought his hip pocket for a handkerchief. He didn't have one. In her brokenhearted fury, Miss Emory watched his agony for only a moment before she pulled him to her, cradled his head in her arms, and pinched his nostrils together so tightly he began to gasp, his eyes wild and mouth gaping like someone trying to scream but with no wind for it. Meanwhile Mrs. Bloxton raced out with a bowl of cold water dripping onto a roll of toilet tissue caught in the crook of her finger. Her intention was to clean Mr. Phillips up but instead, seeing them locked together as obscene as two dogs stuck in the act, she threw the pan of water straight into their faces.

Mrs. Bloxton was certain Miss Emory had not forgiven her

yet, although she'd continued to live in the room to the left of Sara Will's for three years, apparently having no place else to go. It was not, Mrs. Bloxton contended, so much the cold splash of water drenching the two of them that Miss Emory resented as it was the fact that Mrs. Bloxton had been a witness to her madness.

Finding the bathroom empty at quarter of eight, Sara Will studied her own unhappy face in the mirror. She couldn't imagine living here three years or even three more days. Perhaps Lorene Emory had no choice, but Sara Will did. She had a home to go to, a sister, two teenagers in her care, a baby she longed to hold, a man she—she what? What did her face tell her? She felt a wet rush behind her eyes. That she hated her own peevishness, her self-pity, her way of thinking that put a car before a person. She was as bereft as Lorene Emory.

I have to let this feeling go, she said to her reflection. I have to. She opened her mouth intending to scream. The noise she heard was so strident and piercing she thought she must have alarmed the household with it. At any moment Mrs. Bloxton would be knocking at the door demanding an explanation for the disturbance she had caused. The wail continued, filling her up, unstoppable until it died of its own accord. The house was quiet. She knew she hadn't made a sound.

Down at the breakfast table, Sara Will forced a sympathetic smile in Miss Emory's direction. She wasn't surprised to find no response in the angrily made-up face. It was a face painted against bereavement, resistant to any emotion. I have cried for you, Sara Will wanted to say but didn't. The words were there, heavy and wet in her throat, but she couldn't speak them. She had never learned the language of care.

Michael found her. She was coming out of the lunchroom where she'd dawdled over the daily special, when he fastened to her arm and pulled her back into the warmth.

"I'm leaving," he said, still holding her arm as if he were about to embrace her. The cold off his clothing set her trembling, or was it the urgency in his voice? He was doing something while she waited.

"I've already left," she said, thinking she should pull away but not really wanting to. Suddenly she felt flooded with emotion at being almost in someone's arms. She had missed human contact that much, enough to raise her hands to his cold cheeks. "When will you be back?" she asked him.

"There's a spring break sometime around Easter. I'll come then, or sooner if need be. The only way I know to love Eva right now is to leave her alone. Are you all right, Sara?" His eyes, seen through the thick lenses, were glassy and almost colorless. He could have been handsome were it not for the eyes.

As artificial as they seemed, Sara Will knew he could see into her. He was questioning every movement of her face. Her lips trembled, chin out of control. "Oh, Michael," she said, "I feel like I'm the only person in the world."

"It's the same with him," Michael started but then saw she couldn't listen. Already her fingers were fluttering away from his face; her arms tensed under his hands as if trying to break contact. "Well, write to me if you want to. Here's the address." He pushed a bit of paper from his pocket into her hand. "And Sara, thanks for everything."

She stood at the window and watched him revving the motorcycle. The sound sawed through the glass at her. What would happen between now and spring? She turned away from the window, not wanting him to see her there so hopelessly perplexed. She wanted to cry out, Tell me what to do, Michael. You're young and fearless and determined; tell me. But she waited too long. When she looked again, he was gone.

Time was her enemy; there was too much of it. She called the Ford place and learned that the fender and bumper for the Mustang had been shipped but she shouldn't expect to have the car for another week. She hoped the dealer would offer her a used car in the interim, but he didn't and she wouldn't ask. There was no rental company listed in the yellow pages and only one number for taxi service. Her only escape from her cell at Mrs. Bloxton's was to walk.

The days had become warmer, a false spring in the middle of winter, and the air smelled clean and slightly damp, like fresh wet laundry. She could see the smoke from the mill blowing away from town across the ridge instead of settling in a gauzy haze over the valley as it frequently did. She had always resented the mill, although she knew its having been converted to a synthetic-fiber operation was what had kept the little town alive. It was the dam she really hated. She despised the engineering that had turned her valley into a power source, that tamed water but refused to be of use in the building of a bridge.

On the street, she reinforced her isolation, refusing to smile. She stopped greetings that threatened to form on her lips and cast her eyes downward when someone she knew approached. She cringed inside, her face frozen as they passed. But all this energy focused on avoidance hurt her. She felt damaged by it. How much more could she take, weakened as she was by the rigors of her exile?

She couldn't stop thinking about the past. The future seemed totally out of reach but there was no relief from memory, which came uninvited, filling the empty spaces of her days with sights and sounds she thought she'd forgotten. Walking, oblivious of where she was until she found herself stopped in front of a familiar place—the home of an old friend, the theater where she used to see the matinees, the funeral home where she went alone to arrange for her mother's funeral—the memories shot through her one by one, diligent in their detail.

"I have to go somewhere else. Let me go," her mother had moaned during those last bitter days of consciousness which now seemed so close, like yesterday, to Sara. "I have to leave this pain here and go."

Impelled to press those thin, arched shoulders to the bed, Sara Will had anchored her mother in her misery while the woman railed against her weary, sputtering heart and against Sara too.

It was Sara she was mad at, not Swanee, who came bringing a quarter of a fresh-baked cake, a new magazine, or a floral arrangement of pink carnations to brighten the dying light in the room. Thanked profusely and treated to tea, Swanee would sit by the bed, infused with love and duty and fear, and babble on and on about what was happening in Tyler Mills, gossip interwoven with good wishes sent by friends and acquaintances of hers whom her mother had never known. Mama was always tired and complaining after Swanee left, although Sara knew there would be recriminations if Swanee failed to appear every other day in the late afternoon, when Mama was generally at her best. Their mother never wanted Swanee to see her undressed, the iridescent skin of her thin arms, the misshapen chest where heart and lungs bulged against a brittle rail of bone, the swollen legs and feet, skin so tight and rosy even the gentlest touch seemed apt to burst them. Swanee would be protected while Sara saw everything, endured everything, until one day Mama put a stop to the sham they had been playing out.

"Be quiet," she said, interrupting Swanee's chatter with that snapping voice her daughters knew meant business. "Don't you know this is no time for foolishness?"

It turned out to be the last thing Mama said to Swanee, because that night she finally pulled herself free of the pain and never spoke coherently to anyone again; Sara, once in constant demand, hated the apathy that followed more than her mother's angry resistance. The friction between the two women as they battled against the seeping heart had inspired them both, but now there was nothing for Sara to do but watch the feathery motions of death, her mother's hands hovering about her face and neck as if in search of some memory of herself, something to take hold of.

A week later there was a sudden clutching in her mother's chest, a hard pull like string stretched, then the loud singing sigh of an arrow sailing free. Sara had gripped the cool railing of the rented hospital bed while she put her other hand against the shattered heart. She stood there a long time, until both her hands were cool, while that one moment of infinite loneliness stretched on and on, encumbered with a slow dragging ache she knew would never peak or lift her on its crest to take her beyond caring.

It was the same loneliness she felt now; during the past days, an old wound of loss she had thought healed was festering again. Would love always leave her injured?

She moved on the sidewalk, wondering if she'd made a spectacle of herself by standing there locked in memory for so long. No one seemed to notice her. Over the last few days, she had made herself invisible; knowing that, she felt unexpectedly sad.

Back at Mrs. Bloxton's, her mother's memory as close as each dry shuddering breath she drew, it came to Sara that there was no leaving the pain she felt, no true fleeing from affliction short of dying. She lay on her back, longing to fold her arms protectively across her chest or curl up on her side but refusing to. She was determined to keep her body still, to think without closing her mind to all the dark hidden suffering that now seemed unavoidable to her. Dying is not the hardest thing a person ever does, she thought. Sometimes living is harder.

A note came, hand-delivered by a crippled man in an old truck. Mrs. Bloxton laid it in Sara Will's hand and saw her squeeze her fingers around it as if to spill the words out without even looking at them. She took the crumpled paper to the window, her back to Mrs. Bloxton until she heard the door close.

I should be the one to go, she read in a careful, childish hand she had never seen before. *I should, Sara, but I can't because it would break my heart to give you up.*

She pressed the paper against her hand, trying to flatten the wrinkles she had made. Her hands wouldn't be still. The paper shook.

What did he know about broken hearts? She was the one who had questioned her mother's doctor. It was she who furtively drew books off the library shelf to memorize diagrams and explanations. She knew the feel of a rapid pulse, had heard the whispery cry of breathlessness. She knew about slow leaks, bluish skin, the gray edges of afternoon slipping into despairing night when nothing could be done. She knew a heart could stop without breaking, no explosion necessary, nothing dramatic to relate, just a cold weight in the chest, a fixed stare, an expression of disbelief forever trapped on waxen skin.

Why, her own heart had stopped that way. At a moment she couldn't even recall, perhaps in her twenties although she couldn't remember how she looked or felt—maybe it was too gradual to notice—her heart had stopped, her life had stopped simply because she hadn't the courage to get on with it.

A few miles away—oh, how far it seemed!—was her house. She saw, peering out into the early evening which closed around her with its pearly dark, how the house had been her fortress, a prison, and how she had kept the gate. She had locked herself in and others out while the key, as heavy as any jailer's chain, had dangled against her chest, striking worrisome little blows, thumping where her heart should have been.

But she had found her heart now. Alone in a rented room, living a borrowed restless life, hermetically sealed against any invasion, she laid her fearful hand on her own heart just as she'd put her palm against her mother's chest years ago. She expected the same—a shuddering that hesitated and then was dead—but she heard instead a pounding so urgent she thought she might cry out with it. She wanted to go home! Not to the old emptiness, not to barred doors and curtains pulled tight to keep complications out, but to a sister and a teenager with a baby, and to a man who could make her smile. She wanted it all.

21

◆ The taxi that took her home was a last resort. There was no one she could ask for a ride, and she hadn't the courage to deal with Fate yet. She had to give the driver directions. Leaning back to make himself heard over the ragged engine, he shouted to her that he had never had a call out toward Sparrow Creek. The car, smelling heavily of oily exhaust, lurched along on six of its eight cylinders. A pink plastic hand waved in the rear window as they went.

Nobody came out. Sara dragged her bag across the seat and out the door, then paid the man in a fog of fumes. When he'd pulled away, she stood there trying to breathe as the air cleared around her. Nothing felt right. Of course she had no experience with homecomings, was without a frame of reference for the throbbing excitement she suddenly felt.

She had left home only once before, to ride a Trailways bus with her Aunt Saluda and Uncle Charles to Petersburg to visit their daughter. Mama had insisted she go. "You should see something of the world," she had said, although they both knew crossing North Carolina into Virginia did not amount to much of a glimpse. The real purpose of her going was to take care of Aunt Saluda and Uncle Charles, who were as helpless as children outside of Sparrow Creek.

At Durham, Uncle Charles insisted they get off the bus. Nothing Sara Will could say could disprove his contention that another passenger, a young man in a greasy fedora and drab green work clothes who had boarded near Greensboro and taken a seat across the aisle and two rows behind them, was a convict recognized from an FBI poster left hanging in the Tyler Mills Post Office for fifteen years. Uncle Charles had seen the poster long enough to have the face indelibly marked in his frazzled brain, although Sara Will reckoned that fifteen years ago this suspect couldn't have been more than fifteen himself.

There was, however, no convincing Uncle Charles, who stood in the aisle, his neck bulging defiantly out of the starched collar of his one dress shirt, his bag clutched firmly in his hand as he waited for his wife and niece to follow him before they could be savagely relieved of their valuables and the hundred-dollar bill Uncle Charles had in his left shoe. The suspect, who was reading a *Farm Journal,* his thick hand wrapped around the curled binding as he frowned in concentration over a soybean article, never even noticed them.

In the bus station, Sara Will took matters in hand to adjust the tickets without offering an explanation to the stationmaster, who didn't seem to care that three bedraggled countryfolk waited two unnecessary hours in the terminal. Sara sat, sullen and uncommunicative in a straight wooden chair, not looking at either of them, not even poor Aunt Saluda, who, Sara felt, deserved such treatment for having put up with Uncle Charles all these years.

When they finally reached Petersburg, the daughter was waiting at the station, her special dinner ruined, worry written on her hostile face, exasperation in her tone when she spoke to Sara Will, who had, after all, come along to make sure something like this didn't happen.

Sara Will took the bus home the next afternoon, unable to endure her cousin's fine suburban house, her noisy children, her picky reminders that there were ways of handling senile relations who didn't know their own minds. She rode all night, taking restless catnaps interrupted by the glaring streetlights of nameless towns. In the morning, Swanee Hope was there at the station to drive her home in Jonathan's Studebaker. In the car, Swanee made her laugh, although Sara was exhausted and longed for a poached egg on thick toast, a warm bath, and then a long sleep in her own bed. Swanee had seen the humor in Uncle Charles's behavior that Sara couldn't find, and she delighted in telling the story over and over until the trip took on the air of an adventure. Eventually, when the miseries of the journey were dissipated by time and Swanee's rendition of events seemed more true than not, Sara Will was glad to have gone.

"Why, Sara, it's you," Swanee Hope said through a crack in the door. She opened it wider but didn't come out. "I heard an automobile, but I didn't think it would be you. I'm here alone, Sister."

Sara turned wet inside, knees like sponges. He had left. The note had meant nothing or else had been a trick. She had been duped. She couldn't hold her bag any longer, the weight of it pulled at her shoulder socket, but she couldn't let go either. Her fingers gripping were the only things she was sure of—the fingers of her left hand held her to ground, prevented evaporation like a puff of damp smoke hitting clean air. Wait. Who then had Swanee thought the car was?

"Where is he?" she breathed.

"He took Eva and the baby into town to the doctor. Rachel woke up in the night as hot as a pudding. We tried everything—baby aspirin, alcohol rubs, even dipped her in cool water while she screamed her poor little head off. Lordy, what a night it turned out to be! So now they've taken her in to the pediatrician. It's strep throat or something like that," she added confidently. "There's a shot now for everything, not like the old days when babies died of diarrhea and chest colds. Medicine out of mold—now there's a miracle drug for you. Come in the house, Sara. Aren't you cold out there?"

She sat in her own kitchen at her own place and drank a cup of coffee. They were using her mother's china cups, taken out of storage for the Christmas party. There was still a holiday fragrance in the air, a smell of spice and evergreen.

"I just made pumpkin bread," Swanee said. "Have some, Sara."

But Sara refused. She felt uncomfortable, apprehensive. "I should unpack," she said finally, because Swanee wasn't talking to her. Most of her life she'd wished Swanee would shut up, but now she longed for any conversation that would take up time and interfere with her having to think beyond this minute.

"There's plenty of time to do that," Swanee said, "unless you're planning to do something stupid."

Sara couldn't tell if Swanee was serious or not. "I'm not planning anything," Sara said.

"Well, that's a relief. I thought you'd come out here with an ultimatum or something equally ridiculous. I thought maybe you hadn't learned a thing."

"I thought you'd come to see me," Sara said. "You knew where I was."

"What point would there have been? Besides, maybe I thought you ought to suffer some. Is that mean, and spiteful too? Maybe so, but you haven't let yourself have any feelings for so long, I thought you needed to get used to having some. I couldn't help you do that, Sara, even if I wanted to."

"Fate sent me a note," Sara said. "I think he has feelings for me, Swanee. I don't know where they came from or how it could be. I don't know anything about it."

"Some people can see through your smoke screen, Sara, whether you want them to or not. I know you've always thought if you were thorny enough, nobody would try to pluck the rose."

Sara couldn't help but smile. This was the old Swanee, unable to resist any romantic notion that sprung into her head.

"This is not one of your television shows," she said, trying to find the old tone of irritation that had always been so easy to come by. Instead, her voice was light with excitement and fright. "It's real life I'm talking about."

"And about time, too." Swanee sighed agreeably. "You're the same, Sara. I don't expect you'll ever change very much, but I do believe Fate Jessop has found a soft spot." She went on, breathless herself. It seemed strange that there was so much of real consequence to talk about. "I suppose you know Michael's gone. Eva's called him twice already. Never mind about the phone bill—I'll pay it. She's so sweet about it, she gets all whis-

232

pery and serious when what have they got to say to each other we can't all hear? She misses him, Sara. I think something's bound to come of it one of these first days." She stopped, frozen to a sound. "That's the truck now. I hear it coming!"

Sara was up the stairs and in her room before the motor stopped.

"Where is she?"

She could hear him from the moment the front door opened and he saw the suitcase she'd left there by the stair. He wasn't shouting or even speaking loudly, but she heard him clearly, as she would were he out in the hall, already on his way to her. "Swanee, where is she?"

Rachel was crying; her exhausted sobs trailed his question up the stairs.

"How is the little darling?" Swanee was asking. They were coming to her door. Rachel's cries turned to whimpers, heavy shudders of feverish breath Sara could almost feel.

"It's strep. The culture won't be ready until tomorrow, but the doctor's put her on penicillin drops, he's so sure what it is. Now we've got to get it in her."

"Just hold her nose," Swanee said, her voice soothing as if she were talking to Rachel. "That's what we used to do. Hold their nose, they open up to breathe, and you pop the medicine in. Works every time."

"It sounds criminal," Eva said. They were entering the room across the hall. "But we'll do it."

"Sara!"

He was coming. She had only seconds to reason out her actions, to consider the unthinkable. What would she do in his arms? The thought paralyzed her, closed off her brain against logic, put her to imagining. It wasn't that she hadn't been in a man's arms before. There had been high school boys with heavy embraces she had squeezed free of, dancing partners who held her loosely through a familiar two-step, and then Frank Settlemyer with his dry Old Spice scent and smooth, almost beardless cheek. All during the years they had been considered a couple, something thin and dry like parchment paper had always seemed to be between them, keeping them apart. Oh, thought Sara, it was I who provided the distance. Even with her hand held, her shoulder caressed, she was unapproachable. She had thwarted him with her persistent indifference. How much energy, perspiration, sheer power would it take to move her? he must have wondered. Was it worth the effort to separate mind from matter, to make Sara Will Burney generous? Frank Settlemyer had thought not.

But with Fate it would be so easy. With him, she would be taken apart. She knew that. She could feel it happening already. He would touch her face—oh, how she longed to be touched like that!—fingers along her jaw, ensnaring her ear, thumb on her cheek where the bone was so close that even the gentlest touch could go inside her. His hand on her face, then in her hair, fingers pressing to her scalp. With his hand he could press his will into her brain. One hand. If only there were two. She longed to make him whole for both their sakes.

She was so terrified. Her longing terrified her. What if he saw? What if it was written on her face?

The knock at her door seemed distant, even imaginary. Two quick fluttering raps intended not to alarm her, so soft she could pretend she hadn't heard at all. But she had heard. She had actually strained her ears to listen for his step on the stairs, to hear the sound of his breathing, measuring with every breath the distance he had traveled. If it were possible, she would have put her hand flat against the door to hold the knocking, to keep it in her memory. All this atunement was what she wanted, but it was too hard for her. She had never paid such attention to another person, and so all she could do was stand in the middle of her bedroom, hands tightly clasped at her waist, waiting for the event to spring at her. She could see her pulse throbbing at her wrist; one small rhythmic flutter of blue vein was all the proof she had she was alive.

The door creaked open just a crack—why, she hadn't locked

it!—and a hand appeared at the edge. "Sara," he said, and there he was before her looking simply terrible, his hair brittle with static, clothes askew, a spot of slobber on his jacket where Rachel's face had been, a crinkly, anxious, tearful smile ready to break his face. He seemed so fragile to her, so close to exposure that she wanted to stop him, more for his sake than for her own. Any moment now he would be revealed to her, his feelings pouring out of that broken face, the old facade of carefulness shattered between them. She knew he was willing to do that, to lay open to her the man he was. But was she ready for it? Could she say the right words? Could she open her arms that now seemed frozen to her sides? She had done so much harm already, how could she be sure there wouldn't be more wounding between them? Hers was the saber tongue, hers the cold shoulder, the stony gaze set to avoidance. How could she be sure she wouldn't use those old and ready weapons against him again?

"Forgive me, Sara," he said, and a place inside her opened. She could feel it, a gentle unfolding, a slight rippling movement. Her tightly clasped hands drew away from each other, curling outward until her palms were open and almost ready to reach.

"I do love you, Sara," he said now, and the sound of it broke over her like a silky wave she would drown in.

"Sh-h-h-h," she whispered and went to hold him.

22

✦ Early in the morning Fate would go out to the boat. Opening the latch to the barn where the Mustang used to be, he would stand for a moment in the cold gray sunlight and watch the light play on the pale bow of cypress he had scraped clean. The boat was beautiful to him, especially early like this when he approached it in silence, just he and the boat, both of them frigid with cold until he warmed them up with the steady motion of the sandpaper. The sides of the boat would slowly become smooth and warm under his hand, just as he felt his own body warming, muscles loosening with the steady exertion of stroking the wood.

He had bought it while Sara was away, having seen an ad in the paper for a used motorboat. He drove to the address in Tyler Mills without mentioning it to Swanee or Eva, just to have a look. He didn't know much about boats and thought he might be on a fool's errand. He saw right away it suffered from neglect. The paint was splintery; the motor hadn't been pulled in a long time and was rusting in places. Some of the fittings would have to be replaced, the motor overhauled, the boat itself scraped and painted. It felt sound, though.

The elderly woman who had placed the ad told him her husband had paid a good price for the boat years ago when the dam was built, expecting to spend his retirement fishing on the lake. He'd used it quite a lot the first few years, then lost interest. They had thought about selling it several times but never got around to it. Now her husband was dead and she wanted the boat out of her garage for good.

Fate borrowed the money from Swanee, who wanted to give it to him. "I know what it's for," she said. "It's to take Sara to the cemetery." She had tears in her eyes.

So did he. He took the check she'd written, folded it into his pocket, and with his good arm pulled her into an embarrassed embrace. It baffled them both that they were standing there hugging and crying on each other over Sara Will.

"I knew the first minute I laid eyes on you that you were a good person, Swanee," Fate said. He let her go so he could wipe his face on his sleeve.

"I could say the same about you," Swanee said. "I just wonder if Sara's ever going to see it."

"The boat's not something I'm doing to win her over," Fate

said. Sometimes he wasn't sure why he did things, sometimes he didn't want to know, but this time he was sure and he saw the possibility of Swanee's understanding. "Taking her over there is what I want to do whether she cares about me or not." He wanted to see her face with the wind blowing in it while they went. He wanted to make a path for her to the cemetery so he could lead the way and look back and see her coming behind him. He wanted to see her standing there at Serena's grave and then pulling the weeds away and running her hand over the name like Eva said she did in the cemetery down the road. "We'll probably need a machete and an ax and Lord knows what-all to clean the place up."

"The important thing is that you want to do this for her," Swanee said.

First he pulled the motor and got it running. It was twenty-five horsepower, plenty big for the sixteen-foot boat. The intake valves were clogged and the throttle cables needed replacing, but the propeller and drive shaft were in good shape. For several days he worked on the mechanics. The finish on the winch was rusty, but the gears were smooth and sound. Close inspection showed him the galvanized trailer was in good condition, but he needed to buy new tie-downs and a synthetic rope for the anchor. He'd put a trailer hitch on the truck and had wired up the brake light just to get the boat home.

By the time Sara Will came back, all that was done and he had begun working on the boat itself. He didn't mention it to her that first night after Eva had gotten Rachel to sleep, her body finally cool with penicillin and liquid aspirin. Eva fell into bed herself, exhausted by her first ordeal of baby illness, and Swanee followed because she wanted to get out of the way. Sara and Fate were left alone in the parlor before the fire. All the Christmas decorations had been put away, the foolish angel stored at the bottom of a box of Swanee's tree ornaments.

"It seems like a lifetime ago since Christmas when we were here like this," Fate said.

"I think we were just caught up in the moment, Fate," Sara

said. "Maybe that's all there was to it." She was sitting beside him on the sofa, looking at the fire instead of him. Her profile had shadows in it, and Fate longed to touch the contours, search out the hidden places of her face, but he was very still.

"You read my note?" he asked. He wanted to ask if she'd come home because of it, but he didn't dare.

"Yes."

"That next morning after you left, I almost went myself. I didn't want to be here without you, Sara. How can I tell you what it was like? In some ways I reckon I had felt it before, when Vickie left me. Once you've had a feeling like that, a loneliness so hard it knocks you down, you don't forget what it feels like. But this was different, too." He hesitated, anxious to tell her his feelings in a rush of words but knowing the good sense of going slowly. "This is so much your house, Sara, and when you're not here, it's truly empty. It felt cold everywhere. Waking up in the morning, I'd lie there wondering what was wrong. I could feel something out of whack right when I opened my eyes. I don't even know how to English it out so you'll understand how it felt when I remembered you weren't here. I wasn't going to see you in the kitchen looking like a little girl who needs tending—you never get your hair put up exactly right first thing and your cheeks are always puffy when you get up, you wear those funny little thin socks like old men wear and that robe that's about to fall apart. You always look startled, too, like every single morning you're surprised to see me. But you were getting used to me, Sara. I know you were. God, I wish I could tell you how I missed talking to you. Every little thing you ever said mattered. I remember it. I noticed things about you, too. Not just your way of putting things or how you cut your eyes or the sound you make stretching, but things like a button missing on your sweater or the way you lift each biscuit off a hot pan with the tips of just two fingers or the shape of that mole on your neck, just here." He reached out and put his hand beneath her ear where she didn't even know a mole existed. "You see, I had so many things to miss." His fingers moved to her cheek and rested there, one finger ready to catch a tear.

She had never been so touched. "I was angry," she began softly, refusing to cry. She would not succumb to a swelling heart before she'd had her say. "And then I was frightened. I had abdicated my life, it seemed, and there was no way back to it. I hadn't the courage to do anything but grieve. I hated it there; I suppose I would hate anyplace but this house. I'm not very adaptable, Fate. I never was and never will be. I don't expect I'll ever be much different from the way I am today."

"I don't want you different, Sara. I just want you here." He drew his hand away as if he feared his touch could be coercive. He wanted to be honest now. "I want to wake up knowing the day is going to be full of you. I've never wanted anything so much in my whole life."

She caught his hand and held it in her lap. "I didn't want you to drive the car. That's how possessive I am. That's how stubborn."

"I know."

"I didn't want you to stay here at all. You remember how I acted. I have a mean streak."

"I know."

"I've spent my whole life feeling obligations, but I must have wanted to feel that way. I wanted to be tied down. It was easier than anything else. I don't regret doing what I've done, except that now I'm awkward and unpleasant and set in my ways because of it."

"I know."

"But right now, right this very minute"—she squeezed his hand so hard it hurt—"I want to be different. I want to be witty and brave and easygoing. I want to be all the things you'd want."

"You are."

"No."

"All right, I admit you're as disagreeable as the devil." Fate

239

was grinning. "Don't you know, Sara, I've loved you the most when you were the maddest?"

She moved closer until she was resting her head on his shoulder, not quite relaxed but willing to be. "I don't know what we're getting into," she said.

"There's no rush about it—unless, of course, you're planning another vacation."

"Don't talk to me about that. It was your fault, you know." Her voice had that old fractious tone that seemed natural to her, but there was playfulness in it, too, and she didn't move away.

"It's a contentious woman who bears a grudge." Fate touched her forehead with his lips.

She sighed, soothed by his gentleness, the quiet of her house, the firelight that held them close. "Fate," she whispered.

"Hm-m-m?"

"Nothing." She didn't know how to tell him she was thinking of giving him keys to her car. Oh, well, she thought, it's a big decision. Probably she should give the idea more consideration. She nestled closer to him, almost dozing. She would think about it. There was no sense in rushing into anything. Time, so recently her enemy, became dear as she leaned against him. She felt herself becoming subdued, content. Minutes passed, measuring with solemn clicks the peacefulness in the room. The clock and the soft crackling fire were the only sounds.

"What are you thinking?" Fate asked suddenly in her ear.

She was astounded at how easily the spell could be broken. Her reverie was snapped like a piece of kindling and she sat up, bolting with her old testiness. All the comfort she'd felt as she'd rested against his shoulder—he had seemed like an old chair perfectly fitted to her shape—evaporated with his voice. It was a person she leaned into, someone who could disturb her quiet, who expected response, to be noticed and cared for when kindness had always been so hard for her. Would he never let anything be?

She pulled away, but even as she recoiled, she knew she felt as much at odds with her irritation as she did with him. Her old reactions didn't feel right anymore. She strained against them like a bear tugging at the claws of a trap. If she pulled free, she would leave part of herself there.

Fate felt her stiffen and he moved away, too, and stood up. He blocked from her view the red crumbling center of the last log, but she heard it fall into the ashes. The sparks tossed around his legs. She felt cold, although the room was warm in every cranny. It was her anger that put a chill under her skin. Her rage had never been hot, never white heat or a hearty flame that could be extinguished. No, for years it had been cool, living in dark hidden places like a fungus. It had given her a sharp tongue, nettles to stick unsuspecting victims, a cold piercing eye trained to find fault. There had never been an equal to her bitterness, no affection to pour out measure by measure against her ire, no warmth to temper her steel. Now, looking up at him, she saw there could be. He spoke, he laughed, he held babies and stoked fires. He stretched before the hearth, casting his own shadow across her heart. Here he was, willing to love every cantankerous part of her, to warm every chill. She needed only to be patient, to give him a chance. There was enough goodness in him for both of them.

"We ought to turn in," he said, seeing that her frown had eased away. He reached down to pull her up. She came easily, like a stone finally nudged loose from a rutty field. "There's something I want to show you in the morning."

"What?"

"Never you mind."

"Tell me."

"In the morning." He kissed her cheek, then moved his mouth over hers. "You're going to be here in the morning, aren't you?"

"In the kitchen at seven o'clock," she said, her arms locked around his neck.

"It's a date. Now you go on up and I'll bank this fire."

Reluctantly she let her arms fall and, without saying another word, went upstairs. Later, when she was in bed, she heard him moving on the stairs. He paused at her door and then went on. She lay there waiting to hear sounds from the bathroom, then his door closing. The house was quiet. She wondered how he slept; if, like her, he turned on his side away from the empty space. "Oh, Fate," she whispered, and the sound seemed to echo in the room, resounding until it took the place of her breathing, her heartbeat, her frenzied pattern of scattered thought. It filled her up with dreamless sleep until the morning came.

After breakfast he took her out to the barn. He thought, as he led her by the hand across the crusty grass, that he was inviting her into his soul. The boat meant that much to him. It was the only thing he'd done in many years that felt exactly right to him, a pure act unhampered by selfish motives or dishonesty. First there had been the engine to attend to. He had a mechanic's mind, a hand that remembered tools, and so that was the part he'd expected to do well. It was the contact with wood that had surprised him. In just a few days, he'd come to love the boat, to treasure the ribs that held the belly tight, the rich raw odor of wood freed of blistery paint. The boat seemed to expand as if he had single-handedly released it from restraints of neglect. Working, he had felt both himself and the boat becoming useful.

He fumbled with the latch while Sara stood beside him, her arms folded across her breasts for warmth. She was wearing an old turtleneck sweater and his new coat flung around her shoulders. She looked apprehensive and smaller than she was.

The latch sprang loose and he pulled on the door. The hinges creaked and then, giving way to the force of his hand, let go and the door swung open. He didn't know whether to look at her or at the boat. Which did he love more, or was it the same love? Wasn't the boat his attempt to put how he felt beyond words, to act out every silent promise he had ever made to Sara

Will? This was the care he would take, the commitment he would make, if she would only let him.

"What is it?" she asked. Her voice seemed small. She hadn't moved a step but stood looking at the bow straight on. The morning light was so new it barely illuminated beyond the stripped and sanded nose.

"It's a boat, Sara," Fate said. "Come on. You can't see it from there. Look here, I've scraped halfway down the port side. This is the port side, Sara. It's the left side when you're in the boat, which makes it the right side from where you're standing. Of course, you wouldn't be standing in the water, would you, so you can just remember that the port side is the left. The right is starboard. It's simple, Sara." He reached out to pull her inside but she wouldn't come. Her damp sneakers were planted in the gravel.

"What is it doing here?" she asked. "This is where my car belongs."

"I know, Sara. We'll put the Mustang right back in here just as soon as I get finished working on the boat. I'm getting a vinyl-coated cover for it, and we'll park it right here in the yard."

Her face was a blank, completely void of any understanding. "The car will be ready in just a few days," she protested.

"Sara, forget about the car for a minute." Fate took her arm more roughly than he'd intended. "Just look at the boat. She's a sturdy one with a good motor. She's old but I got her at a fair price, and now I'm fixing her up. I'll have her ready by the time we have a nice warm spell. I've already thought of a name for her—*Three Sisters*. What do you think? That's for you and Swanee and Serena. That's what the boat's for, Sara. To take you to Serena."

"But there should be a road," Sara said, brittle with terror. If she moved an inch, she would shatter. "A road and a bridge. It doesn't have to be much of a bridge. There could be limited traffic on it. Even a footbridge would do, although they promised a real bridge."

"There isn't a bridge, Sara. Do you think there'll ever be one? You just keep kicking a dead horse. Nobody cares but you. Don't you see that? But now I've come up with this solution, this boat here, and I've been working on getting it ready. I'm going to take you to Serena the first spring day that comes along."

"I couldn't," Sara said. "It would be giving in."

"No, Sara, it would be doing what you could. It would be making yourself satisfied with less than you'd intended—that's what I did for years. Why, Sara, you're as bad off as I was if you don't make the best of what comes to you."

She was trembling. He thought at first it was from the cold, because she was yet to come into the protection of the barn and a little wind was flapping some towels left frozen on the line the night before. Then he saw she was crying. She bent her head, the collar of his coat hiding her face, and sobbed out loud, big aching cries that bruised them both. He didn't know what to do, hurt as he was by her refusal to look at the boat but torn, too, by the pain he felt for her.

"Oh, Sara," he said and put his arm around her. He pulled her against his chest while her sobbing shook them both. He thought he might cry too. Why was everything so hard? he wondered. He kissed her forehead, put his lips along her hairline. She was trying to be still, but her body shook as if all the crying she'd needed to do years ago when her sister died was pouring out, washing over both of them in a storm of grief.

"Dear Sara," he whispered. "Dear, dear Sara, it'll be all right. You don't have to give up on the road and the bridge. I wouldn't expect you to. But here is something we can do. Here's something I can do for you. Please let me, Sara. Come, look at the boat. It's beautiful. There's an understanding between me and this boat, a kind of pact we made to take you across the lake. Touch it, Sara. Feel how strong it is."

She moved with him to the boat and put out her hand to lay palm flat on the wood. His hand came over hers, holding them together. "I'm afraid," she said softly, her breath shuddering from her chest. "I'm afraid of the water."

"Oh, Sara," he said, putting his arm around her once more so she was close, held between him and the boat. "So am I."

23

◆ The flurry of activity surrounding Rachel's birthday subsided quickly. The baby, still half sick with strep, slept on Fate's chest through most of the festivities. Eva snapped pictures of everyone with Swanee's new Instamatic so Rachel would have a record of the event. She sent the pictures to Michael, except for one which she put in an envelope to her parents. It was a picture of Rachel with her cake, one hand dug into the pink frosting, her silver paper hat sliding on her feathery hair, her pale bewildered face startled by the flash.

Some of the other pictures were fuzzy. Eva couldn't make everyone be still at the same time. Here was a turning head, a mouth trapped in speech, a hand flung out of focus, but she mailed them anyway, along with a note to Michael that read: *Fate has bought a boat for taking Sara across the lake. We are going the first spring day. Come with us.*

How would he know the first spring day? he wondered, slipping the letter into an old stationery box he'd gotten from his mother. There were two other letters in the box, each written on notepaper bordered with violets that Fate had given Eva for Christmas. How had Fate known this would happen, that she'd have someone to write to after so long a silence?

Michael tore a sheet of paper out of his notebook, wrote

Dear Eva on the first line, then stopped. He stripped the ragged edge off the paper and chewed on it while he thought of what to say. He'd never had to write letters before, so every time a purple envelope appeared on the desk in his room, he had to try again to think of something to tell her. There was nothing newsworthy in his life. He went to class and spent his free hours in the same library carrel day after day, working algebra problems, diagraming sentences, memorizing the strata of rocks. Then he went to work at an all-night superette, came home after midnight, and slept until six, when the monotony started all over again. He did it all without thinking about how bored he was or how lonely until a letter came and he was forced to respond to the reality of Eva in the world. What could he say but that he missed her, that he was well? How is Rachel, he would ask, my would-be daughter? And Fate and Swanee and Sara Will? How was his life now that he was away from it?

He sat there looking at the pictures, the faces caught at peculiar angles, some awkwardly posed, the subjects never quite ready. Were these the people he loved?

He didn't have to open the note to remember what it said. He had memorized it in a glance. *Come with us.*

I will, he wrote. *Love, Michael.*

His mother, seeing his reply stamped and ready to mail on the hall table, marveled at his new efficiency. Perhaps he hadn't been crazy after all, just young and spirited, floundering in the fluky waters of indecision and inexperience. It wasn't that she expected him to get over Eva Jessop—did anyone ever completely recover from first love?—but at least he was doing something purposeful like going to college instead of flying all over creation after her. He's settling down, she thought, and felt that momentary lightness mothers feel when struck with the prospect of their children's successful passage out of adolescence. Michael was going to be all right.

———

Rachel's first serious illness did something to Eva. "I think she's just tired," Swanee said, looking for the most comforting possibility. "She's been up so much at night."

"No, it's more than that," Sara said. "I think she's trying to make some sort of decision about herself."

"Well, she's hardly old enough." Swanee folded the corner of Sara's sheet and slipped the triangle neatly under. They were spending the morning turning mattresses and washing linens. "She ought to wait awhile. Why, there's no reason in the world to be deciding anything more worrisome than the pattern for Rachel's Easter dress. I'm going to make her an outfit, Sara, bonnet and all. I'm about as rusty as that old machine because I haven't sewed anything in years, much less smocked a yoke, but I intend to see it through no matter how hard it proves to be. Remember how I used to make the sweetest little rosebuds? Why, I made them for every little girl in Tyler Mills for a while. I wanted to send something smocked to my little grandchild, but her mother says she never wears anything like that. Everything is so sporty in California. The child doesn't appear to have a single dress to her name, and she's never had her hair curled." Swanee gathered up the dirty sheets and looked sheepishly at Sara. "It's not wrong to want to do things for Rachel, is it?"

"Of course not. Let's do Eva's room next."

Eva and Rachel had gone into town with Fate who was buying paint for the boat. Their room had a fresh powdery smell lingering above the musty odor of old curtains and clothing left too long in closed drawers.

"Eva won't be with us much longer," Sara said. Speaking the words sent a quick ache into her chest. She missed the girl already. This minute, with her things scattered about the room so it had an air of abandonment, Sara could feel her absence. Eva's life was bound to be elsewhere, away from the confinement of this dreary old house. It was only right, but it hurt Sara to think of it.

"Why, Sara, you're not planning to send her home," Swanee

cried, flinging back the sheets and dragging them off onto the floor.

"Of course not, but she'll go, if not directly to Michael then at least where she can be near him. She doesn't want to be like me. Coming here taught her that much."

"Help me lift this." Swanee was tugging on the mattress. "Now turn." The mattress flipped over, landed askew, and the sisters pulled it straight.

"Fate will be so sad when she goes," Sara said.

"Not necessarily."

"She's his child, Swanee. You know what that's like better than I."

"I know you spend most of your life learning how to give your children up. I learned it. Fate will, too." Swanee was frowning at her, but then she brightened a little. "Besides, it's not like he'll be alone. He's got you now."

Sara looked at her sister's face, so incapable of subterfuge, eyes she knew saw into her muddled worries and confusion, and felt herself go soft inside.

"While we're on the subject, Sara, I think I should tell you that I'm thinking about moving back to town." Swanee expelled an anxious little sigh, her brow knitted in her struggle to get the words right. "I feel like I want to be in my own house. I'm not afraid like I used to be. I might even start driving again. It's been years since Jonathan died. Fear just might be a bad habit with both of us."

"You'll have to decide about that for yourself," Sara said quickly before panic could set in. "But you'll always be welcome here."

Swanee wiped her face against the top sheet. "I hear the truck. I'll take these on down," she said.

Sara went on to the next room, hardly aware of what she was doing. The conversation blurred in her brain. What did it all mean? Methodically she began stripping the bed. Swanee was leaving. Eva and Rachel were bound to go too. It was only a matter of time until she would be alone in her house.

What was it she felt? It wasn't the pressing loneliness she'd lately come to fear or the panic that sometimes blasted her like an icy wind, so severe and quick it took her breath. This was different. It was a settling in, as if she'd finally seen a way of coming to terms with herself. Like a warrior surveying the dead, she felt the hollowness of her victory. How could it be that she had both lost and won?

I am going to be fine, she thought, although she was weighted with exhaustion. She tugged wearily at the covers, pulling the mattress bare. She was in Fate's room. This was where he slept. This pillow she pressed to her chest was where he laid his head, this blanket held his warmth. How much courage would it take to love him? Could she possibly have enough?

"Sara! What are you doing?" Surprise that she was in his room showed on Fate's face, but she knew he was glad to see her. When had anyone ever been glad to see her?

"Changing the beds," she said, dropping the pillow.

"You shouldn't be doing that, at least not for me," Fate chided gently. "I always do for myself." He gathered the load under his arm, then stuffed it between his chest and his injured hand. He had learned ways of doing things. He could change beds and cook and hold down a job and make ready a boat, just because it was there to be done and he wanted to.

"I love you, Fate," she said, hardly above a whisper. She felt as though she'd blurted out an answer only to realize mid-sentence that she'd misunderstood the question. She was clammy with embarrassment, awash with regret. Maybe he hadn't heard.

"You're just trying to get on my good side." Fate grinned, but he let the laundry fall back on the bed.

He could always make her bristle. Irritation was a relief to her. "Can't you be serious just this once?"

"Are you?" He put his hand on her neck and waited, expecting her to stiffen, but she didn't.

"I'm always serious."

"Well, then, I reckon that means we have to get married."

Fate pulled her down on the bed beside him. They could see their faces in the dresser mirror. Both were pale and foolish looking, as if they'd just received news of such mixed content they didn't know whether to laugh or cry.

"No, it doesn't mean any such thing," Sara said, miffed by their awkwardness.

"I hope you don't think I can live out here with you much longer without us married, Sara. That's not the way I was raised."

"The way you were raised? And what about the way I was raised? Don't talk to me about upbringing and what's proper."

"Then you'll marry me?"

"I suppose I'll have to," she conceded, looking belligerent. He could see she was smoldering, eagerly awaiting the chance to make sparks.

Well, he could stir the coals. "Are you always going to be so prickly, Sara? I tell you the truth, it rankles me sometimes how hard I have to work to get a little pleasantry out of you."

"So you want to discuss faults," she burst out, a bright lick of flame. "All right! Do you really think that was any way to make a proposal of marriage? Of course, I don't know a thing about how it's done, but as you're the one asking, you could have thought of something more fitting. 'I reckon that means we have to get married!'" she mimicked. "It's just about what I would expect from somebody who shows up uninvited and stays three months."

"I knew that was coming! The day I leave this world, you'll still hold that against me. Forget all the good times I've brought you, forget my putting life back into this run-down old place— things around here was looking piss-poor when I came, Sara, and don't you deny it. You had a lip as tight as a cork and a way of thinking that belonged in the Dark Ages. And now, just when you've started acting human—why, I've heard you laugh out loud at least twice, you've rocked a baby to sleep, you've shown me a certain amount of unsolicited affection—you want to start in berating me when I'm directly responsible for most of your good fortune. But never you mind! Call the wedding off! The bed's already stripped. I'll have my things out of here in thirty minutes or less. You can have everything just like it was, Sara, as bare as bones." He jumped up, spilling the sheets on the floor, and then stepped into them, stumbling on his way to the closet.

It never would have occurred to her to laugh. She was a solemn person, a bitter relentless woman just like he'd been describing, out of sorts with the times and as uncompromising as a cloudy day. But laugh she did. It bubbled up, startling them both as if they had blundered into a lighthearted moment incongruous to their predicament and found themselves unable to resist being happy in it.

"What are we doing?" Fate wanted to know, grinning at her.

"Fighting." She laughed.

"Will you marry me, Sara?" he asked, halfway between going and staying.

"I most certainly will," she sighed and caught him where he stood.

In front of the fire, their lives unfolded. She told him how once, when she was a child, the three girls had been playing at the creek near a place where the water spilled, rushing over rocks and rumbling with a disgruntled roar. Swanee and Serena had waded across, holding their skirts around their thighs, to search the upper bank for wild strawberries and patches of trillium and she had been alone, the swift icy water separating her from her sisters. She watched them moving up the bank, laughing together, swinging around trees, ducking under branches. Swanee slipped and Serena grabbed hold, the two girls leaning into each other, giggling at the prospect of Swanee going home soaked to the skin, teeth chattering, lips blue with cold. For a moment they disappeared around a tree whose roots, partially exposed where the water had washed out the bank, looked like snakes half buried, their heads dangling toward the water. "Come back!" she called to them. "Come back now!" But they

251

didn't hear. She could hardly hear herself over the rushing water. It echoed down the valley, a collection of deafening sounds carrying her pitiful voice with it. At that moment she knew what a mute felt like, she knew the handicap of silence. She hated the water.

"Then I saw them coming down, holding hands and sliding on the moss. They skipped across the rocks and tossed a handful of tiny strawberries to me. The berries weren't quite ripe. They had a sour, gritty taste, but I ate every one of them. It was penance for my fear."

"The first car I got was a jalopy. I bought it for fifty dollars and fixed it up. It needed everything done to it, and so I learned a lot. I found parts in junkyards—now there's a good business; you can make a fortune with a junkyard if you understand the merchandise. Why, we could start one, Sara. That's just the thing, seeing how you're land-poor. That field out there to the left of the lane, it's a perfect spot for a business. I could build a little shack. Of course, we'd have to put up hurricane fencing to protect our investment." He was patting her hand enthusiastically while he visualized it.

"You're not serious," Sara said, pulling her hand away.

"Of course not." He took her hand back, chuckling at her. "But you thought I was. I had you going, Sara." He kissed the tips of her fingers. "The truth is, I'm going to look for a job. I've got an appointment at the mill tomorrow. I don't know what will come of it, but if I get something I need to finish the boat pretty quick."

"You don't need a job. There's enough work around here to keep you busy for months," Sara said.

"Don't worry, I'll get things done little by little. You'll just have to be patient about it. I don't want a honeydew instead of a honeymoon."

"What's that?"

"Honey do this, honey do that."

"You needn't worry," Sara said, curling close to him, "because I will never ever call you honey."

Eva came in with Rachel. They had been out walking in the stubby winter grass, and the knees and seat of Rachel's overalls were damp where she'd stumbled. Both their faces were red with cold and Rachel's nose was running. Eva wiped it hard with a tissue while Rachel squirmed away, trying to get out of her mother's reach. Eva pulled off their coats and laid their mittens on the hearth.

"Come to me, sweetheart," Fate said, lifting Rachel onto his lap.

Eva sat down on the floor beside Sara's feet, and they watched the fire together. "I wish it was spring," she said, rubbing warmth into her stockinged feet.

"Young people always want time to go speeding along," Fate said. "As for me, I'd like to stop it right here."

Swanee came to the door. Her mouth open to say something, she stopped suddenly, filled with the moment, the peacefulness of it, the completeness of the picture they made. Oh, she thought, touching her hand to her lips to prevent the escape of a sigh. Oh, how beautiful they all are. And she went in to join them.

24

✦ Fate painted the boat below the waterline with green marine paint. He wanted to paint a border of lapping green waves along the line, a blatant expression of the buoyancy he felt, but he knew Sara, though of late stoically tolerant, would think it foolish. He ran the brush carefully against the rib to make the marking straight and clean. The top half he painted with white enamel, so glossy it seemed to be taking the sun into itself. The inside he varnished, then attached lights to bow and stern and reset the molded plastic swivel seat that had been attached to the middle bench when he bought the boat.

"What is that for?" Sara wanted to know. She came out every day now to view his progress. Fate could see she was gradually becoming comfortable with the boat. She ran her hand along the slick surface, then across the vinyl letters that spelled THREE SISTERS at the bow. This touching made her less apprehensive about the trip Fate was planning. "That seat up there in the middle, what's it for?"

"The old man used it fishing, but I can see you sitting on it, Sara, looking like royalty."

The very idea made her feel foolish. Besides, it wouldn't be safe balanced up there a head above everybody else, but she didn't say anything. When the time came, Swanee could ride on the throne.

Sara called about her car and was told it was ready. Fate would drive her into town. "There's some shopping I need to do so I'll stay on awhile," she explained. "I haven't bought any clothes in years," she added casually, although she felt awkward mentioning something as personal as her wardrobe. She wanted to let him know he needn't wait for her.

"A wedding dress," Fate concluded, undeterred by her perplexity. "I'm going to call Michael to come Sunday week. I want to invite Clement and Harriet too, if that's all right with you and Eva. Swanee's already asked the preacher for me, Sara, she did it yesterday, and he said there wasn't a thing he'd rather do that Sunday afternoon than get us married. So now there's the blood tests and the license to take care of. I can't afford a new suit of clothes at present, but I can eke out enough for a shirt and a tie that's not a foot wide. And a haircut. Can you make do with me like that?"

"I believe so," Sara replied, revived by his easiness, and went inside to get her checkbook and purse.

Fate stopped first at the jewelry store. "This is as good a time as any to look at rings," he suggested. "It'll have to be a plain one, Sara, just a gold band is all."

"That's all I want," Sara said.

In the jewelry store, surrounded by polished glass cases, tables set with lace cloths, and place settings of china and crystal, silver trays and bowls leaning against blue velvet backgrounds, she felt her old fearfulness. They were both misplaced. The woman who waited on them was wearing a soft woolen suit of a purple shade Sara had never seen before but which she suspected was the color of heather. The woman's gold chains slid on her silky blouse, in and out of her soft collar. From one dangled an antique watch, its tiny gold hands moving ever so slowly across the minutes as her hands moved patiently, elegantly, between the glass and the blue velvet, searching by touch for the right box of rings.

The rings were all plain, although of different widths and sizes, and a few had beveled edges. The woman waited silently for Sara to pick one. There was nothing to say about the rings, no inducements or bargains. Either a woman had need of a wedding ring or she did not.

Sara stared down at the case with the gold circles neatly lined up in their slots, but her fingers refused to come forward. Her hands tightly planted across the warming surface of her purse, she felt beside herself, as if she had floated out of her head and was seeing this awkward, unfashionable woman who had never felt comfortable in jewelry or high-heeled shoes, had never owned a piece of silk or had her hair done, who was afraid even to touch a perfect circle of gold for fear of damaging it in her clumsy hand.

"Sara wasn't looking to marry anybody," Fate said too loudly, as if her hesitation had embarrassed him. "Lucky man that I am, I guess we're both still a little surprised. Here, Sara." He grabbed her hand and shoved one of the rings on. It was a perfect fit, a flat broad cylinder with only a little weight to it. It would not impede her. Sara was light-headed with relief.

"Now you," she said to Fate.

"Not me."

"These are for men," the woman said, coming forward to lift out another tray. Immediately she deserted them again, backing away to look out the window as if she expected an argument she should get clear of.

"I want you to have one," Sara said.

"On this hand?" He nodded toward the gnarled fingers pressed to his stomach. "On this, Sara?"

"Yes," she hissed, although she'd intended to whisper. "On that hand. Or on the other one, for heaven's sake. What difference does it make?"

"You don't mind my wearing a ring on this crippled old hand? You're sure, Sara?" He looked bashful. A slight blush rose across his cheeks. She wanted to wipe it away, to save him from any exposure that would show the saleswoman how wounded he had once been.

"It would be better not to wear a ring on my good hand when I'm working," he began, his voice rising with blustery excitement. "I thought—well, I reckon I thought we were going to keep on avoiding my being handicapped. I mean, I ignore it most of the time because I'm so used to it, but I can't expect you not to have feelings about it."

"I want you to wear a ring on this hand." She ran her fingers gently over the lifeless shape of heavy bones and drawn flesh, then took a ring from the display, pushed it over the frozen knuckle, and stood looking at it. She had tears in her eyes and a tremble at her mouth that made her look very young and helpless. "Don't you see, Fate," she said softly, so that no one else could hear, "that I am more damaged than you?"

Next, at Fate's insistence, they looked in Broydan's Store for a dress. The one he liked best was on display in the window, a lavender chiffon party dress with a fitted waist and petaled sleeves and hem.

"I can't wear a dress that was on a mannequin," Sara protested. "Besides, I've got auburn hair. People with my coloring don't wear lavender."

"Black, then," Fate said. "It goes with everything. Or white, Sara! Why not white?" He was making fun of her, but she was too distracted to object.

She tried on the lavender chiffon but refused to come out in it. Standing barefoot before the dressing room's mirrored wall, her chest and arms partially exposed out of the soft material, her body outlined by the taffeta slip underneath, she glimpsed something pretty in the reflection, something alive and joyful barely hidden under the surface of her gooseflesh.

This was the dress she would be married in. In this dress, wearing silvery shoes and her mother's pearls, a single winter rose in her hand, she would promise things so hard, so complicated, so risky that the thought of them made her nerves turn raw, her pulse scamper, her hands tremble on the soft folds of her skirt. And yet she was glad. Gladness sprang up, toppling her fear, overrunning like a swift current the boundaries of her narrow life, widening her spirit, reaming her heart, making her ready for whatever was to come. "I do love him," she said into the mirror. "I do."

The Mustang looked perfect, but it had a different smell to it. The wheel felt odd, too, and she thought at first that the brakes grabbed. But once she was alone with the car on the open road, she began to feel easy. She hadn't driven in weeks—it was her own movements that were out of kilter, her awkward reactions that made the car lurch while her foot rediscovered the particular angle which lightly tipped the accelerator and put the right pressure on the brake.

The smell was an irritation, though. It was a heavy odor of sweat and smoke. With the window partially down to let fresh cold wind in, the stench hovered at the dashboard, forcing her to inhale lightly and breathe out heartily as if she could blow the smell away. The ashtray, she thought suddenly, and pulled it open. The butts of three cigarettes lay in a pile of soft gray ash. She tried to be angry. Surely this violation of her car was reason enough. Someone had driven the Mustang, and more than just around the lot to test the repairs. Maybe the mechanic had taken it for a road test, then stopped at a drive-in for lunch and a smoke before heading back to the shop; maybe teenagers had hot-wired it off the lot and raced through the midnight streets of Tyler Mills, screeching and yelling, the radio blaring staticky rock and roll. The thought of the Mustang out for a joyride made her smile. No damage done, she thought. Tomorrow she'd empty the ashtray and spray the interior with disinfectant. Just having the windows down in the winter air would make some difference. Life's little wrinkles only took a bit of smoothing.

Fate followed her home in the truck. The sky they drove toward was snowy, the color of slate. It was dark when they turned off the road onto her lane. The blinker light on the Mustang flashed a left turn and disappeared between the trees. Fate slowed the truck to make the turn, then stopped, his headlights beaming along the edge of the ditch, skimming the mailbox, exposing the black wet trunks of pines and the clay sludge where the gravel had washed out on the edge of the lane.

Except for his truck's unsteady beams of light, he was in the dark. He felt a surge of doubt, a flapping bitter rush of wind through the floorboard as if his unreliable old heater had finally failed completely. He should stop here. He should back out of Sara Will Burney's life as quickly as shifting gears; he should leave Eva and Rachel and go, never looking back, disappearing like Vickie had. No one would follow him. Sara Will had too much pride, and Eva had Michael. She had a family, a life starting to bloom. He would end up on the periphery of Eva's future no matter what. And who knew what life with Sara Will would bring? No bed of roses, that was for sure; no past full of memories to rely on. Everything with them was here and now. There didn't seem to be adequate time left to know enough about each other—no time and a reticence that came from years of holding back, of refusal to question how they got this way. They would be stepping from one hard place to another, stumbling along because both of them were stumblers; he'd seen that already. They weren't the kind of people to do anything with ease.

Through the trees he could see her parking lights like two red beacon fires set to keep someone like him from running aground. Oh, Lord, he thought, feeling the cold around his feet blow up his shivering front into his face, let me do right by her. Let me quit being a fool right this minute. He turned the truck down the lane, following the light. The old truck rumbled in and out of chugholes, jostling loose whatever fear was left in him. She was waiting beside the car, her lights still on to guide him.

"I thought I'd lost you!" she called and reached back into the car to click off the lights.

He cut his engine and then his lights. The heavy slate of sky reached down to them, filling in every empty inch of the valley with its thick dark. Only the dull curtained light from the kitchen windows saved them from blindness.

"One of these first days I'm going to set a light post out here," Fate said, "and run a spot out to the barn, too. Put the switch by the kitchen door and we're all set for going out of an evening." He reached forward to lead her toward the kitchen light.

"You stopped at the lane," Sara said. "I felt you stop like I had put my ear to the ground. I can tell you I held my breath. Here I was with two rings in my purse, a dress at Broydan's being taken in, and you were changing your mind."

If he hadn't been holding her hand, he wouldn't have been able to turn to the voice, it was that distant, that fearfully breathless. "Whatever it was, it passed on by me," he said. He felt one of her knuckles, which was slightly turned and swollen. She would soon be feeling arthritis in it if she didn't already. "I came on."

"So you did," Sara replied and went up the steps ahead of him to open the door.

It was, of course, a sight Swanee Hope Burney Calhoun had never expected to see: her sister in lavender chiffon and their mother's pearls coming down the stairs with a white rose in her hand on her way to get married. The parlor looked like a dream. She and Eva had seen to that. They'd bought out the florist's supply of fern, hothouse glads, and snapdragons, put a bowl of pink tea roses and baby's breath on the hall table, banked the mantel and the top of the pump organ in the parlor with magnolia leaves. It looked like a funeral, Michael said, but where was the body? It was Fate he meant, and he took the stairs two at a time to determine the duties of best man in the room he'd once shared with the groom.

Michael pinned a pink rosebud to Fate's lapel, then to his own, and the two men stood looking at themselves in the wavy mirror. "My hair never looks right," Fate complained, patting one side of his curls to make them balance with the other.

"You look fine."

"And this suit. Here you come all spruced up in new duds and I'm wearing the only suit of clothes Noah had on the ark. Thirty-five dollars twenty years ago, and it shows."

"You look like a million bucks."

"No honeymoon either. I told her we could go down the road to the Holiday Inn in Whitney for a night or two, but she says no, she wants to spend her wedding night right here in this house with Swanee and Eva and Rachel. We won't have them forever, she says. Can you believe that? So I says fine. Then Swanee pipes up and says how she's not staying here if that's the case. So this afternoon when you and Clement and Harriet leave, you're taking Swanee and Eva and the baby to the Holiday Inn where they can have a nice dinner and go swimming in the indoor pool, and tomorrow Sara and me will go get them. Don't that beat all? But I kept my mouth shut. It's a treat for Eva, you know, and it puts Sara and me alone." He saw his own embarrassment. His collar choked him and he ran his finger inside it, freeing his esophagus so he could swallow again.

Eva was playing the organ. Her pumping was irregular because she'd begun practicing only last week. They had no music but the Baptist hymnal and some old sheet music from Sara and Swanee's lessons years ago. Upstairs the wedding party heard her struggling through an easy-to-play version of "Träumerei," which sounded like a dirge. The bass notes hung in the air, unforgiving and mournful. Then she played "My Wild Irish Rose" and "Let Me Call You Sweetheart," fingering both of them hesitantly as she searched for the notes. The tunes were hardly recognizable.

"It's time!" Swanee called through the closed door. "You men come on down here!"

When they were standing before the fireplace, Eva started playing "Here Comes the Bride" with one finger. She had figured out the melody on her own but hadn't had time to put accompaniment to it.

Upstairs, Sara heard the tune like an alarm in her head. There was no shutting it off, so she followed the sound out of her room and down the hall to the landing. She held the rose securely but slightly away from her body so she didn't crush it or pick her dress. The chiffon skirt billowed a little with each step, and her impulse was to press it down to her knees but she didn't. Swanee was waiting in the doorway to the parlor. The women let a brief smile pass between them and then looked away as if the sight of their own faces would bring them to tears.

The organ echoed its reedy notes even after Eva had moved away from the stool to stand with her parents. Harriet was holding Rachel, and Eva didn't try to take the baby back. Clement put his arm around his daughter lightly, not tugging her toward him but nevertheless holding her. Michael stood beside Fate, the ring on his little finger. Swanee took the opposite place beside Sara, a gold band on her thumb.

Mr. Barlow was quick and to the point. He had agreed to

this arrangement, although he believed marriages should be solemnized in church with more witnesses than this. He liked the prenuptial parties, the counseling, the big receptions that turned the vows into events. Still, when Swanee Hope asked him to perform this ceremony, he'd consented. Sara Will Burney might be peculiar, a recluse with a bee in her bonnet about a bridge across the lake, but she and Fate Jessop were baptized souls—Swanee Hope could vouch for both of them—and this was God's work he was doing.

He read about the marriage at Cana, the first miracle, because this wedding, like that one, had its own strangeness, its private mystery. Besides, the story of Ruth, his personal favorite for weddings, didn't fit the circumstances. This couple would do well to stay at home out of harm's way. From all he'd heard, Sara Will Burney seemed likely to die in the same bed she was born in.

The couple repeated their vows with firm voices, their inflections matching the minister's. There was only one stumble. Fate hesitated on his own name, Lafayette, as if being named that came as a surprise to him. For the recessional (there was no place to go—the group simply modulated, a rippling little wave of whispery hugs and pats), Eva played "Love Lifted Me" out of the hymnal. It was a tune she knew, and she made the old organ shudder with it. All of them heard the ill-fitting words in the backs of their heads while they spoke congratulations. "But the Master of the sea, / Heard my despairing cry, / From the waters lifted me, / Now safe am I. / When nothing else could help, / Love lifted me." It was all they could do not to sing out on the second refrain. Then she played one stanza of "Love Divine, All Loves Excelling" and was finished.

Congratulations having been said, everyone stood waiting to be called to the kitchen, where the wedding cake had been set out on the table, a strand of polished ivy curling around it. Harriet had brought the cake, insisting on taking this opportunity to make her first wedding cake after investing over a hundred dollars in equipment and completing a six-week decorating course. It was a two-tiered cake frosted as smooth and white as ice, with glittery plastic wedding bells stuck on top. Harriet had ridden most of the morning with the cake balanced on her lap, calling out admonishments to Clement every time he was forced to touch the brake or negotiate a curve. The cake arrived in perfect condition, but Harriet's shoulders were knotted with tension and Clement wasn't speaking to her. She had brought her silver cake knife in case the Burneys didn't have one.

Escaping the parlor, which now seemed close and funereal with flowers, the wedding party took on an accommodating ease that the comfortable kitchen could provide. Here there were no decorations except for the table, with its trail of ivy linking cake and punch bowl, from which Eva ladled punch floating with lime sherbet without splattering a drop. Swanee had bought her a dress for the occasion, winter white with crocheted collar and capped sleeves, which made her look positively angelic. Nobody would have ever guessed this was a bleached-blond runaway unwed mother who set cups so carefully on gold-rimmed glass plates. Michael couldn't take his eyes off her. He was holding Rachel who had come into his arms easily, as if she had some memory of his care. Maybe, he thought, it would be the same with Eva.

"The poor thing is nodding right there on your shoulder. I think she needs a nap," Swanee cooed, wiping the baby's fingers before she could leave a smudge across Michael's new suit. "I wouldn't be surprised if you had to rock her a little, though. I'm afraid we've been spoiling her something awful since you left."

Upstairs, he slipped off her dress and tried to take off her shoes but Rachel refused, stiffening her toes and beginning to pout, eyes glazed with sleep but hostile. Her cheeks puffed as she tuned up to cry.

"You can wear them," Michael said happily, eager to give in to her. He wrapped a light blanket around her and they settled in Sara Will's rocker. Content with her shoes, Rachel seemed ready to drop off but Michael wanted to hold her. Her warm weight—heavier than he'd remembered—seemed to settle him, and he felt calm for the first time since he'd been invited to come for the wedding.

The invitation had unnerved him, coming suddenly as it did—a phone call from Eva's mother saying Sara and Fate were getting married on Sunday and he was to come along with them. He felt unprepared, off balance. This was not what he'd planned. Another few weeks, he'd thought with despair, he would be ready to accept whatever Eva wanted.

Lately he had been noticing a girl across from him in algebra class who had a worried look, forever frowning at the blackboard or her book, her brain knotted as she struggled to make sense out of the hodgepodge of letters, numbers, and signs. She chewed on a fingernail, picked at the tip of her eraser or the ruffled edge of paper in her notebook. She worried but she never truly concentrated, fearful, Michael thought, that even if she gave a problem her full attention, she still wouldn't get it right. If only she could let the numbers flow into her head like a story, a ribbon unfurling gracefully, she would lose her fear. He'd thought about telling her that—stumbling into her going to class, he would take her despair in his arms and shelter her; he would kiss her wrinkled forehead and take her hands in his to smooth the tension out. The girl was not pretty to him, not even especially interesting, but he watched her anyway. Was it her helplessness he cared about? Was he simply so weary of the battle with Eva that he was willing to settle for less, this girl who would fall into his arms as easily as his pencil moving through her elementary problems, tidying her desperate scribble with orderly care? In algebra class he rarely thought about Eva.

It was at night that her familiar image appeared to him, more concrete than a dream. Sometimes he awoke to find his arms outstretched above him, reaching for her. Remembering his search was over, his heart recovered, pulse slowed, and he would see Eva in the shadows of his bedroom wall as she moved through Sara's rooms, saw her at the kitchen table crumbling a biscuit into Rachel's dish or licking a drip of maple syrup from her fingertips. He could visualize the exposed breast as she nursed; he saw her arched back, neck straining as she leaned her flat stomach against the sink rim and sang in a rollicking, twangy voice, "I'm going to hire a wino to decorate our home." She never turned to him when he saw her like that. She didn't need him. Or did she?

Her frantic little notes, her frenetic giggle during their brief and oddly hesitant phone conversations, made him doubt his own memory. Could it be that his absence had made her less content with television game shows, quick paperback reads, magazines full of colored photos of remodeled kitchens, floral bedrooms, recipes for homemade astringents and grainy herb bread? Was she exhausted with the slow, careful dusting of bric-a-brac, the changeless winter scenery outside her bedroom window? Once he'd thought he heard tears in her voice, some wild fluttering, a desperate wing-beating as if she were suddenly conscious of entrapment. What does she want? he wondered helplessly, and yet he couldn't ask, not on the phone or in one of his pitifully inept letters. He had thought face to face he would see the truth. Now two hours had passed and she was still an enigma to him.

"You could put her down," Eva whispered, tiptoeing in.

Michael didn't move. "I don't want to give her up."

Eva sighed and studied herself in the mirror. "That's what you used to say about me."

"I'm not a crazy person, Eva. I never have been."

"I know that, although maybe it would be better if you were. Then I could have you locked up. It would be safer away from me, Michael." She pulled at the rim of dark curls at her temples and then stared critically at her frowning face. "I'm almost seventeen years old. How can I be so young and so old at the same time?" She sat down on the bed. Her feet didn't touch the floor and her legs looked skinny dangling there. He wanted to take her in his other arm and hold her and Rachel together, but he was a little afraid of her.

"Swanee's talking about moving back to Tyler Mills to her old house. I could go with her, I suppose. There's plenty of room and we get along. I could stay here, too, now that this is Uncle Fate's home, but I wouldn't want to do that. Sara and Fate need to concentrate on each other for a while, see if they can get one bit used to each other, which I doubt they can. They're about as unlikely a pair as I've always thought you and I would be."

"And now? About us, I mean?" Michael asked, so softly Eva had to strain to be sure she heard.

"I don't know." She stopped looking in the mirror and turned to him. "I just know I wanted you to come today. I want you to come and go across the lake with us, too. I can't think of anything important happening to me without your being part of it, that's how simple it seems. But I know nothing's simple, I've learned that much." She waited for him to say something, but he didn't know what to say. Inside his head there was a stillness like the quiet before a trap springs and something is caught forever.

"I'm going to ask Mama and Daddy if I can come home this summer. I think they'll let me. I still want to make something of myself, I don't know what exactly, but something I can have some pride in. There are day-care centers where Rachel can stay, and I think Mama would be good about helping out as long as I can get a few things straight with her. I want to get my high school diploma and start college. Do you think, Michael, that we could go on a real date?"

"I think we could," Michael breathed. Rachel stirred in his arms as if she had heard his hammering heart in her sleep. "I'll put her down." He moved slowly to the crib, turned the baby carefully onto her stomach, and laid her on the mattress. He unbuckled the tiny shoes and slipped them off, his fingers trem-

266

bling. Every moment was slow and fraught with care. He laid the blanket over the sleeping form and stood looking down at her as if she were his anchor, his safety. "I love you, Eva," he said, looking at the baby.

Eva wrapped her arms around him from the back, hands pressing his rib cage where no breath could stay. Her head was against his back, her body curved to his. "Oh, Michael," she said, her voice a whisper at his shoulder blade. "I don't know, but I think I love you too."

He put his hands over hers and there he stood, ensnared between them, tethered at head and heart. For the first time in years, he felt free.

25

◆ Fate Jessop was throwing up. It was seven o'clock in the evening on her wedding day and Sara Will, alone in the kitchen, the top tier of the cake safely stored in the freezer, cups and plates washed and put away, heard disrupting her quiet a muffled retching, sporadic and deep, coming from the bathroom across the hall.

She knew it was the champagne. They had eaten fat slices of Harriet's sugary cake and drunk the sweet sherbet punch on empty stomachs, then made toasts with the champagne Michael had brought—cheap champagne, she supposed, that left a dull ache in her sinuses but tasted good, icy cold and dry, bubbling in her mouth and throat as it went down. Fate had drunk several glasses, downing big swallows with every expression of good wishes anyone could muster, and now he was losing it all.

She had no idea what to do, although she assumed leaving

him alone was the best thing. He was, after all, a grown man capable of managing his own distress and cleaning up after himself. Didn't he frequently remind her he was accustomed to domestic duties, undaunted by the daily tasks most men found demeaning, difficult, and time-consuming? He was used to being alone. A rank odor eked around the door. The smell, putrid in her close kitchen warmth, set her nose to twitching and her throat burned spontaneously as if she were about to gag. Whatever should she do?

She stood at the sink, thrown back in time to the child who had been terrified of the unexpected, accidents that would demand quick thinking, situations that required expert responses, where there were no second chances, no room for mistakes or alternative plans. No time to figure or practice.

She could feel the clammy desperation with which she'd listened to her father tell about a neighbor man touching a hot wire, the current flashing through his body, jolting him again and again while his wife raced screaming to him, overrun with fear. In her panic, she put out her hands to pull him free but her touch bonded them instead, his body the conduit that seared her fingers to his flesh. They had died there together, locked in the surge of volts, charred head to toe, her screaming dead in her throat.

"She should of knocked him loose with a stick," their daddy said to the three sisters, fixing his stern gaze on their white faces. "That's what she ought to of done." And, terrified, Sara had filed the remedy in her memory of collected horror stories gleaned from news stories and local lore. Her child's mind was compartmentalized in rows of specific instructions entered under appropriate headings: Snakebite, Grease Fire, Tornado, Steaming Radiator, Flesh Laid Open to the Bone.

"What do you say if somebody tries to pick you up along the road? Tell me quick, Serena." She had forgotten the exact words, the magical phrases of protection their mother had given them.

"Say 'My daddy's just down the road a piece and I'm meeting

up with him.' Then when the car pulls away, you skedaddle through the woods and don't show your face on the road that whole day. That's all there is to it, silly." Serena was never worried; it never occurred to her that the next thing that happened would be too big to handle, an unsurmountable problem that would doom her to failure.

It was Sara who was frightened, forever watchful, unsure and questioning. What is the right thing to do? she would ask herself, never willing to concede the possibility of several solutions. She had painted her child's world black and white. The shading of circumstance she had ignored.

But there was no ignoring the sounds from the bathroom. How many minutes had the retching lasted? Was his stomach empty now, twisted dry but still heaving? If she went to him, what would she do? What if she gagged herself? Her stomach felt weak, hot with sweet food and guilt. Now that they were married, wasn't it her duty to go to him, to offer consolation no matter how helpless she felt?

She went to the bathroom, started to knock, then opened her fist on the wood and pushed the door open. He was kneeling in front of the toilet in which floated green slime, its sweet stench thick in the close air. He took no notice of her, caught as he was in the violence of his own body, which rose slightly, contorting over the bowl. Holding her breath, she reached across him and flushed the toilet, then pushed open the window a crack. Her hands had memory. Without her bidding they became her mother's hands holding a cloth under cold water, wringing it damp, holding it across his forehead, supporting his head with it. She laid her other hand on his neck, a thin neck, pitted with smallpox or acne scars, sunburned to leather. She could feel the cords beneath the skin, the spasm of muscles as his body lurched again over the bowl, spewing colorless liquid.

"I think that's all," Fate said while she wiped his face with the cloth. She held the cloth under the water and wrung it out again, ran its coolness over his neck, across his temples, and into his sweaty curls.

269

"Just rest a minute," she said.

"I feel like a fool, Sara," he said, straightening his shoulders, although he still knelt in front of the toilet.

"Too much excitement for us old folks," she said. "Too much champagne. I'm surprised it didn't happen to me."

"You wouldn't have allowed it," Fate said, pulling himself up. His face was ashen and his eyes squinty with tears. He took the cloth from her and rubbed his face with it, then ran water in a cup, sloshed it around in his mouth, and spit into the toilet.

"I think you should lie down," Sara said.

Too weak to protest, he followed her into the parlor, where he stretched out wearily on the sofa, his feet hanging over the arm. "Some wedding day," he said, trying to smile. "I'm sorry, Sara. Should of known I'd start off having to be sorry about something."

"Just sleep a little while and you'll be fine," Sara urged, although she didn't like his color. Dark circles around his eyes gave him a hollow, sickly look; making himself comfortable on the narrow sofa space, he had folded his hands across his chest like a corpse.

After his eyes closed she went back into the kitchen, away from the festive floral displays, the limp ribbons trailing from the mantel. If it weren't already dark she would take the baskets of glads and snapdragons to the cemetery. They wouldn't last long in the cold but she wanted them there, a message to her parents that all was well with her. All was well, wasn't it? she asked herself. And if it weren't, hadn't she always wanted them to think so?

We'll take them tomorrow, she decided and sat down at the table. The parlor clock chimed the half-hour. She should eat something. A poached egg would settle her stomach, feed her brain. No, she would wait for Fate. He'd awaken famished. She would cook for them and they would eat slowly, aware of the long night, then tomorrow, stretching out before them full of sunlight and brisk cold air to walk in.

The wedding rose was in a vase on the table. Stimulated by

the kitchen heat, the petals had already begun to curl back from its golden heart. She felt like that, no longer a bud wired tight to hold herself in secret. She felt free and yet contained. She was the same person in the same house but there was another dimension now, an inevitable flowering she couldn't avoid. I will never be beautiful, she thought, touching a velvet petal with her fingertip, but I can be useful. I can learn.

Hadn't she proved that just moments ago in the bathroom? In sickness and in health, she had said. She knew about sickness, how even at their age—and she had felt so young today—ailments would creep up on them. Her gallbladder answered fried food with fierce, back-splitting cramps. Her fingers ached in the cold. They were afflictions she could live with, but she knew about life-sapping illnesses, too; she had seen infirmity invade her parents' bodies so gradually she hadn't even recognized the thefts of atrophy—the weakening grasp, the translucent skin, wrinkles like webs to be brushed away—until suddenly their voices called out in the night to her, food required soft cooking, itchy skin massaged, pills doled onto tongues, dribbles wiped, thin hair brushed gently to avoid tender scalps. She had nursed both her parents, their needs absorbing her own so that eventually it was like caring for herself. Was that what she had loved most about them—their needs simplified by bed care, body functions finally more crucial than opinions? Had she loved her own usefulness more than she had loved them?

She had always blamed Swanee for not helping her more, resentment never spoken but forever alluded to, twitching angrily on her quick tongue. But she had not really wanted Swanee's suggestions or interference. They had all played their parts.

I have always known what to do when the time came, Sara thought suddenly. What terrible blunder had she ever made? What unforgivable mistake had colored her life? None that she could think of. I can take care of myself, she thought, looking closely at the rose as if seeing herself revealed there. One petal fell, lay curled near her hand. She sat absolutely still, waiting patiently for Fate Jessop to wake up.

He didn't sleep. Instead he waited, eyes closed, for the hour to strike. When it twanged dully through the house, as solemn as a death knell, he intended to get up although he was bone-tired and his muscles ached, badgering him with reminders of old age across his shoulders, down his arm, into his chest. He had thought in the bathroom that he was having a heart attack. The flood of nausea in his throat, the hot tearing of his gut that spread through his lungs—a crushing pressure there so he couldn't draw a breath—had frightened him unspeakably. When he'd tried to cry out, to warn Sara, the raw bitter taste of sour liquor had filled his mouth and he'd vomited. There is no reason to alarm Sara over an upset stomach, he'd thought grate-fully as he retched over the toilet. Marriage hadn't killed him yet.

But it had left him worn out. He lay immobile on the sofa, his heart pounding noisily, his pulse racing as blood surged into every internal cranny, battling weariness even down into his cool tightly clenched fingertips. It was no use, he thought. He would have to lie there for days to recover, if he ever did. She had married an old man, a one-armed son of a bitch who couldn't hold ladies' liquor. That was a fine how-you-do, and there was no telling what she was thinking about it. Or about tonight either. Why hadn't they discussed it? Young people didn't bother to talk about sex, as far as he knew. They just got on with it, too hot to use their heads. But he and Sara weren't like that. There was no excuse for their reticence or for their not making use of opportunity either. Here he'd gone and mar-ried a woman he'd kissed on less than twenty occasions, if he could make his feeble brain remember them all, sweet kisses every one of them, unthreatening and—well, if he had to put a word to it, pure. Too pure to make tonight fathomable. Why, Sara should have been given a chance to float before she was forced to swim. Why hadn't he seen that before now, when it was a whole lot too late for any sort of remedy? They might both be taking a bitter dose of medicine before the night was out.

Good Lord, if the truth were known, he'd never been inside her room for more than a brief conversation, once to take her coffee—so long ago that seemed now, such a fleeting, inspired moment that he couldn't recall it properly—the second time when she was leaving without letting him say a word to make up to her, a dismal angry confrontation that had defeated both of them; and finally there had been the time he'd first told her he loved her, when he'd truly known it himself just by the look of terror on her face. Her fear had loosened his tongue for words he hadn't expected to speak, at least not at that moment. But he had loved her, seeing her face blank, body stiff and untouchable as she guarded herself. He had known the words to break her down and he'd used them. "I love you, Sara," he'd said, and it had been true, both then and now. He did love her, and that feeling would overcome any awkwardness they felt, the gnarled stomachs, the weary limbs.

The clock chimed eight, each tone lingering on the next. He sat up and pushed his fingers through his thick curls. His shirt was wrinkled and smelled sour. There were splattery circles down his tie. He would clean up before he approached her. He could imagine a slow circling, she with darting eyes as he pretended to preen and strut. She would be dizzy from following him, brittle with tension as she waited for him to pounce. That was what she expected, wasn't it, a silent desperate encounter he would win? He grinned, revived a little by his mental foray into the future. He took the stairs two at a time on his way to get presentable.

Sara Will heard the water running into the tub upstairs, the quick sloshing, the rumble of water coursing down to her. So the time had come. She got up and put coffee on to perk, then set two places at the table, the rose in the center. She put water in a pan to simmer and stood two slices of bread in the toaster.

When Fate appeared in the doorway, all spruced up in clean clothes, he looked pale, almost frail to her. What if he were truly sick, a hidden malady spreading across flesh she was yet to touch? The thought of it didn't repulse her. Instead she wanted to touch him so acutely that she could hardly stand where she was before the stove, gentle steam from the poaching pan wafting into her face.

"Do you think you could eat a poached egg?" she asked.

"I think I could worry it down."

He came and stood beside her at the stove, watched her fingers tremble as she cracked an egg into a bowl and slid it into the swirling water. The egg glazed over while she watched it.

"I should have thought ahead," she said, slipping in another egg. "It's not much of a meal. I suppose you know by now I'm a plain cook. It's the way Mama cooked, using what she had. Swanee is the fancy one."

"I've never complained." He put his arm around her shoulder.

"Day in and day out, you might," Sara said, reaching away from him to push the toast down.

"Vickie couldn't boil water when we got married. She put butter in the pan to fry bacon, that's how bad it was. Things got some better but not much. The main thing she learned was to put fruit in everything. Many a dinnertime I wished to God she'd been doing something else the day she discovered mandarin oranges."

"I've never even bought any," Sara said. She put the hot toast on plates and lifted an egg out onto each one, then handed them to Fate. "You never talk about Vickie."

Fate sat down at the table, waiting while she brought the coffee. "There's nothing to say. I don't think about her and you shouldn't either. I won't have her haunting us. She's gone, and I wouldn't have her back if I got the offer. Time moves on. One day we're young, the next we're old. Right here in the middle, the two of us have been given this minute—that's all it is by

God's time, a minute or two—to feel right with ourselves, to be content. I'd hate to see us waste it."

"That egg's getting cold," Sara said, putting his cup down. But instead of going to her place, she pressed her hands gently to the sides of his head, then bent lower to kiss his cheek, urging as she did his face up to hers. Her kisses were light and yet he felt the weight of them, the initiative, the deep care of every feathery touch. His hollow stomach bounced, bringing a lump of desire into his throat. There would be no preening, no pouncing, no advantage given or taken. He knew the truth of this night, felt it in her lips, a touch that shot through him, making every nerve alive and waiting. He would, he knew, in the end be still and let her love him.

The moon hung in the sky above the woods like a porcelain plate casting sheer, exquisite light in her room. Pale beams framed the window on her floor, gave texture to the wall and dimensions to the heavy furniture, her rocker pitched backward with clothing dropped hurriedly across it. The air was chilled but the bed was warm, had trapped their damp body heat inside its clothing and dried them while they dozed the light, new sleep of lovers. She at least had slept lightly, waking to the progression of moonlight across her room, measuring pulse and light, binding time and space together. The moon influenced the tides, a grade-school fact she'd paid little attention to. The moon's cycle also described her own—a woman's magic was in the heavens; conception linked her to moonbeams. Times to plant and harvest were traced across the expanse of sky. In that regard, time had passed her by. There would be no conception; seeds dropped in her barren field would die there. It is right that the young have children, she thought, holding her breath while Fate moved against her. He slept flung out, loose and full of motion. His constant tossing didn't awaken him, but, for her, it would take getting used to. She felt his breath on her shoulder and eased her arm under his pillow, tugging him gently into her arms. This is enough, she thought, breathing out a sigh that whispered in the room. This moment is enough.

Waking early in the morning just before first light when the room was dark and still, Fate felt her wakeful presence beside him without touching her, knew by her breathing that she was waiting for him.

"The morning of Clement and Serena's wedding," he began, his voice whispery and dry with sleep, "that very morning before Clement brought Serena home, Mama made up their marriage bed. It was a plain, sturdy poster bed, made of oak and pegged by Mama's old dad years ago. We had always had it—I reckon Mama and Daddy slept in it themselves when they first got married, until they could afford to replace it with a mahogany one with fancy pineapple knobs and brass plates to hide the screws. The oak bed ended up in the guest room, and that's where Serena spent her wedding night. I remember Mama bringing in fresh sheets for the bed although the old ones hadn't been slept on. Her shoulders were shaking while she tucked the corners smooth. I wanted to help her but she shooed me away. I don't think she even wanted me there watching, but I stayed. I believe she was connecting herself to them by making that bed, or else she was letting go. I think that was it—she was letting go of Clement and taking Serena in at the same time. The marriage wasn't one she'd bargained for. She'd never laid eyes on Serena, so here was this stranger coming into her house, taking her favorite son. But she made the bed perfect, as smooth as silk and sweet with sachets of rose and lavender under the pillows."

"I never could forgive what happened to her," Sara murmured into the silence he left. "I've held it against God, against life itself, for all these years."

"I know it." Fate turned toward her in the darkness and with his good arm drew her on top of him. She rested against him easily. "She was happy with us, Sara. She and Clement were fine together. Her dying wasn't a punishment for anyone."

Her mouth stopped him. Her hair fell thick and warm across

his chest, shielding his injured arm as she rose above him. She was the moon, opalescent and full, shining whitely in the gray dawn. She swayed there, touching him with her eyes, then with fingertips, lips, tongue, searching, finding, lifting him upward until he felt suspended between her and the earth, held in the warm air like spindrift. And deep inside him, there was a rippling tide.

26

✦ Leaving land, Sara felt herself stepping onto the unsteady surface of water. Fate held her hand at the bow, supporting her with a heavy grip until her feet found the buoyant support of the slick hull and she swayed there for a moment, afloat for the first time, her arms awkwardly thrown out for balance as if she were about to dance or wave to someone on the other shore. She caught herself on the swivel fishing seat and leaned limply against it, the energy of anticipation sapped by an ancient terror of breathlessness, air usurped by water, limbs held fast in murky tides, thick slime greening her hair, her skin poached as white and flaky as a fish.

How could it be that this fear remained when so many others had been struck down almost carelessly, she thought, because she didn't have time for worries anymore? She had read that water was supposed to be her natural primordial habitat, or had her ancestors merely escaped into it, forced to swim for their lives? Was the whale truly God's plaything, created out of sheer joy, or was the beast the result of failure, trapped between air and water and denied the slow light of sunrise, the colors of morning that now shimmered across the water, weakly green here at the dock but deep blue across the expanse of the lake, dappled with sunlight?

She would watch the sky, she decided, the cloudless eggshell blue fringed on its lower rim with evergreen, spruce pointing spiky fingers heavenward, pines lifting above the crowded thickets of wild rhododendron and blackberry bushes, limestone knobs reflecting white sunlight. She would focus on familiarity, but, even while the possibility of surviving brought her a moment of relief, she lurched backward, grabbing the chair with a vicious grip as the boat dipped under her, settling now to another's weight. Swanee had come on board, puffing with worry and excitement, her head tied tightly with a thin gaudily painted yellow scarf. She had an old raincoat pulled around her shoulders.

She sat down in front as close to dry ground as possible and cried out to Sara, "Oh, Lord, I'm petrified." But she wasn't. Her nervousness bubbled out of her, freeing her from the twisting panic that turned like a vise in Sara Will's stomach.

Still holding to the seat, Sara stepped across the bench and sat down in the stern beside where she knew Fate would have to sit to man the engine and navigate. The boat dipped to her movement, rocking heavily. She studied the shore, her hand holding fast to the white rim of wood. Every day she had gone out to watch Fate work on this boat, had noted the smooth joints, the solid, curved wood shaped to defy water, had eventually reveled in the airy strength of it. She had believed she could trust what was seen with her own eyes and tested with her hand. Now she knew it was the water she had no faith in. It was unknown to her, unknowable, moved by wind and gravity; the icy trickle that fell through her fingers could not be contained and studied, could not be conquered when she dipped her hand along the edge as if she thought that making this small, secretive contact could provide a defense. Her fingers ached with its cold. She could drown just from the shock of water. Even a good swimmer would be helpless against the slowed pulse, the numbed limbs. And she could not swim at all.

"You hold on to that baby, Eva," Swanee called, because the

girl was coming down the dock now, she and Rachel hooded and fat with warmth in their winter jackets. "You take her, Michael," Swanee called, standing up to make herself heard over the slapping water. "You hold the baby for her!" The boat rocked, nudging the dock. It tipped deeper as Eva stepped onto the bow, then was handed down by Fate, who was straddling the first bench.

"Who's taking the throne?" Swanee cried. "Not Eva! No, no! Michael, you'll have to sit there!"

Fate went back to the motor and pulled the cord while Michael loosened the line, ready to cast them off. Fate didn't look at Sara. He was afraid of her expression, dreading the panic he would find there or, even worse, the regret. He prayed the motor would start. Twice he'd brought the boat to the lake to practice lowering it down the concrete ramp into the water, starting it up, leaving the dock, all the maneuvers he would be responsible for when he brought her. Everything had worked a week ago.

The motor chugged on his second pull and started up, a ragged, unmuffled noise. Fate adjusted the throttle and put them in reverse as Michael jumped on board. They swooped backward around the dock, then moved forward, the motor roaring smoothly over the wind they made, the sleek surface disappearing beneath them as they cut into the water. If only he had a free hand, he thought, so he could touch Sara Will, who looked away from him, eyes trained to the rocky shore and the wild woods above the sheer clay banks where she thought safety was. Here I am, his hand would say, resting firmly on her shoulder, keeping her steady against the kick of wind, the bouncing slap when they crossed the wake of a speeding boat. Trust me.

"Life preservers!" Swanee cried, tugging them out of the storage space at her feet. She handed them back, three old fat orange ones smelling of mildew, which had come with the boat, then new slick nylon ones for herself and Eva, and a tiny one for Rachel that slid up around her face so she was hidden in it.

Taking Rachel from Eva, Michael held her in the fishing seat, her eyes squinting into the stark sunlight and cold wind above the life jacket. She was subdued, content, as if this adventure were no surprise to her, the seasoned traveler among them who expected no permanence beyond the arms that held her. Sara put her hand on Fate's knee.

The boat beetled down the lake, leaving a spreading wake of pale foam behind them. In front of her, where the sun fell on the undisturbed water, it seemed laid with pinstripes, a translucent cloth spread out and held down at the edges by stobs of weathered oak, old trees thick with black moss but bare of leaves, dying from the relentless damp at their roots. Once these trees had fed on solid stuff; pure forest soil had nurtured their deep-stretching roots on the hillsides. Lightning thinned them, an occasional saw rasped into their innards, giving up hardwood that was brought down for firewood, but mostly these upper crests of hills, the ridges that bordered the sky, had been left untouched. Farmers had preferred the valley floor for crisp rows of cabbage, the thick, weedy, tasseled corn, the low leafy green of burley. All that was underwater now. She was skimming over trees, hastily felled, which once had made shady spots beside fields or in pastures where cows huddled at midday. There had been springs which never clogged, not even in the coldest weather, forced out of the hillside rocks with such pressure that they bubbled icily down to springhouses, to freeze finally in the still pumps. Beneath her the springs still moved, bubbling into piles of rotted lumber that had once been houses, window glass standing on edge to cut fishing line, tin from roofs caked with slime and rust. She knew most of the buildings had been burned. She had watched the smoky sky day after day, had smelled the rich blaze of bonfires when the wind was right. Funeral pyres, they had been, purging the valley, leveling it before the rising water.

"Sara!" The voice made her surface and she traced it on the wind, turning toward Fate, who was looking down the bow, straight ahead. "There, Sara!" he called, forcing her to look.

It was the island, with its tiny cove locked between boulders torn loose and abandoned where they fell in a ragged line down into the water. The boat slowed, easing toward the narrow ribbon of sand.

"Watch for me!" Fate called to Michael, who gave the baby back to Eva and jumped on the bow, crouching there to watch for rocks and stumps. They eased in, almost carried on the current, the engine sputtering to hold its pace. Michael jumped off, his rubber boots sinking into the soft shore, and pulled the boat up until its nose rested on the sand. Then all was still. They sat there, feeling the lapping water at their sides, the gentle swaying comfort like a cradle.

"Well, Sara," Swanee said, looking back at her sister, "here we are." She seemed about to burst into tears but she didn't. Instead, she struggled out of her life preserver and stood up. "Michael, come get me out of here," she cried, climbing up on the bow where she could step off onto the sand. "Are you all coming?" she asked them. "Fate, don't forget all that trailblazing equipment you brought, because we just might have to blaze one. Eva, hand Rachel to me and you get that basket. I put a thermos of coffee and one of lemonade in it, along with a wedge of pound cake. Sara, are you coming?"

"How about it, Sara?" Fate said, tugging at her life jacket. Freed from it, Sara stood up and moved a little, testing her sea legs. She watched Swanee going up the beach toward the woods, Eva following with the basket, Michael with Rachel on his back bounding past them, Rachel shrieking as she clung to his neck.

"Come, Sara," Fate said, for he'd finished flinging his tools onto the beach. He put out his hand to help her across the benches, then stepped onto the bow, pulled her up after him, and jumped down, sinking slightly in the thick mud. He lifted his arm to her and Sara stepped off, expecting to sink as he had, only to find herself instead on solid ground.

This was the earth: ruffles of dark sludge layered with dirty new sand, sparkling with mica, stone once at home in thick clay now moved, pulled forward, falling back, smoothly shaped by water. To the sides beyond the rocky harbor, water licked the edge of woods, tangled roots of gigantic oaks exposed at the water line, dangling driftwood as light and frail as old bones. The road, abandoned thirty-five years ago but still a visible slash inward, was choked with weeds and dotted at the entrance with little pines. The stand of pines on either side was open, thick with needles but clean, for not even weeds could thrive on that shadowy, acidic floor.

They walked inward, leaving the watery light behind them, following the gullies of the trail, past the pine forest, climbing slightly, feeling a tug at the back of their knees, the weight of jackets and equipment already heavy on their shoulders and arms. Only a little way in, the road narrowed abruptly, grown dense with scraggly scrub oak and maple seedlings already stunted by honeysuckle. The woods were thick now and dark with chokeberry and necklace weed. They came upon a spring trickling down between a stairstep of rocks. The ground was damp along it and trout lilies bloomed there, their yellow heads nodding toward the ground. Above them was a narrow strip of sky like a faded chalky line, almost colorless.

"Nothing looks the same," Swanee fretted. "Sara, are you sure this is right?" She was panting, her face rosy with exertion. "You're the one who remembers everything."

Hornets blew up next to them, hung in the air for a moment, then buzzed away from the disturbance. They climbed over a fallen tree, black with rot and smelling damp and woodsy. The bark stuck in big flecks to their clothes, marking them with decay. No one bothered to brush it off.

"Tell us what you think," Swanee cried. "How much farther is it, sister?"

"Close," Sara said, because now she could see the slight opening high above them to her right where the sky let in a patch of brightness and the wind moved slightly in the open air. It was the knoll she'd remembered, a carved-out place, slanted but not steep, where headstones could stand straight up and the hard spring rains wouldn't wash the soil out.

"We're walking straight uphill," Swanee said, talking just to Sara. The rest of them remained quiet, as if they realized they were not important to the event.

Rachel, lulled by Michael's steady tread, was asleep on his shoulder. When the old roadbed narrowed, Michael had found himself in the lead, and he stopped occasionally to look back at the rest of them, the pale faces now flushed with color, eyes straining to avoid the briars and gullies hidden in the underbrush. Once there was a rustling to the right of him and he stopped, watchful for the movement of snakes, but he saw nothing. He was glad he'd worn his rubber boots, although they weren't good for hiking. He slid sometimes, but only he noticed; the others, confident of his lead, were too busy pulling their own weight.

Once he held a branch away for Eva, who slipped silently in front, then moved behind him to her original place in line. At a fallen tree, he held up to take her hand as she scooted over, then let go quickly, for he was determined to be the one to sever contact. His hands would demand nothing; he had given too much in his search for Eva to risk losing her in too tight a grip. Easy does it, he thought, and concentrated on Rachel, who never struggled in his arms. He was damp through to his skin where she had fastened to him, solid with sleep. Sometimes he put his hand on her head or back to shield her from a wayward limb or prevent a jostling when he lost his stride, and that gentle touching, her soft shoulders hardly wider than his hand, her cool ear ringed with silky hair against his finger, triggered such joy in him that he could only sigh heavily with it, making both of them tremble.

Fate, who had intended to take the lead, found himself the cow's tail of the caravan and glad of it. This way he could watch Sara Will's back, the determined set of her shoulders, her surefooted steps moving solemnly upward. She never meandered or stumbled, never reached out to grab hold of rough bark to pull herself up. She was the only one of them not carrying something. She had brought only herself.

Chances were she'd never expected to arrive at all. It was her own watery grave she'd imagined, not this ragged trail of shaded earth leading deep into a wilderness. They had walked uphill most of the way, and Fate was tired. The tools he'd thought to bring—hoe, ax, rake, shears—dug a ridge of pain into his good shoulder and kept him off balance, so he had to compensate by angling his body to the left. His sides ached from the twisting motion he made.

Breathlessly he concentrated on Sara, hoping to ignore his own misery. She had handled everything fairly well so far. Last night she'd welcomed Michael with a hug, graciously set out the big dinner she and Eva had spent all afternoon cooking. Later she'd even come into the parlor with them to watch television. During the commercials, when she usually complained about the content of the last fifteen minutes, she kept quiet. Sara could find fault where there wasn't any; give her a go at television and she was a wild woman, attacking every plot line with a vengeance. The movie they watched, some silliness about a woman being in love with three men at the same time, was evidently too trivial for Sara to abuse. Either that or she had her mind elsewhere—on swift undertow, most likely, white water coursing over stone, the explosion of wood shattering on rock. They had gone to bed early, hoping to give Michael and Eva some time together, but he'd heard Michael come up soon afterward, leaving Swanee and Eva to secure the house and negotiate the dark stairs together.

He and Sara had lain quiet, each trying to give the other a chance to doze off. Sleep eluded them both, although drowsiness traced fuzzy patterns on his brain whenever he closed his eyes. He felt himself lurch with it once and caught himself falling.

"We should just get up," he whispered finally, knowing Sara was awake although she hadn't moved. He knew her breathing now, and the wakeful silence of her hands pressed together at her waist.

"No," she said with soft weariness, "but you can. I'm too tired to move. Too tired to sleep, too. My mind won't be still."

"I'll bring you something warm to drink," Fate offered, wanting an excuse to loosen the knot of nerves that tangled at the back of his neck.

"All right." Sara reached out for his hand. "I'm not afraid about tomorrow, Fate. I'm glad to be going."

Now he wasn't sure. The tension around her mouth at breakfast, the stiff silence in the truck, the panic that struck her on the boat—he recognized every symptom of the sadness that seeped like water into her pores. She did not have a bridge, only this flimsy boat, this temporal, unsatisfactory substitute for her solid vision. All her dogged persistence had come to this: a brambly woods gathering the trail to itself, a cemetery hidden in weedy neglect, a man at her back forcing her on this circuitous route to what could be, at best, only a puny victory.

Well, he had done the best he could. Fate shifted the angle of the tools away from the cut they were making into his shoulder. What he needed was a walking stick. All of them did. He could see them with shepherd's staffs, oak crooks like ancient weapons lifting above their heads. Such paraphernalia would supply dignity to their trek, lend form to their ragged collection of tools, baskets, coats, swinging from shoulders and arms.

Up ahead, Swanee Hope had halted and was fanning herself with the loose sleeve of her raincoat. "Sara!" she called down to them, "if it's not close by, I'm going to have to take a rest."

"There," Sara said. She stopped on the trail, her gaze lifted, face open to the clear air of the spring morning, as fresh as April itself and glowing with a lushness Fate had never seen before but loved instantly.

They followed her gaze, peering into a sparse rim of pokeweed, through a lining of dogwood just beginning to flower, until their eyes rested where hers had stopped—on dull stone set unnaturally upright, incongruous and unyielding to the slope.

Sara left the trail, pushing through the pokeweed, stepping easily as if this were her own lane she traveled, as familiar as that. They watched her go, then one by one pushed through themselves, moving like a battle line until they arrived at the barren place, almost treeless but thick with wild, tangled growth. At the edge of the opening under the dogwoods, trillium bloomed. Wake-robin stood straight in their path, and they moved silently around it, careful not to step on the purple heads. Finally Swanee rested her hand on a hand-carved stone, weathered and trapped in weeds.

"Where is it, Sister?" she puffed. "How do we begin to find it?"

"There was a Judas tree. It was just a little thing when I last saw it. Mama wanted to leave it there, thinking it would eventually make shade over the place."

"Is that it?" Michael called, pointing into the center, where a display of fuchsia rose above the briars.

"I think so," Sara answered. She didn't say more because she'd felt her voice begin to tremble. Muscles held tense for days shuddered, sending a chill through her.

"You stay here," Fate said. "I'll see." He went, hacking at thorny arms that caught on his clothes, stepping high over the bushes until he reached the Judas tree and knelt down at it, momentarily hidden from them. He was glad he couldn't be seen as he held back the weeds and saw the words carved there. They sent an ache into his own heart. He saw Serena's face as if its image were shaped there on the stone. He saw his brother bent low, unsupportable in the heavy grief of youth, when life seemed stopped, forever locked in the pain of parting. He saw Sara, the despairing girl's face opened once in a scream, a face he'd wanted to touch even then.

She was there beside him; silently she had come through the pass he'd made and now she knelt with him, her knees sunk in the damp earth, her hand tracing the letters he had exposed. "Thank you, Fate," was what she said to him.

"I thought there for a while you'd be having to bury me up here too," Swanee wheezed, coming in to them. She held her coat out from her body, protecting herself from the briars with it. Pulled threads puckered where she'd been caught. "Ah, me," she said, reaching where Fate and Sara knelt, "here it is, here we are, Sara, after all these years." She wiped her face on the cuff of her coat. "I could burst into tears over this, but I'm too tired. I think we should have lemonade or some coffee and a piece of cake before we do another thing. Come on in here, children!" she called to Eva and Michael, who had stopped under the dogwoods.

"I think this ought to be for them alone," Michael said to Eva. "I just came to help Fate clean the place up."

"That's your only reason?"

Their halt had awakened Rachel, who rubbed her face against Michael's shoulder and then pulled away, wanting to get down. He stood her on her feet, his hands ready to embrace her if she toppled over. Rachel steadied herself, looking from Eva to Michael.

"I wanted to see how you were," Michael said, forcing himself to be quiet. "I wanted to see Rachel. You invited me, Eva."

"I've been like a crazy person waiting for you to come, but now that you're here, nothing seems right." Eva watched Rachel's steady flat-footed steps into the trillium. "I thought you loved me, Michael."

"I do."

"Then why is everything so different? You used to be after me all the time."

"Harassment was what you called it." Michael lifted Rachel out of the trillium and turned her in the opposite direction.

"I was so mean to you, Michael. I want to die every time I think about it."

Why wasn't she looking at him? She peered up the hill into a distant thicket as if she were on the lookout for someone unexpected, some peril that would swoop down on them. She was still holding the peach basket tight to her chest.

"We were both different then," Michael said, unable to stay away any longer. He took the basket out of her arms and set it down. "I didn't know back then that there was but one way to love a person."

"And now?" She was finally looking at him. Those eyes he'd longed for searched his face and he felt himself exposed, the passion he'd been holding onto as open as a new wound.

"Now I know it's more complicated than that, and more wonderful, too. Now I guess I just want what's best for both of us. I hope we'll find out that we're good together. I still want that chance with you, Eva, because I'll always love you. There's no way around it. Besides, you know me better than any other living person does. That counts for something." Rachel tugged at his pants leg, fussing up at him, and he lifted her back into his arms. "What is it, sweetheart?" he crooned to the baby.

"I'm coming home with you, Michael," Eva said. "Last night when I saw you'd come in the car, I called my folks about it. Fate and Sara said they'd come next week with the crib and whatever else we can't get in."

"Why didn't you tell me?" Michael asked, hugging Rachel to his shoulder and watching her mother, who put out her hand to touch the baby's back, then slid her fingers onto his arm and moved that one step that brought her to him.

"I needed to know if you still wanted me to come. It's not that I'm asking for a commitment, Michael."

"We'll go tomorrow," he said and pressed his cheek to her hair.

It was the moment he'd waited for. His cheek was damp on her hair. At first he tried to squeeze his eyes shut against the tears, but then he simply let them flow under the rim of his glasses, giving in to his emotions just as he'd always given in to Eva. What he felt for her would always have pain in it, would always hold the memory of a dark beginning, but there were

288

good memories, too, and good times to come. He was sure of it. He bit the salty edge of his lip and held her tight.

They gathered at the edge of the cemetery to share Swanee's refreshments before the work began. Eva discovered other Burney stones, so after Michael had cut the larger brambles away with the ax, she and Michael left Fate and the two women at Serena's grave to begin weeding among the markers of the relatives.

Eva kept wanting to touch him. Her hand grazed his shoulder as he bent to the work. She picked sticky seeds from his sleeve, brushed bark from his hair. The roots were tough and deep. Sometimes he grunted loudly as he pulled heavily at a tangle of deep brush, only to find it caught in a subterranean vine that came out of the earth dripping dirt from its tendrils, leaving a trench of upturned soil beneath it. Some of the vines couldn't be broken and there was no end to them, so he hacked them in two with the hoe and left the juicy root standing up in the ground. He was damp all over with dirty sweat within the hour but still Eva touched him, her hands constantly running across the stretched muscles in his back, massaging his shoulder or arm. He felt naked under her touch. Even as he worked, knees bent forward on soggy ground, or turned away from her while she chased after Rachel, he felt her presence. The sense of her mingled with the smell of earth, the loamy grit that clung between his fingers and under his nails, the steady chopping of the hoe across the way that reverberated like a heartbeat beneath him. He didn't have to see her to know she was there. Smoothing the turned-up soil over a grave with his bare, aching fingers, he felt her body under his hand, pressed his thumb to her pulse, and felt the peacefulness of having come to the end of a long journey to find himself at home.

27

✦ Sara remembered how the stone had been quarried farther east, someplace their daddy knew about, and he'd gone there in his truck, picked out the granite himself, and printed on a slip of paper what the carved letters should say. Two weeks later, he'd returned to see it lifted onto his truck bed, laid flat like a useless dead thing wrapped in a quilted shroud.

Back at home, he stopped alone at the Sparrow Creek Cemetery, dragged the stone off the truck, and pulled it to the place where he'd already dug a trench above the fresh red pile of earth strewn with withered flowers. He settled the stone in, pushing it upright with all his weight behind it. He shoveled dirt around it, metal now and then scraping the stone, then tamped it with the back of the shovel.

All the while Sara had stood on the edge of the cemetery watching him. She saw his hand crossing his eyes, rubbing out tears and gravel because the wind was stirring, tearing at the ground. Thick black clouds banked and slid down toward them. It was a cold bleak afternoon, and yet the polished surface of stone gave off its pink glow as if the sun were touching it. The only expensive marker among the hand-hewn gray and white native stones, it sparkled like a ruby washed up in a pan of gravel.

Her father stood there for a moment, bent over his shovel in his Sunday clothes, not old but broken by the labor of the soil—years of furrows dug, plants stood upright in clay, seeds buried, tenacious rock dug from fields. This was no place to farm but he had loved the land in spite of himself. Until now. Until it swallowed his child and he was obliged to set hostile stone back into the earth.

Sara had watched him there, his coat blowing up, wind ruffling his thin hair, and had longed to comfort him with her warmth, but she couldn't move. His grief was as private as hers, so she stood silently while he brushed his hand across the face of the monument one last time and moved away. He went back to his truck, leaning on the shovel like a cane, so hobbled by his own sorrow that he never saw his youngest child standing there.

After the truck had rumbled away toward home, the young Sara moved between the stones to the grave. She saw the ripples of dirt, where the shovel had pressed, and bent down to smooth them, falling to her knees as if she could no longer support herself. Her body was empty, bereft of all but primitive sensations. She felt the cold moving inside her clothes but could not bring back the musky closeness of Serena when they'd danced together in the kitchen, Serena loose and laughing as she showed off the newest steps, while Sara held herself tight, her lips moving with the count, anxious to hide her awkwardness with proficiency.

With her open hand she felt the stone itself, as cold and hard as a jewel. She read the words cleanly etched and perfectly aligned but they meant nothing to her. There was no face there, no scent of lemon water or vanilla, no shoulders smooth with sweet talc that dusted the air. She saw that the flowers were dead, wilted with cold, thin petals tipped with rot or dried brown. She began to brush them away. Her penchant for tidiness sprang unabated into her hands and she worked frenetically, gathering stems, scooping up petals, flinging tied bouquets away. She nudged at the earth, licking it with her hands like an animal trying to revive its dead. What she could not change, she would at least shape. Under her quick icy fingers the mound found form, was smoothly molded.

Rain had begun to fall with splattery drops on her back and shoulders; it slipped down her loose hair and formed small separate craters like decorations in the dirt where she worked. The clouds dropped down, suspended low above her head. The rain fell hard, pelting her with sharp stinging drops turned to ice. She smoothed the mound frantically, destroying the pattern of rainfall on its loose surface. For every stroke she made, the rain defied her with another lashing, until she could only watch helplessly as the thick clay soil splashed up, water running in muddy rivulets across it and down into the grass on either side. She had pulled herself up then. Bedraggled and soggy, she stood beside the spreading mound, watching the mud soak through her shoes. Soon she would be ankle deep in it, locked in and battered by icy rain. She heard a horn sound over the pounding water but she didn't look up. All her attention was on the desecration of her work, the sight of nature's relentless hold on what she treasured most.

"Sara Will!" a voice called out. She could feel the soaked ground giving as someone ran to her. It was her daddy, who flung a coat over her head, pulled her free from her muddy stance, and, with his arm tight around her, forced her into the truck. They were both drenched through. The truck's heater sent out a blast of warmth and they steamed with it, the air smoky around them.

"Oh, Sara," her daddy groaned, wiping her face with a towel he'd brought. There were trickles of water running down her slick hair, and her clothes were splattered with mud. "You shouldn't have come."

"I had to see, Daddy." She was looking straight ahead at the cemetery, oblivious of her chattering teeth, the sudden shocks of cold that made her body tremble. "I had to know the place where Serena is."

"But you could have caught your death," her daddy said.

Sara saw it looked the same. How could that be, when everything else in her life had changed? The polished blush of the stone could have held her reflection if she'd stayed there on her knees, but she stood up abruptly, stumbling with the wrenching accuracy of her memory. The sun, approaching noon, hung at her neck, sapping her strength after the hard walk, and she paused a moment to recover, her hand pressed to her forehead as she shielded her face from Fate's view.

"I'll dig out the big stuff," he offered. "There's no need for you to help."

"It's mine to do," Sara replied, retrieving the hoe before he could stop her. She hacked at the earth without looking at Fate and Swanee, who backed away, unwilling to do battle with her.

They pulled weeds under the narrow shade of the Judas tree.

"A futile task," Swanee said, "what with summer coming."

"We're doing it for her," Fate whispered, "not for the dead."

"Then she could show some consideration," Swanee complained softly. "After all, we've braved the elements getting here. We came for her."

Sara could hear them talking. Over the steady chop of the hoe, voices moved, whispering toward her. Rachel's squeal cut the quiet like a shattering thump on a piece of glass. Sara grimaced and drew her shoulders up against the disturbance. Her vision of this place had been a solitary one: she alone tending, repairing. It was lonely work which demanded muscles, not camaraderie. She needn't think beyond the task at hand; she needn't let her heart take part. It was like tending a garden. You turned neglect into order just for the moment, without expecting permanence or promises. You tugged at nature with little hope for success. Unwanted roots were too deep; every raw stub left buried in the ground would find nurture and push itself up, leafing out toward the sun. She was like that. She had been pruned and weeded but the roots had remained; spiny thorns grew beneath her surface.

"I wish you'd let us help," Swanee complained, edging toward where Sara broke into the brambles with her hoe. "We didn't come along just for the ride, you know." Wobbly from having bent over to weed, she supported herself on the warm edge of Serena's tombstone.

"Don't!" Sara cried out, stopping the hoe mid-stroke.

"Don't what?" Swanee asked. "Don't lean on this—this *thing?* Don't what, Sara? Don't disturb you since you're the important one here, the one with a mission? You're the only one with *purpose?*" Swanee straightened herself, but the tiny whiffle of breeze that played in the midday heat caught her like a leaf and set her trembling. Her head shook, chin limp with hurt. "Or is it more than that, Sara? Hasn't it always been more than that? Don't be alive when Serena is dead! That's what you really mean! Do you think I haven't felt it, but what could I do about it? I had a baby when she couldn't—it hurt like the dickens; nobody bothered to tell me it was going to hurt like that— but I did it. I didn't die from it!"

The cemetery was quiet. It was just as Sara had wanted it to be except that the silence wasn't whole anymore. It floated in and out like breath.

"How could you ever think I wished you dead?" Sara asked bitterly, cutting the silence that seemed about to strangle her. "It's never had anything to do with you."

"No, Sara, that's where you're wrong," Swanee cried, her head shaking as if a spasm had overtaken her. "It has everything to do with me—with us—because we're sisters. We ought to be doing this together, Sara. Don't you see that?"

Sara looked down at the rectangle of earth, sunk in from years of battering weather, a tangled hopeless mess, resistant to all her plans and visions. She didn't know what to do. There was no answer carved in the stone. "When the water started rising, I didn't come over here," she said suddenly. "I could have, but I thought there'd be a road and a bridge. I thought there was no reason to say good-bye."

"You should have said good-bye when she died." Swanee was calmer now. Her stare was hard, but the words were gently said. "You made a treasure of your grief, Sara, so all this time that's where your heart's been."

Somewhere above them a bird screamed, a squawking angry cry that startled them, then lingered in the stillness like a moan.

"We could plant something," Sara said finally but almost to herself. "After this mess is cleared away," she turned to

Swanee, "we could put in wild ferns, something green that could choke out the weeds. The fiddleheads are up so we can see where they are."

"I'll look for them," Swanee said, turning away. She tottered a little, her shoulders slumped with exhaustion. She looked old.

Fate took the hoe from Sara. "Rest a minute," he said, "just while I get the worst of this out. Then you can have your hoe back, I promise."

After relinquishing the hoe, she watched the tossing dirt at her feet, iron edge striking again and again at soil she'd once smoothed with her hand. The loneliness of that stormy afternoon swept over her where she stood, the same frenzy to make contact, to reach into the grave and lay her hand on the dead, as if that cold touching could bring her consolation, could give her rest. She shuddered with the scream she felt but could not make.

"Sara." It was Fate at her arm, urging her out of the sun. She sat down where he and Swanee had weeded under the Judas tree. The branches, heavy with their deep pink flowering, made a crimson shade. She leaned against the trunk, now grown strong as her mother had predicted it would. She wondered suddenly if her mother had really expected the bridge. Could it be that she had said good-bye to her child years before, when the grief was new and defenseless, before it had months and years to weight her down with regret? Had she gradually discarded the remnants of sadness that clung to her mother's heart in order to make room for the sweetness of memory that had no failing in it? Was that what people did who loved life more than they feared death?

A soft murmuring in the air brought Sara back. She heard it gratefully. Eva and Michael were speaking again; their voices drifting over her had harmony in them. Swanee, passing between distant stones with Rachel held high in her arms, talked the soft garbled baby talk Sara recognized and understood.

While she sat there, their scattered voices reached inside her. She held her breath while the sounds imprinted her with this moment, this treasure she would carry for the rest of her life, this place she had found among the living.

28

✦ Fate and Sara took Swanee with them to Eva's house. They planned a picnic lunch, using Swanee's old peach basket to pack a fried chicken, cheese, and rolls because Sara still had an aversion to restaurants.

"If we're late coming home, we'll stop someplace and have supper," Fate said.

"Just if we're starving," Swanee added, and they both laughed at Sara Will, who, unaccustomed to being the butt of any joke, vacillated between embarrassment and irritation. She was pouring cold tea into the thermos. "Have we got anything sweet?" she asked to bring order to the preparations.

"Just you." Fate grabbed her from behind so she staggered backward, spilling tea on the counter. It dripped off the edge onto the floor.

"I'll get it! It'll be as clean as a whistle," Fate said, spinning paper towels off the roll.

"I'll do it," Sara said. "Both of you get out of here. I'll never get through this with you two standing around aggravating me."

"It's not such a big deal," Fate said, handing her the towels but refusing to budge. "We're just taking the crib and high chair to Eva. We're going for a visit, that's all. Why can't you relax and enjoy it?"

"I don't know, I just can't." She bent down to wipe up the tea.

"Of course you can't if you don't want to. That's it, Sara. I don't see why you're not a dried-up prune of a woman, the way you fret all the time." He reached down and pulled her up. "Instead you're not a bit wrinkled and as pretty as a picture."

"I'm not pretty." She dropped the soggy towels in the sink, refusing to look at him.

"Of course you are."

"It's ridiculous to even talk about," Sara said. "I know I'm not pretty, I never was, I never will be."

"That's the truth," Swanee said. "Sara thought everybody was pretty but her when she was a child. Serena and me, we got our way of looking from the McElroy side and Sara, except for that reddish hair of hers, got her looks from the Burneys. I can see her right now frowning at herself in Mama's mirror, her face all scrunched up like she was something sad the cat brought in. She couldn't see how that face of hers was a pretty one no matter what anybody told her to the contrary, and, when you're a little thing and you start believing something like that about yourself, you always believe it no matter how smart or pretty or successful you turn out to be. The fact is, even if I were to get real skinny, I would still look in the mirror and see a fat little girl, so why bother, is what I say."

"Why, Swanee, you were never fat!" Sara laughed. "Pleasingly plump, maybe, but never fat."

"I was a little porker," Swanee said, lifting the basket off the counter. "Now let's go before we've spent the entire day in this kitchen."

They settled themselves as comfortably as they could in the old truck. Fate's new air cushions rustled and sighed under them. Sara Will felt they sat too high, the same toppling sensation she'd felt on the bus, and she was glad to be between Fate and Swanee, her shoulders pressed tight on either side.

"I hope you enjoy this trip, Sara," Swanee said as they rumbled along, "because you'll be needing to take another one."

"Why? Where to?"

"To the airport all the way in Charlotte. I've made up my

mind I'm going to see my Bill. All this time goes by while I'm waiting for him to come to me when I've never even seen California." She sighed on a shallow breath, already wound up with fright and excitement at the thought of such a trip. "Those grandchildren of mine don't know a thing about growing up on Sparrow Creek, so they've got a lot to learn. They've got McElroy-Burney blood in them no matter what they act like."

"When are you going?" Fate asked because Sara was too flabbergasted to speak.

"Next week. Thursday at twelve forty-five, to be exact, so you'll have to get me there on time. I'm planning to stay a month if I can stand it that long—I don't know but what all that sand and sun will get the best of me right quick. I suppose I'll come home whenever I get ready or they kick me out. And Sara, when I do come home, I'm coming to my house. I've given my tenants a month's notice to vacate the premises. I should tell you there're some pieces of furniture I want to take with me, things Jonathan and I bought together. They never went right in your house anyway, and I know where every piece truly belongs. You don't mind, do you?"

Sara could see her house uncluttered, all those empty spaces bare again after so many years. Maybe she and Fate could buy some things together. "I'll get used to it," she said, wishing she could take Fate's hand but he needed it for driving.

Michael was at Eva's. He and Clement unloaded the truck while Harriet served cake and coffee in the dining room. The house was beautiful, like rooms in a magazine, but warm, too, and receptive to spring sunlight. Sara didn't even try to imagine Serena in it, or Fate either. She knew it wasn't really the house they'd lived in.

Eva was beaming. She was going to study for the high school equivalency test all summer and, if she passed, start to college in the fall. Nothing was said about her and Michael, but his place in the family was obvious to everyone.

"Well, it's all working out, honey," Fate said to Eva on the porch. He had just given Rachel back to her after kissing the baby good-bye. "I just wish I could have made it easier somehow."

"It didn't seem to be in the cards, you know," Eva replied, putting her hand on his cheek. "But now there's a good chance I can do something positive with my life, and that makes everything that's happened seem worth it."

"If things don't go right, you let me know, you hear?" Fate pressed his hand over hers.

"If things don't go right, I'll just have to make them right," she said and moved in to kiss him.

"That's my girl," he whispered.

"No matter what happens, I'll always be that."

The airport had brightly colored molded seats bolted to the floor, with little television sets locked in front of them. Young soldiers, wearing stiff new uniforms and glossy shoes, rubbed their shaven necks and yawned at the snowy screens. Across the way, a mother turned her shoulder away from the traffic to nurse her baby. An old couple dozed together, their heads bent to their chests, jaws loose. At their feet were an assortment of mismatched luggage, a box advertising rum tied tightly with twine, and a gigantic straw basket with *Puerto Rico* stitched on it.

"That's us twenty years from now," Fate said, nudging Sara as they passed. They went around the lighted cylinders of Plexiglas advertising local industries and real estate, past an open snack bar and a newsstand, as they followed behind Swanee, who waved her ticket and jogged down the tile corridor in front of them as if she were fleeing. "She's got a whole hour to spare. We left home before day."

"I doubt she closed her eyes all night," Sara said, watching Swanee's sudden halt in front of one of the monitors stuck to the concourse wall. "Look at her. I just hope she doesn't collapse before she gets on the plane. Then there's that stop in Atlanta to worry about. She ought not be doing this alone."

"She'll manage. She'll ask in Atlanta and somebody will tell her what to do," Fate said. "You're more worried than she is."

"It's right down here!" Swanee called before they could catch up. "I have to go through this security gate right up here. They're checking us for guns, Sara, and bombs. Thank God they do that. The travel agent told me they even X-ray the suitcases. That's why I folded my new gown right on top as neat as you please with the lace showing. They might as well have something pretty to look at! What do I do now? What do I do?" she cried. They had arrived at the checkpoint, where a grim couple wearing blue uniforms with black gun cases strapped at their waists were waiting.

"Carry-on on the belt, please," the woman said, hardly looking at them.

"Carry-on? What carry-on?" Swanee cried frantically.

"Your pocketbook, ma'am," the man said, coming to lift it off Swanee's shoulder. "That your hand luggage?" he nodded at the case Sara was holding.

"Do like he says, Sara, put it down there," Swanee cried. She watched her bags disappear through the flapping tunnel gate. "Well, if I understand everything correctly, I go right down there and there's a waiting room where I stay until they call my number. Two-o-six to Atlanta. And then I wait in Atlanta in a similar place till they call seven-twenty-five to Los Angeles. I don't see my suitcase again till I get all the way there."

"What about this stuff, ma'am?" The guard motioned to Swanee's bags at the far end of the conveyor.

"I'm coming!" Swanee said, exasperation bubbling up. "This is my sister I'm saying good-bye to."

"You have a good time, Swanee," Sara said, opening her arms. "You tell Bill I said to show you a real good time."

"You'll have to come sometime, Sara. We'll all go to California together!"

Swanee was soft in her arms. It surprised Sara that so active a form could fit so easily against her own bony frame. "Go on through there," Sara said, but she was still hugging her sister. "Let's make sure you're not concealing a weapon somewhere."

"Good-bye, Fate," Swanee sobbed, turning out of Sara's arms into his. "You take care of her."

"You do the same for yourself. We'll be right here waiting whenever you let us know. I'll see to your house, too, while you're gone, so don't worry about a thing."

"Lady, there's a line forming," the guard said.

Swanee turned her back on them, stepped through the frame where the green light blinked, swung her bags over her arm, and was gone.

"We'll watch the takeoff," Fate said. "We can go outside and watch it."

Sara was blowing her nose in a tissue. "Who would have thought this would have gotten to me?" she sniffed.

"Sara," Fate said. "Sweetheart." He wrapped his one strong arm around her. "Everything gets to you."

What was forbidden her here? In her sleep she put out her hand, touching Fate with the back of her fingers as if she were testing a fever. It was the coolness of his flesh that awakened her to the delicate light of their room, dawn breaking slowly as the days lengthened into summer. She reached down carefully to draw the sheet across his back and shoulder, shielding him with warmth.

She lay there contentedly, listening to the sounds her house had always made, those creaks and groans of age she'd grown used to, as familiar as breath. Once she had loved the house too much, had guarded it jealously, fearfully, knowing how quickly it could burn, how defenseless it would be against a heavy wind. What would I do? she had thought for years, seeing in her mind's eye the ashes, smoldering beams fallen into themselves, the charred chimneys standing defiantly in the cinders of treasured belongings, handwoven linens, photographs melted to curls of blurred color. How could I live?

Now she knew. She turned slowly on her side toward Fate's

back, closing her eyes to the room. She put her face against his shoulder blade as gently as she could, not wanting to wake him but heavy with longing; nascent desire, undeniable in the fingertips that grazed his shoulder, left feathery strokes on his ear. She waited, willing him to turn to her, even in sleep. Her breath fell on his neck, deep trembles of breath that made them both twitch. She pressed her lips to his spine, light kisses against the knobby bone. His secret white skin had a taste to it, a scent only she would recognize. She ran her tongue along his weakened shoulder blade, held awkwardly even as he slept. Her ministry was not to make him well again. He was whole to her now.

"Sara."

"Yes."

"What are you doing?" He turned toward her, his injured arm falling under him so he was free to hold her.

"Making love to you," she said lightly, because the words were new and untried. He stopped her wrinkly look of embarrassment by pressing his mouth to hers.

"Oh, Sara."

"Did you know that in a balloon," she said slowly, her mind slipping away while his mouth touched her neck, her shoulder, then moved across her breast, "floating high above the trees so the ground becomes a separate element, you don't hear sounds, you don't even feel the air? Did you know that?" She waited, not expecting an answer, just the gentle passion which, at this moment, would separate them from ordinary things. "You become the air," she said.

He left her sleeping. Going barefoot down the hall to the landing, he stopped at the window that looked out on the front lawn, the lane curling out of the woods, the woods themselves which camouflaged the highway and hid them from the world. The prospect—wisteria dripping purple blossoms from its ropes, the random flowering of dogwoods, the startling hue of the flame azalea—astonished him with its beauty.

This is where I live, he thought. He would see summer here

and then the beginning of fall, the quick bright color of the sweet gum, the blood-red scattering leaves of the dogwoods, the bending tufts of goldenrod. He tried to remember how the place had looked an October ago, tried to see what Sara Will had seen from the roof, but imagination failed him. This year he would be on the roof himself, ready to mark the landscape in his memory just as he now framed forever this picture of the spring morning he looked out on. He had plans. There were still repairs to make, small jobs Sara had managed to overlook for years. Some big ones, too, such as thinning the woods out front, which would eat into his free time once he had a job. There would always be something that needed doing, and when there wasn't, there were projects all his own he intended to see to, like paving the lane. He wanted to make it smooth and inviting for when company came.

He went down to the kitchen and put the coffee on, although the house felt too warm for coffee. He got out eggs to scramble, found sweet rolls left in the freezer he could pop in the oven. Before he began to cook, he fixed a tray—Burney china crackled with age, as delicate as shells; silver from the hidden chest, curved spoons thin enough to warm in his hand. He found damask napkins smelling faintly of must. It was the first smell he'd noticed in Sara's house, before he and Eva and Rachel had settled in and obliterated it with their mingling odors.

It was almost ten o'clock. Well, they could have brunch instead of breakfast, like they'd done on Christmas morning. That wintry day seemed so long ago, as if a long journey separated him from that turbulent time. He didn't want to remember how he'd played the fool back then, trying to win Sara over with tricks. A flimflam fool he'd been, always selling a bill of goods to somebody, but mostly to himself. What had he ever done that was worth a damn? He hadn't made Vickie happy, although he still didn't know what that would have taken. He'd never had his parents' approval. They had died leaving him unatoned, he felt. They went to their graves never knowing how separate he'd felt, how unreconciled. Even his accident, his crippled body, was his own fault. Had he been careful enough? Had he been too cocky, too bumptious, to adjust the jack properly? Wasn't he alone to blame for his shoddy past, his useless slide into middle age? He had made such a mess of it until he found Sara. She had done as much for him as he had done for her.

He went back upstairs and eased through the door he'd left partially open. She was sleeping, her head turned on the pillow, her hair in loose tangles around her face. Leaning over her, he watched the fluttering eyelids that struggled to resist the midmorning sun, the tiny throb of pulse at her throat, the shuddering sigh on her lips as she broke away from sleep. I could not love you more, he said silently and lifted a burnished curl on his hand to kiss it.

"Good morning," Sara whispered and reached up for him. In her arms, he felt himself forgiven everything.

They put the garden in. Sara hired someone to plow up part of the open field between the woods and the yard where years ago her mother had always had a garden. She stood on the porch, watching the clumpy furrows pile up where ragweed and clover had grown as dense as a carpet. The tractor battered the quiet with its clacking roar, diesel exhaust discoloring the still air, but Sara turned her mind away from the racket to watch the field becoming useful under the twisting blades. Everything changes, she thought, even me. To plant a seed the ground must be disturbed, a surface altered.

They knelt together in the turned-up dirt, putting in beans, summer squash, okra, a row of sweet corn, tomato plants. The dirt smelled green and fresh, and Sara took long slow breaths of it as though it were a smell she'd longed for.

"What's this?" she asked when Fate dropped seed packets on the ground in front of her. They were zinnias to put a burst of color along the final row. How had he known that years ago zinnias had bloomed there?

She dug a trench with her spade along one long side of the

garden, then on the end that edged the road. That done, she followed the little ridge she'd made, dropping in the seeds. Fate came along behind her, smoothing the dirt over with his hoe.

"I'll run the hose out here," he said when they had finished. "If we don't get a normal amount of rainfall, I'll have to figure out some sort of irrigation system, but until then I can just add a little water when need be."

He came back from the house dragging three hoses linked together, his thumb over the open end. At the edge of the garden he planted his finger on the rim of the opening, making a fine spray over the garden and where the zinnias had been sown. The mist rose in the air and blew across the dark plot, making the soil look richer than Sara could ever remember it. Then she felt the mist against her shoulder, as cool as rain.

"What are you doing?" she cried, but she was laughing as the spray washed over her head, dampened her hot face, trickled into her shirt.

He just stood there grinning at her, his thumb controlling the gentle spray that watered her like a flower.

After a real bath, Sara was in the kitchen making lunch. Fate's tape player was on the windowsill behind her, and from it Kenny Rogers whispered in that husky, heart-rending voice she'd come to listen for, "Lady, I'm your knight in shining armor and I love you. . . ."

She cut across two sandwiches with one quick motion of the knife. The kitchen was still except for Kenny's singing; the sun flooded across her golden floor, striking everywhere so the room glowed with quiet light. In the stillness, Sara felt herself flooded, too. Contentment poured over her like warm water, as sunlight penetrated the leafy vault of her woods, making every bud visible, every leaf transparent and singular.

She felt right with herself. Oh, every day she thought about Eva and Rachel and Michael. She loved the sound of Rachel's gurgles on the phone and the brief, busily written notes that Eva sent. She had never expected to have such people reaching

305

into her life, and she relished the sight of pastel envelopes among the junk mail, the sudden shrill beckoning of the telephone. I am not forgotten, she would think.

Of course, it was Swanee she really missed. Why would anybody want to go to California? she asked herself while setting the table for two or dusting over one of Swanee's knickknacks she was refusing to pack until the moment of Swanee's move. She thought about all the women who went west in wagons, day after day, with the morning sun to their backs, facing heat to the west, the slow purple sunset that fell over discarded heirlooms, shallow graves, family histories abandoned along the trail. Where did they find the courage? Sara wondered. It was for love they went, she reasoned, knowing now what love could do.

"Sara, come here. Quick, Sara, hurry!" Fate yelled over Kenny's pulsing rendition of "Ruby."

She took flight, leaving the sandwiches on the counter, her hands clutching her apron, down the hall to the parlor door.

"Look!"

The television was on. A lighted board on the screen flickered with blinking lights. An organ rippled through one of those fanfares she abhorred.

"And now," the plastic-faced emcee bellowed over the music, "let's give a warm welcome to our next contestant! All the way from Tyler Mills, North Carolina—"

"Just look at her," Sara said over the applause. She sank into a chair, weak with a tide of affection as true and conscious as her own heartbeat. "Just look."

For there on the screen, her head of bouncing curls surrounding her like a white halo, her trembling face bursting with excitement and pleasure, cheeks puffed out with that little gust of breath Sara knew would come with the first words she uttered, was Swanee Hope Burney Calhoun, smiling out at them from a gaudy game-show set.

Sara smiled back. She sat there in her parlor trembling herself as she looked into the face that spoke to her, even from

such a distance, of constancy and determination and the complicated, tenacious, sometimes even joyful connection of sisters.

Sara felt drawn into that face as if it were her own. She
watched breathlessly as the contours went soft. It was a baby
face, but Sara knew where the wrinkles hid, laugh lines at eyes
and mouth, those narrow slashes of worry that could appear
instantaneously across the knobby forehead. She knew the nervous gesture, too, of fingers tugging at a waistband; she recognized the tiny explosions of sighs pulsing at her on the
airwaves. If only she could reach through space to put her
hands on those shoulders lifted so anxiously against exposure,
against saying one foolish word that would bring embarrassment
to any Burney anywhere, living or dead. If only she could show
Swanee how glad she was, how proud.

"I should have known—" she began and then halted, surprised at how truly happy she felt. She put out her hand to
Fate, who looked from one of them to the other, then reached
toward the trembling fingers that connected him to them both.

"Well, Sara," he said, "you know she always did have all the
answers."